CU01508375

CRAVED BY A WOLF

ETERNAL MATES BOOK 20

FELICITY HEATON

Copyright © 2022 Felicity Heaton

All rights reserved. No part of this publication may be reproduced, stored in a retrieval system, or transmitted, in any form or by any means mechanical, electronic, photocopying, recording or otherwise without the prior written consent of the publisher, nor be otherwise circulated in any form of binding or cover other than that in which it is published and without a similar condition being imposed on the subsequent purchaser.

The right of Felicity Heaton to be identified as the Author of the Work has been asserted by her in accordance with the Copyright, Designs and Patents Act 1988.

First printed April 2022

First Edition

Layout and design by Felicity Heaton

All characters in this publication are purely fictitious and any resemblance to real persons, living or dead, is purely coincidental.

THE ETERNAL MATES SERIES

Discover more available paranormal romance books at:
http://www.felicityheaton.com

Or sign up to my mailing list to receive a FREE vampire romance ebook, learn about new titles, be eligible for special subscriber-only giveaways, and read exclusive content including short stories:
http://ml.felicityheaton.com/mailinglist

CHAPTER 1

Life was pretty sweet.

Hella ambled along the lakeshore, the heels of her black knee-high boots clicking on the pale golden flagstones that formed the broad promenade and her gaze on the stunningly blue water to her right as it twinkled in the artificial sunlight. She sipped her iced coffee, a bounce in her step, her whole body feeling lighter—brighter—for finally having swept off the oh-so-clingy nymph.

Ethyrian had been fun for a while. Charming. Rich. Handsome—no—beautiful. Hella wasn't sure a man should be beautiful, but that was nymphs for you. They weren't gorgeous like incubi, who all looked as if they had just stepped out of Hollywood and easily gave Brad Pitt and Ryan Reynolds a run for their money. No. Nymphs crossed the line into beautiful, every single one of them looking for all the world as if they had just stepped out of the wood elf kingdom in *Lord of the Rings*.

Man, she could really go for some Legolas right now.

She scowled, pushed that thought aside, and stopped her roaming gaze before she could single out any eligible males in the crowded promenade. She wasn't going to backslide. This was going to be her year. One devoted to exploring everything the fae town she lived in had to offer.

Which was a lot.

The damned nymph popped back into her head.

Hella booted him back out of it.

She had a policy when it came to her bedfellows. She didn't do commitment. She didn't do clingy. She most definitely didn't do men who cried like babies and begged her to take them back.

Hella had flatly told him no and goodbye and had kicked him to the curb.

For a man who had been desperate to stay with her, he certainly hadn't been calling all hours of the day or making wild attempts to change her mind. Which was strange.

It might have been a bit disappointing if it hadn't allowed her the space and freedom to expand her horizons.

Hella flashed a saucy wink at a pair of panther shifters loitering outside one of the taverns to her left that lined the broad pavement, facing the huge lake. The younger of the two took the bait, his smile nothing short of salacious as he gave her a sexy, slow once-over, raking his golden eyes from her hair to her boots and back again. Currently, she was working her way through all the eligible males in the fae town.

She glanced at the buildings that encircled the lake, crammed into the cavern that sat beneath a mountain, and realised that was a lot of men. Fenix, her incubus best-bud, was going to be kept in tonics and pills for a long time thanks to her current foray into sexually exploring every possible species—bar those classified as demon breeds like incubi—to see what suited her tastes best.

She hadn't tried panther yet.

She twirled a strand of her wavy blue hair around her fingers and sipped on her drink, making sure he got a good eyeful of the way she wrapped her glossy lips around the straw.

His low growl sent a thrill down her spine as he stepped towards her. His friend put a halt to everything by grabbing his arm and tugging him back, and saying something that had the handsome shifter frowning at him. Maybe they were going to fight over her. Two females stepped out of the tavern holding four tankards and made a beeline for the males. Hella shrugged. Or maybe not.

She turned her cheek to them, no longer interested in what either male had to offer. She also didn't do cheats. Anyone who warmed her bed for a night or two needed to be unattached.

The last thing she needed was angry females banging down her door or spreading malicious talk about her. It was bad for business.

No one wanted potions, ointments or spells from witches liable to screw others over. People tended not to separate a witch's personal life from their business practice. If she was known to cheat when it came to pursuing pleasure, she couldn't be trusted to not cheat when it came to the wares she sold. Plenty of witches had fallen foul of that and had been driven out of business, or worse, out of the fae town in which they lived.

Hella took in the elegant pastel pink, cream and dove-grey four-storey buildings that lined the promenade, their lead roofs absorbing the bright sunlight that bathed their façades. They resembled the buildings in Geneva, the nearest mortal town, a classic European air about them. The ones that acted as hotels for visiting immortals had French doors and balconies for each room rather than windows, offering a view of the lake to everyone who stayed there. Others were taverns with apartments above them, and some were shops and other businesses.

She drifted towards the large windows that lined the lowest floors of a row of stores, admiring the colourful glass bottles in the perfume emporium and the latest fashions displayed in the next building. Her gaze dropped to her black dress. Witches had to wear black dresses. It was tradition. No one wanted to buy magical goods from a woman in a pink dress or linen slacks and a camisole. A witch had to look the part.

Hella had pushed the limits of what was acceptable, testing out several dresses in her years to see how far she could go without turning off her clients and driving them elsewhere. Rather than the drab ankle-length dress many witches wore—mainly those fresh from the coven—she chose to wear knee-length empire-line dresses or summer dresses that cinched in at the waist and were stitched with faint violet stars. She even wore corseted dresses that showed a little more of her wares than was appropriate according to most circles in witch society.

Today, she had picked her favourite strapless empire-line dress, one that had a sheer black layer over the silky underlayer. That top layer was folded into pleats around her breasts, and beneath them there was a delicate band of ribbon embroidered with silver swirls and dots.

She always felt good in this dress. It drew the eye to her best assets.

She also didn't do ankle boots. She pushed the boundaries there too, choosing knee-high leather boots that laced up the front and had a comfortable three-inch block heel.

She eyed a pretty amethyst brooch on one of the dresses in the window display and drifted towards it, her gaze transfixed on it as the polished stone and gold filigree that surrounded it glittered in the warm light. If she couldn't wear colours other than black, maybe she could accessorise. She had never tried wearing jewellery before. Surely that wouldn't turn her clients off?

"Want it?" A male voice rolled over her and she tensed, her head whipping to her right. Disappointment flooded her when she found herself face to face with a squat, ageing man who was wearing half a tankard of ale down the front of his leather jerkin. He slurred, "I'll buy it for you."

In exchange for what?

Hella really didn't want to know the answer to that question, so she politely smiled and moved away, heading at speed for the lake and not slowing until she was sure she was alone again.

She dumped her empty drink in the nearest bin and surveyed the lake, losing herself in it as the water sparkled and its beauty hit her all over again. She was sure she would never grow tired of this view. The elegant buildings hugged the shore as far as the eye could see, ending only at the far side of the manmade lake where a slice of bright green replaced them. A dense forest rose up beyond the park, clinging to the rugged slope. Above the trees, the rocky roof of the cavern curled towards her.

Hella had helped with the spell that turned the ceiling of the cavern into a sky for the most part. Originally, it had channelled whatever weather was happening above the mountain they were under. The town hadn't particularly been happy when they had discovered that weather included snow and rain too, so on days when it was inclement topside, the spell defaulted to a fake blue sky and sunshine.

Which had led to the town demanding they do a new spell that made the days always sunny and warm, and the nights always clear and moonlit and blanketed with stars.

She tipped her head back and bathed in the warmth of the sunlight, and was humming to herself before she realised what she was doing. What could she put on the menu tonight? Maybe she could find some eligible bachelor panthers and convince them to warm her bed. If she wandered south, into the network of alleyways that connected the broader avenues in the town, she would eventually end up in the area of the cavern where the townhouses and apartment buildings gave way to sprawling walled compounds. The shifters liked their space and had established themselves quickly in the town, grabbing a lot of the vacant land for themselves. One of the compounds belonged to panthers. The one next to it belonged to tigers.

The two breeds were always fighting like cats and… cats.

Still, if she couldn't find a panther to sample, she could always bag herself a tiger. They were excellent lovers, incredibly acrobatic. She had learned a few things from the tigers she had bedded over the years.

She turned towards the next alley, feeling more positive about the evening ahead of her as she recalled her past exploits.

Her step slowed as she experienced a sudden sensation that something had shifted. Her mood? The air? She wasn't sure.

Whatever it was, it felt off.

Wrong.

She slowly took in her surroundings, that feeling growing at an alarming rate. The promenade was busy, with a lot of groups hanging out in front of stores or beside the lake. Other groups were moving, chatting animatedly to each other, and there were some solo people like her too. Some of those males and females meandered as she was, enjoying the warm sunshine, while others moved with purpose through the crowd, heading somewhere. She scanned them all, seeking the source of the sensation building inside her, and her fingertips tingled as her magic rose to the fore.

Hella looked over her shoulder in the direction she had come.

And spotted them.

A dozen burly, drop-dead-gorgeous men heading her way.

Hella hitched her skirts with her left hand, aware this was going to come down to a chase, and possibly a fight.

Because apparently, nymph kings didn't take no for an answer after all.

She summoned a protective spell and a speed spell in her mind, chanting the incantations as quickly as she could manage, and twisted back in the direction she had been heading.

And slammed straight into a broad, impressively cut bare chest.

Hella tilted her head back, her gaze roaming up the thick slabs of his pectorals to a strong but elegant neck, the spells forgotten as her stomach dropped.

The beautiful blond's lips quirked into a satisfied half-smile, the pointed tips of his ears showing as the breeze caught his long hair and shifted it across his shoulders, and his blue eyes piercing her.

Hello, Legolas.

She might have purred if it wasn't for one small fact.

He was a nymph.

His stunning eyes narrowed and his hand shot forwards, his grip bruising and unyielding as it closed around her arm, fingers pressing deep enough that pain shot up to her shoulder and down to her hand.

Life suddenly didn't look as sweet.

Panic seized her as firmly as his large hand as she heard the other nymphs closing in and the air hummed with familiar power. He was preparing to teleport. She swiftly raised her left knee, aiming for the sweet spot between his green leather clad legs as she quickly worked through the incantations.

He released her and blocked her leg.

And slammed a cold metal cuff around her right wrist with the other.

The power that had been surging through her disappeared, the incantation in her head nothing but empty words as the bespelled shackles did their work, severing the connection between her and her magic.

Hella grunted as two more nymphs grabbed her from behind, slamming her forwards into the larger male. She elbowed one in his stomach, hard enough that he loosed a very satisfying grunt and stumbled back a step. She was quick to seize the small amount of space she had gained, leaning away from the one who was trying to shackle her and cocking her fist. Another of the nymph's stopped her before she could punch him, tightly gripping her arm and holding her back.

The male with the shackles pulled her arm free of his grip and yanked it towards him, hard enough that pain shot through her shoulder as she fell against him. He shoved her back a few inches and she could only glare at him as he fastened the other cuff around her free wrist, his satisfied smirk growing wider, and teleported with her.

But in the breath between the fae town and an unfamiliar room, a sound rang in her ears, one that sent a chill skittering down her spine and spread strange warmth through her veins.

A beast howled in rage.

CHAPTER 2

If Grant MacKinnon had been one to wax lyrical, he might have written a poem or two dedicated to the comely redheaded lass who towered over him, but her small, booted foot pressing hard against his throat to keep him pinned to the cobbles didn't sit well with him so he growled at her instead, flashing his emerging fangs.

The witch merely smiled in response, her purple-painted lips curling in a way that was mocking.

Because it wasn't only her boot keeping him down, making him look like a weak pup in front of half the subterranean fae town near Fort William in Scotland as they gathered to see what the commotion was. He slid a glare at several of the males and females, wanting to growl again as he saw the amusement in their eyes.

He wasn't their entertainment.

Entertainment.

Shadows crowded the corners of his mind as it latched onto that word and echoes of faded feelings rose from the dead like wraiths to torment him as he battled both the witch and his past. The memories he had shoved into a deep, dark box within him threatened to break it open and he fought for air as panic swelled.

He pulled down a ragged breath and held it, focusing on it as he centred his mind, calming it enough that he could keep the lid on his past closed. Some days it was easier than others. Some days he couldn't even leave his damned cottage, wound up a wreck in the corner, jumping at shadows, snarling and snapping at ghosts, an embarrassment to his pack.

Thankfully, today he had a nice distraction to help him through the attack.

The female sighed at his apparent lack of focus, or maybe the fact he wasn't paying her as much attention as she desired, and pressed harder, reinforcing the weight of her foot with magic that swirled around him, lacing air that was already thick with the scent of herbs and spices, and other things, with a coppery tang.

MacKinnon struggled to suck down a vital breath as she crushed his throat, cutting off the growl he had intended to aim at her.

Fire surged through his veins, had him restless with a need to shift even when the pain kept his wolf form in check, holding it back. Probably a good thing. He wasn't sure what he had done to deserve being trampled on by this witch, but shifting into a wolf and ripping out her trachea with his fangs wouldn't go down well with the locals. One angry witch was dangerous enough—a whole horde of them would be a guaranteed death sentence.

But as air became an issue, and those shadows grew darker—stronger—he couldn't stop himself from reacting. He seized her ankle, closing his fingers tightly around it just above the leather of her boot, and shoved upwards.

The little witch refused to budge.

MacKinnon strained, every muscle in his body tensing as adrenaline surged, as he began to feel caged and panic broke to the surface, lacing the rage burning up his blood. His fingers pressed into her flesh, digging deep as his claws emerged, adding the metallic scent of her blood to the air, and he shoved upwards again as he called upon all his strength, sure it would be enough to remove her.

He was an alpha after all.

A position he had attained through a series of battles to the death, as was the way with his clan.

He had cut down no fewer than four contenders, laying even the biggest of them low, so a delicate slip of a female shouldn't be a match for him.

And yet he couldn't move her.

Didn't even make her sway as he exerted all his strength, gripping her ankle so fiercely that he had to be hurting her. Her eyes didn't even water. Her lips didn't even twitch. Not even when he dug his claws deeper and shredded the leather of her boots to slice through the flesh beneath. Her blood spilled over his fingers and their audience tensed.

MacKinnon tensed too, waiting to see how she would react.

She cast a black look at her leg and the blood that glistened on his fingers, huffed and pressed harder, shoving the heel of her boot into his throat with enough force that dark spots winked across his vision.

The redhead leaned over him, her hair swaying away from her ankle-length black dress, and planted her hands on her shapely hips.

She sneered.

"Hear me and hear me well, Grant MacKinnon of clan MacKinnon."

And then she spewed something that might have been Latin, or Ancient Greek for all he knew, and the hairs on his nape rose to stand on end and his wolf cowered as a current ran down his spine and the air around him charged with electricity.

The bitch was casting magic on him.

MacKinnon grabbed her ankle in both hands now, his wolf lunging forwards to snap and snarl as that part of him detected the threat, saw an enemy it wanted to take down and a cage it needed to free itself from. A cage. The lid on his past blew right off the box and all the dark, ugly things spilled out. He growled and bared his fangs, snapped them as fur rippled over his skin in response to the fierce need to escape, to the memories that surged up like a black tide, threatening to swallow him. When he still couldn't move the witch, he cast a desperate look at several males.

None of the bastards looked inclined to help him.

Several of them looked away, suddenly interested in their boots.

Kin howled as his bones ached, as his muscles clamped down on them with enough force that they felt as if they might snap, and put everything he had into one last effort. Her foot lifted. His eyes widened and he didn't miss a beat, shoved harder as victory appeared within his reach, fuelled by hope that he would be able to escape her before she could complete the spell.

But then she smiled wickedly.

He howled again as every molecule in his body vibrated, a chain reaction that began in his toes and his fingers and swept through him to collide in his chest. His heart seized, his body feeling fit to burst as he arched off the cobblestones, as pain stole his breath and fire branded his bones.

The world wobbled, the ground pitching, and he laboured for air and fought the encroaching darkness as his vision tunnelled, the witch becoming little more than a smear of crimson and black against a blur of white and turquoise.

Her words warbled in his ears.

"Find your fated one and bring her to me."

Kin mentally flipped her off as he clung to consciousness, as the pain tearing through him began to ease and the fire began to abate, and his muscles turned liquid. He wasn't about to hand over his fated female to anyone. He didn't even know who she was. In all his two hundred and fifty-seven years, he had never even come close to finding her. He had grown convinced that she didn't exist.

Destiny hadn't made a female for him.

He was clinging to life for no good reason.

MacKinnon sagged onto the cobblestones, the taste of his own blood strong in his mouth as he breathed, on the verge of chuckling at the witch. He wasn't sure what he had done to deserve her wrath, but the moment she let him go, he would tell her whatever she wanted to hear and then he was gone and he was never coming back. Unless she had compelled him in some way, he would be fine.

The witch leaned closer again, slowly coming back into focus as the pain ebbed away, leaving only weakness behind. That weakness increased as she pressed her foot down on his throat again, cutting off his air supply. Maybe he wouldn't leave. Maybe he would kill her and be done with it. She deserved death.

No one treated him like this and got away with it.

Not anymore.

Her dark eyes glittered and swirled with silver stars as she stared down at him and hissed, "I'll be kind enough to give you a clue, and a warning that I'll be keeping tabs on you. Don't think to play me, wolf. The curse I placed on you is strong. You're going to crave your mate, will wither and fade to nothing unless you find her and she accepts you, and then you're going to betray her by bringing her to me. I have a feud to settle."

Rage scorched his blood to ashes as it hit him that he really hadn't done anything to deserve this curse. He hadn't crossed this witch in any way. The female she believed to be his fated mate had crossed her and now she was using him to get to her.

Expected him to go against his very nature, his every instinct, and betray his one true mate.

MacKinnon snarled as he pushed her foot up, black fur sweeping over his bare forearms from beneath the rolled-up sleeves of his dark grey Henley and his nails lengthening back into claws. He pinned her with a glare, channelling all the anger he was feeling into it.

"I'll no' be doing what ye want, ye hackit bint, so piss off," he growled, aware of everyone's eyes on him, of the judging looks he would be receiving from the nobles among the crowd.

Under normal circumstances, he could tame his tongue and talk as eloquently as the residents of the fae town, not betraying his deep Scottish roots.

But he was pissed.

The witch flashed him another smile, one he wanted to punch off her face. "I don't remember giving you a choice... unless you think to choose death? If you do not do this for me, that is the fate that awaits you."

She went to remove her foot and then paused and leaned over him again.

"I almost forgot!" Her dark eyes brightened again. "Your clue. I did promise you one after all. A scent for the wolf to follow, as it were. Your mate is a hella bad witch."

Kin frowned at her and opened his mouth to ask what the hell that was supposed to mean.

But she disappeared.

He popped to his feet, fury rolling through him in powerful waves as he lifted his head and scented the air as he turned in a circle. There was no trace of her. The crowd backed away now he was standing and they could get a good look at him, the glances they cast him as he stretched his acute senses out to cover almost every inch of the bustling fae town making it clear they wanted nothing to do with him or any trouble he might be bringing.

People tended to react that way to him.

Either that or they got out of his way, giving him a wide berth.

MacKinnon liked to think of it as a perk of being six-ten. It certainly made up for all the times he banged his head on a doorframe or was asked to reach something for someone in a supermarket. He had lost count of the number of older mortal women who had requested assistance and then snared him in a ten-minute round of complimenting his height and his build, and complaining how there hadn't been men like him when they were young enough.

There had been men like him around when they had been young enough, because he had been around. Only he had never been interested in human women. They were too delicate. Breakable. As fragile as glass.

Kin preferred a female with spirit and strength, one who could handle him.

Was his fated one such a female?

He huffed as he realised the witch was gone. There was no trace of her for him to track, and all he had to go on was her word that he was cursed and a clue that didn't make any sense. He scrubbed the day's worth of growth on his face, scratching the stubble as he went over everything she had said, giving his body time to recover before he dared to move. The benefit of being an old wolf was that he healed fast. In less than a day, his throat would be as new.

His mood, however, looked as if it was going to be in the ditch for a while at least.

What the hell was the clue?

The hackit witch hadn't told him a thing he could use. Not even her name, so he couldn't hunt her down and press her for more information.

Or kill her and hope it lifted the curse.

He growled. If there even was a curse. And even if there was, he couldn't—wouldn't—trust a word the witch had said. She had known him, sure, but that didn't mean she was telling the truth about the existence of his fated female. He had a reputation around town and there weren't many other six-ten alpha wolves in the area. In fact, there weren't any. She had probably decided to target him because he was easily distinguishable from the other wolves and most of the patrons and residents of the fae town. He had been an easy target, one she could cast a spell upon to make him believe whoever she wanted was his fated one, giving him a reason to find her.

Doubt began to spread through him, his logical mind swift to lock on to his theory that the female this witch wanted him to betray wasn't his mate. She was just another witch and he had just been in the wrong place at the wrong time.

Kin shoved his fingers through his dark hair, tousling it as the crowd dispersed, returning to their business and leaving him standing on the cobblestone road that arced through the witches' district in the direction of the town square. He drew down a deep breath, coughed as his throat ached and the thick scents from the copper stills bubbling beneath the colourful canopies that stretched outwards from the white two- and three-storey buildings burned his lungs. A few of the shop owners had remained outside and were watching him with curious eyes. Several of them went back to tending to their collections of clay pots and jugs as he glanced at them, making it clear they didn't want to help him.

There was one way of finding out whether he had been bespelled and if it was possible that spell was a curse and one designed to trick his mind and his body into believing this witch he was meant to find and betray was his mate.

He could ask another witch.

Kin made a beeline for one of the shops.

For a breed that preferred to wear black, the witches loved a splash of colour. The roofs of every building in the district were made of green, blue and gold tiles that undulated like great serpents, and jewel-tone canopies adorned with crests and writing extended from every one of them, providing shelter for the stores that spilled out onto the wide pedestrian street.

He ducked beneath a violet canopy and reached for the painted wooden door, but it opened before he could touch it. The petite white-haired witch that filled the doorway smiled up at him, her green eyes bright with mischief.

"Been a while, Kin. What brings you to town?" She cast a glance over her shoulder. "Need some more smartphones?"

This witch peddled phones that worked on a magical network her sister had built, a method of communication that even functioned in Hell, and he had purchased several from her in the past. His pack had members who worked with others in that dark realm, and he didn't like being out of touch with them for long periods. Hell was dangerous. No place for a wolf.

"Came to meet with a pack. Was waylaid by a redheaded witch." He rubbed his throat, drawing her gaze there, and her eyes slowly widened.

She eased back and to one side, and held her arm out. "Come inside. I'll take a look at that for you."

"I'll heal," he growled and squeezed past her, ducking low to avoid banging his head on the top of the doorframe. "I need answers. Am I cursed?"

"Cursed?" She peered back into the street, a worried edge to her expression, and then closed the door and locked it. She flipped the sign on the glass around and came to him, her eyes glittering with concern. "What makes you think you're cursed?"

When she raised her hand, he instinctively backed off, his wolf side driving him to keep his distance as it sensed magic. While he and his wolf were really one and the same—two halves of a whole—the human and beast sides of him reacted very differently in most situations. It was the reason many of his breed viewed the two separately and could distinguish between what reactions came from the wolf and what came from the human. His human mind used logic, employing a broad range of emotions and experiences to draw conclusions about things and react to them. His wolf mind operated on a more basic level, fuelled by strong instincts to survive, breed and protect. Emotions were boiled down to only a handful and any recent experience coloured his reactions, which meant in the eyes of his wolf side, magic equalled bad.

And something to avoid.

Unfortunately, he backed right into one of her rotating displays of phone cases. He grimaced and twisted as it toppled, tried to grab it and caught it at the last second, but not soon enough to stop it from spilling half its contents across the floor. He grunted as he righted it and moved to one side too much, knocking against another display stand.

"Your bloody shop is too wee." He seized the second display before it could fall too, growled as he cast a glance around him and realised there was nowhere he could move without being in danger of causing mayhem.

Abigail sighed and took hold of his arm, pulling him towards her as she waved her other hand. The air charged and the hairs on his nape rose again, and everything in the room scooted away from him to line the edges, giving him space.

MacKinnon barely leashed the urge to wrench free of her grip and lash out at her in response to her using magic so close to him. He clenched his fists and gritted his teeth so hard he felt sure they would crumble under the pressure, and told himself that she wasn't a threat.

She was a friend.

It didn't stop the darkness that teased the edges of his mind, vile thorny tendrils that sensed the weakness in him and saw an opportunity to strike. This darkness wasn't one born of recent experiences but of those deep in his past, and it wasn't welcome. He focused his thoughts, blocking the memories that tried to come, pushing them back down into the shadowy box where they belonged, and won his fight against them just as Abigail's hand slipped from his arm.

"Better?" She went to the counter, picked up a metal bottle and sipped from it.

It looked like a water bottle—the sort humans used when exercising. He had seen a few mortals running in the streets topside with such canteens. He focused on it and the witch, narrowing the world down to her and his current predicament, using them to banish his memories.

As those memories lost their grip on him, his wolf side lunged back to the fore, snarling and pushing him to shift in order to face the current threat.

The current non-existent threat.

He wasn't in danger. Not anymore. He told himself that on repeat, but it didn't calm his wolf side.

Abigail hopped up onto the counter, between a display stand filled with gift cards and the cash register, and crossed her legs. Unlike the witch who had cursed him, she was one of the types who preferred to wear a more fashionable style of black dress. It ended at her knees, flashing violet stockings and ankle high pointed black leather boots.

"Come closer." She waved him towards her. When he didn't move, she rolled her eyes. "Wolf giving you hell?"

Was it ever? He clenched his fists, curling his fingers and digging his claws into his palms. His instincts could sense the magic in her and it had his wolf side on the defensive, wanting to keep his distance. He sucked down a breath, making his throat burn, and told himself that she wasn't a danger to him. Abigail was a sweet lass and had always been nice to him and his pack.

His wolf growled anyway.

MacKinnon huffed and pulled down another breath, stared at Abigail and forced himself to move towards her, because she couldn't help him unless he trusted her. Trust wasn't easy to come by for him, but Abigail had earned it.

She set her bottle down beside her hip and held both hands out in front of her. Her eyes slipped shut as she murmured something beneath her breath and the air vibrated around him. His wolf side battered the cage of his mortal body, growling and snarling, but he breathed slowly and evenly, doing his damnedest to calm himself, aware that if he didn't, he would shift. Shifting right now would be dangerous. His human mind—the logical side of him— would be subdued by his animal instincts. He would end up lashing out at every perceivable threat.

Which meant every witch in the town, including Abigail.

"There is a spell on you. I can't tell what it is though, and I really can't help you break it if that's what you want. I'm not that good at this sort of thing." Abigail's voice held a note of apology, or possibly regret. Her eyes opened and lifted to lock with his as her pale eyebrows furrowed. "Any info you can give me might help me figure out what this spell is and I could find a witch who has the right skill set in order to undo it."

"A curse," he spat and paced away from her, unable to keep still as the anger that had been drifting to the back of his mind surged to the fore again, stoking the embers in his veins back into an inferno. "I'm to find my fated one and betray her by bringing her to this witch. Redhead. Nasty. Dark eyes. Wee little thing like you."

"Everyone is *wee* compared with you." Abigail shrugged. "Doesn't sound familiar. Why does she want you to betray this other witch?"

He shrugged now, hefting his shoulders as he pivoted and growled. "I don't know. The witch did something. Is it… is it possible she might not be my true mate?"

He hadn't realised how badly he needed to know the answer to that question until it burst from his lips. His gaze collided with Abigail's again as his entire body tensed, every inch of him going rigid as he awaited her answer.

She sipped her water and then pursed her lips. "It is possible. A spell can make you believe anything."

"Fuckin' knew it." He snarled and twisted, stalked away from her to the other end of the shop, which took all of three strides, and barely leashed the urge to lash out at the bottles and boxes stacked on a cabinet there. Abigail would make him pay for any damages and the price tags on some of the items was enough to put him off unleashing his rage on them. He settled for growling instead. "She's playing me."

"Or not," Abigail put in. "It is entirely possible this witch you're meant to betray is your fated one."

He huffed at that. "No way. How could a witch know who my mate is?"

"A spell, maybe? Imagine the money you could make off it!" Her eyes lit up, as if she was already counting the cash in her head, and then she sobered. "But it would be one hell of a spell. Something like that… it would cost a witch a lot. I'm not talking coin either. Dark magic… I've read books… Heard rumours like any other light witch. Some dark spells want blood."

"Doesn't sound so bad," he muttered.

"I'm talking blood like shaving years off your life blood. Dark magic likes a sacrifice. It craves power and it gets it from leeching the life from the witch casting it. I even heard a rumour once that a spell killed a dark witch the second she cast it." Her tone was matter of fact, but there was a wariness in her eyes, as if just talking about such things was forbidden and liable to get her into trouble. Light witches tended to avoid anything to do with their darker counterparts and Kin was beginning to see why.

"Why would a witch be willing to put herself through that just to settle a feud?" MacKinnon frowned at her as he tried to think of a good enough reason for a witch to want to risk death in order to have revenge upon someone.

"Who knows?" She gave him a look that said they would have to be crazy.

"But a spell could find my mate? This could be real?" He tried to keep the desperate need to know the answer to that question out of his voice and failed, sounded far too eager as he stared at Abigail.

"Maybe. Maybe not. If a witch had figured out a way to find someone's fated mate for them, you think they wouldn't have cashed in on it by now? Witches love money. MacKinnon… I'm not sure it's possible for a witch to divine another person's mate for them." Abigail's shrug said it all.

The redhead had probably been lying.

It strengthened his belief that she had targeted him because he had been in the wrong place at the wrong time and because she had known he would be driven to find the witch. He had been the perfect candidate for her curse.

His wolf side wouldn't want to rest until it had tracked down this female who could potentially be his mate.

Already the need to see if this witch triggered an urge to mate with her, rousing instincts in a way only his fated one could, was building inside him, steadily stealing control and blurring reality to make him believe the witch was his true mate. Even if the redhead hadn't told him he was cursed to die if he didn't find his fated one as she wanted, he would have eventually succumbed to the deep need to find her.

Or he would have if he could unravel her clue.

"If you can't lift the spell, maybe you can help me in another way. I was to be given a clue." He crossed the room in two strides and stopped close to her. His mood took another dark turn as he thought about how the redhead had mocked him and what she had told him, which hadn't been much. "All I know is my fated female is, according to her, a hella bad witch. The fuckin' bampot."

Abigail slowly smiled. "There's your clue."

He scowled at her, in no mood for games. "That's no' a clue. That's a manglin' of the English language."

She gave him a pointed look and he glared now. She was lucky he wasn't spewing curses and cutting loose in a way that would have her looking confused rather than irritated. It was hard enough on the best of days to keep his Scottish brogue dialled back enough that the innkeepers didn't roll their eyes at him and ask him to repeat everything three times. For a fae town in the heart of the Highlands, there was a lack of locals running the taverns.

Bloody imports.

"Hella is a witch. I've heard of her."

That had all his focus locking on Abigail again, the innkeepers forgotten as his heart thumped against his ribs and his blood pounded with a need to make her repeat what she had said so he could be sure he had heard her right.

"Is she local?" Kin tried to imagine what kind of wild lass would come with a name like Hella. Probably the sort who would kick his arse to the moon and back if she knew what he had planned for her.

Could he really hand over his fated female to the redhead?

He scrubbed that thought. She wasn't his real fated one. If she triggered any instincts in him, it was thanks to the spell. The redhead had employed a cunning trick to make him do as she wanted, because as much as he wanted to return to his pack and forget about this so-called curse she had cast on him, he couldn't.

He needed to find Hella.

He needed to see her.

"She's not local." Abigail slid off the counter and moved around it.

Damn it.

It made sense he supposed. Why would the redhead send a wolf to track a female if she was already in the vicinity? He frowned. Why send him at all? Witches could use spells to access the portal pathways that linked the fae towns and places around the globe, and Hell. The same spell they placed on tokens that shifters and other breeds that couldn't teleport needed to use the portals, making a small fortune off his kind.

The witch could find this female if she wanted it.

Which led him to suspect that he was an important part of her plan.

She wanted him to be the one to find this Hella.

This whole thing was beginning to smell a lot like revenge. Hella had done something to aggravate the redhead and now he had been dragged into their feud, was a tool the redhead was using to execute what she must consider to be the ultimate revenge. He wanted no part of it, but the feeling building inside him, compelling him to find Hella, said he wasn't getting a choice, just as the redhead had warned.

The thought of finding a female who might trigger his mating instincts sat like acid coated lead in his stomach though. How long had he waited for his fated female? How long had he been clinging to the hope that there was someone out there who had been made just for him, with whom he could share the deepest of bonds?

A female who would give his life new purpose and light, chasing back the shadows that had long darkened it.

Could Hella really be his mate?

There was no way for him to know.

He frowned at his boots as one dawned on him, whispering through his mind to tease and tempt him. He could find the lass, bring her to the witch, and break the curse. Then he would know.

Although betraying his fated one might not make her feel particularly warm and fuzzy towards him.

Kin shrugged it off. He would worry about the finer details later. He needed to find her first.

"Where is this Hella?" He lifted his gaze, settling it back on Abigail.

She glanced up from counting the coin in her register. "According to my friend, she lives in the fae town in Geneva."

"Geneva." He had never left the country before and now he was meant to head halfway across Europe?

He wasn't sure what to expect, had never really paid much heed to his pack members who had gone abroad and returned with tales of their adventures, because he had been too busy running the clan and keeping it safe, and more concerned with what was happening at home rather than hundreds of miles away.

But visiting Switzerland couldn't be any worse than staying here and slowly dying.

Kin reached into his jeans' pocket and tossed several gold coins onto the counter in front of Abigail.

"I'll be needing a token then."

CHAPTER 3

MacKinnon twitched and whipped towards the lake to his left as the air there shifted, suddenly growing cooler. His claws punched long from his fingertips, ready in a heartbeat, and didn't retract even when he saw the towering jet of water that rose high into the air and thundered down into the lake around one hundred feet out. A fountain. It resembled the one in the nearby mortal town of Geneva.

In fact, the whole fae town resembled Geneva, as if someone had copied it building for building. Although, this immortal town was much smaller than the one topside. It was just as bright and elegant though, with warm sunshine that beat down on the pale sandstone pavement and reflected off the balconied buildings to his right.

Several of them were hotels, and he had been tempted to call into one and secure himself a place to stay, but when he had approached the doorman, the male had looked aghast and Kin had caught his reflection in the revolving door.

Since then, he had been keeping his head down, deeply aware of the way many of the townsfolk paused to stare. He had never felt so conspicuous. He glared at a trio of black-haired females who stood by the shore, their violet eyes and pointed ears betraying their breed as much as their antiquated corseted dresses did. They all stared at him and only one of them looked curious. The other two looked disgusted.

Sure, he was a big male, and he probably had a face like a smacked arse right now because his mood was still deep in a ditch and showed no sign of improving thanks to the attention he was attracting, and his throat looked like someone had used it as a punchbag, but there was really no reason for all the finely dressed males and females to gawp at him.

He levelled a black look at the trio of elves, causing them to turn away.

He heaved a sigh as he looked ahead of him and saw only more nobles, coming and going along the promenade as if it was the fashionable thing to do. The gods only knew it probably was in a town like this one. It reeked of wealth.

Kin denied the urge to keep his head down as he walked, tipped his damned chin up and shoulders back instead, because he wasn't going to be intimidated or cowed by these noble folk.

His gaze narrowed on a group of pointy eared males ahead of him, ones who wore green leather trousers and white shirts beneath a matching jerkin. Gold glittered around their wrists and adorned their ears, and their finely boned features settled into scowls as they caught sight of him. Kin scowled right back at them, barely leashing the urge that surged through him and had his claws itching to rip into their flesh, to wipe the haughty smirks off their fae faces.

Nymphs.

He growled through his clenched teeth, battling memories that bubbled to the surface. A darkened room. Candles bursting to life. Fae nobles forming a ring around him, seated on opulent gold and velvet chairs as servants scraped and bowed to them.

The crack of a whip.

Pain echoed down his spine, a ghost of his past that continued to taunt him whenever he let the memories come, whenever he wasn't strong enough to deny them and they slipped free of the box he had locked them away in. It would be days before he had fully rid himself of them, freeing himself of their torment.

The sensible side of him said to move on, to ignore the nymphs because they couldn't provide him with the information he needed and, therefore, they didn't matter. The side of him that had been born in that dark part of his past, that refused to be tamed, rose to crush it and he pivoted towards the blond males, unable to stop himself. His claws lengthened further and his fangs bit into his gums as he strode towards them, rapidly crossing the span of flagstones that separated them. His breathing quickened, deepened, sending vital oxygen to his blood as he geared up for a fight.

One of the nymphs noticed him approaching and tapped another on the arm, and before Kin could kick off and grab at least one of them, the whole group had disappeared. Kin stopped where they had been and glared at the rippling blue water of the lake, breathing hard and struggling to rein in his anger and the urge to lash out at everyone who moved behind him. He fixed his focus on the water, staring beyond the surface to pick out the flora and fauna that called the lake home. He tracked a school of small fish, bewitched by how their silver sides made them flash whenever they changed direction and how they moved as one, in perfect symphony.

The scent of herbs and metal filled his nostrils.

MacKinnon turned and looked over his shoulder, seeking the source of it. He pivoted when he spotted two witches strolling along the street. They paused in front of the window of one of the stores.

He crossed the broad stretch of pavement to them, not failing to notice how their slight shoulders tensed beneath their plain black dresses as he closed in. He glanced at his reflection in the window they faced, locking gazes with the one on the left, and swallowed to wet his throat as he ran his hand over his wild dark hair.

"Excuse me, lasses, I was wondering if you could tell me where I could find a witch named Hella." He made a point of stopping a good six feet from them, attempting to show them that he wasn't a threat with his body language as well as his gentle tone of voice.

They turned to face him as one, ran an assessing gaze down him and then spoke to him.

In German.

Their tone wasn't even close to gentle.

It was abrasive, with a dismissive note.

Before he could try again, they hurried away from him.

Kin growled at his reflection in the clothing store's window, baring his fangs, because he must have asked at least two dozen witches about Hella now and none of them would tell him. He doubted they didn't know her. There was always a glimmer in their eyes, a spark that betrayed them and said they knew exactly where to find the female he was seeking.

They just didn't want to tell him.

He took in his appearance. Taller than most witches by a good foot and a half. Probably three times their slender weight in muscle. Scruff on his face. Unkempt hair that looked exactly how it should given how many times he had clawed, raked and shoved his fingers through it in frustration over the last few hours.

Eyes that were currently more gold than grey because his wolf side was at the fore, his temper way beyond his control.

And a pretty black and purple bruise across his throat.

He could hardly blame the witches for not wanting to tell him where to find one of their own.

Kin huffed. Maybe if he schooled his features a little and tried to appear more approachable and less homicidal then they would speak with him.

He doubted it.

Witches were quite protective of their own, but it was worth a shot.

He tried out a few faces, attempting to appear charming as he smiled at his reflection, and probably looking like he was losing his mind. A shiver skated down his spine and his wolf instincts growled at him that someone was watching him. He shifted his gaze to the left, catching the reflection of the three females who lingered a few feet behind him. Pretty wee lasses. All of them wore provocative leather corsets and mini-skirts in glaring colours, designed to draw the attention of males to them.

Succubi.

They sidled over to him and he turned to face them, flashing them all a warm smile that had their eyes brightening. Maybe he could get information on Hella from someone other than a witch. Witches did business with other immortals after all. Chances were high that several people in this town would have gone to Hella for a potion or spell.

The tallest of the succubi, a delicate pink-haired beauty who stood a good foot shorter than him despite her stiletto boots, offered a smile in return and stepped ahead of her sisters. She paused only inches from him and stroked a small hand down his chest as she faux-purred at him.

"You look like you need to let loose," she murmured, her voice like honey, sweet and tempting him to dip his head and have a taste of what she was offering.

He kept his spine straight and resisted her allure, letting her feather her fingers over his chest to the open vee of his dark grey Henley. She teased the strip of flesh there, her glittering blue eyes growing hooded.

"Been a while since we had one as strong as you in this town. Visiting someone?" She grazed her fingers across the dip between his pectorals.

The shorter of the other two came up beside him and stroked her hand down his forearm and pushed the long sleeve of his top up to reveal skin.

She leaned in and licked it, and groaned. "He tastes like sunshine."

"No tasting," the third one barked and pulled her off him, shoving her aside. She grinned wickedly. "At least not unless I can get a lick of this pop too."

"Lasses, there's plenty o' me to go around." Kin held his hands up and smiled.

The three succubi sank into each other on a sigh.

"Did you hear that voice?" Pink-hair said with a dreamy smile at her sisters.

The shorter, brunette female swayed towards her. "Did I? When was the last time we had a Scot?"

"Makes me ache just hearing it. Do you think he knows how to put it to good use? I could probably feed off him just talking to me!" The older of the three, a pretty button-nosed blonde, edged her hand towards him.

Kin grinned down at them, aware they were saying whatever it took to lure him under their spell and make him part with his coin, but enjoying it nonetheless. "I'm here on business, but perhaps I could be enticed to take a small break from my hunt… if you would be so inclined to help me."

"Be so inclined?" Pink-hair swayed towards him now, hunger lighting her eyes. "Darling, I'll do whatever you want if it will get you into my bed for the night."

"*Our* bed," Brunette snapped.

"Yes, our bed." Blonde licked her lips.

All three of them sidled closer, crowding him as they gazed adoringly at him, as if he had just fallen out of Heaven or a dream. Their scents swirled around him, fogging his head a little, and he focused his mind, on his guard against them because he had no intention of parting with his coin or indulging these succubi in any way.

Mostly because he would probably end up parting with his life.

As strong as he was, he wasn't sure he could handle three succubi feeding on him.

He drew down a breath as he tried to decide how to ask them about Hella and the fog in his head grew thicker as an intoxicating scent filled his lungs.

Like a blend of fresh rain on heather moorland faintly spiced with cinnamon.

Kin breathed deeper, unable to get enough of the scent, and his muscles clamped down on his bones as his blood heated. His wolf side lunged to the fore and his fangs lengthened, his claws emerging as hunger rolled through him, fiercer than he had ever felt it before.

It was a trick.

A power the succubi were wielding to pull him under their spell and into their bed.

Only when he bent his head to sniff their necks and scent them, it wasn't any of them who smelled so enticing.

He groaned as his cock stiffened in response to the scent as it grew stronger and seemed to invade every cell in his body and hijack it. His head clouded more rapidly, thoughts blurring and fading to the background as instinct stole control. He desperately scanned the crowd on the promenade, seeking the source of the scent.

And froze when his gaze landed on a stunning, blue-haired lass with emerald eyes.

A chill skated down his spine and his shaft went hard as stone.

It was her.

She was the source of the scent.

She was his fated one.

He felt it in his bones. His soul. This female had been made for him, was meant for only him, and she would be his. He shoved the succubi aside, unaware of them now, the world narrowing down to the beautiful lass fate had created for him.

Hella.

MacKinnon drifted towards her, powerless to resist her pull. The need to be close to her was strong and she hadn't even noticed him yet. How desperate would he be to be near to her, pressed against her and holding her in his arms when she did see him? The urge to gather her to him was already overwhelming, his awareness of the world coming back as instinct growled that his female was parading down a busy street in a black dress that highlighted her figure.

Drawing the eyes of other males.

She stiffened, her body locking up tight.

Was she aware of him?

He tracked the path of her gaze as she tossed a look over her shoulder.

To a group of bare-chested nymphs.

Her panic hit him like a shockwave, rocking him back on his heels, and he growled and kicked off as the dozen blond males made their move, launching towards her. He wasn't sure what his female had done to deserve the wrath of a witch or a pack of nymphs, and he didn't care. Every fibre of his being howled at him to protect her and he would do just that. He charted an intercept course, shoving men and women aside, not caring where they landed as he locked his gaze on the two nymphs leading the charge.

He sensed the female move.

Felt her fear.

Instinct demanded he go to her, had him twisting on his heel and barrelling into two shifter males. The black-haired men went down hard and he leaped over them, ignoring their yells, his gaze wild as he sought the witch.

A larger nymph had her in his clutches and was holding her tightly despite her attempts to break free.

Kin snarled and gnashed his fangs when her fear cranked up a notch and he spotted the reason why.

The bastard had cuffed her.

The bright silver band of metal around her delicate wrist glinted in the sunlight as she desperately struggled.

Kin grabbed a female and pushed her out of his way, into a group of males, his heart hammering as the other nymphs reached Hella.

Her green eyes shone with terror as she looked up at the male who held her, one who towered as tall as Kin and probably weighed as much in muscle. Not that it was going to stop Kin from tearing the male a new one and teaching him the error of his ways.

No one touched his fated female.

Kin cocked his fist as he lunged towards the bastard, aiming at the back of his head, determined to knock his teeth out from behind.

He threw the punch as soon as he was close enough.

And hit nothing but air as the fiend teleported.

Taking his wee witch with him.

Rage burned up Kin's blood and he couldn't hold back the feral howl that rolled up his throat, tossed his head back and let loose, pouring all his fury into it as his spine bowed forwards, his claws like talons as he dragged his hands down to his sides and every muscle in his body tensed.

Black fur swept over his skin and he itched all over, his bones aching as anger had him close to shifting, the need to track his female bringing his wolf to the fore. He managed to find the strength to deny it and clung to his mortal form as he twisted towards the succubi who had been flirting with him.

They were huddled together in front of the shop still, a sea of fallen men and women between him and them, all of which looked ready to tear *him* a new one as he stalked through them, heading for the succubi.

"Where do the nymphs live?" he snarled as soon as he was close enough to his prey, and when none of them answered him quickly enough, he shot his hand out and gripped the throat of the pink-haired one. He dragged her against him and flashed his fangs in her face. "Tell me where the nymphs live in this town."

Her eyes widened and she shook her head, her hands coming up to grip his arm as she choked.

"Not here." The brunette pressed her hands against his chest, trying to push him away. "They don't live here."

"Lies," he spat, because he had seen other nymphs during his search for Hella. They had to have a building or two here in the town somewhere, a place they called home. He snarled, unable to hold it back as he thought of his female at their mercy.

Nymphs were sexual predators, using their beauty and charms to seduce unwitting females. He had seen the breed at work with his own eyes, had watched them pull even unwilling women under their spell, convincing them to surrender to them.

The blonde sank her little claws into his hand, drawing blood and earning herself a glare. "They bore the royal seal. Hella will be in Lucia by now. Let her go!"

Hella.

The confirmation that the ethereal blue-haired female had been the one he had come to find shook him, had his grip on the succubus relaxing against his will as he struggled to keep his mind on the hunt and off how beautiful Hella was.

Was she really his mate?

He shook that thought away with a growl, unwilling to trust his instincts. The feeling she stirred in him was a fabrication, a lie meant to make him do as the witch wanted and a method of punishing Hella for whatever sin she had committed against the one who had cursed him.

He would be a fool to allow himself to believe Hella was his fated one.

Yet he couldn't stem the need to find her and save her from the nymphs.

Kin shoved the pink-haired female at her companion. "Lucia? Where is that? Somewhere in Switzerland?"

Pink-hair laughed and he had half a mind to grab her and choke her again for mocking his ignorance. She rubbed her throat. "Lucia isn't a town. It's not even a country."

He flexed his fingers, tired of dancing around the answer, because he needed to be moving. He needed to find the nymphs who had taken Hella from him and take her back.

She noticed his subtle threat and blurted, "It's the faery realm."

"Fuck," MacKinnon bit out.

First another country. Now another realm. Add the fact that his wolf instincts had recognised Hella as his fated one and it was all becoming too much. He missed the uncomplicated nature of his home in the Highlands already, ached to return to the clan and rest atop his favourite spot, taking in the rolling moorland that embraced the munros and waiting for the gloaming, when a sense of magic and wonder filled the air.

His mother had held him on her lap many times as a pup to tell him the gloaming was when the faeries came out—in that brief moment between day and night.

Between light and darkness.

Now he was expected to go to a place of faeries and he was unsure what to expect when he got there. There were other stories about fae-kind. Darker stories. The ancient books in his possession, passed to him by his mother, were filled with tales of the seelie and unseelie, and their eternal war.

The thought of stepping into their realm had him hesitating, lingering in the mortal one, where he was safe.

But the vision of his female being held against her will, shackled and stripped of power, and the lingering scent of her that swirled around him had him gearing up for a battle.

He couldn't bear the thought of her in danger, so he would place himself in the path of it by pursuing her into another world.

Kin flexed his fingers into fists.

He'd had to fight for everything he had ever wanted.

It looked as if this time would be no different.

If it was war the nymphs wanted, it was war he would give them.

CHAPTER 4

If Hella's magic hadn't been bound by the infernal shackles weighing her arms down, she might have been tempted to hit the nymph who dogged her every step with a spell or two. Turn him into a eunuch. Elevate him to a soprano. That sort of thing.

As it was, all she could do was glare at him as she paced around the circular room, her anger at a constant rolling boil.

She passed a very expensive looking vase, the sort humans paid millions for, and swiped it from the polished wooden sideboard, turned in one fluid motion and launched it at the guard. He swayed to his right, easily dodging it, and it landed on the pretty parquet floor and smashed into a thousand pieces. Part of her had expected him to at least attempt to catch it, saving the precious object for his master.

Hella reached for a nice crystal sculpture of a man and woman going at it, the temptation to see if he would catch this one and the desire to smash more of Ethyrian's belongings too powerful to deny.

Her guard gripped her arm before she could grab the statue and hauled her away from it. He twisted with her and shoved her towards the centre of the room. Her prison. She curled a lip at it. She was being held by force by a man she had dumped.

In a sumptuous room that had every luxury imaginable, but it was still by force.

Just this one room put her home to shame. It put every home in the Geneva fae town to shame. She had been in the most opulent of them, attending soirees thrown by the nobles, or peddling them a potion. This room made them look shabby in comparison.

The gold and crystal chandelier sparkled in the candlelight that illuminated the intricately painted domed ceiling of the huge circular room—a painting that depicted a lot of naughty things—and caught on the gilded mirrors that lined the ivory walls, mimicking the two arched windows and the arched doorways.

Between the two windows, there was a large circular mattress covered in colourful silk pillows. Four posts enclosed it, carved to look like trees, their branches reaching and entwining and studded with diamonds. The wood was as pale as her skin, finely grained.

It looked like bones to her.

Hella kept her distance from the love nest side of the room, opting to pace on the side that had been turned into a lounge area, with a chaise longue and two couches made of the same bone-coloured wood and turquoise velvet. She pretended not to notice how the two couches faced the chaise, as if they had been positioned so people could watch whatever was happening on it. She also pretended not to notice that the carved wooden frame that ran over the top of the back of the chaise had two worn patches that looked awfully as if someone had been regularly tied down there.

She pivoted towards the door that was open and drifted towards it, breathing deep of the fresh air that rolled into the room through it as her panic mounted. This wasn't her home now. She wasn't going to become part of whatever weird kinky things happened in this room. She would speak to Ethyrian and convince him that he was being unreasonable, and he would let her go.

She chuckled at that, the mirthless, desperate sound bursting from her lips, loud in the thick silence. Her guard tensed and she glared at him when he gave her a look that questioned her sanity. So, she was losing her mind a little. Who wouldn't when they were being held in a nymph king's sex den with no way to escape and no real hope of convincing him to let her go?

Ethyrian would keep her here. No matter what she said or did. She knew it in her gut. He had been wounded when she had last seen him, hurt by her rejection and the fact she hadn't believed his continuous declarations of love, and she had foolishly thought it was over.

But it looked as if the male really didn't know how to take no for an answer.

And wasn't above kidnapping to get what he wanted.

Typical king.

She huffed, her strides growing more agitated as her mind raced, as her fingers were drawn towards the secret pocket in her black dress. She focused on her guard as her hand brushed across it and she felt the vial that had survived the brute's rough handling of her. Maybe she did have a way to escape. Although she wasn't sure it would work.

Chances were the magic imbued into her restraints would negate the potion even if she could reach it, uncork it and swallow it before her nymph shadow could stop her.

She pivoted at the closed wooden door, not daring to get too close to it. The one time she had moved within six feet of it, the guard had grabbed her and tossed her into the centre of the room, and she had fallen, almost landing on the vial.

Hella strode towards the open door, one that led onto a balcony and revealed a slice of green mountains and too-blue sky that weren't the product of a spell.

She wasn't in Kansas anymore.

Her nymph guard had teleported her elsewhere, to a place few non-fae got to see, and even fewer survived to tell tales about.

Lucia.

Realm of the light fae.

The door behind her opened before she could step out onto the balcony and she spun on her heel to face that direction.

Ethyrian swept into the room, looking as good as always in his tight green leather trousers that hugged his long lean legs and a loose white shirt that somehow revealed his honed torso even as it concealed it. Something was different about him though. His long blond hair was held back by a delicate knotted gold band that sat across his forehead and held an oval sapphire above his nose.

His crown.

If she had known the nymph was a king when she had met him all those months ago, she might have rejected his advances and spared herself all this trouble. She had figured him for a noble though, someone with only a little power, not enough to make him dangerous. Throughout history, kings had proven themselves to be a terrible lot, corrupted by their position, expecting everyone to fawn over them and do as they pleased.

To serve them.

To obey them.

Hella wasn't exactly obedient material. She hadn't even been able to obey the rules of her coven. She certainly couldn't be expected to obey one man.

His blue eyes met hers, as bewitching as ever, like a tropical ocean that glittered and tempted, sparkling with flecks of gold. Even now they made her want to dive into them. She had fallen for those eyes more than his impressive physique and his good looks. Those eyes had beckoned her, had been the first thing she had noticed about him.

There wasn't a male in this universe who had eyes as interesting and entrancing as his.

Hella shut that line of thought down, refusing to let him cast a spell on her again, and reminded herself that he was holding her captive.

His firm, broad mouth curled into an easy smile, one meant to charm and disarm her. He had used that smile on her too many times to count, and each time she had fallen for it, forgetting her anger or her desire to be rid of him and ending up in bed with him.

She glanced at the bed off to her right. One she would not be falling into with him. No backsliding.

"Hella," he murmured, saying her name in a sexy way that had heat flushing over her skin. "Come, my love."

He held his hand out to her.

Hella sneered at it. "I'll do no such thing."

His fair eyebrows pinched and then relaxed, and he slid a look at the guard. The male dipped his head and left, taking all the air in the room with him as the door closed behind him and she found herself alone with Ethyrian.

"Come," Ethyrian repeated, harder this time, and his irises darkened a shade.

Warning her that she was treading on thin ice.

He was close to losing his temper. That was the reason he had sent the guard away. Heaven forbid one of his subordinates witnessed her rejecting their king and disobeying him, or what he would do to her as punishment.

She kept her distance from him when he moved a step towards her, her pulse picking up pace as she glanced over her shoulder at the balcony again. A balcony that was high up. She could hear water though. Distant. Muted. If she had to guess, she was in a tower and there was a river somewhere below her.

Could she jump?

She strained hard, listening to the rushing sound, her stomach twisting and knotting as she considered it. The river was probably a long way down. She might not survive the drop, especially if the water wasn't deep. But then, she didn't have to hit the water. If she was fast enough, she could reach the vial and drink it before she hit the river.

And what if the potion didn't work because of her restraints?

Hella swallowed hard at the thought of hitting a shallow river and going splat.

Maybe she could tough it out a little, play along with Ethyrian until she could convince him to remove her cuffs and then she could escape using the potion. One problem with that plan though. Ethyrian would have her naked before she could work her charm on him, placing the potion beyond her reach. Or worse, he would discover the vial.

Her mind raced, thoughts colliding as she looked at him again, as he stalked towards her, all gorgeous glower that heated her blood and made her body remember the good times they had shared. It wouldn't exactly be a chore to sleep with him until he let her go, but the idea rankled her, had her wanting to strike him and keep him away from her.

"Sweet Hella," he started.

"There's nothing sweet about me," she bit out and waggled the shackles in his face, and it hit her that they were the reason she was mad as hell at him and didn't want to sleep with him anymore. He had chained her and had her brought here, and that wasn't the way someone who was apparently in love with you behaved. "There's nothing sweet about you either, is there? You declare your undying love for me, swear to the moon you will be forever mine, do all in your power to convince me that love is real, and what… when I don't return the feelings you resort to kidnapping? They make TV programmes about obsessive types like you all the time."

"My love for you *is* real. I will make you see it," he gritted and lunged for her.

She sidestepped and hurried towards the door, placing more distance between them.

"Just let me go, Ethyrian. We can forget this ever happened." She clutched her dress, keeping hold of the hidden vial.

Could she reach it and drink it? Was it worth the risk? If the spell in the shackles worked on the potion too, she would have sacrificed her only method of escape. As tempting as it was to risk it, she couldn't. She had to bide her time until she was free of the cuffs. Maybe she could speed that along.

She lifted her hands and moved them apart, snapping tight the chain between the two thick silver cuffs. "If you remove these, it will go a long way towards convincing me that you're not a psychopath and you meant those pretty words. If you love me, you'll do it."

He glared at her, his lips flattening as his eyebrows drew down and he stalked towards her. "If I remove those restraints, you will teleport. I will not lose you again."

"I can't teleport. I'm a witch. We didn't get that nifty perk." Not technically true. She could teleport. The potion would make it happen. She resisted the temptation to touch it again. "I'll stay if you release me."

She would be gone in a flash.

Hella smiled sweetly, the one she had always used on him whenever he had been in a bad mood. It usually worked like a charm, but this time he remained at a distance, glaring at her. Aware that she was going to have to work a little harder than just smiling at him in order to win him over this time, she sidled towards him, her heart thumping hard. She wouldn't fall for his charms again. She wouldn't fall into his bed. She would just make it appear as if she was doing both of those things.

"I do love you," he husked as she drew closer, his gaze growing unfocused as he skimmed it over her body. It sharpened again as it locked with hers and he rocked her entire world on its axis. "That is why I am going to marry you."

She spluttered.

"I'm sorry… you're going to what now? For a moment there, I was sure you said marry me." She back-pedalled. Hard. Placing more distance between them as her pulse skyrocketed.

"I am going to marry you. You are to be my wife." He smiled at her, as if she should be thrilled by this turn of events and not terrified.

Convincing him to do anything flew out of the window, because she could see in his eyes that he had made up his mind and he was going to marry her whether she liked it or not. She wasn't getting a say in things, and that really pissed her off. She had to escape. If she didn't, she was going to end up wed before she knew it, enslaved by a male she didn't even like.

No. Thank. You.

He wasn't in love with her, not like he believed. He was obsessed with her, and she had the feeling it was because she had dumped him. Ethyrian had never been the dumpee. He had always been the dumper. She could see that now. He had never even told her that he loved her until she had been breaking up with her. It was obvious now that this was new to him and he didn't like it and rather than ridding herself of him, she had made the whole situation worse.

Now he wanted to wed her.

If she had let things between them fizzle out naturally, she wouldn't be in this mess. Her rejection had caused this turn of events, making Ethyrian obsessed with her.

Making him a danger to her.

"You shall be a queen." He strode towards her, using her temporary inability to move thanks to shock to his advantage, and was only inches from her before she roused herself. He stroked his hand down her bare arm, his blue gaze adoring as his smile widened. "A fitting position for my beauty. You shall take your rightful place at my side and I shall dote upon you. I will even visit my harem less."

"How generous of you." Hella twisted free of his grip and walked away from him, struggling for air. "I never would have dreamed you'd place me first before your concubines."

Concubines she hadn't even been aware of when they had been together. How many times had he slept with them before coming to see her? After coming to see her? She vomited a little in her mouth.

"My wife will always come first." He sounded as if that would be the most magnanimous thing he had ever done and she should be falling at his feet and telling him he was too kind—too generous.

She glared at him over her shoulder instead. "I highly doubt that. I seem to recall you always came first."

He scowled at her, crossed the distance between them and had her arm in a bruising grip before she could even blink. He loomed over her, darkness in his eyes as he stared at her, and her pulse spiked again as his fingers pressed into her flesh. That show of strength was a warning, and he looked close to showing her in other ways that she would do better not to speak to him like that.

Hella tried to break free of his grip, but this time he tightened it, refusing to release her.

"My stubborn wife will learn her place in time." He lifted his other hand and smoothed his knuckles across her cheek, and the touch felt more like a threat than a caress.

Her entire body locked up tight in response as his hand drifted lower to graze her neck, her legs trembling as she forced herself to hold his gaze, to keep her head tipped up and not let him see how afraid she was. She would escape this.

Sooner rather than later.

In fact, she was thinking right now might be as good a time as any.

She plastered a smile on her face and made herself lean into his touch as he opened his hand and cupped her cheek in his palm. She resisted the shudder that wracked her as he stroked his thumb over her lower lip and his gaze fell there.

"You will want for nothing, Hella, my love," he murmured, his eyes growing hooded and his breaths shallowing as he continued to stare at her mouth.

"Except my freedom," she whispered and rattled the chains, reminding him of the fact he had made her his prisoner, stealing her power from her and dragging her to his realm.

And now he intended to enslave her with another band around her flesh, this one made of gold and placed upon her finger, and she had no doubt in her mind that ring would be bespelled too, ensuring she never used her magic against him.

Never escaped him.

He smiled sweetly and caressed her throat as his grip on her arm loosened, allowing blood to flow back into her fingers. He lifted that arm and pressed a kiss to it, never taking his eyes from hers, as if the brush of his lips could take away the pain he had inflicted. She had half a mind to clock him with her restraints.

It wouldn't get her anywhere though.

The way to disarm Ethyrian wasn't being violent towards him. It was being sweet towards him. Adoring. As much as it sickened her, she had to pander to his inflated ego if she wanted to get away from him.

"Will you remove them once we are wed?" She lifted her hands and stroked his chest, feeling his heart picking up pace against her palms.

She didn't miss the press of his erection against her hip as he angled them towards her either.

"Of course." He brushed his fingers over one of the silver bands. "Although I would not be averse to restraining you in such a manner from time to time."

She bet.

She stroked her fingers down his broad chest. "And what if I was inclined to restrain you?"

His blue eyes darkened, and not with anger this time, and he swooped on her mouth on a low growl, claiming her lips in a fierce kiss that did nothing for her. Had no female ever offered to tie him up? Maybe she could use his excitement about the prospect of being restrained and at her mercy to aid her escape.

A chained king couldn't exactly stop her, not if the shackles he wore inhibited his ability to teleport, and she would use exactly that sort of handcuffs on him.

Although, she doubted he would remove her restraints first, which meant she couldn't conjure manacles that would stop him from teleporting and she would still be in the same predicament. The balcony was looking more tempting than ever. How far below her was the river? How deep was it?

Hella subtly manoeuvred him towards the door to the balcony, kissing him and fisting his shirt to keep him in place. He tensed when a breeze swept around them and she deepened the kiss, fearing he would pull back to see what she was up to.

When they reached the balcony, she pushed him back against the arched stone doorframe, keeping him distracted as she cracked an eye open and scoped things out. Only she couldn't see a damned thing. The stone wall around the balcony ran at hip height to her and it was solid, not a crack in it for her to see through.

So she broke away from Ethyrian and fanned herself, pretending his kiss had made her far too hot rather than ice-cold and she needed a little air.

She stopped at the wall and looked down, and discovered the true definition of ice-cold as the several hundred-foot drop to the broad canyon below froze her blood in her veins.

Mother earth.

That was a long way down.

Water churned white in the bottom of the canyon. If she didn't hit the rocky walls, she would probably drown in the rapids.

Maybe the potion would work.

Ethyrian came up behind her and nuzzled her neck, peppering it with kisses as he murmured stomach-turning things in her ear. Maybe going splat would be better than subjecting herself to the twisted things he had planned for her.

"And then my head concubine, Iryna, will be chained on her knees and you and I shall watch as Lesharius, my commander, punishes her with his cock and when you are aching, my sweet, I shall unlace myself and make her swallow my shaft until you are begging for me to plant it between your thighs." He stroked his hand down the flat of her stomach, edging towards that place.

She was learning something new about Ethyrian every second, and she wasn't enjoying it. He had never shown this side of himself to her before. She hadn't even had an inkling that he was this dark and perverse. How long would it be before she was the one strapped down on her knees, being punished by him and his commander?

She swallowed the bile that rose into her throat and made her decision.

Hella turned in his arms and he caged her against the wall, pressing the evidence of his arousal against her stomach. She tensed when he reached for her skirts, fisting them and dragging them up, his blue eyes so bright with hunger that they glowed in the waning light. Cool air kissed her bare thighs, panic lanced her, and she pressed her hands to his chest.

And pushed as hard as she could.

He stumbled away from her.

And she tipped backwards.

Over the wall.

And screamed as she plummeted towards the river.

CHAPTER 5

Finding the portal to Lucia hadn't been easy, but MacKinnon had managed it. It had used up several of the charges in the token Abigail had given him, a small wooden skull-shaped disc that was firmly tucked in the pocket of his jeans. He checked it again, not wanting to be stuck in this mystical realm because he had lost the damned thing.

Although, it was a beautiful place.

Green. Ethereal.

White buildings rose like great sharpened bones from the dense forest of pines that were each as tall as a redwood, spearing a turquoise sky that sparkled with faint stars. The glade around him was vibrant, the grass threaded with violet and golden flowers that shifted in the breeze, releasing a sweet fragrance. Mossy boulders dotted the clearing, strange colourful birds landing on them to peck for insects or chirp at him before flying away into the trees. Water as clear as diamonds ran in a sweeping shallow stream to his right, rippling over crystalline boulders.

It didn't seem real.

Even the light wasn't right. It was warm—magical—and the air sparkled as if someone had tossed handfuls of gold glitter into it.

This whole place was like a dream.

Kin had never felt so out of place or so far from home. He kept his senses sharpened as he quietly moved along the riverbank, every step he took crushing blooms to make them release more scent into the thick air. He glanced off to his left, his gaze lifting beyond the treetops to the arch-shaped towers that rose beyond them, and the sensible part of him said to head that way, towards civilisation.

The cautious part of him warned to keep his distance.

He was a stranger in a land of fae, and he doubted they would welcome the intrusion. The few fae he had questioned in Geneva about Lucia and how to get there had all warned him to forget his mission. When he had told them that he couldn't, that this was a matter of life and death, they had said it would be his death but had reluctantly told him what they knew.

One of them had left him with grim words about staying out of the shadows.

Whatever that meant.

Kin didn't understand the warning, but he still found himself instinctively staying in the light, charting a course that followed the river. He had been walking for what felt like hours, avoiding areas where he sensed there were people. The urge to approach some of them was growing stronger as the minutes ticked by and he still hadn't found Hella. Maybe they would be nice enough to point him in the direction of the nymphs.

Maybe they would gut him where he stood.

Or worse.

He barely bit back the growl that rumbled up his throat as fur swept over his forearms and his claws lengthened in response to the imagined threat to his freedom. Never again. No one in this world or the mortal one would shackle him. He would be no one's prisoner.

No one's entertainment.

So approaching the fae and asking them if they knew where the nymphs were or had seen Hella was out of the question. He couldn't reveal himself. It was too dangerous.

But he was getting nowhere.

And it was getting dark.

He thought.

Kin looked at the sky, at the stars that were no brighter now than when he had arrived. Faint aurora chased around them, coming and going in waves. Did time not move in this place? Was there no day and night?

He rounded a bend in the river and wove through a thick copse of saplings, some of which reached over the water, desperately seeking more light. Afraid of the shadows? He mulled over what the fae could have meant by that warning as the trees thinned and the moss gave way to glittering stones. The river deepened, the sound of water rushing filling the still air, and he was tempted to bend and drink some, but his instincts whispered that thirst was better than potentially poisoning himself. He wasn't sure if the water in this realm was the same as it was in his own world.

Nothing felt the same here.

He tilted his head back as he reached a broad clearing where the grass and flowers had grown tall enough to reach his knees and his step faltered.

A castle.

The ivory fortress towered atop a cliff, stones shimmering in the warm light. It looked like something out of a fairy tale, with towers that speared the high walls at intervals, their conical roofs made of dark blue tiles. In the centre, trees surrounded a cathedral-like structure that had curving arches supporting sections of it, and a gold and blue domed roof. On the other side of the wide river, atop another cliff, a smaller palace stood. A bridge connected the two, spanning the deep canyon the river cut through. From this angle, it looked as if the smaller side had only a low wall around it and a single domed building. He squinted, sure he could spy people near the balustrade and crossing the covered bridge, appearing and disappearing between the columns supporting the blue roof.

Kin found himself drifting towards it, wanting to get a better look. Would there be other buildings in the woods that hugged it? A whole town he couldn't see from this distance? It was different to the other buildings he had seen. He looked back over his shoulder in their direction, taking in the great white towers that curved to a point like an arch, looking more like the tips of swords now he was at a distance.

He turned back towards the castle, the rush of the river becoming a thundering roar as it cut through the gap between the two pale cliffs. He studied the building again as he approached it, and there were people on the other side of the river, moving around the open space there and crossing the bridge. They were blond. Nymphs? He couldn't be sure from this distance.

He focused his senses and pulled down a deep breath, attempting to catch Hella's scent. The smell of water and flowers was too strong, drowning out everything else. He huffed and kept walking, gaze scanning the building now, seeking a way to it that wouldn't draw attention to himself.

A figure suddenly plummeted into view, falling from one of the ivory towers.

His stomach plummeted with her when he noticed the colour of her hair.

Blue.

Hella.

His heart thundered, hammering a painful, hard beat against his ribs as he stood immobile, shocked by the sight of her and struggling to process what he was seeing. She flipped and fought her short black dress.

And hit the water feet first.

MacKinnon kicked his boots off and dove into the water, swam hard with the current and fought to keep his head above the surface as he was swept along. The water was colder than he had expected, sapping his heat, but the adrenaline that spiked his blood as he saw she hadn't emerged yet was enough to keep him going, had him kicking harder, desperately propelling himself towards where she had struck the surface.

He dove the moment he reached it, legs pumping furiously as he scoured the water for her. He grimaced as the current slammed him into a rock, knocking vital air from his lungs, and gripped it and shoved off. The river had to be at least thirty feet deep. Where was she?

There.

She tumbled head over heels, legs flailing, and he wanted to growl when he saw her hands were still bound. What the hell had the nymph been thinking? Why take her and push her off a tower?

His heart lurched as she was smashed against a boulder and spun away from it, her actions growing weak and sluggish. He kicked harder and reached for her, stretched his arms as far as he could and tried to grab her. He missed. Godsdammit. He growled, releasing precious air, grabbed the nearest rock and pressed his feet to it. He kicked off, shooting towards her, and snared her.

The moment he wrapped his arms around her, his strength tried to leave him, relief that she was safe in them stealing it from him. She wasn't safe yet. He clung to the remaining shreds of his strength and kicked upwards, propelling them both towards the surface. He gasped for air as they breached it, his head fogging as his body greedily devoured the oxygen.

Hella spluttered and coughed, shaking in his arms as she tightly gripped his forearm.

Kin turned her to face him.

Could only stare as he got a good look at her, struck dumb by the sight of her.

She was beautiful.

He told himself it was just the spell. It was all a lie.

But gods, she was beautiful.

She looked as if she fitted into this realm, as if she belonged in it, with her wide luminous emerald eyes, flawless pale skin and her rosy cheeks. She could be fae. He tucked her to his chest with one arm and brushed the tangled threads of her azure hair behind her ear with his other hand, revealing her very human ears.

She stared at him as they were swept downstream, not resisting him as he carefully navigated the river with her, pushing off boulders that were in their path and keeping her safely tucked against him.

As they entered calmer waters and their pace slowed, she finally spoke, and the sound of her voice altered something fundamental inside him, stirring his soul and warming his blood.

"You're not fae," she murmured throatily, a soft but flinty quality to her voice that plunged his thoughts firmly into the gutter. His lass had a voice for the bedroom. "You're not a nymph either. If I had to guess—" She looked him over, heating his blood now, making him burn for her as she took him in. "Some kind of shifter maybe?"

"Wolf," he grunted, unable to manage more than that. Something about this female had his tongue tied, his heart thundering, and him trembling like a lad as her soft curves pressed against him.

"What's a wolf doing in Lucia?" she whispered and then undid him by clutching the front of his Henley, twisting it into her little fist as if she didn't want to let him go. "Although, I'm not going to complain about the rescue or anything. It's quite appreciated."

She didn't seem inclined to get away from him. Kin wasn't sure he had ever felt quite as pleased by something as he was by that or how she nestled closer to him. His wolf calmed as she pressed against him, clinging to him, her gaze on his face. His female was in his arms. Safe. Close. He gathered her closer still, unable to stop himself, and wrapped both arms around her, pinning her to him.

Her green eyes sparkled, bewitching him.

Beckoning him.

The cliffs gave way to gentle sloping banks lined with pines and she glanced at them as the river slowed to a crawl. He wanted to deny her even when he knew he couldn't. They could safely leave the water now. There was no reason for her to remain in his arms. He reluctantly swam towards the bank, stood when the water was shallow enough and carried her onto dry land.

Kin set her down on the soft moss and stepped back, trying not to notice how her wet dress clung to her body, revealing it to his hungry gaze, or how her little nipples beaded before his eyes, as if they ached for his touch. He shifted his right leg forward a little, attempting to alleviate the ache in his cock, as hard as stone for her.

She had to see what she was doing to him.

There was no hiding it in his wet jeans.

She backed off a step and fidgeted, wringing some of the water from her dress. The silver shackles around her wrists glinted in the light, drawing his gaze to them, and he growled at the red marks on her skin where they had rubbed it raw.

She froze and lifted her head a little, enough that she could meet his gaze.

And flash cleavage at him.

He would have growled at that too if it hadn't been for the wary edge her eyes gained or how cautious she sounded as she asked, "What's a wolf doing in Lucia?"

"I came for you."

She stiffened and straightened, her chest rising and falling more rapidly as she stared at him. "Came for me?"

Kin reached for her cuffs and she darted back and tucked her hands against her chest as her eyes widened and she swallowed hard.

"You're the one who howled." She blinked at him and the sight of her afraid of him tore at his soul, had him aching with a need to comfort and calm her, and show her that he wasn't a danger to her. Not like she was thinking. "What do you want with me?"

He lined up some bullshit about seeing her in trouble and playing the white knight, it being just something he was prone to do.

And then blurted, "You're my fated female."

He was sure of it as he breathed in her scent, as it calmed his wolf and gave him strength, and drew him to her. His gaze lowered, taking in her curves, and he wanted to growl. Wanted to howl. Throw his head back and let it all out because he couldn't contain this feeling of sheer joy that swept through him.

After all these years, he had found her.

This lass had been made for him, and he wanted her as he had never wanted a female before her.

The mulish twist to her lips and the amount of distrust that shone in her eyes said she didn't want him though.

His instincts demanded he seize her and bend her to his will, because she was his and she would surrender to him.

Kin tamped them down and relied on his mind instead, because letting his instincts steal control of him was a sure-fire way of losing her. She had been through a lot, had been taken by force by nymphs and he was sure now that she had chosen to leap from the balcony of the tower to escape them. Everything about this female screamed that she would put him in the dirt if he made a wrong move with her.

So he needed to make the right one.

He needed to earn her trust.

Saving her from the river should have been enough, but she had a wild look about her, one that would have told him she was frightened even if he hadn't been able to sense it in her. She needed more than a rescue to win her over. She needed to see that he was on her side and not interested in treating her in ways other men had.

And he knew the perfect way to show her that.

"I can break those cuffs." He jerked his chin towards them.

Her green eyes darted down to them and back to his, and she scoffed. "I doubt that."

He frowned at her, because in all his years, no one had taken a look at him and questioned his strength. "I can, lass. I'm old. Strong."

And he wanted to show her just how strong he was. He wanted her to admire that strength and fall into his arms, as his fated female should. He huffed. He was getting ahead of himself again, letting his instincts influence his thoughts. Many a male at his pack had made the mistake of trying to win a female by bending her to his will, convinced that she would give in and accept him.

Not one of them had that female now.

He was damned if he would drive his fated one away from him like that.

He leashed a growl. If she really was his fated one.

She reluctantly edged her hands towards him.

Kin was the one who hesitated now. A war erupted inside him as he stared at her outstretched hands and the silver manacles that linked them. He really shouldn't do this. He fought the need that pressed him to say it, that pushed the words up his throat as he lifted his gaze to her face and lost himself in her eyes again.

"I want a boon in return," he murmured, feeling hazy as he breathed in her scent, as his wolf side paced and growled, goading him into obeying his instincts.

"What?" She frowned at him, a wary edge to her green eyes as she held his gaze.

Her pulse was off the scale, rocketing in his ears, and he told himself to forget it, to take back what he had said because he was pushing her too hard. So much for not listening to his instincts. It had been two seconds and he was already trying to dominate her, to make her his whether she wanted it or not.

"A wee kiss." He braced himself, sure she would lash out at him or storm away, that he had ruined everything by being too forward with her.

She looked as if she was contemplating striking him, but then she thrust her hands towards him and tipped her chin up, a fire in her eyes as she glared at him.

His bonnie lass was a wild one, just as he'd expected.

Kin flexed his fingers and shook them to try to stop them from trembling, not wanting her to notice how she fired him up and how deeply she affected him, stealing his strength and making him weak.

He drew down a breath as he took hold of her right cuff. It hitched as their skin made contact, as a sizzle chased up his arm and his gaze leaped to meet hers. Her green eyes were wide again and gods, he was close to her. Her scent and heat swirled around him, fogging his mind, making it hard for him to focus on anything other than how tempting her soft pink lips were.

Lips that would yield to him soon.

He bit back a groan and went to work, careful not to rub her wrists with the sharp edge of the shackle. They were stronger than they looked. He had figured he could easily break them, but they were more than just steel. It struck him that was the reason she feared him, and the reason she was happy to pay his fee for her freedom. There was a spell in the restraints, one that had to be inhibiting her powers.

His beautiful lass had been more than chained. Her magic, a fundamental part of who she was, had been stolen from her.

He growled and dug his fingers beneath the thick metal, strained and refused to give up this time. His wee witch wouldn't be treated in such a manner. Not when he could do something about it. The edge of the shackle bit into his fingers, drawing blood, but he kept at it, yanking the two sides apart.

The lock gave, the cuff opening so suddenly he almost hit Hella in the face as his hand flew up. She ducked backwards and scowled at him. He issued her an apologetic look and then tackled her other cuff.

The second it opened and the restraints dropped to the ground, he reached for her, eager for his reward.

Only the wily witch snatched something from her pocket, brought it to her lips and disappeared with a single finger salute in his direction as the small bottle fell towards the moss.

Kin snatched it on a vicious growl before it could hit the ground, and wanted to howl when he straightened and opened his fist and spotted a label on the dark blue bottle.

Drink me.

He sniffed it. Some kind of potion? In her haste, she hadn't drunk it all. There was a drop left.

Shouts echoed through the trees from the direction of the castle and Kin stared at the bottle. If this didn't work, the nymphs would hunt him down. The shackles the witch had worn would become his prison instead. He sucked down a steadying breath, brought the bottle to his lips and tipped the drop onto his tongue.

A howl tore up his throat as every molecule in his body vibrated and then burned, and he was sure the damned potion was rearranging his entire body into a new order.

And then suddenly he was standing where he had been in the fae town in Geneva.

"Oh, *fuck*," a sultry, oh-so-bewitching voice muttered, rousing his blood and sharpening his senses.

He locked gazes with Hella.

A heartbeat passed, a moment in which he felt sure she would do the sensible thing and not provoke him any further.

And then she pivoted on her heel and ran.

CHAPTER 6

Hella cursed herself as she sprinted along the promenade, weaving between people in a poor attempt to throw the somewhat annoyed looking wolf off her trail. She shouldn't have dropped the bottle. The huge dark-haired shifter was a clever one, was far more intelligent than she had given him credit for. She risked a glance over her shoulder as she grabbed a female elf and shoved her into his path.

He didn't even slow down.

He barged into the female, knocking her down, his sharp eyes more gold than steel-grey now as they remained locked on Hella. A shiver traipsed down her spine at the intensity of his gaze on her, the way his eyes brightened towards glowing gold, heating her blood and bewitching her.

She took it back.

There was another man in this world with eyes as enchanting and captivating as Ethyrian's.

But that didn't mean she was going to fall head over heels for the wolf.

She was going to make him fall head over heels.

She grinned as she swept her hand out behind her, magic surging to her fingertips as she chanted the incantation in her mind. A bright blue orb shot from her palm, rocketing towards him, and those stunning eyes widened.

He reacted impressively quickly, kicking off on his next step to propel himself to his right, behind the cover of two fair-haired fae males. The spell struck them instead, sending them flying like bowling pins, and they bellowed in unison as they tumbled through the air. Damn. She faced forwards again, pretending not to see the smug grin on the wolf's face as he ran at her, and redoubled her efforts, her gaze leaping around to chart a course through the crowd that would give her the most cover.

She silently apologised to all the poor unsuspecting people as she wove through them, aware that the wolf was going to maintain his straight as an arrow course, knocking them out of the way. Their grunts as the wolf hit them filled her ears, churning her stomach and making her want to look back and yell an apology for the brute's behaviour. She focused on outpacing him instead, while at the same time rattling through every incantation she knew in the hope she would find one that would be more useful.

And wouldn't level half the town or harm innocent people.

Too many of the spells that would have removed him from her tail and freed her from his wrath involved ingredients, something she didn't have at her disposal.

But she did have at her home.

If she could just put more distance between herself and the wolf, she could buy some time to put a proper spell together, one that would rid herself of him.

She glanced back again as a shriek sounded.

Wolf gruffly muttered, "Sorry."

It didn't stop the two females he had sent flying into a group of men from looking as if they wanted to claw his eyes out.

Hella summoned another spell as the crowd thinned, making it easier for the wolf to close in on her. Desperate times called for desperate measures. She had been through enough today without letting an angry wolf get his paws on her.

Her blood heated a little, an echo of the fire that had burned through her when he had demanded a kiss as his prize for freeing her from her shackles. Just the thought of him claiming her mouth with his firm lips ignited an inferno in her veins, one that had awareness of him growing stronger inside her, pulsing through her with every hard beat of her heart. She had come close to going through with kissing him, had been so bewitched by the thought of discovering just how a male like him would kiss that she had almost fallen back into his arms.

But there had been too much at stake.

If she had let him kiss her, it wouldn't have stopped there.

The wolf thought she was his fated mate.

That couldn't be good.

So she set her sights on a group of men ahead of her, completed the spell in her mind and felt the power of it flow to her hands. Twin orbs formed, violet and green that swirled together, and she hurled them at the unsuspecting group, stretching her hands out in front of her. She yanked her hands back as the spell hit two of the black-haired demons, dragging them towards her and then past her, hurling them at the wolf.

Roars sounded behind her, pure fury that had a cold shiver bolting down her spine now, and then a series of muffled grunts and wings beating the air. Wolf growled, his displeasure clear in it as his gaze caressed her back and she glanced over her shoulder at him.

He wrestled with the demons, taking blows as he attempted to break past them and continue his pursuit. The demons didn't let up and she breathed a sigh of relief as the wolf turned his focus to dealing with them, his handsome face a mask of rage as he swung hard punches at his foes.

Hella faced forwards again, aware she didn't have much time. Eventually, he would either lay the demons out cold or would escape them. She sprinted as fast as her tired legs would carry her, her wet black dress clinging to her thighs. The witches' district loomed ahead of her, the elegant three-storey buildings a sight for sore eyes as she raced towards them. Colourful canopies stretched out into the street from each of them, the rich jewel tones a contrast to the cream, white and pastel façades. Her boots pounded the flagstones, her pace drawing curious gazes from the witches attending to their wares beneath the canopies, stirring copper pots and topping up crates of herbs and spices, or dealing with customers.

She could only imagine what she looked like. Wet dress. Damp hair. Running for her life. She was never going to live this one down. They would probably all think she had fallen in the lake or something equally as ridiculous. She could only imagine how dire the rumours would become if they saw the wolf chasing her. It wasn't going to happen.

She banked right, down a narrow alleyway between two buildings, and crossed over the next street. When she reached the end of the next alley, she veered left and ran harder, forcing herself to keep going. Her home, a pastel blue townhouse with a cerulean canopy that was currently rolled up against the building to signal she was closed for business, came into view and she almost stumbled as relief blasted through her.

Hella skidded to a halt at the dark blue door set between the four windows on the ground floor and muttered the incantation to open it. The locks clicked, and she pushed the door open and slammed it behind her. The temptation to sink against it and catch her breath was strong as she stared at her shop, feeling safe now that she was home.

Only she wasn't safe.

She forced herself to move, hurrying for the stairs at the back right of the room, beyond the long wooden counter. She took them two at a time, not slowing even when she reached her private floors.

She grabbed her favourite carpet bag, one she had enchanted a long time ago after watching a movie called *Mary Poppins*, and began tossing everything she might need into it. Bottles, jars, spell books, ink and a few clothes. She needed to cover all her bases. The bastard nymph would come for her again. She was sure of it. It wouldn't take him long to figure out that she hadn't drowned in the river.

She had to move house at the very least, and country at most. Maybe even spend some time in Hell until everything died down. She rushed back down the stairs to her shop and began grabbing more ingredients. You could never have too many, and who knew when she would be able to come back here. It might take months or years for her to rid herself of her pest problem.

The thought of leaving her home for that long—her business—had her stalling in the middle of the room and looking at her shop. An ache bloomed inside her, sorrow swift to sweep through her, and she wasn't sure whether she wanted to scream or cry.

Hella opted for screaming when the door behind her burst open.

She pivoted on her heel and locked up tight.

The wolf filled her doorway, his broad chest straining against his damp, dark grey Henley with each hard breath he sucked down. Mother earth, he was a big bastard. Far bigger than she had thought. He had to stoop to fit through the door, had to be over a foot taller than her five-seven. He growled as he panted, looking like a feral beast with all the scratches on his chest and in the dark stubble that coated his square jaw and the blood that stained him in places.

His eyes glowed gold in the low light, a fire in them that beckoned her together with his raw strength as he stepped into the room and straightened, sucking the air from her lungs.

Hella knew how the three little pigs felt now.

Because this wolf had just blown her house down.

CHAPTER 7

Furious. It was the only word that could sum up the raw, burning anger that blazed in MacKinnon's blood as he ducked beneath the blow a black-haired demon aimed at him. He swung left, dodging another blow the second demon made with his dark leathery wings. The air whistled as the wing cut through it and Kin didn't want to be on the receiving end of a blow from it. He was sure it would slice him clean open.

He grunted as the first demon caught him off guard, seizing hold of his arm and digging claws into his flesh as he dragged Kin towards him. Fiery lightning arced across his forehead as the demon's connected with it, the pain blinding him for a moment. He recovered swiftly, brought his knee up and slammed it between the male's legs, ripping a bellow from him.

More demons joined the fray, three in total, and he cursed the name of the witch who had gotten him into this fight. When he found her, he was going to spank her until she had apologised enough times to make up for the cuts and scratches that already littered his aching body.

Or maybe he would kiss her.

One of the demons landed a vicious blow on Kin's jaw, pain he deserved for being so distracted by Hella in the middle of a fight—when his life was on the line. He was strong, but no match for five demons. He leaped backwards, placing some distance between him and the towering males, not ashamed to admit that. He knew when he was outmatched.

The smallest of the demons rushed him, a fire in his dark eyes as he roared a battle cry.

Kin dipped low as the male reached him, evading his right hook, and slammed his shoulder into the demon's bare stomach. He gripped the male's black leathers and shoved upwards, lifting the male's boots off the ground.

Growled as he ran with him, charging towards the other demons. He hurled the male when he was close to them, sending him slamming into his friends, and grinned as the demon took most of them down and they landed in a tangled heap on the flagstones.

Kin kicked off, sprinting hard, his bare feet aching with each harsh landing they made. What he wouldn't give for his boots right now. The pair he had discarded in his haste to save Hella had been his favourite. Still, at least this fae town had nice smooth paving rather than cobbled streets.

When he was satisfied he had lost the demons, he slowed to a jog. His pulse steadied, his breaths coming more easily, and he focused his mind.

He sniffed the air, picking through the scents of the town, seeking rain-soaked heather. Grinned when he found a trace of it on a broad street where the elegant three-storey buildings had colourful canopies stretching out from above their ground floors. Witches.

Kin tracked the faint scent, locked on to it now. He glanced at every store he passed, seeking a sign of Hella, more determined than ever to get his kiss. She owed him, and he would be taking payment for services rendered.

And maybe he would make her buy him a new pair of boots while he was at it.

His mood darkened as he stalked through the streets, trying to shut out the muttered comments about his bedraggled appearance. He glowered at a few of the witches, silencing them and making them shrink back with only a look in their direction. He had been in a bad enough mood the last time he had been in this town, and then he had been dry, fed and fully clothed. Now he was wet, hungry because he hadn't eaten in over a day, and missing his boots.

The scent led him down a side street, growing stronger. His head fogged a little, filling with a vision of moorland and Hella among the heather, her blue hair tumbling around her slender shoulders and her green eyes bright as she spun to look at him, a smile on her tempting lips. He growled, the low rumbling sound echoing around him as he crossed a street and followed her scent down another alley. He paused at the end of it and breathed deeply, trying to figure out which way she had gone. He took a few steps towards the middle of the street and the scent grew weaker. Same thing when he tried heading right.

Which meant she had gone left.

Kin stormed up the road, his pace quickening in time with his pulse as her scent continued to grow stronger. Tension built by degrees as he closed in on her, an ache growing inside him as his wolf latched onto her signature, pinpointing her inside one of the buildings.

He breathed harder, couldn't stop growling as he thought about kissing her, as his mind filled with how good it had felt to have her curves pressed against him and her hands on him and the way she had looked at him, a spark of fire in her eyes that had called to him.

By the time he reached her door, he was too far gone to be civil.

He kicked the blue door in, burning for that kiss—for her.

A mindless slave to his need for his female.

Her scream pierced the fog in his head, dissipating it in an instant, and she twirled to face him.

Gods, she truly was beautiful.

Her blue hair hung in tangled threads, clinging to her pale skin in places, and her dress still stuck provocatively to her curves, teasing him to the point of madness.

MacKinnon stalked towards her, growling as his wolf instincts demanded he claim what was his.

Her throat worked on a hard swallow and she backed away from him, her blue eyebrows furrowing as her eyes remained locked with his. She tensed as her bottom hit a long counter, glanced back at it and then her gaze darted to him, and her lips parted.

He glanced at the wooden counter too, a growl pealing from his lips as he stared at it. It would easily support her weight while he took her. Flickers of the other witch's words ran through his hazy mind. Hella had to accept him. It was the only way to satisfy this curse.

This craving he felt for her.

He shifted his gaze back to meet hers and didn't miss the spark in them that said she might accept him—that this attraction wasn't one-sided.

On another low growl, he closed the distance between them down to nothing, bracing himself for her retaliation.

Only she didn't fight him as he swept her into his arms and his mouth descended on hers, claiming it as his prize.

He groaned as his entire world crumbled around him, reshaped by the feel of her soft lips yielding to the hard press of his. She opened for him, an eager wee thing that roused his passion and had his mind leaping forwards as she deepened the kiss. Her sweet moan sent a shiver down his spine and he clutched her tighter, drawing her closer as it filled him with a need to devour her.

To stake a claim on her.

Her small hands brushed down his arms from his shoulders to the point where they met her waist, and she reached behind her. They gently took hold of him and she tried to prise his arms away from her, but he refused to let her as he angled his head and stroked her tongue with his. She trembled and loosed another sultry moan, lightly ran her blunt nails down his forearms and tried again. He sensed the need in her and let her have her way this time, curious as to what she wanted to do with him.

When her hands curled around his wrists and she brought them up between them, he thought she meant to make him cup her breasts. He opened his hands, eager to touch her, to tease the hard little points that her dress concealed.

And snarled when cold metal kissed his skin.

His wrists dropped as she released them, weighed down by something.

Kin reared back and looked down at them, and his throat closed in an instant, the haze of passion clearing in a heartbeat.

Manacles.

She had shackled him.

He turned a vicious growl on her that came dangerously close to a whimper as a chain appeared on both of the heavy silver cuffs and snapped to an anchor point near the door behind him, yanking him away from the witch. Panic lanced him, fear swamping him to extinguish every other emotion as he looked from one wrist to another and fought his bonds.

"This cannae hold me," he snarled and kept fighting, every muscle on his body flexing as he leaned forwards, straining against the chains. "I broke those shackles you wore in Lucia."

"Good luck breaking these ones." She casually flicked her messy blue hair over her shoulder, regarding him with a cool stare as he fought harder and harder, sweat dotting his brow as the chains refused to give.

They had to give.

His breaths shortened, his lungs feeling too tight as his struggle made zero impact on his bonds.

She waved her hand and the door behind him repaired itself.

Kin moved a step back, turned towards the door and the anchor point and gripped the chains. He heaved backwards, gritting his teeth and growling as he strained. They would give. They would. He exerted all of his strength, his fingers aching as he gripped the chains so fiercely that he felt sure he might break his bones before he broke the metal links holding him.

He bared fangs at Hella as she approached him, curiosity filling her green irises as she looked him over.

"Why do you think I'm your mate?" Her soft voice teased his ears, rousing the fierce ache for her for a moment before fear overwhelmed it, pushing it back out again. She canted her head to her right and frowned at him. "Why are you so insistent on having me?"

He refused to answer those questions, kept up his assault on the chains, sure they would weaken and give way if he only kept at it. He breathed harder as his panic mounted, as his wolf paced and growled, battered the cage of his body. If he shifted, he could escape. He stilled and focused, breathed through the fear and summoned the shift.

"No escape that way. The cuffs will morph to fit the size of your paws if you shift." She said that in a far too bright and breezy tone, as if his panic and suffering meant nothing to her.

So he flashed his fangs and snapped them at her, savagely lunging towards her at the same time.

She stumbled backwards into a long wooden display case filled with books, knocking several of them off the shelves as it wobbled.

With renewed focus, he yanked on the chains and heaved backwards, his body arching towards the ceiling as he growled. Every muscle screamed in protest, but he refused to give up, even when he knew it was pointless. The witch was right. There was no escaping these bonds.

"Fuckin' witches," he snarled and struggled to keep breathing as the panic really set in, as his mind ventured down dark paths that would only lead to oblivion and the lid on the shadowy box containing memories of his past began to vibrate and lift. Any moment now they would hit him. He needed to escape before it happened. Needed to break his bonds before he was left at the mercy of a witch who had none. He sneered at her. "I hope you both burn in Hell."

Hella arched an eyebrow at him. "What other witch deserves a curse from you?"

He glared at her and spat, "The one who cursed me."

His breaths quickened, heart labouring as he pulled at the chains, the manacles cutting into his wrists to spill blood down his hands and make his grip slippery.

Her green eyes darted to his bloodied hands, her brow furrowing as she saw them. "You need to calm down."

"No," he bit out, not because he refused to do as she had ordered but because he couldn't. His breaths shortened again, his chest constricting. He recalled what the witch who had cursed him had said—he would die if Hella didn't accept him. He tried to focus through the riot in his mind. Forced a shaky smile in her direction. He could be charming. Females liked a charming male. "Be a nice lass now and unchain me."

She shook her head.

He lunged for her again, the chains tightening to yank him back before he could reach her. "Ye have no bloody right to be chaining me!"

"Call it self-defence," she snapped back at him.

He narrowed his eyes on her. "Ye liked that kiss o'mine, wee witch. Ye cannae deny it. I felt it. Your wee body was begging for mine."

She slapped him hard enough that his cheek stung.

MacKinnon snapped fangs at her again, his wolf side lunging to the fore to have fur sweeping over his skin as he realised she wasn't going to let him go. He growled and attacked the chains again. Smelled hot wax. Heard the crack of a whip. The cry that burst from his own lips as fire arced down his spine. He snarled and fought to focus, to purge the memories before they fully hit, but he was too far gone. They seized hold of him, shadowy hands that dragged him down into the darkness.

Into despair.

Laughter echoed around him as he desperately tried to escape.

Shame swept through him as he was forced to entertain them, so desperate for a scrap of food that he had been willing to do anything, had swallowed his tattered pride and done whatever he could to please them.

Whatever they asked.

They had broken him so easily.

His vision came and went, his hands flickering between manly and those of a boy, the shackles he wore switching between bright silver and rusty.

MacKinnon wobbled on his feet, labouring for air as the darkness swept up on him.

He had sworn no one would ever hold him again.

He lifted his bleak gaze to Hella and stared into her eyes as they widened.

And now his fated female had him chained.

CHAPTER 8

The wolf exploded towards Hella, his golden eyes holding a feral light and his fangs enormous as he snarled at her. She stumbled backwards, hitting the low bookcase again, her heart shooting into her mouth. The chains snapped tight and he grunted as the momentum yanked him backwards, away from her. He turned on them with a savage growl, desperately attacking them, and she fought to catch her breath and calm her racing heart.

The ground beneath her shook with each violent lunge of his body as he battled the chains, his muscles bunching beneath his dark grey Henley, bulging with each fierce tug he made. The edges of the metal cuffs bit into his wrists, spilling his blood down his hands and all over the floor.

Hella stared at it as it splattered across the floorboards, her mind full of his grunts and growls, the desperate sounds tearing at her together with the sight of so much blood.

"Stop!" She jerked towards him, her hands flying up, desperation flooding her now.

He turned on her with a vicious snarl that peeled his lips off his fangs, his expression savage as he lunged for her again. She reared back, fear sweeping through her as he turned his wrath on her for a moment before he returned to fighting his bonds.

"Calm down," she murmured, hoping the soft tone would soothe him, even when something inside her called her stupid. There was no calming this wolf down. She had set fire to his rage, ignited this wild and dangerous side of him, and he was the one paying for it. Blood rolled down the chains as he heaved backwards, straining to break the chains, and she shook her head and whispered, "Stop. You're hurting yourself."

Mother earth, if she had known he would react this way to being chained, she never would have done it. Her stomach churned as she slowly approached him, fearing the moment he noticed her closing the distance between them, aware he would turn his rage on her again and this time she was close enough that he might actually strike her.

"Calm down." She held her hands up, feeling sick as he didn't let up, his violent attempts to break free shaking the ground beneath her feet. When he turned his claws on himself, shredding his top and catching his skin beneath it as he ripped it from him, panic and guilt had her lurching a step towards him again. "If you calm down, I'll—"

She had wanted to say she would release him, but he twisted and launched at her, and she staggered backwards, narrowly avoiding his claws as they slashed through the air in her direction. She fell, landing on her backside, and stared up at him, her breaths coming so rapidly that she felt dizzy.

The wolf breathed faster too, the crazed look in his eyes relaying his panic as it mounted.

"Just calm down. Breathe." She didn't dare stand up, not while he was glaring down at her, liable to strike her if she moved. "Like this."

She fought to breathe calmly and evenly, denying her need to keep on panting for air, battling the panic that closed her throat. For a moment, she thought it was working and his breathing was growing more even, and then he twisted and snarled, wrapped the chains around his hands and pulled on them, every muscle in his body straining with effort.

Calming him down before releasing him wasn't going to work. She could see that now. Something about being chained had triggered this reaction, and that revelation only made her feel worse. This wolf had done nothing wrong. He had saved her in the river, preventing her from drowning, and she had repaid him by tricking him into lowering his guard so she could chain him.

And why?

Because he had declared she was his one true mate?

She felt like a fool, was sure she should be stronger than this, but something about that scared her. Too many men had suddenly decided she belonged to them, were trying to strip her freedom from her. It had rattled her and she had reacted badly, stealing his freedom instead.

She should have considered the consequences of her actions.

The wolf breathed faster, his panic a palpable thing now, sucking the air from her lungs as guilt rushed through her. He attacked his cuffs, clawing at them and cutting himself in the process, and she couldn't take it anymore.

"Hold still." She summoned the counter-spell that would remove the shackles, quickly working through the incantation in her mind.

But not quickly enough.

The wolf cast her a bleak, wounded look and then staggered and dropped hard.

And passed out on her floor.

The shackles disappeared, exposing the damage he had done to his wrists, the deep lacerations that continued to spill blood on the wooden floorboards.

Her eyes widened as he shifted, transforming into a large black wolf, but it wasn't the sight of him changing that shocked her.

It was the scars that littered his body, cutting through his fur. The long pink streaks arched over his back, all of them heading in different directions, and a few cut over his muzzle too.

Hella had the dreadful feeling he had been whipped.

Held captive and abused.

Cold stole through her, her guilt weighing her down now to have her falling to her knees beside him. She hadn't known. She reached a trembling hand out to his face, aching inside as she took in all his scars and replayed how he had reacted to being chained. The pain of his memories had to be severe, the things he had suffered during his captivity horrible enough that just the thought of being chained had sent him off the deep end, turning him wild with a need to escape his bonds.

"I'm sorry," she whispered, her heart going out to him as he panted, his breaths still too fast for her liking.

She had caused this, but perhaps she could do something that might go some way towards making amends. She reluctantly pushed to her feet and went to her bag, hefted it onto the counter and rifled through it. She pulled out all the ingredients she needed and an empty flask, and set to work, mixing just the right amounts to make the potion.

A tonic to calm his turbulent mind and help him rest and recover.

And it didn't hurt that it would keep him asleep while she decided what to do.

She swirled the liquid in the flask, watching the powders and fine herbs melting into it as it changed colour, going from green to red to violet. When it turned inky blue and specks like silver stars emerged in it, twinkling at her as the liquid shifted, she decanted a dose into a smaller bottle.

Hella took it to the wolf and sank to her knees again, not hesitating to touch him this time. She carefully lifted his big head, marvelling at how soft his fur was, and angled it onto her bare knees. His rapid breaths shifted the skirt of her dress, pushing it up higher to expose more skin, as if even in sleep he was trying to make a move on her.

She poured the tonic into his mouth, spilling some on her thighs. Apparently, it wasn't easy pouring liquid into the mouth of a wolf. The gap between his teeth was too large and she couldn't angle his head any better than she already had. All she could do was continue and hope that he drank enough of the potion for it to be effective.

When the bottle was empty, she set it down beside her and watched him. She brushed her fingers through his thick fur, the feel of it mesmerising her, and stroked his ears. He slowly calmed, his breathing becoming more even, and she wasn't sure whether it was because her tonic was working or because she was petting him.

Hella bit the pad of her thumb as she gazed down at him.

She wasn't sure what to do with him.

But a few things kept popping into her head.

That kiss had been toe-curling after all.

Again, she almost hadn't done as she had planned. This wolf had a bad habit of making her do that, and part of her felt that was dangerous. The rest of her had enjoyed the kiss far too much, had been swept up in the moment and had almost fallen under his spell.

She carefully stroked her palm across his cheek, feeling as if she was on a precipice and no matter what she did, she was in for a painful fall. Her fingers drifted to his muzzle and she traced one of the scars as she murmured.

"What shall I do with you?"

CHAPTER 9

MacKinnon raced across the moorland, crushing heather beneath his paws as the last light of day painted the sky with threads of pink and gold above the munros that protected the glen. He paused atop a hillock, the magic of the gloaming reaching right down to his soul to warm it, but at the same time he felt agitated.

Restless.

He needed to keep moving.

Couldn't stop to watch the light change as he often did.

Not this time.

He kicked off again, heading in the direction he had been, running as fast as he could manage. His steps were sure and light as he navigated the rough and broken ground, leaping between clumps of heather, using them as a guide as to where was safe to place his paws and avoiding the boggier parts of the valley floor. Water trickled, heavy with the earthy smell of peat, but another scent overpowered it.

Heather.

Fresh rain.

Faintly spiced.

He breathed deep of it and calm coursed through him, as if that scent was a balm for his weary soul.

Weak sunlight bathed his black fur as he crossed the glen, heading for the green mountains on the other side, where heather painted the lower slopes purple. He needed to be there. He felt it in his blood, like a compulsion, a powerful need he could only obey.

The sound of running water grew louder and he scented the burn ahead of him, the small river in full flow as the recent rainfall ran off the peat into it.

When he reached it, he leaped clear across it, landing on the other side and not missing a step.

His sharp eyes locked on to a small house ahead of him, nestled in the shadow of the tallest munro and standing alone among the heather. White-painted stone. Mossy slate roof.

He was drawn to it as the light changed in the valley, the air charging with magic.

Aware of what he would find inside.

A delicate blue-haired lass stepped out of the door, her face turned towards the sunset, and his heart thumped harder at the sight of her. Her corseted short black dress was a stark contrast to the white wall as she stopped near the door, hugging curves that inflamed him and had him running harder to reach her.

Aching for her.

She serenely turned and looked down at him as he approached, heading up the slight incline to her.

Didn't say a word as he shifted and rose naked before her.

Her green eyes beckoned him, filled with sparks of fire, bewitching him.

Kin seized her on a growl, pinned her to the doorframe, and claimed her mouth in a bruising kiss. He groaned as she yielded to him, her soft lips opening and her tongue coming to brush his, to tease him with the taste of her.

Turning the kiss against him.

She claimed him with it instead as she wrapped her arms around his neck, as she pushed delicate fingers through his dark hair and clutched him to her. She moaned as their mouths clashed, as the ferocity of the kiss shook him to his core, her desperation flooding him to fill him with a single need.

He needed to please his mate.

To satisfy her.

Kin grabbed her backside and lifted her, and she didn't stop him as he wedged himself between her slender thighs. She kissed him deeper, urging him on with little moans that made him mindless with a need for her. Savage.

One hand slipped from his shoulder, trailing fire over his biceps as he held her aloft. She pushed him closer to the edge, raking blunt nails over his flesh as she shifted her hand between them. Her fingers skimmed over his stomach, heading downwards, cranking his temperature up until he was burning.

His cock kicked as she neared it, hungry for her touch, but she denied him, brushed her fingers upwards instead and curled her hand around his nape. He shivered as she stroked it, teasing it with her nails, maddening him and pushing him to the point of no return.

He needed her.

He needed his fated one.

He pulled back and stared at her, lost in her enchanting eyes, in her kiss-swollen lips and the hunger that blazed inside her.

A hunger he could satisfy for her.

Her hands dropped to her hips and she pulled her skirts up, tugging them from between them, and he groaned as he realised something.

She wore no panties.

Her soft heat met his hard shaft and he couldn't stop himself from rubbing against her, gliding up and down and covering himself in her moisture. The scent of her filled his lungs, had control slipping as he drowned in it and visions of the things he wanted to do to her. He groaned as she rocked her hips forwards, pressing her heat against him, pushing him right to the edge.

On a low growl, he gripped his cock and breached her.

She wrapped her legs around him and eagerly sank onto him, taking him into her, stealing his breath as her tight heat encased him, scalding him.

"Hella," he moaned, unable to hold it back as she tugged him to her and rotated her hips.

"Kin," she murmured, desperation lacing her bewitching voice that he felt as a command in his soul.

In his heart.

He dropped his head and seized her lips at the same time as he dug his hands into her bottom. He kissed her deeply, not holding anything back, letting her see how mad she made him, how crazed he was for her, as he pinned her to the doorframe and plunged into her. Each press and withdraw was as frantic as his kiss, had his heart thundering as pressure built inside him. She tightened her legs around his waist and moaned as she rode him, her thrusts taking him back into her the second he withdrew, forcing him to take her harder.

His lass was a wild one indeed.

Kin pressed his claws into her backside and pumped harder, taking her deeper and stealing control from her. She arched against him, her fingertips digging into his shoulder and nape as he angled his hips and thrust deeper still, making her take all of him, a slave to the urge to brand her and make her want no other. He wanted her to feel him for days, to know that she was his now.

He grunted and broke the kiss, buried his face in her neck as he focused on the way it felt to be inside her, how hot and tight she was around him, perfectly gloving him, and how she moaned each time he thrust to the hilt, the head of his cock striking deep inside her. He lengthened his strokes and her moans grew wilder, her head tipping back as she bowed towards him.

"So close," she whispered, desperately clawing at his shoulders.

His shaft thickened and hardened, his balls aching as they drew up, and he grunted as he took her faster, unable to slow down now, to hold himself back. She gasped with each brutal plunge that drove her into the wall, surprised him by letting her legs fall open, surrendering to him. An urge rolled through him, commanding him to obey. On a feral, wicked growl that echoed around the glen, he bit down hard on her shoulder.

Hella cried out her release, the feel of her body pulsing around his cock and the trickle of her pleasure that ran into him propelling him over the edge with her.

He threw his head back and howled as he thrust into her, as seed boiled up his shaft and stars winked across his vision. Bliss swept through him as he clutched her in place, holding her at his mercy as he throbbed, flooding her with his essence.

When his body stopped trembling and his mind cleared, he cracked his eyes open and gazed down at her.

His mate.

Rose coloured her cheeks, her green eyes still hazy with satisfaction, and he found he wanted to put this image of her to memory, so he could recall how she looked after being thoroughly loved by him.

But he wanted to do something else more.

As the last light of day faded and the darkness swept in, he bent his head and kissed her.

Sinking his fangs into her nape to claim her as his eternal mate.

CHAPTER 10

Hella hurried back upstairs when a growl curled through the air, abandoning her mission to pack everything she could into her carpet bag. She crossed her cream living room to the white door at the far end of it and eased it open to peer around it. The wolf sprawled in the middle of her double bed, the dark blue covers tangled in his legs, thrashed his head side to side and arched off the mattress. The violent action shook the wooden bedframe, slamming the headboard against the wall, and she hoped to the gods that her neighbours didn't lodge a noise complaint. They probably thought she was giving him the ride of his life.

Which was awfully tempting.

She shut down that dangerous line of thought and focused on viewing him as a problem, not something she could use to scratch her itches.

She still wasn't sure what to do with him.

He had shifted back soon after she had dragged his dead weight up the stairs and onto her bed and had been restless ever since, rubbing himself all over her sheets.

Gloriously naked.

She glanced at his hips.

Gloriously hard.

She had wanted to make him more comfortable when he had been in his wolf form, so she had removed his jeans without considering the fact that when he returned to his human form, he would be nude.

She eased into the room, doing her best not to stare as she moved to check on him and make sure the spell was holding. He sank against the mattress, every muscle on his honed torso flexing with each hard breath he pulled down.

Heat scalded her cheeks as he rocked his hips, his impressive erection thrusting into the air.

Mother earth, it really was tempting to drop her hand and stroke that solid length of steel, running her hand from the broad dark head to his tight balls.

She kept her hands to herself instead, reminded herself that he was a problem, and one she would only make worse if he knew she wanted him.

Hella grabbed the duvet, pulled it out from between his long muscular legs, and tossed it over him, covering his lower half. It didn't stop him from rutting the air and didn't stop her from staring at his chest as it shifted in a powerful symphony that rocked her, shook her, made her ache to climb on top of him and help him deal with that pesky hard-on he was sporting.

He groaned, the sound pure male and wicked, sending a thrill chasing through her that had her nipples beading against her dress and heat pooling low in her belly.

His head tipped back into the pillows as he strained, his big body bowing off the mattress again.

White-hot jealousy coursed through her as she watched him.

Because it had to be one hell of a dream.

"Hella," he grunted.

She locked up tight, her eyes widening as she stared at him, trying to convince herself she had imagined him calling her name in a passion-drenched voice. No one had ever moaned her name like that and she was only a dream. How rough and low would his voice go if she climbed on top of him and rode him to oblivion, waking him by taking him inside her and not stopping until they were both sated?

Hella shook her head, trying to dislodge that thought, but it was too late. It planted roots and grew, had her feeling hazy and achy, fevered as she pictured him below her, her hands against the hard ropes of his stomach, his guttural cries filling her ears.

She tried to turn away, meant to leave, giving him some privacy, but her gaze fell to his broad chest and the dusting of dark hair that covered the heavy slabs, concealing more scars that called to her, rousing a feeling inside her that had desire falling away. This wolf had been through hell in the past. Before she could stop herself, she was leaning over him, charting one of the long silvery lines with trembling fingers.

His big body tensed, his biceps flexing and forearms cording. Biceps she wouldn't be able to encircle even if she used both hands. Her fingers wouldn't touch. He was huge—everywhere.

He suddenly threw his head back and howled, arching off the bed as a shiver bolted down her spine and warmth skittered over her skin. He grunted with each roll of his hips, and she didn't need to use a spell to peek into his mind to know that his wet dream had just reached an epic conclusion.

Hella twisted to leave.

Froze as his heavy eyelids cracked open.

He gazed at her, his striking silver eyes hazy, flecked with gold around his dilated pupils.

And then they narrowed and his gaze shot down to his hips.

And back to her.

And he blushed hard.

She swore his entire face went red as a beetroot.

"Nice dream?" she said, shooting for casual even as her pulse was off the scale, her body shaking as adrenaline rocketed through her veins, the fact that he had caught her watching him dream-fuck her making her feel more than a little naughty, uncertain and guilty.

"Dream?" he rumbled, deep voice raw from all that sexy yelling he had done. Hello, bedroom voice. She shivered for another reason, flushed all over as she tried to rein in her imagination and stop it from traversing wicked routes. He lifted his left hand from the sheets. "Would rather it be a reality. Come, bonnie lass. Your male has need of you."

She scoffed at his outstretched hand. "Need of me? I'm not your serving wench or a whore. You can't order me around."

She denied the part of her that was pushing her to take his hand and show him just how good they could be in reality, and backed off instead.

Which didn't please the wolf.

"You're my fated one." He glowered at her and threw the covers back to reveal himself in all his glory. "You would deny me?"

She told herself not to look.

But ended up glancing at his hips anyway.

He hadn't spilled seed as she had thought, and he was still hard.

Hella stared temptation in the face and waged a war with herself, his words ringing in her mind. Maybe if he hadn't been so insistent on making out she had been put on this planet to serve him, if he hadn't used the fated word in a way that made her feel as if she was an object rather than something to cherish, she might have decided to be nice to him.

Might have even tolerated him enough to fool around with him.

But her eyes were open now and giving this male any part of herself would end with her chained in a different sort of way, this one in the form of a bite mark on her nape.

No one owned her.

No one told her what she could and couldn't do.

And she didn't have room in her life for antiquated bastards who couldn't see that.

She stormed to the chair in the corner of the room, picked up his jeans and turned on him. She glared at him as she threw the jeans, hitting him in the face. He dragged them down, a stupid dumbfounded look on his face.

One that told her he couldn't see what he had done wrong.

And he couldn't believe she wasn't doing as he wanted.

"Get out," she snapped and flung her arm towards the bedroom door. "And never come back here."

He growled, "I cannae do that. If I leave, I die."

Colour her curious.

He pulled down a breath and his lips flattened, and he looked as if he was fighting himself.

When he spoke again, his tone was softer, his brogue less pronounced.

"If you don't give me release, I die, Hella. You must accept me." He cast a glance at his hips and then lifted his gaze to lock with hers again. "I'll be gentle with you, if that's what you fear."

Hella rolled her eyes. "I had lion twins splitting me in two the other day. I don't need a gentle man."

He growled again, flashing his fangs this time, and tensed as he fisted his clothing. "How many males have ye accepted into your wee body? It matters no'. You'll bed no more."

His accent seemed to be an emotional barometer. The more heated he got, the less understandable he became. She was tempted to roll her eyes at him again to see just how deep into his Scottish roots she could push him.

"I'll do what I want and who I want, and if you try to stop me—" She hesitated as the way he had reacted to the shackles filled her mind. She didn't want to torment him like that again. Maybe she could try something else.

If he wouldn't leave, then she would make him.

She pivoted on her heel and swept away from him, her shoulders tipped back and her head held high, the perfect image of a witch one would be wise not to mess with. The wolf's gaze scalded her back, tracking down to her bottom, and he loosed a low, sexy growl.

Hella refused to let it affect her.

The wolf was about to be shown the door and if he had any sense, he would take the hint and leave her alone. She had her own problems to deal with and every second she wasted on the wolf was a second Ethyrian drew closer to realising she had escaped Lucia.

She hurried down the stairs to her shop.

The wolf followed.

Still naked.

Hella huffed as she glanced at him and he leaned against the wall, folded his arms across his chest and crossed his ankles. Shameless male.

"Put some clothes on," she snapped and tried to shut him out as she unlocked a case behind the counter and plucked a book from the shelves.

When she turned back towards the counter, her gaze collided with his.

He grinned salaciously at her, irritatingly sure of himself while she was flustered and unsteady, rattled by his presence. "You don't want that. I can see in your eyes you want me, lass. I can smell that you need your male."

Hella gagged. "Gross."

And diligently kept her eyes off the impressive hard-on he was still sporting as he pushed away from the wall and stalked towards her.

He was far too big.

If she did *accept* him, as he kept putting it, he *would* split her in two.

She was just considering possible spells that would help her get around that when his knees gave out, he went down hard and clocked his jaw on the edge of the wooden counter.

Ruining his carefully affected image of confidence and swagger.

Hella resisted the urge to peer over the counter and check on him, and continued leafing through the book instead as she dryly said, "Have a nice trip? Send me a postcard next time."

The wolf's arm shot up from behind the counter, his hand slammed down onto it and he hauled himself up. He growled as he shook off the blow to his ego but he looked groggy, which worried her.

Was he telling her the truth about the curse?

Would he really die if she didn't add him to the tally of notches on her bedpost?

She intended to find out the answer to both of those questions.

Her finger settled on the yellowing page just below the name of the spell she had been looking for. The language was old, one witches had used centuries ago, a strange blend of Latin, Old Saxon and Greek. She had studied it in school at the coven, but had never been good at it. There was a chance she might get an ingredient or measurement wrong and the spell wouldn't work, or would have terrible consequences, but needs must.

"What are you doing?" he muttered, a wary edge to his voice as he watched her working, sorting through her ingredients to find the ones she needed.

"Making a potion." She lined all the jars and bottles up in front of her, relieved that she had everything she needed.

Or everything she thought she needed.

One of the ingredients was either frog spawn or snake milk, and she only had frog spawn, so she crossed her fingers that was the right one.

"What will it do?" He tried to pick up one of the bottles and she swatted his hand to stop him, mostly because he would probably refuse to drink it if he realised it contained newt entrails.

She had to admit, it wasn't the nicest sounding potion, and she did feel a little bad about the fact she was going to trick him into drinking it, but then he deserved a little payback for demanding she just spread her legs for him because she was his fated one.

If she was his fated one.

She wasn't convinced of that.

"It'll make you stronger for one." She mixed several of the ingredients in a dish, mashing them together into a paste, and was tempted to weave another spell into it, one that would reveal if she really was his mate and it wasn't just something the witch who had cursed him had made him believe so he would come after her.

She was a master combiner, but mixing another potion into one that was already a blend of two and included a spell she was already having her doubts about, was a guaranteed way to make it backfire on the wolf, and as much as he annoyed her, she didn't want him dead.

Yet.

He grunted, "I'm strong enough."

Hella rolled her eyes again. "No need for the macho attitude. How about I word it a different way, one that won't dent that precious overinflated ego of yours? It will keep you strong and buy me some time to look into this curse you claim someone put on you."

He muttered, "I dinnae claim anything. A witch cursed me."

"You must have done something to deserve it." She sprinkled ash on the paste and watched it closely. Nothing happened for a few seconds and then it hissed and smoked. The delayed reaction probably wasn't a good sign. Were her ingredients a bit old? She couldn't remember the last time she had taken the time to burn cedar and sage to make ash.

The wolf growled now. "I did nothing."

She looked up at him and the indignant look on his handsome face said he was getting tired of her blaming him for this mess. Rather than responding with another taunt, she focused on her work, adding drops of frog spawn to the paste and then mixing it with a silver spoon to loosen it up. What if the wolf was telling the truth and he had done nothing to deserve being cursed by the other witch?

That would only leave one answer.

The witch had a problem with her and the wolf was collateral damage.

Hella scraped the gloopy liquid into a flask and added distilled water, several drops of different extracts, and some vodka. The alcohol wasn't listed in the ingredients. It was just something she always added to a potion to make it go down smoothly. Some potions tended to be rather thick.

Case in point, the liquid currently turning into a black jelly-like substance in her flask.

There was no way the wolf would be able to drink it, so she added a couple more shots of vodka and mixed it in with a glass stirrer. The jelly loosened, becoming more like yoghurt. It would have to do.

She set the flask down and looked for a nice cup to put it in for him.

The wolf snatched it and lifted it before him, his silver eyes bright as he stared at it. "Will this reveal I did nothing to deserve being cursed?"

"No, but it will reveal if you are cursed." She tried to take it from him and he held it higher, beyond her reach.

And eyed it suspiciously.

"What else will it reveal?" There was worry in those words as he glared at the potion and then her.

"Keeping secrets?"

He scoffed. "No."

Which was a definite yes.

"It's not a truth serum." She bent over and looked under the counter, found an old pink teacup with a chip in it that she had used in her fortune-telling days, and straightened. She set it down on the counter in front of him. He curled a lip at it, as if asking him to drink from such a delicate, feminine vessel was insulting. She sighed. "I'll only know if you're cursed, and the other active ingredients will work to restore your strength. We can go from there."

She smiled sweetly at him when he still looked as if he would sooner die than drink the potion.

"Trust me."

The wolf huffed but downed the potion, and she grimaced with him as it oozed towards his mouth. Maybe she should have added a dash more vodka to loosen it up further. He pulled a face, and she was sure he might vomit, but then he swallowed the last of it. He slammed the flask back down on the counter and covered his mouth with his other hand, his skin paling, and tense seconds passed as she waited to see if the potion was going to come back up.

Hella edged to her left, out of the line of fire, just in case.

He finally lowered his hand from his face, swallowed again and aimed a scowl at her. "Couldn't make it a wee bit more palatable?"

She shrugged. "A potion is what it is. Not all of them taste like candy and flowers."

Most of them didn't. She had been made to take many potions during her education and nearly all of them had tasted disgusting, ranging from old sweat to vomit. Although, the vomit tasting ones were usually because they had come back up, their consistency turning her stomach.

The wolf cast a look at his bare body and then her, an air of expectation about him. "Well?"

She waved him away. "Give it a minute. Spells take time to work."

Like the one built in on a delayed timer.

She was about to check the list of ingredients, worried that she had missed something or it had called for snake milk and not frog spawn, and then crimson symbols shimmered over every glorious inch of his body.

She hurried to catalogue as many of them as she could, aware she only had a few seconds to read them. Interlocking glyphs made up of circles and hexagons laced with runic symbols and slashes glowed against his skin and then were gone, and she only caught a few of them.

But it was enough for her to know the truth.

"You're not lying. You are cursed," she said, casting him a look that she knew revealed the depth of her surprise because his scowl deepened, his handsome face hardening as his jaw flexed.

"I told you as much," he barked.

She almost regretted the second half of the potion now, because she really wanted to know who had done this work on him and why.

"Now will you accept me?" The wolf's gaze darkened and he reached for her.

And locked up tight.

His eyes widened, horror and dismay flashing across them, together with a look that called her a lying bitch.

He looked horribly as if he thought she had betrayed him.

"Why?" he uttered, that word like a knife in her chest, slashing clean through her as the urge to apologise to him shot to the tip of her tongue, guilt pushing it there.

She didn't get a chance to tell him she was sorry.

He disappeared with a faint pop.

Hella stared at where he had been, acid churning inside her, a feeling she was beginning to associate with the wolf. What was it about him that made her feel terrible about the things she did? She had never had trouble doing this kind of thing before, had always been ruthless when it came to retaining her freedom and living her life the way she wanted. The wolf wanted to take that freedom from her.

He expected her to do as *he* wanted.

She steeled herself, denying the urge to go after him and apologise, to even go as far as offering to help him. No good would come of it. It was better she felt guilty than she found herself shackled by a mate bond to a wolf who would treat her no better than the nymph king.

She had no intention of sacrificing her independence.

Although. She looked at the flask he had placed on the counter and recalled the way he had looked at her at times, with a softness that had warmed her soul and stirred her heart in a way no other man had. Maybe if she found a man worthy of her, one who would walk by her side and not seek to restrain her, would be her equal, she might just do it.

She might fall in love for the first time.

Hella put everything back into her carpet bag, including the book, and shut out thoughts of the wolf.

There was no point in going after him to offer him assistance with breaking his curse.

She wasn't done with him. He would be back and madder than ever, and she would deal with that when it happened.

But right now, she had an entire nymph army and their obsessed king to escape.

She had to move.

Literally.

CHAPTER 11

MacKinnon was furious.

Again.

He yelled as he fell from the air and hit a freezing lake from a great height, his exposed balls taking the brunt of the harsh landing. Momentum plummeted him deep into the frigid water and his muscles cramped as it stole the heat from his body, had his lungs feeling too tight. Good thing breathing was a bad idea right now.

He kicked upwards, focused on the clear surface above him, on reaching it before the need to breathe became too strong to deny.

Kin breached the surface, lurching into the air and gasping at it, greedily sucking it down into his aching lungs. He sank back into the water.

And his jeans materialised and dropped on his head.

He growled and swiped them from his face, looked up at the clear sky and wanted to yell again, cursing Hella's name and demanding his ancestors give him the strength to deal with her. Wily wasn't a strong enough word for his wee witch. She had tricked him into drinking a potion designed to make him leave, tearing him away from her.

Damn her.

He frowned as something else materialised above him.

A folded scrap of parchment.

It fluttered down towards him, dancing in the air like a butterfly, using the two halves of it as its wings.

Kin reached a hand up and caught it when it was close enough, flipped it open and read the single word scrawled on it.

Sorry.

"Sorry, my arse," he muttered and scrunched the paper into his fist.

The witch was playing games with him. They both were. Neither cared that his life was on the line. Well, he didn't care about them either. He was done with them.

He turned in a slow circle, treading water, and arched an eyebrow as he realised Hella had dropped him in a glen close to his home. Did she know this place, or had the spell picked it because it *was* his home?

He clung to his jeans with one hand and swam towards the shore, his eyes on the evergreens that hugged it, a deep band of green between the dark blue of the water and the lighter green of the mountain that rose beyond the forest. His muscles protested with each stroke, the ache in them worsening as the cold continued to steal his strength, and he was freezing by the time he reached the pebbly shore.

Kin stomped up the shallow incline to the shadow of the trees, where mossy grass provided some protection for his feet. His teeth clattered as he struggled with his wet clothes, trying to get them on.

And gave up.

Wolf shifters weren't known for caring whether anyone saw them naked, often stripped before a shift and walked around in the nude after one. It wasn't like his clan would see anything they hadn't before if he walked into the small group of houses as he was now.

But they would know something had happened to him.

He huffed. They probably already knew something had happened to him. He had been gone for days, something that was unlike him. Hadn't even sent word to his pack before going after Hella.

MacKinnon bundled his jeans up in his fist and strode towards the heart of his territory, following a path worn into the earth that wound through the pines and spruces, steeling himself as he walked. There would be comments. He would keep his chin up and not let them see a slip of a witch had rattled him and had him unsure of what he was doing.

Had him craving her.

His thoughts turned to her, summoning memories of her and the way she had looked at him at times. He didn't want to soften towards her, but just before he had been teleported by the potion, there had been regret in her eyes.

As if she hadn't really wanted to send him away.

He recalled the nymphs and how desperate she had been to escape them, and it struck him.

She feared they would capture her again.

She feared someone taking her freedom from her.

He groaned and palmed his face, feeling like a colossal fool even as his instincts whispered at him that she was his mate, that she was his to claim and he needed her. She belonged to him. It was hard to deny that feeling as he stepped out from the trees onto a broad swath of grass and saw the single-storey white cottages of his pack's home ahead of him.

They were nestled in the shadow of a great curving munro, bringing to mind his dream of Hella and the lone white cottage where she had been waiting for him.

His wolf side began to pace, as agitated as he felt as he stared at his home and for the first time ached to be somewhere else.

Somewhere far different from the simple, quiet life he had at his pack.

Kin blamed the curse. He still had no proof that Hella was his fated one. He only had the feelings she stirred in him to go on and those could easily be a fabrication. He probably wouldn't be the first male a spell had tricked into believing he had found his mate.

Ewan, a young male with auburn hair, came out of his home as Kin neared it, took one look at him and hurried towards him. "Are ye hurt?"

Kin shook his head. "Took a swim in the loch."

Ewan looked as if he didn't believe him. "You've been gone for days. Gregor was fretting something terrible."

Gregor, a big blond male who came close to rivalling Kin's height, stepped out of his cottage on the other side of the square of grass they kept clear in the centre of the village. The male watched him with worried blue eyes and Kin gave him a look that told him not to fuss. It became a scowl as Gregor's pretty little black-haired mate came out of the house too and glanced up at him, and the male slung his arm around her to reassure her.

Gods, Kin ached to hold Hella like that.

To have her by his side here in this glen.

He had never felt his home lacked something, but now he did.

It lacked a wily, wild wee witch.

Gregor levelled him with a look that said they would be talking later. Kin huffed and strode to his own small cottage, one that faced the square and had a door that matched the colour of the slate roof. He paused before it and tilted his gaze upwards, to the green mountain laced with patches of soft purple heather, and sighed. This was too much like his dream, only there was no witch waiting for him in his cottage, ready to welcome him with open arms.

She wanted nothing to do with him.

And could he really blame her?

MacKinnon pushed the door open and stepped inside, closing it behind him before any of the pack could get ideas about paying a call. He didn't need their questions right now. He needed whisky. Copious amounts of whisky.

He glanced at the black log burner that stood against the wall to his right. Someone had kept the fire going for him. Gregor probably. His second in command had always worried about him—always took care of him.

The male had been the only one to stand by him when their previous alpha had been killed and Kin had put himself forward for the position, willing to fight for it as was tradition. When he had won, defeating every challenger, he had made Gregor his second in command.

Kin dumped his wet jeans, found a pair of black trunks in his bedroom and tugged them on, and then went to his small kitchen at the front of the house. He grabbed a glass and the whisky, and poured until the amber liquid was close to the brim. He downed that one, savouring the burn and how it rid his mouth of the foul taste of the potion Hella had given him, and poured a second, smaller glass. He carried that one and the bottle with him to his favourite armchair, a dark grey wingback that had seen better days, the material patchy and worn in places. It was comfortable though.

Bliss as he sank into it and leaned back to stare at the fire. He stretched his legs out towards it, warming his bare feet, and sipped the whisky.

Doing his damnedest not to think about Hella.

His eyelids grew heavy as he watched the flames dancing, as his body slowly warmed and the whisky did its job, taking the edge off his mood.

He poured another glass and his body warmed for another reason as Hella danced into his head. Beautiful. Bewitching. Images from his dream came to him and blurred with memories of her. Her gaze had been dark with need when he had come around from that dream to find her standing over him. It had flickered with interest when it had landed on his aching shaft.

And for a moment, he swore she had been tempted by his offer to bed her.

Kin palmed his length, unsurprised to find it as hard as steel. He wasn't satisfied. The dream had been great, but he needed release. He was still primed for a female, his thoughts constantly conjuring wicked images to keep his passion at a steady boil.

He stroked himself as he watched the fire, restless with need, aching to sink himself into the wet heat of a willing female and spend himself. On a low growl, he pushed to his feet and stalked across the house to his wet clothes. He grabbed his jeans, his actions rough as hunger rolled through him, and checked both pockets.

It was gone.

The token was gone.

He tossed his jeans away from him and paced, his cock bobbing with each step, the way it brushed his trunks sheer agony. He palmed it again. Even if he hadn't lost his token, he still would have needed to reach the nearest portal to make the teleport to Geneva. And then what? Hella didn't want him. She might have looked hungry when she had been watching him, but by her own admission she was a horny little thing and took many males to her bed.

Gods. He scrubbed a hand down his face. Was she out there now, seeking a male to satisfy her? He turned on a vicious growl, swept his arm down to his right and caught the edge of the small wooden coffee table. He followed through with the motion, sending it flying across the room to crash into the wall near the door.

Why didn't she want him?

He looked himself over, not seeing anything that would turn her off. He was a strong male, a perfect physical specimen, and plenty of females hurled themselves at him, wanting to share a night in his bed.

But not the witch.

She had teleported him away from her to stop him from making advances, ridding herself of him.

Because he had let his instincts and upbringing get the better of him from time to time? Whenever he had heard wolves talk of how the mating instincts hijacked control, he had thought them weak, males who had lacked the willpower to keep those instincts in check.

How wrong he had been.

Several times he had slipped up and tried to coerce Hella into a union with him. Every time she had spurned him and rage had flashed in her eyes.

Kin poured another glass and drank it down. It didn't help matters. He stared at his tented trunks, aware it wasn't going away on its own. He needed a female. His head swivelled towards the window above his kitchen counter. Any female would do. He needed to be logical about this. He was cursed. A witch had told him Hella was his mate. It was a lie. The witch was using him to get to Hella, wanted to hurt her for some reason. Hella was nothing to him. She was beautiful, sure, but she wasn't his fated one.

He kept telling himself that as he grabbed the coffee table and set it back down near his armchair, and placed his empty glass down on it. He had gone too long without bedding a female and Hella's beauty had fired him up, not the fact she was his mate. Her sinful curves and beguiling eyes, and the way she had kissed him had ignited this lust in him.

And it was just lust.

Which meant any female could satisfy it for him.

Kin strode to the door, opened it, and peered out into the fading evening.

Magda, a pretty brunette who had been more than happy to share his bed whenever they had both gotten too lonely in the past, paused as she neared her door and glanced his way.

He crooked his finger at her and went back inside, leaving the door open.

And wasn't surprised to find her standing in it as he turned to sit on his armchair.

She closed the door behind her, her cheeks flushed and eyes already gold with interest.

Kin poured another glass of whisky and stared at her. "Strip."

She hurried to unfasten her deep green dress, the sound of the zipper lowering rousing anticipation in his veins and sending more blood rushing south. He purged the witch from his mind when she tried to invade it and focused on Magda's lush curves as she revealed them to him, slowly lowering the dress. Her bare breasts were large, more than a handful.

Unlike the witch's, whose breasts would just nicely fill his hands.

Kin banished her and stared at Magda, forcing his focus back to her. Her dress reached her hips and slipped over it, revealing a neat thatch of dark curls at the apex of her thighs, and he pulled down a breath, catching the scent of her desire.

He jerked his chin, silently commanding her to come to him.

She obeyed.

Unlike the witch.

Kin gritted his teeth. Kicked her out of his head and slammed the door on her arse. He raked his gaze over Magda. She was more than pleasing, could satisfy these needs for him and then he would forget the witch. It was only lust that made him want Hella. She wasn't his mate.

He stared at Magda, recalling all their past encounters in an attempt to make his desire about her instead. At times, he had felt she had a thing for him, but then there had also been times where she had made it clear she wasn't interested in him beyond warming his bed from time to time. She had talked of finding her fated mate once, a long time ago, and the glint in her eyes had revealed how deeply she wanted that to happen.

And gods, he felt sure that he would look the same way if he spoke of his fated one right now. He would look as if his heart was fit to burst, as if he wanted to howl in joy, and that he wanted to cherish his female because she was precious and perfect.

Had he really found his mate?

Or was it all a cruel lie?

He shook those questions from his mind, forcing his focus back to the female here with him now, and away from the one who didn't want him to cherish her, to protect her and love her.

Magda eased to her knees before him and stroked his thighs, and he spread them for her, watching her as she eagerly leaned forwards to kiss his skin, so eager to please him.

Unlike the witch.

He growled and Magda froze, her golden eyes lifting to his face as fear flashed across hers. Because she thought he was growling at her because she had displeased him. She hadn't. He was angry with himself for not having more control over his own mind and body, furious at Hella for muddling his thoughts and his feelings, and in a rage at the witch who had cursed him to believe Hella was his mate.

Determined to rid himself of those feelings, of thoughts of Hella, he grabbed Magda by her nape and hauled her up to him for a bruising kiss. He wasn't gentle as he took her mouth, wasn't at all sweet or charming. He was every bit the alpha he was, taking what he wanted without bowing to anyone else's desires, without caring about the feelings of the woman in his arms.

She moaned regardless and sank against him, a compliant little thing that didn't seek to stop him or make him gentle his kiss.

Didn't slap him away.

Or chain him.

She surrendered to him.

Rubbed her bare curves against him.

But for some damned reason, no matter how fiercely he kissed her, no matter how she worked her body against him, he felt only rage.

Resentment.

All of it aimed at himself.

This wasn't right. This wasn't what he wanted. He was acting out because Hella had rejected him and he was hurting, and frustrated. This wasn't like him. He had never been like other alphas of his breed, had never taken what he wanted from females with little care about what they wanted.

When she brought her knees up beside his thighs and eagerly reached for his trunks, Kin seized her wrist and stopped her.

Because this wasn't right.

She didn't smell right.

Didn't taste right.

She wasn't the one his body wanted—the one his soul yearned to have in his arms.

Kin pushed her away, angrier than ever. Only that anger was mixed with frustration and despair, and a whole lot of disappointment and despondence.

"Leave," he muttered, unable to bring himself to look at her.

"Did I... did I do something wrong?" She gathered her dress and covered her body with it.

He clawed back his rage as hurt flashed in her eyes and heaved a sigh, his tone softening as he dragged a hand down his face and added, "It isn't you. I just have too much on my mind. It's best if you just go... And speak to no one about this, Magda."

Because the last thing he needed were rumours circulating that he couldn't bring himself to sleep with a female. It would lead to whispers that would be far too close to the truth—or at least a truth wrought by a spell.

He had found his fated one and she had rejected him.

The door slammed, leaving him alone, and he sank into his armchair and stared at the fire, savouring the quiet that was a contrast to the riot in his mind.

Hours ticked past as he watched the flames slowly dying and a feeling steadily built inside him.

He was like those flames.

He could feel it now as the alcohol wore off and his mind calmed. He could deny things all he wanted, but it didn't change them. There was a curse on him, just as Hella had revealed, and it was eating away at his strength, slowly devouring him from the inside.

As much as he hated the thought of making another attempt with Hella, wasn't sure he could handle another rejection, he was aware that he would die if he didn't succeed in seducing her. The curse wanted it and it was the only way to make himself strong again.

Strong enough to find the redheaded witch and end her.

MacKinnon scoffed. He didn't need to kill the witch. He didn't even need to fight her. He just needed to give her what she wanted.

He needed to hand Hella over to her.

He didn't owe Hella anything, not after the way she had treated him. She wasn't his true fated one. It was an illusion. A fated female would never act in such a manner towards their male.

But in order to hand her over to the witch, he needed to do the impossible.

He needed to seduce Hella.

But how was he to soften her and make her lower her guard enough that she accepted him, and agreed to come with him to the fae town in Scotland?

He grunted as he thought about it and realised it wasn't going to be as easy as it sounded. His wolf instincts would do their best to influence his actions, and if he was to seduce her, he needed to approach her in a different manner to how he had been with her so far.

He needed to be charming, not brutish. Smooth, not coarse. He needed to win her over, not command her to obey him.

He slowly smiled as an idea formed.

The perfect way to make her fall into his bed.

And under his spell.

He would help her with her nymph problem.

CHAPTER 12

The rent was sky high and the lodgings had seen better days, but Hella's new temporary single-storey home—*shed*—was deep in the shifter district, a place where she doubted Ethyrian's men would come looking for her. She peered at the stains on the cobbled floor that were old and refused to come up, and curled her lip at the faint lingering scent of animal that clung to everything in the single rectangular room. She tried not to think about what beasts had called it home in the past.

Possibly horses.

When the old panther shifter had shown it to her, he had embellished a lot. According to him, it wasn't a shed previously used to house animals. The stable door was *cottage chic*. The peeling white paint on the outside was *authentic*. And the missing terracotta tiles on the roof lent it *character*, apparently.

It was a shed.

But beggars couldn't be choosers.

In reality, it was the perfect hiding place.

No self-respecting witch would live in such a hovel.

So the nymphs were unlikely to look for her here.

Still, she couldn't hide here all hours of the day and night. She would have to go out at some point. She was going to need supplies and was worried about her shop, not that she was crazy enough to go and check on it. She had her spies keeping an eye on it for her. By spies, she meant young witches who lived in the surrounding buildings and who were her eyes and ears when it came to all the juicy gossip in the town. In exchange for lessons, they kept their ear to the ground and told her everything.

Who was having an affair. Which businesses were in trouble. Which witch was making a play for more power. Who was sleeping with whom. Who was in the market for an affair. Fine, there were a lot of affairs involved, but it made her little town far more interesting when she knew which couples were on the verge of breaking up and who was sleeping together. The more unlikely the pairing, the better.

She stared into the mirror that had seen better days, was patchy in places and had been hanging on the yellow wall for decades judging by the fact the paint behind it was a darker shade of dandelion. Odd that there was a mirror in the shed.

Unless the previous occupant had been a horse shifter.

It would explain the smell.

Male horse shifters loved spending most of their time in their animal forms. Apparently, it got them a lot of attention from females. A fine-looking and well-groomed horse could easily draw a crowd of twittering women who wanted to pet and stroke, and *ride* it.

She twisted a length of her blue hair around her finger, desperately trying not to think about what kind of sordid things had happened in this building.

Should she dye it?

A ruckus outside in the street had her fingers tensing in her hair, yanking on it, and she hurried to the single sash window, her heart thundering as adrenaline shot through her veins. She sagged against the wall as she saw it was only two groups of feline shifters fighting in the alley between the tall walls that enclosed two of the compounds and not an army of nymphs come to grab her. The shifter district was lively to say the least. She had never realised it before, but having been here for two nights, she had learned that every shifter breed had a problem or two with the other ones who occupied the area.

Fights were far too common.

Her nerves were shot.

She couldn't get a decent night's sleep because there was always a fight or four that broke out and had her flying to the window, terrified of what she might see.

Hella watched as the six males went at it, clawing and hissing at each other, not really paying attention to them. Maybe she needed to move again. What if she went to the fae town near Fort William in Scotland? Fenix, her closest friend, had often spoken about it and owned a home near there. She could drop in and check on him while she was there. It had been months since he had come to see her for more pills to keep his incubus hunger in check, and she was worried.

It wasn't like him to go this long without coming to see her. The number of pills she had given him the last time she had seen him hadn't been anywhere near enough to cover this many months between visits. She tried to look on the bright side, telling herself that he might have found his mate and things might have worked out for them this time, but deep in her heart she knew that if that was the case, he would have brought the female to meet her.

He had always talked of doing just that.

Hella had always talked of him watching his back and that one day the blood mages he targeted were going to take him down, but he had never listened.

And she understood why.

He was cursed.

Seemed to be a theme these days.

The wolf was cursed too. There was no doubt about that in her mind now. She did have other doubts though—like the claim she was his fated one. Someone was 'yanking his chain' as Fenix would put it. She didn't know who she had crossed to get the wolf cursed, but she had added finding out to her to-do list.

Together with breaking the wolf's curse.

Hella abandoned the idea of changing the colour of her hair and drifted to the table she had placed her bag on, opened it and sifted through it. She pulled out two of the books she had brought with her and set them down, and carefully eased onto the wooden chair, not trusting that it wouldn't collapse beneath her weight.

The fire in the ancient log burner crackled and popped, filling the silence as she leafed through the first book, looking for anything that might help her with the wolf's curse. Her fingers brushed the page, lovingly stroking it, and she glanced at the other book. She had left so many of them behind.

How were they doing?

She hoped the nymphs didn't rip them apart in a fit of pique when they discovered she was in the wind. Some of them were old, as ancient as this shed she now called home. They were precious and irreplaceable.

She was tempted to sneak to see one of her friends, a witch who had seen her hauling arse across town. She had asked Greta to keep an eye on her house and send any nymphs that came asking about her in the wrong direction.

Or better yet, dispose of them.

The less of the king's men in town, the easier she could move around.

Hella sagged against the back of the chair, not caring when it creaked ominously.

She just wanted her old life back.

She huffed. If she had known who Ethyrian was when she had met him at the masquerade ball in Paris, she would have steered well clear of him. Kings, princes and alphas had a terrible habit of thinking they could just take what they wanted.

Case in point, the wolf.

She bet her left tit he was an alpha.

He had that dominant, overbearing attitude she now associated with men drunk on their position of power.

Although, Ethyrian had been nice to her. A little simpering at times, and broody, but he had been nice. Only she had apparently seen just one side of the nymph king, and he had been concealing the one that had reared its ugly head the moment she had dumped him. She sighed. She had been in a bit of a dry spell when she had attended the ball and had figured nymphs for an easy lay, a bit of fun, like an incubus but without the drawback that their semen could affect her connection to nature and therefore ruin her magic.

And her.

It turned out that nymphs were sexually highly charged, but they were also seriously high maintenance. They wanted to be petted and cooed over, desired and adored.

Which really wasn't her scene.

Any man who took that much effort to please and keep happy was a man she didn't need.

Hella moved her focus back to her book, drifting through the pages as the fire warmed her back. The world outside was quiet and peaceful, and for a moment, everything felt right in the world.

And then a big bad wolf came barrelling backwards through her door.

Shortly followed by five nymphs.

CHAPTER 13

Kin's plan was going well. He had found Hella's house empty, a lot of her belongings gone, but he had chanced upon a very helpful lass a few doors down who had muttered that he wasn't a nymph and Hella hadn't said anything about non-nymphs. She had been more than happy to tell him that Hella had moved to the other side of town, and when he had pressed her for better directions, she had shrugged and told him that was all she knew.

He had spent a day moving around the other side of the fae town, trying to pick up Hella's scent, and had ended up in the shifter district. There, he had asked around about the blue-haired witch and had struck gold.

An old panther shifter had pointed him to what Kin could only describe as a dilapidated stable.

MacKinnon had checked it out and discovered the reason he hadn't been able to pick up Hella's scent was because the place she was staying in reeked to high heaven, the odour of horse so strong that it masked her subtle fragrance of rain-soaked heather and spice.

He had been tempted to knock and check on her, by which he meant he had ended up fighting the urge to bang her door down, sweep in and sweep her off her feet and into his arms for another kiss. His instincts as her mate had gone haywire the moment he had sensed her moving around inside the white building and he'd had a hard time denying them.

A fight had broken out in the alley between him and the building though, and she had appeared in the window.

And gods, he had been bewitched all over again.

Had stood there like a dolt staring at her, aching for her to look at him, his wolf side placated by just the sight of her and the knowledge she was safe.

For now.

It hadn't taken him long to realise she was scared, or to figure out the reason why.

She wasn't afraid of the panthers and jaguars who had been brawling in the street.

She had feared the ruckus had been caused by nymphs who had come for her.

Seeing her shaken like that had roused something dark and powerful inside him, had set him on a course that had taken him away from her, back towards the busier and more elegant side of the town.

Hunting for nymphs.

He had been stalking the streets ever since, seeking nymphs who wore the same clothing as those who had abducted her last time. Several of them had borne a silver crest on the leather strap that crossed their bare chests, holding their swords in place on their back. He scanned every nymph he came across for that same seal.

His plan was simple.

He was going to find the nymphs she feared and deal with them, and then he would return to her triumphant and she would be so grateful that she would fall into his arms and accept him. Once he was strong enough, he would cart her back to the Fort William fae town, hand her over to the witch and be done with this whole affair.

Life would return to normal.

His wolf side growled at that, pacing within him, making him restless.

He steeled himself, refusing to listen to his instincts. He didn't want to keep Hella. She wasn't his true mate. In time, he would find his real fated female and he would win her heart. That was enough for him.

Kin stopped in the middle of the promenade, earning a few glares as people had to abruptly change course to avoid colliding with him. He curled his fingers into tight fists as an urge built inside him, one so powerful that it had him on the verge of turning around and heading straight to Hella. He wanted her to belong to him.

He wanted her to be his mate.

He didn't want to go back home without her.

He didn't want to betray her.

He closed his eyes and drew down a breath, tired of this internal battle that was happening more and more frequently as the hours ticked past. He had made up his mind and he would see his plan through. When he handed Hella over to the witch and she lifted the curse, he would see that he was right.

Hella wasn't his true fated one.

His fingers relaxed and his shoulders sagged, and he opened his eyes and stared at the flagstones in front of him.

But what if she was?

What if he handed her over and the witch lifted the curse, and he still felt that Hella was his fated one?

Gods. He scrubbed a hand down his face, weariness invading his soul. He wasn't sure he could live with himself if that was the case. He would have done the unthinkable.

The unforgivable.

He would have betrayed his mate.

He wasn't sure how he would handle the shame of his pack knowing what he had done, and they would know. Word would spread through the fae town and beyond.

Grant MacKinnon had betrayed his fated mate.

He sank to his haunches in the middle of the street, uncaring of the way people were no doubt looking at him as they passed, and rested his elbows on his knees, his hands dangling before him. Could he really do this?

If Hella did turn out to be his mate, then he would have only one recourse. Death.

He would deserve it for committing an act so reprehensible and destroying the sanctity of what it meant to find your fated female, something all mature wolves yearned for.

And even then, he wasn't sure his death would atone for his sin.

His eyebrows knitted hard and his jaw tensed as he ran through his options and found they were limited. The curse was active. It was real. Even now his strength was waning. How long could he go without luring Hella under his spell and into bed? How long could he then go without handing her over to the witch? Bedding Hella wouldn't lift his curse. It would only negate its effects, and for how long?

He was no fool.

He had felt fine before he had kissed Hella. That kiss had triggered the current weakening of his body, his grim march towards death. If he bedded her, the effect would no doubt be worse.

His strength would most likely leave him faster, forcing him to bed her again to keep it up, and then what? Would the drain happen faster still? Each time he slept with Hella, would the effect of the curse speed up? The redheaded witch would have taken measures to ensure he had to bring Hella to her in order to break it.

Which meant his suspicions were probably right.

The more he bedded Hella, the faster his strength would leave him.

Until sleeping with her had no effect and he had to take her to the witch to end his suffering.

He growled through his emerging fangs, despair swift to flood him as he realised how hopeless it was. Even if he wanted to deny the witch, which he did, he couldn't. It would be the death of him.

He chuckled mirthlessly.

Betraying his fated one would be the death of him too.

There had to be another way.

But the more he thought about it, the more his situation began to feel like another cage, and the shadows locked deep within him fed on his rising panic as everything closed in on him. They grew stronger as he battled them, until they began to unfurl dark tendrils that reached into the very pit of his soul. Sharp tendrils that pierced him and held him, dragging him down into the mire. He stared at the pavement, losing sight of the world around him as the shadows seemed to engulf him.

Devour him.

This curse was another cage. No. It was worse than any physical restraint.

Restraints he could break. Cages he could escape. This curse felt inescapable. Whatever he did, he would lose—either his life or his mate.

His eyebrows knitted hard and he clenched his jaw as his claws pressed into his knees. There was a third option. There had to be. He just needed to find a way to end this curse without sacrificing himself or losing his mate. He refused to listen to the dark whispers that taunted him, trying to hold him within the cage of his memories, and steeled his heart. He would find a way. The voices grew distant and quietened, and the shadows fell away as he gathered his strength and shirked his past, letting it roll off him as he focused on his future.

On moving forwards.

Kin pushed to his feet and lifted his head, intending to mull everything over and find a solution to his problem while he searched for the king's men.

Only he spotted a group of five blond nymphs ahead of him, all of them wearing only green leather trousers, with daggers strapped to their hips. They drew the glances of every woman who passed them, looking every bit the bastard fae they were as they seduced them with easy smiles and murmured comments.

Kin narrowed his eyes on one of the long-haired males as he turned side-on to him.

He recognised the crest on the dark brown sheath of his dagger.

And grinned.

He needed a method of winning Hella over and needed to blow off some steam, unleashing the aggression and anger he felt whenever he thought about his situation, and the gods had just placed five of them in his path.

He rolled his shoulders, twisted his neck, and flexed his fingers into fists and clenched them, causing his forearms to tense beneath his navy Henley.

Kin strode towards the males, his focus narrowing down to them, the rest of the world falling away as he drew down deep breaths, gearing up for a fight. His gaze leaped over each male, cataloguing everything from their height and build, to their potential age.

And the fact all of them were armed with only daggers.

Score a point for him.

He stretched his fingers and his claws emerged, his own little daggers. His wolf side paced back and forth, hungry for contact, snarling and growling as he closed the distance between him and the nymphs. His mate feared these males finding her. No more. He would eliminate them, protecting her and showing her that he could be trusted.

And earning her gratitude.

Everything hinged on that.

He needed to win her over with the prize he intended to present to her and then she would fall into his arms, would welcome his kiss and so much more.

But first, he had to secure that prize.

MacKinnon walked up to the biggest of the blond males, cocked his fist and smashed it into the side of his head, cutting him off mid-sentence and knocking him into one of his comrades. A heartbeat passed and then pandemonium erupted, all five nymphs turning on him as one as they processed what he had just done.

He grinned and leaped backwards as one lunged at him, easily evading his wild swing. The other four were quicker to gather their wits, including the largest nymph. He came at Kin on a furious bellow, unsheathing his dagger at the same time, and slashed the silver blade through the air at stomach height the moment he was close enough to land a blow. Kin sucked his stomach in and bowed his body away from the dagger, his arms coming forwards to balance himself. The moment the threat had passed, he leaned his upper body backwards, brought his left leg up and slammed his shin into the nymph's stomach. The male grunted. Kin followed through and sent the bastard flying towards the lake.

He continued to turn, brought his foot down and pressed it to the flagstones and brought his right leg up, higher than his first kick had been. He nailed another of the nymphs in his face. Blood and what looked a hell of a lot like a tooth flew from the male's mouth and he went down, coughing and spluttering, painting one of the pale flagstones crimson.

The youngest looking nymph, a male who had been keeping back, took one look at his fallen comrades and charged Kin on a battle cry, his dagger held before him in both trembling hands. A greenhorn.

Kin felt bad about what he was going to do to the male, but all was fair in love and war.

He let the young male come at him, waited until the nymph was close enough, his blade in danger of piercing Kin's stomach, and then stepped to his left, hooked the nymph's throat in the crook of his right arm and brought it up, twisting the male around so his back was to Kin's front. Before the nymph could recover his wits to attack him, Kin seized his hand with his left one and bent it backwards, snapping his wrist.

The dagger dropped as the nymph cried out.

Kin shoved the male away from him as the weapon hit the pavement and two nymphs came at him, one aiming for the young male while the other brandished his dagger and came at Kin. Kin swept low as he stepped to meet the male, scooped the dagger up off the ground and spun it in his grip, so the gold pommel was near his thumb and the cross-guard was snug to the edge of his hand. The nymph slashed at him with his blade and threw a punch with his other hand, both of which Kin dodged. He continued to evade the male's attacks, moving backwards.

Luring him away from his comrades.

Divide and conquer.

When the gap between him and the other four nymphs was over forty feet, he attacked. He lunged with the dagger, forcing the nymph to block, and as the male brought his arm up, he struck him hard in the stomach with a vicious right uppercut. The male grunted and bent forwards from the force of the blow.

And Kin twisted his hand and brought the blade across his throat.

Blood fell like a waterfall from the thin line that cut from one side of his neck to the other, saturating his bare chest in an instant, and horrified gasps and screams sounded around him as their audience caught up.

His senses sparked and he growled as he dodged to his right, grunted as a blade slashed across his biceps, slicing through his Henley. Dammit. He cursed again when he saw it wasn't only the biggest of the nymphs who had launched another attack. The one who had lost a tooth and the one who had rushed to check on the youngest nymph surrounded him too.

He desperately blocked the dagger one thrust at him, bracing his forearm against the male's and stopping the blade from piercing his shoulder. The nymph drove forwards, forcing Kin backwards. Kin watched the dagger inching closer to his right shoulder, dropped his own weapon and desperately grabbed the male's wrist and tried to shove him away. The nymph sneered and pressed harder, his muscles bulging as he pushed the blade back towards him, and Kin grunted as his back met the wall of one of the buildings.

Not good.

The nymph grinned now and Kin growled as he battled to match his strength, to keep the blade from piercing him as he fought to twist the male's hand away. He gritted his teeth as he slowly turned the nymph's hand, refusing to give up when the male realised his intention and shoved the flat of his free hand against the hilt of the dagger.

The point came dangerously close to piercing him.

Kin weighed his options as he wrestled to turn the blade away from his chest, aware that they were limited. He went with the first one that came to mind.

Kneed the nymph in the crotch.

The male grunted, shock rolling across his face, and Kin took advantage of his momentary distraction. He quickly turned the male's hand towards his chest and shoved, driving the blade deep into his shoulder. The nymph bellowed and stumbled backwards, freeing Kin.

He was quick to kick off and swipe up his fallen dagger, to turn and aim it at the male to finish him off.

Only the nymph disappeared.

One of his comrades came at Kin, lunging wildly with his dagger.

MacKinnon leaped to his right, narrowly avoiding being skewered by him, and huffed as the male's blade slashed across his left hip, slicing through his shirt and the skin beneath. Pain blazed a path across his flesh and he growled as he pressed his hand to it and leaped back to gain more space.

Placing him right back near the biggest nymph.

That male grabbed him before he could move again, twisting him into a chokehold. Kin snarled as the nymph arched backwards, placing more pressure on his throat, cutting off his air supply. His lungs burned as he hooked his hand over the male's forearm and dug his claws in. The nymph Kin had stabbed came at him, bloodied dagger aimed at his chest, and his lungs burned for a different reason as he stared at it.

Panic made his wolf wild and he couldn't stop the shift.

Fur swept over his body as his bones shrank and his face morphed. His vision sharpened, his hearing growing so sensitive he could pick up the heartbeats of everyone in the area, and the scents around him grew stronger. Blood. Sweat. Fear. He growled and twisted as he completed the shift, turning from man to wolf in only a handful of seconds.

His emotions dulled, their range narrowing as his animal instincts seized control. Panic boiled down to fear.

To an urge to survive.

Kin twisted his head and sank his fangs deep into the arm of the male holding him, savagely ripping at his flesh as he pumped his hind legs in an attempt to jerk himself free of his grip. The male who had been coming at him hesitated at the sight of him and Kin used it to his advantage as he broke free and his paws hit the ground. He kicked off, sailing through the air and leaving his jeans and boots behind. Shock shone in the nymph's eyes as they reflected Kin.

He landed with his front paws against the male's chest and angled his head as he lunged forwards, his momentum knocking the nymph backwards.

Before he could even hit the ground, Kin had torn his throat open and the male had drawn his final breath.

The largest male came at him, making a wild lunge for Kin's scruff. Kin leaped sideways away from him, tugging a shriek from a female he landed near, and bared his fangs at the nymph. He circled with the male, lowering his head, keeping all of his focus locked on him as he continued to growl and snarl. The male was a threat, one that needed to be eliminated.

The safety of his fated female depended upon it.

The nymph bent and retrieved a dagger from the flagstones, arming himself with a second, and flexed his fingers around them as he drew down a steadying breath. Kin stilled and waited, barely breathing, his sharp vision detecting even the tiniest twitch in the nymph's muscles.

The barest flex of his left deltoid was enough to give him away.

Kin sprinted around him before he had even begun to move, was behind him as he took his first step in the direction Kin had been, and was leaping on his back just as he caught up. Kin snarled and sank his fangs into the male's shoulder. The male bellowed and twisted, trying to dislodge him, and Kin scrabbled with his hind legs, seeking purchase to stop himself from falling off. His claws dug into the waistband of the male's green leathers and he risked adjusting his grip with his fangs.

Buried them deep in the nymph's spine and bit down hard.

The nymph jerked as bone crunched and then slumped forwards, and Kin landed on top of him.

He released the dead male and lifted his head, and growled when he saw the other two nymphs running into the distance.

Kin licked his lips, clearing the blood from his muzzle, and huffed as he stepped down from the nymph. He surveyed the three fallen nymphs, growing aware of the people who were watching him. He bared his fangs at them, driven to chase them off, feeling they were a threat to him too.

A few of them were giving him strange looks rather than fearful ones.

He looked down at his front legs and then back at one noble male in particular, and focused on shifting back as an urge to wipe the amused look off his face rushed through him. His bones ached as they lengthened and transformed, his face morphing back as his black fur receded to reveal pink skin.

When he was back in his human form, he glared at the male and grunted, "Never seen a wolf in a Henley before?"

He strode to his jeans, swiped them from the ground and tugged them on, shutting out the irritating males who had found the sight of him wearing clothing while in his wolf form amusing. He had to admit, it did somewhat ruin how frightening he looked when he shifted into an animal, and he usually made an effort to remove his clothes before he transformed. Sometimes he didn't get the luxury of stripping off though.

Like when a nymph was choking him to death.

He shoved his feet into his boots. He couldn't exactly ask for a timeout in the middle of a fight so he could remove his clothing and then shift.

Kin stomped to one of the dead nymphs, grabbed him by his hair and hauled him towards the others, earning himself disgusted and horrified looks from many of the gathered. He shrugged it off as he gathered his other two prizes and began dragging them through the streets, leaving a bloody smear in his wake.

By the time he reached the road that led from the promenade to Hella's stable, he was growing tired of how the people in his path would gasp at the sight of him and how some of the females, and males, would fan themselves and look away. A few vomited.

He adjusted his grip on the trio of nymphs, fisting their hair closer to their scalps, and trudged onwards, deeply aware that he was a grim spectacle in this pristine town. In the Scottish fae town, no one would have batted an eye. Here, everyone stared and spoke in whispers, discussing how shocking it was and debating whether he intended to eat the nymphs.

MacKinnon grunted.

He never had liked the upper classes of his world and this place was home to that entitled, elitist breed of immortal.

It was probably good for them to see an angry wolf dragging his victims through their town. They needed a dose of reality. Not everywhere was as sanitised as this place, and not everyone in the world was as civilised.

Kin hauled his prize to Hella's door and hesitated. He released the dead nymphs and preened his appearance, wiping any remaining blood from his face, neatening his dark hair and inspecting the gashes in his Henley as he tried to figure out what to say to her when he presented his prize to her.

Would she react in the same way as the other townsfolk had and be horrified, her delicate sensibilities shaken by what he had done?

Kin didn't get a chance to find out.

His senses sharpened and his spine stiffened.

He wasn't alone.

He turned on his heel, his eyes widening as he spotted seven nymphs charging towards him. He stooped and grabbed a dagger that was still in its sheath on one of his prizes and hurled it at the male in front of the group. It nailed him in his shoulder and he went down.

Leaving Kin without a weapon.

Fuck.

He extended his claws and launched at the next male, slammed into him and drove forwards, propelling the male backwards. He punched the nymph in his side. Once. Twice. A third time. The male grunted with each blow, and coughed up blood on the third, splattering Kin's cheek with it. Kin growled and slashed at the male's stomach with his claws, slicing long deep gashes in it and then shoved him in his chest.

Sending him flying towards the group.

He huffed when they all dodged and kept coming at him.

Double fuck.

The biggest of them barrelled into him, knocking the wind from him and sending *him* flying.

Right into Hella's door.

He grunted as he crashed through it, landed on his back and used the momentum to his advantage. He rolled heels over head to hit his knees, ending up facing the doorway as he came to his feet and the nymphs shoved into the room.

Behind him, Hella shot to her feet. "What the hell, wolf? You led them straight to me!"

He grimaced at how furious she both sounded and felt on his senses, wanted to look back at her, but feared what he would find. There went his plan. Rather than being grateful, she was madder than ever at him, and sure, he got why.

But it didn't stop her from spelling it out.

"I'm in hiding, you idiot." She cuffed him around the back of his head and he flinched and glared over his shoulder at her.

She glared right back at him, her emerald eyes bright with silver and gold stars that shifted and swirled. Magic charged the air, the tinny scent of it strong, and he hoped to the gods that she wasn't about to unleash it on him because they had bigger problems to deal with than her being upset with him.

"Stay back." He held his left arm out before her.

"I will do no such thing," she snapped.

Kin glanced over his shoulder at her.

And was blinded as she unleashed a bright bolt of red light from her hand.

He reared away from her as he blinked hard, clearing his vision in time to see the spell strike the nymphs. A huge crimson glyph appeared, shaped like an octagon with a star inside it surrounded by circles filled with a large symbol. Electricity pulsed in the air and then a thick beam shot from the glyph.

Knocking every nymph flying and clearing a path to the door.

Kin could only stare as she went on the offensive, casting a glowing green orb at one of the nymphs who had ended up hurled to the right of the room, close to a rickety bed. The second it hit the male, he screamed and contorted.

"Look out!" she yelled and he swivelled towards the door just as a nymph kicked off and plunged a dagger towards his chest.

A wall of pale blue interlocking hexagons appeared between him and the nymph, and the male grunted as he slammed into it and staggered backwards, losing his grip on his dagger as he tripped and fell on his backside.

Incredible.

A thrill bolted down his spine.

He had never fought beside a female before, got a little caught up in her as she directed another blast at the nymph before he could recover, hitting him with the same green orb she had used on the one in the corner, ripping a high-pitched scream from him.

In his world, females didn't fight.

But then, she was nothing like the females in his world.

She was something else.

Something incredible.

Amazing.

She waved her hand over her belongings and everything flew into the carpet bag, and then it shot into her grip and she was moving.

Leaping clear over the fallen nymph near the door.

And she was leaving.

His mate was running from him again.

MacKinnon howled and gave chase.

CHAPTER 14

Hella was beyond furious now.

She ran hard, panic at the helm, aware from the howl of rage that the wolf was going to pursue her again. Great. Just what she needed. She looked over her shoulder and sure enough, he was bearing down on her, his face a mask of pure fury and his eyes like liquid gold.

Gorgeous.

She shivered as a thrill chased down her spine, the foolish part of her wanting to accidentally, on purpose, slow down so he could catch her. She shoved it aside and clung to her anger.

"Thank you *so* much for leading them right to me!" she yelled at him, pouring every drop of sarcasm she could into her words.

His golden eyes narrowed on her and his lips flattened, drawing her gaze to them. Her blood heated and an unruly thought curled through her mind. Would that dark scruff that coated his jaw be soft against her lips or scrape them until they were sensitised?

Hella cursed herself and dragged her gaze away from him, making a valiant attempt to shut out rogue thoughts of the wolf.

She faced forwards again, banking right on a street that ran parallel to the promenade, not daring to hit it in case more nymphs were waiting there. She had five of the bastards hot on her heels. She really didn't need to add to that number when the spells she had used to take down just two of them and clear a path to freedom had left her shaky.

The wolf barked, "Ah didnae ken them bawbags was gonna folla me!"

If it wasn't for the fact she was being chased by the group of nymphs he had sicced on her, Hella might have found it endearing or possibly alluring that his Scots got way more pronounced when he was in a rage. As it was, her blood heated again, desire licking through her, and she had a hard time resisting looking back to drink her fill of him.

"Eyes forward, Hella," she muttered to herself.

She struggled to keep hold of her bag as she ran, clinging to it with both hands and fighting the weight of it. Like this, she was vulnerable. She needed her hands to cast spells, but the bag was too heavy to carry in one hand, meaning she would have to stop and put it down in order to attack the nymphs. If she did, she risked losing her most cherished possessions. She needed what was in the bag.

But mother earth, it was getting heavier by the second.

Her breaths sawed from her lips, her heart pounding so fast she felt sick as her legs tired and she forced herself to keep going.

She cursed when she began to slow, the drain of using her magic to cast such powerful spells combining with adrenaline to steal her strength despite how desperately she clung to it.

The wolf caught up to her. "Can ye no' run any faster?"

Hella shot him a look.

Was about to yell at him again when he shrugged.

And swept her into his arms, relieving her of her carpet bag at the same time. He tossed her over his shoulder and banded his forearm over her thighs, pinning them to his chest. She opened her mouth to protest, but snapped it shut as she realised that with the wolf carrying her and her bag, she had both hands free and was facing the nymphs.

She would yell at him later.

Right now, she had five nymphs to get off her tail.

Hella lifted her hands before her, jamming her elbows into his muscular back to stop herself from jiggling around so much. She stared at the spot between her palms as she moved them to face each other and summoned a spell. Five pinpricks of violet light appeared between her hands and grew into small discs.

They shot towards the nymphs, expanding as they approached them. She grinned as only two of them managed to evade them and the spell struck the other three. One nymph shot over sixty feet into the air and disappeared. One went flying to his left as if someone had attached a rope to him and pulled, slamming him into a building and sending him through the window. The third was blasted backwards and landed with enough force to shatter several flagstones.

"Careful no' to burn my arse hairs, witch," the wolf growled, each long stride jostling her on his shoulder.

Hella looked down. He did have a fine backside. It would be a shame to burn it. His navy Henley had ridden up, revealing flashes of twin dimples in his muscles just above the waist of his jeans, and she was sorely tempted to reach down and stroke them with her fingers.

"Anger me again and I'll burn more than your arse hairs, wolf," she bit out, holding on to her anger and refusing to let him see how badly he flustered her.

He chuckled, the warm sound out of place given they were still being pursued. Two of the nymphs had re-joined the group, but the wolf was outpacing them. He was fast, she gave him that. There was a chance they might survive this.

"Grant MacKinnon," the wolf muttered.

Her eyebrows shot up and she twisted to look at the back of his head. "What?"

"My name. You never asked for it."

She huffed. "I never wanted to know it."

He didn't miss a beat. "Most call me MacKinnon and those I like call me Kin. You can call me Kin."

He liked her? She refused to let the warm fuzzy feeling that stirred take hold of her. He only liked her because he thought she was his mate.

He planted his hand on her backside and she scowled and awkwardly reached around to swat him away.

"Quit getting handsy, wolf." She slapped his large hand until he moved it away, taking hold of her legs again.

It didn't stop the heat that rolled through her, a hazy quality to it that had her tempted to ask him to plant it back on her bottom again and palm it this time. Good gods, she needed to get laid.

And not by the wolf.

Hella focused on pulling together what remained of her strength and drew down a slow breath as she emptied her mind. She muttered the incantation under her breath and the wolf tensed, and she knew why. Magic charged the air around her as the spell gathered strength, rapidly forming between her hands.

The black-purple orb twisted and distorted, jagged violet ribbons crackling over its surface, and she stared at it as it grew, as she funnelled more of her strength into it, aware this was her last and best shot but hesitant to take it.

Abyssal magic was dangerous.

Forbidden for a reason.

If she screwed this up, the black hole she was creating could swallow half the town.

"What the bloody hell are ye doing, witch?" MacKinnon growled and she ignored him, because she couldn't risk losing her focus.

One slip was all it would take to wipe out everyone in the immediate area, including her and the wolf.

"Just a little more," she murmured, shaping the spell now, keeping it low level enough that it wouldn't place her beloved town in danger but would deal with her pest problem.

The moment she felt it was ready, she released it.

It bobbed towards the group of nymphs, gently rising and dipping through the air around fifteen feet above the ground, moving slowly.

The foolish males were too focused on catching up with her and the wolf to pay attention to the innocuous five-inch sphere heading towards them.

The moment it was above them, it expanded with a deep humming sound that hit her in her chest and swallowed them whole, together with a neat section of the pavement, and then shrank back in on itself and disappeared.

"What the bloody fuck was that?" MacKinnon twisted with her, swinging her around on his shoulder so violently that her queasy stomach almost rebelled, and then a split-second later continued the pivot so she was facing the shallow crater in the street. He grumbled, "Starting to think you're a wee bit dangerous, lass."

"You're only *starting* to think that?" She couldn't hold back her smile as she said that and was glad he couldn't see it and know she was beginning to enjoy their banter. She didn't want him getting ideas. Speaking of which. She pressed her hands to his shoulders and shoved upwards. "You can put me down now."

"No." He tightened his grip instead and kept running. "Not until you're safe."

"I am safe," she countered.

The low, vicious growl that pealed from his lips and the way his fingers dug into her thigh told her that he thought quite the opposite. Because of his instincts? She had never delved too much into life as a shifter, because it had never really interested her.

Until now.

Was MacKinnon a slave to his instincts? She had heard tales of male shifters losing control to their instincts, unable to resist obeying their animal side, and she had heard even more frightening tales of what a male like him was capable of when it came to their fated female.

She had no desire to find out whether MacKinnon would be just as wildly possessive and dangerously protective as the males in those stories.

She kept shoving against his shoulders, but he refused to release her, even when she bashed her fists into his back and took to elbowing his thick head. Everyone they passed stared at her and a thought pinged into her head, but was quickly shut down. She couldn't call for help. If she did, there was a danger that MacKinnon would attack anyone who tried to rescue her, believing they meant to take his fated one from him.

A flash of the three dead nymphs she had leaped over when escaping the rest of Ethyrian's guards filled her mind and she stilled. MacKinnon wouldn't just attack anyone who tried to take her. He would kill them.

The streets around her changed as he carried her further from the centre of the town, into the outskirts at the other end of the cavern to the shifter district and far from the one where her real home was. The buildings grew smaller, two-storey detached affairs that had peeling pastel paint and roofs that had seen better days, and the flagstones gave way to cobbles. Where the hell was the wolf taking her?

He slowed at last and began breathing hard, huffing at times, and she angled her head in an attempt to see his face.

When it failed, she muttered, "What are you doing?"

"Scenting," he grumbled, his voice gone low, far too sexy.

"All I smell is old blood, urine and other things I wish I couldn't." She glanced around her again, not missing the vampires that skulked in the shadows between the buildings, able to walk in the light here because the sun was false.

They all looked horribly hungry.

She focused on her fingers, but they didn't even tingle with magic. She was tapped out, needed to sleep and maybe whip up a rejuvenation potion to help her along. The sensation that she was powerless wasn't a welcome one, had her easing closer to MacKinnon, if that was possible. He seemed to detect her fear, because he gently brought her down from his shoulder and pinned her to his chest.

Or maybe he was just taking advantage.

In order to avoid sliding right off him, she had to wrap her legs around his waist, which only encouraged him to plant his hand on her backside again.

This time, Hella didn't complain. She was too busy keeping an eye on the vampires, hoping that the fact she was with a werewolf would keep them at bay. The two species never had seen eye to eye.

MacKinnon turned and she glanced over his shoulder in time to see him shove open the wooden door of a small white house. It smelled musty as he carried her inside and she wrinkled her nose.

He set her down by the door, closed it and hemmed her in, pinning her back to the wall, his big body crowding her and stealing the air from her lungs as he made the room feel far too small.

"What are you doing?" She pressed her hands to his broad chest and shoved, not moving him an inch.

"Shh," he hissed and canted his head, his glowing golden eyes fixed on the door, a look of sheer concentration etched on his face.

She froze and listened too, but heard nothing. What could he hear? He was strong and clearly had sharp senses, which meant he had to be old, but he didn't look much over forty-five to her. There was a little age showing in just the right places on his face. Smile lines bracketed his mouth and his eyes, telling her that he knew how to laugh and have a good time.

Part of her wanted to say she found that impossible to imagine given the fact he was prone to glowering and growling at her, but she had seen flickers of it at times, enough to know that if she wasn't so caustic towards him and he wasn't so obsessed with the fact she was meant to be his, that she might find she actually enjoyed his company.

MacKinnon's striking golden eyes slid to meet hers, his voice gone low and husky. "They're definitely gone."

"Doubting my spells now, wolf?" She rolled her eyes at him, bringing up the only barrier she could as he pressed closer to her and his voice did wicked things to her body, making her ache and yearn for him.

"Would never doubt you, my wily wee witch."

"I'm not your anything." Her heart shot into her throat as he lifted his left hand and she ducked to her left, making a break for it. He pressed his hand to the wall there, blocking her exit with his arm, and when she turned the other way, he did the same there. Her eyes darted up to collide with his.

"I'll be having another kiss now," he murmured throatily, just the sound of his voice making her thighs quiver and nipples bead.

She swallowed to wet her parched throat and leaned back.

"What for?" Her eyes widened as something hit her. "Oh my gods, you led the nymphs to me just so you could stage this rescue!"

She couldn't believe his audacity.

No. Actually, she could.

"I did no such thing," he barked, his handsome face darkening, and she almost believed he was being sincere, only she wasn't about to trust a word that left his far-too-kissable lips. "I killed three nymphs and the others scattered. I thought they were gone for good. I brought the three to you as a peace offering."

Hella pulled a face. "I thought it was cats that brought dead things as presents?"

MacKinnon brushed his right hand lightly down her bare arm, sending heat shimmering over her skin and stealing her breath.

He murmured, "If you want a present, I can give you one."

She rolled her eyes again, adding a touch more theatrics to it this time. "I'm not interested in the sort of present you want to give me."

He smiled slowly—panty-meltingly—so confident in his charms that she was torn between slapping him and kissing that smug look off his face.

"Ah can feel ye, lass." His voice went lower, his brogue cranking her temperature up, and she was sure he was doing it on purpose, knew how he affected her when he sounded so rough around the edges. He dropped his left hand to her chest, stealing her breath all over again as the heavy weight of it settled between her breasts, and stared at his fingers. "Ye be needing your male."

Hella caught his wrist and shoved his hand away from her, sense slamming back into her to knock the part of her that kept falling under his spell out of her.

"You're not *my* male." She ducked under his arm and moved deeper into the room, turning to face him as her pulse thundered in her ears. "You're a confused, cursed wolf. You're being manipulated and enslaved by your instincts, and they're wrong. I'm not your fated one."

He slowly pivoted towards her.

The glow in his golden eyes unsettled her as he stared at her in silence, his expression giving nothing away now.

"My lass has spirit," he murmured and the corners of his lips twitched. "I like that... but I will have my kiss."

Persistent, irritating, and gorgeous wolf.

"Come and get it then." She crooked her finger at him, feeling it tingle with magic as a sliver of her strength returned.

Just enough to carry out a plan that would no doubt make him angry with her again.

He stalked towards her, all predator and male, tearing her between going through with it and giving him the kiss he wanted. His golden gaze dropped to her lips and they tingled in response, an ache rolling through her as she recalled just how firm his lips had been against hers the last time they had kissed, and how thoroughly he had kissed her, stamping his mark on her.

It had been far too long since she had been kissed like that.

Hella forced herself to focus, because she wouldn't be kissing him again.

When he reached her, his hands coming up to claim her hips, she lifted her hand and brushed her finger over his lower lip, stopping him in his tracks. His eyes grew hooded, another look she found far too sexy, and then drowsy as she swept her finger back again, savouring the softness of his lip.

"What?" he mumbled and blinked, frowned and tried to look at her. "Wha'd'you do to—"

He dropped to his knees and sank forwards, and Hella stepped aside so he didn't collapse against her legs. She grimaced when he faceplanted on the dirty wooden floorboards instead, out cold.

"I gave you a goodnight kiss," she whispered.

She sank into a crouch beside him and brushed her fingers across his brow, clearing his dark hair from it, and then feathered them down to his temple. She stroked the smile lines beside his closed eye and then caressed the sculpted plane of his cheek. His whiskers were coarse, just right for making her lips tingle as he kissed her, and she almost wished she had laced her lips with the spell and not her fingertips.

For the second time in a week, Hella found herself looking down at him and asking, "What am I going to do with you?"

She knew what she had to do with him, and it was enough to make her hesitate. He wasn't to be trusted though. He truly believed she was his fated one and that meant he wasn't going to stop trying to place a claim on her—a claim she didn't want. She didn't want to be his.

And there was only one way to make him see that.

She had to do the unthinkable.

Just remembering how badly he had reacted the last time she had chained him was enough to make her hesitate, to have her stalling and staring at him, simply watching him sleep. She told herself she had no choice, even as some distant voice inside her screamed that she did. She could help him. She shook her head. She wanted to help him, but she wanted it to be on her terms, not his. If she let him run free, he would keep trying to seduce her, and she wasn't strong enough to keep on resisting his advances.

He was right.

She did want him.

But he wanted something far different to what she did.

He wanted to chain her with a bond.

His instincts said she was his mate and that was all that mattered to him. He didn't care whether she wanted him or not. He wasn't here to woo her and court her, to take her on dates and get to know her, and make her fall madly in love with him.

He was here to take what he wanted.

And she couldn't allow that.

So she went to her carpet bag, opened it and rummaged through it until she found a small tear-shaped vial. She removed the wax and stopper and drank the potion, closed her eyes and waited for it to take effect. It was slow to come, telling her that she needed more than this rejuvenation spell to restore her magic back to its usual level. She would rest later, once she was safe from the big bad wolf.

Hella summoned the shackles she had used on him before, carried them to him and sank to her knees near his head.

And hesitated again.

Her gaze shifted from his wrists to his face and her stomach turned, her heart aching and growing heavier by the second. Could she really do this to him? By his account, he hadn't meant to bring those nymphs to her door. He had been trying to make amends in his own way, and he had helped her escape Ethyrian's men and had brought her to another safe house.

"Too late now," she muttered. "When he comes around, he's going to be furious."

She stroked the line of his brow. It was relaxed now but she could easily picture the glare he would aim at her when he regained consciousness. It was better he wasn't free to launch at her in a rage when that happened.

Maybe she could explain things quickly and make him see that she would help him if he could manage to be reasonable and keep his paws to himself.

She highly doubted that.

He wasn't going to be in the mood to listen to her when he woke to find himself chained to a bed.

She looked up at the old wooden ceiling. If there was a bed here.

Hella stood and went upstairs to check, and sure enough, there was an ancient four-poster bed in the single room there. It looked ready to fall apart, so she used a little magic to make it sturdy enough to withstand an angry wolf, and then went back downstairs to him.

Another spell made it easier to drag his dead weight upstairs, but it also made her head turn. She settled for using what physical strength she did possess, which was nothing compared with his, to manoeuvre him into the room and onto the bed. It took several attempts, during which she accidentally lost her grip on him twice, causing him to faceplant on the floor again. At this rate, he was going to wake angry and with a headache.

When he was finally on the bed, she hesitated again and then forced herself to chain him to it.

And hurried away from him so she didn't have to see what she had done.

She went downstairs and used the last of her magic to cast a protection spell on the building that would keep out foes and dampen the noise MacKinnon was going to make when he came around.

Her head fogged and she stumbled to an ancient brown leather armchair near a long bench table and sank onto it, fatigue rolling up on her.

Her eyes slipped shut and she sank towards what she hoped would be a deep, restful sleep.

Only MacKinnon was there waiting for her in her dreams.

CHAPTER 15

Hella wove her way through the saplings that lined the mossy bank of the dark loch, drifting from tree to tree. The lingering heat of a summer's day caressed her skin, had her stroking fingers over her cleavage to catch the dampness that gathered there and had her itching to remove her black corset and shed her skirts to cool off in the water. The air was thick in the birch forest, hard to breathe as she meandered towards the lake, drawn to it. She carefully stepped over a fallen log, the moss and grass cushioning her bare feet.

Light twinkled through the trees, threaded with flecks of gold that glittered as she gazed up at the verdant leafy canopy.

This place was beautiful.

Breathtaking.

She had never felt so immersed in nature, so surrounded by the goddess's power and her life-giving force.

Hella reached out to brush her fingers across the silvery trunk of one of the saplings, feeling the soft texture of the bark beneath their tips, and kept drifting forwards.

The loch beckoned.

Moss and grass gave way to a pebbled shore. The trees gave way to open air.

Hella stepped out onto the pebbles and kept walking forwards, not stopping until the water lapped at her toes and dampened the hem of her skirts.

She looked down and canted her head as she frowned.

Her long skirts.

It wasn't like her to wear such modest clothing, but as she took in her black dress, she found she liked that it concealed so much of her body, keeping it a mystery, even as it revealed her best asset. She stroked her breasts again, skimming fingers over the twin mounds, and lifted her gaze, settling it on the loch.

Green mountains laced with pale purple and pink heather enclosed the water, their gentle slopes appearing brown near the top and dark green at the bottom where trees hugged their foothills. The water rippled and sparkled in the sunshine, the way the light played across it mesmerising her for a moment before her gaze was drawn to one of the islands that dotted the loch. There were several of them, some large and home to towering pines, and others little more than rocks jutting from the surface.

She found her focus drifting to one in particular as a sensation built inside her—an island that had several trees clustered together in the centre of it.

She stilled.

That wasn't the only thing on the island.

MacKinnon stood on the shore, his loose white shirt billowing in the breeze, held in place by the waist of a red and green kilt.

Her pulse quickened, heart thumping harder as she stared at him and he stared at her, and awareness of him reached right down into her soul.

She had been mistaken.

He was the breathtaking thing in this place.

His dark hair was tousled and wild, his eyes more gold than silver, and the few buttons of his shirt were undone, revealing his broad chest and making her itch to brush her fingers through the hair that covered it.

Her breath hitched as he moved forwards, as he waded into the water.

Heading for her.

Her pulse fluttered and she looked away, knew she should leave but couldn't bring herself to do it as he dived into the loch and began swimming towards her. Anticipation thrummed inside her, had her restless and unsure what to do as he closed the distance between them, his powerful arms and legs making swift work of crossing the water that separated them.

But not quickly enough for her liking.

Her entire body felt as if it was on fire as she waited. She burned for him.

Hella looked down at the water that caressed her feet and then at MacKinnon.

And found she couldn't wait.

She waded into the water, her skirts growing heavy as it soaked them. She wrestled with them, struggling to lift them as the water reached her thighs, the coolness of it a relief from the summer heat but not from the fire blazing within her.

That fire only grew hotter still when MacKinnon reached a point where he could stand. He rose from the water and stole her breath. Mother earth, he was glorious. His white shirt clung to his body, revealing it to her hungry gaze, and she barely bit back a moan as he swept his hands over his wet hair, slicking it back from his face.

Droplets of water rolled down his sculpted cheeks to caress the straight line of his jaw, tempting her fingers to stroke the same path.

Eyes that were, in fact, more silver than gold locked with hers, bewitching her.

Such striking eyes.

How could she have ever thought no man in this world could have eyes more interesting and entrancing than Ethyrian's?

MacKinnon's eyes could cast a spell on her, were black magic that destroyed her defences and tore down her control.

He waded towards her, powerful legs cutting through the water, making it surge around him, and her breaths came faster, her heart thundering as she waited to see what he would do.

Hoping it was what she needed him to do.

The moment he was close enough, he snagged her wrist and pulled her into his arms.

And kissed her.

Not a gentle, tender kiss.

His kiss was rough and commanding, meant to bend her to his will and make her submit to him, and gods, she loved it. She lost herself in it, her hands coming up to fist his wet shirt as desperation rolled through her, shattering her control. He was right. Damn him. He was right. She did need him.

She had never needed anyone as fiercely as she needed him.

And here in this dream world she could have him.

Here there were no consequences to her actions. She could take what she wanted and give what he needed, and nothing between them would change.

On a low, strangled moan, she tugged at his shirt, the need to get it off him more important than air at that moment. He broke the kiss and reached over his back, gripped his shirt and pulled it off, revealing every inch of his delicious torso. Hella groaned and swooped on it, kissed a path across his chest that had him moaning and clutching her to him. She circled his left nipple with her tongue and then moved downwards, her hands joining in the fun, exploring every inch of his hard pecs and the heavy ropes of his stomach. Gods, this man was pure strength, hard beneath her greedy hands in a way that spoke to her on a primal level, firing her up.

Hella reached for the waist of his kilt.

MacKinnon beat her to it, unfastening the red and green tartan and opening it to reveal himself. Sweet gods. She groaned and reached for the hard length that jutted towards her, determined to fulfil her fantasies about touching it. He trembled as she brushed her thumb over the broad head, smearing a pearl of moisture into his skin, and stroked her hand downwards. When she cupped his balls, his hips jerked forwards, his growl wicked and low. It curled through her, heating her blood another few degrees.

His mouth descended on hers again, his hands coming down to fist her skirts and pull at them. A moan escaped her as he kissed along her jaw and down her neck, as he nipped at her skin and sent a shiver rolling through her. She tilted her head back as his right arm banded around her waist and he dropped his head to her breasts, kissing and laving the swells of them.

Distracting her.

She didn't realise what he was doing until her corset loosened.

Hella stilled as he peeled it away from her, revealing her to his gaze. He loosed another low growl, this one a rumbling sound that reverberated through her as he dragged her to him and lowered his head to her bare breasts. She moaned as he licked and sucked her nipples, as his fingers dug into her upper back and her bottom. She dug her own fingers into his shoulders, gripping them fiercely as he drove her out of her mind, as he ignited her body and torched her control. An urge ripped through her and she dropped her hands from his shoulders, grabbed her skirts and pulled at them, freeing her legs.

She hopped up and wrapped them around his hips, and reached between them, seized hold of his cock and guided him into her. He grunted as she pressed down on him, his entire body tensing as he clutched her to him, and a heartbeat passed in which he didn't move.

And then he snarled and claimed her mouth in a hard kiss as he gripped her hip and began thrusting, each plunge and withdrawal wilder than the last. Hella's breaths quickened in time with his as her body came alive, as he stretched and filled her, the size of him making it impossible for her not to feel every inch as he slid into her, not to mourn them when he pulled out only to fill her again. His hips pumped harder, faster as he kissed her deeper, and she worked her body against his, desperation mounting inside her as need coiled in her abdomen and flooded her mind, leaving only sensation, only the fierce and frantic reach for release.

She threw her head back and screamed when it hit her, rocked her with such force that she knew she would never be the same. Her body quivered, thighs shaking as he pumped her harder and faster, burying his face in her neck now.

He clamped down on her flesh with his blunt teeth and growled as he came.

Hella moaned with each hard pulse of his cock, each hot jet of seed, and clung to him.

Fearing she had been wrong.

There would be consequences to her actions here in this dream.

Because now more than ever, she needed to know if MacKinnon would make her feel like this in reality.

She needed him.

And resisting him was starting to feel impossible.

CHAPTER 16

MacKinnon came awake with a jolt that snapped him into an upright position.

Or it would have if something hadn't held his wrists in place above his head, stopping him from moving more than a few inches.

He cast a panicked look at his arms and the silver cuffs that were snug against his wrists, chains attaching them to the two posts on either side of the headboard. His breaths shortened, his mind darkening as memories pushed to the surface. He fought them, sharpening his mind and focusing it on something else to keep them at bay so they didn't overwhelm him.

He breathed slowly, evenly, and closed his eyes, willing himself to relax and not fight his bonds. If he did that, the memories would take hold of him. He focused on his breathing, on keeping it calm and measured, shutting out the sensation of cold metal around his wrists. It wasn't there.

Focusing on something else became easy as he caught Hella's scent in the air. Heather and rain, laced with something more than spice this time. Desire. He pulled down a deeper breath, letting the scent of her desire seep deep into his pores, until she was all he could smell.

His shaft swelled and hardened in response, his body aching for her, the need she stirred in him swift to roll back to a boil. Where was she? He focused his senses, seeking her, and found her downstairs. But she had been here a moment ago. Her scent was fresh. Heated. Had she been watching him again?

Desiring him?

Another potential answer came to him, one that had him restless with a need to see her and on the verge of calling out to her.

She had dreamed of him.

He had noticed how tired she had looked before she had cast that little spell on him, knocking him out. She must have fallen asleep and had dreamed of him. Gods, just the thought of her fantasising about him in such a manner had him as hard as stone in his jeans.

Kin remembered something else that had happened.

And grimaced.

He had been so fired up from the fight and the chase and his mate being in danger, that he hadn't been able to deny the needs she roused in him. He ached for her. Burned for her. Needed her more than the breath in his lungs or a beat in his chest.

A kiss had seemed like an innocent enough request.

But then he hadn't made it a request.

He had made it a demand.

He pulled another face and huffed.

He needed to stop letting desire and instinct steal control of him. Which was easier said than done. Even now, the scent of her had him itching for her, desperate to call out to her and make her come to him. When she came to see him, he would cajole her into lowering her guard, would be sweet and charming so she would kiss him and then he would seek more while she was swept up in the moment.

Seducing her.

He grunted.

It was what he had decided to do, wasn't it? He had come here to seduce her and bed her, and then take her to the witch and be done with her.

So why did he want to rage at just the thought of betraying her like that?

Why did he already hate himself for something he hadn't even done yet?

He blamed his instincts. The urge to claim her was strong, had his fangs descending against his will. He told himself that she was most likely right and she wasn't his fated one, but his instincts weren't listening. They saw her as his mate.

As the one female in this world he needed in his life.

The only female he would want from this point forwards.

Kin closed his eyes and exhaled, purging all the air from his lungs as he cleared his mind. She wasn't his true mate. His fated female was still out there somewhere. Everything he felt for Hella was a lie.

Her scent teased him.

Warmed him.

Calmed him.

Wasn't it?

His brow furrowed as he opened his eyes and stared at the ceiling. Maybe he could find out. She was a witch and had been able to reveal there was a curse on him. He could convince her to help him remove it. It was in her best interests too. She didn't want him any more than he wanted her.

A lie.

She wanted him as fiercely as he wanted her.

And what did that mean?

Witches didn't have fated mates, so she couldn't be caught up in the fever of finding her one as he was. Which meant she truly desired him.

And she didn't even know anything about him.

Most females in his life had wanted him only after discovering he was an alpha. His status had made him more appealing, and oftentimes he believed it was all that made him appealing. Plenty of females had seduced him purely because of his position, hoping to secure a place at his side and gaining power as his female.

Kin had despised them for it.

But now he had a beautiful witch looking at him with desire in her emerald eyes, with need only he could satisfy, and he wanted her.

Would give up everything he had fought for in life if he could only have her.

He leashed that desire and reined it in, because no good would come of allowing his instincts to colour his judgement and his actions. He needed to break this curse. Once it was broken, he would know if Hella was his mate and then he could work towards claiming the forever he wanted with her.

If she wanted him.

He groaned and it became a growl as he imagined how furious and hurt she would be if he handed her over to the witch. She wouldn't listen to him if he tried to explain his reasons. She would probably kill him.

His thoughts circled back around. But what if he didn't hand her over to the witch to break his curse? What if Hella could break it for him somehow?

Then he would stand a chance with her.

Wouldn't he?

He opened his mouth to call for Hella.

Snapped it closed when a knock sounded.

Kin strained, sharpening his senses and locking them onto the floor below him. At the edges of the room, things felt fuzzy. Because of a spell? Had Hella cast a barrier to protect them from the nymphs? He didn't like the way it dampened his senses, making it difficult to discern who was outside.

He also didn't like the fact that Hella was tense, unmoving, and her heartbeat was off the scale.

His fated female feared and he needed to reach her, needed to wrap her in his arms and hold her so she knew she was safe. He would never allow anyone to hurt her. He tugged at the chains holding him in place, growing agitated when they refused to give, keeping him from obeying his desire to take care of his mate.

Another knock.

This time, a muffled voice joined it. Masculine. That was all Kin could tell. The spell made it sound wobbly and disjointed. Or maybe that was the panic setting in again now he had remembered he was chained. He breathed deep and sagged against the mattress, calming his mind again and focusing on Hella.

She moved and he tracked her with his senses.

Big mistake.

A riot started in his skull as he felt her moving towards the door and his wolf side grew wild, the need to protect her seizing him in sharp talons that pierced his soul and spread vile poisonous words through his mind. His mate was in danger. He growled and wrestled with his bonds, his rage mounting as they refused to break and the wooden posts remained in one piece. There was another way out of these shackles. Black fur swept over his body and his bones ached, and agony tore through him like white-hot fire when his shift failed to happen. He clenched his teeth and bit back the cry that rolled up his throat as he tried to stop the shift instead. Impossible. Sweat beaded his brow and soaked his chest as he breathed harder and faster, battling the agony that churned inside him, threatening to steal consciousness from him. He couldn't pass out.

He cursed his shackles.

He cursed Hella.

The foolish witch had done something to them that prevented him from shifting.

He struggled to focus, desperately trying to calm himself now, choking back another bellow as his body again tried to morph into his wolf form. He had never failed a shift before, wasn't sure how many times his body would attempt it before it gave up, but each time lightning seared his bones and his muscles clamped down on them, and he grew weaker.

On the third attempt, he twisted left and vomited all over the bed, his entire body quaking as his muscles turned to liquid instead. He sagged with his head on his left arm, his right one bent at an awkward angle behind him, and fought for air. No more shifting. He didn't want to shift. He kept telling himself that, trying to convince his body to give up and his wolf to calm.

Hella needed him sharp and focused, not weak.

She was in danger.

His wolf calmed in an instant, that part of him perking up to focus on her.

The sense of calm flowed from his soul and through his tired body too, easing his tension away and clearing his mind. He closed his eyes and flopped onto his back again, seizing that calm and clinging to it as he locked his senses back on Hella.

It was difficult to keep hold of it when he heard her speaking to a male.

One who reeked of sex.

A fucking incubus if Kin had to guess.

"Oh, Fenix." Hella sounded far too soft and tender and he growled low when he sensed her move and her signature blended with this Fenix's one. She was touching the male. Rage poured through him, scouring his veins like hot acid, and it only grew worse when she continued. "You've lost so much weight. Hang on… I have just the thing. I've been saving it for you."

What had she been saving for this male in particular?

Kin tugged at his bonds again, unable to resist attempting to break free of them, and not because he didn't like being chained or his memories were in danger of overwhelming him this time. He wasn't sure his memories could steal his focus away from Hella, not while she was pressed close to another male.

He didn't relax even when he felt her move away from the incubus. Glass clinked. Something rattled.

"It's here somewhere." She made a small noise of frustration, one that Kin echoed as a growl as he shifted his focus to the incubus and couldn't stop himself from wondering something. Was he handsome? Had Hella slept with this male? She stole his focus again as she announced, "It survived!"

What survived? MacKinnon grunted and yanked on his bonds again, needing to know the answer to that question. Was this incubus just a client? Or something more? She sounded fond of him. In fact, he had never heard her sound so warm. Tender.

She cared about this male.

"I'll stand, thanks." The male's deep voice held a warm note too, a teasing one.

"I knew you'd be back, so I continued our work." More glass clinked and Kin smelled different odours. Was she making a spell? She sounded bright as she added, "I have a whole bunch of leads for you. Several locations of mages I think you should definitely check out. I'll dig them out of the bag when I'm done with this."

"That's the best news I've had in a long time."

Kin glared at his hips, staring through them to the floor below. This incubus cared about Hella too. Was working with her. Why were they looking for mages?

"Still seeing the nymph?" That question leaving Fenix's lips had Kin stilling and holding his breath, curious as to how much Hella would tell him.

This male knew about Hella and the nymph, a subject Kin wanted to know more about.

"No." There was a sharp edge to her tone and her movements grew jerky and irritated. "He got too clingy."

Her mood shifted, turning darker but laced with a dash of fear that had Kin idly tugging at his restraints, wanting to obey his need to go to her and hold her and tell her that she didn't need to worry about the nymph.

He would take care of the male for her.

"He the reason you're in some back-alley squat?" Fenix said and he was playing with fire.

Hella's mood took a very sharp turn now, her rage a palpable thing that had Kin restless and his wolf pacing and snapping his fangs.

The incubus needed to die.

No one upset Hella like this and lived to tell the tale.

"Change the subject," she snapped and the tense air filled with the sound of glass clinking. "I am so over him already."

"If he's giving you trouble, Hella, you're welcome to stay with me for a while."

The incubus was apparently determined to incur Kin's wrath.

He strained against his bonds now, gripping the chains in his hands and heaving forwards, determined to break them so he could make the male pay for trying to steal his fated female from him.

"Things would have to be dire for me to throw myself into the lion's den." She sighed, the soft sound enough to steal Kin's focus away from the incubus and back to her. "I think I have this under control."

Her uncertainty was a knife in his gut and he wanted to call out to her and tell her that *they* had it under control. He would protect her from the nymph. No one would take her from him. He protected what was his, and by the gods, Hella belonged to him.

"You know they'd behave themselves. You know you're welcome in my house." Fenix dug his grave a little deeper.

She heaved another long sigh. "I know, Fenix. It's just… things are complicated. Now drink up before it spoils."

What had she made the incubus? MacKinnon found he really wanted to know the answer to that question, enough that he was tempted to bang on the floor with his boot to get her attention. Witches didn't have strong senses. Hella probably didn't know he was awake and listening.

She proved that by saying, "Like it? It's pure, unfiltered passion. I distilled it myself."

Passion. Distilled by herself. Meaning either she had been in the presence of people making love while she used the spell or she had been the one bedding someone else and profiting off it.

Either way, Kin didn't like it.

He had thought her a lusty one before, but he was learning new things about her and he was beginning to wish the spell had kept him asleep for longer. He breathed hard, trying to quell his turbulent mind as it filled with images of Hella with other males, giggling and moaning, savouring their attention while she rejected his.

"So you broke up with the nymph." Fenix's voice lured Kin back to the room, had him purging the vision of Hella with other males from his mind and focusing back on her again.

Because he wanted to know more about her and the nymph.

"And he wants me back. Let's leave it at that." Her tone said to let it go.

Kin willed the incubus to not do it.

"So who's warming your bed these days then?" Fenix moved on his senses, most likely to the other side of the bench.

Hella remained where she was, barely moving. He heard glass clinking and smelled machine oil. What was she doing?

She kicked Kin's rage into the stratosphere as she said, "It's not a single who. I've decided to dabble in everything the town has to offer. I've even been mixing my flavours."

A red haze descended and Kin's fangs lengthened, his claws punching from his fingertips as the urge to shift came over him. He growled low and wrestled with his bonds, his mind filling with the faces of males he had seen around town. How many of them had Hella welcomed into her bed? How many times had she invited more than one at once?

He twisted his wrists in the cuffs, not caring that the metal cut into them. He would risk losing his hands if it meant he was free and could hunt down every male Hella had slept with and end them. She was his.

His beautiful, blue-haired lass.

Kin lost himself in a fantasy of cutting through the males in his wolf form, killing every single one in the fae town while Hella watched. Her green eyes were luminous and wide, filled not with horror but adoration when he returned to her. She slowly morphed into the Hella who had been in his dreams, the one who waited for him at the cottage door, beckoning him with a warm but sultry look.

The scent of his own blood joined the different smells in the air, overpowering them, and he kept fighting his bonds. Not because he wanted to go on a rampage.

But because he wanted to reach Hella.

He wanted to go to her and have her look at him as she had in his dream.

He wanted her to accept him.

To love him.

"Here. Leaf through these while I finish these pills for you." The sound of her sweet voice teased his ears, drawing him back to the world.

To her.

"The ones in England and America sound most promising," she said, and his mind latched onto the thought that she intended to travel with this male, was going to leave him and be with the incubus.

She was going to leave him chained and without her.

And gods, he probably deserved it, but he couldn't allow it. She was vulnerable without him. In danger. He needed to protect her. He needed to stay by her side until the threat to her was over and the nymph was no more.

And she needed to break this curse for him.

So, she couldn't go with someone else and help them.

He needed her.

He needed her, dammit.

He dropped his left foot over the side of the bed and banged the floor with his boot, making sure she knew he was awake and angry, and that she hadn't forgotten about him.

Something smacked the ceiling in response and Hella yelled, "Keep it down. I'm doing business here."

"I will no' keep it down, lass." Kin stomped harder in response. "You're my mate. I'll no' be letting this sex demon steal you from me."

And what was it with Hella and males who used sex as a weapon? First a nymph and now an incubus. He really didn't want to know the answer to that question, shoved it from his mind and kept banging his boot against the floor.

So hard the entire room shook.

She grumbled, "Don't ask."

"Ashamed of me now? I helped you. I saved your life. Why don't you tell your lover that?" he growled and tried to sit up, remembered he was chained and bellowed, "Let me out of these chains, you wee bitch."

"He was asking for it," Hella muttered and Kin growled louder.

Sure, he had sort of been asking for it with his demand that she kiss him, but still. She was asking for him to be furious with her by flirting with the incubus within earshot of him. He kicked the floor again and this time she ignored him, earning the boards a glare because other than smashing his foot through them, that was all he could do. He growled and tugged at his bonds again, cursing them and her as crimson spilled down his arms and soaked into the sleeves of his Henley.

He willed her not to leave him.

Darkness encroached at the corners of his vision as his breaths shortened, his mind seizing on the fact it was too late. He had driven her away from him with his actions and now she was going to leave him here.

Chained forever.

To die.

CHAPTER 17

Hella tried to tamp down the feeling squirming in the pit of her stomach as she approached the stairs, determined not to feel bad about what she had done, even when it was impossible. Guilt gnawed at her. It had her hesitating when she placed her foot on the first wooden step and listened to MacKinnon growling. She wasn't sure she was strong enough to brazenly walk upstairs as planned and lay down the law. The second she saw him chained to that bed, she was going to feel more wretched, just as she had when she had gone to see him after waking from her delicious dream.

This wasn't like her.

She wasn't the kind to hurt others like this, punishing them so cruelly for something so slight. He had only wanted a kiss. It wasn't as if he had demanded she bare her nape for him to sink a claiming bite into it.

It wasn't as if she hadn't wanted to kiss him too.

She was feeling bold enough to admit that the chase had been thrilling and had fired her up too.

Only fear had kicked in when he had demanded a kiss.

She had panicked.

The bed rattled, slamming violently against the wall, and she hurried up the steps, her heart in her throat as MacKinnon grunted, sounding pained.

She drew to an abrupt halt when he came into view and her pulse rocketed, panic seizing the helm to steer her towards him. She raced across the room to the side of the bed and froze as he turned murderous silver eyes on her, tying her tongue in a knot so she stood there like an idiot, unsure what to do.

MacKinnon lurched forwards again, spilling more blood down his arms and onto the ancient bedclothes.

She couldn't bear it.

"Stop struggling!" She lunged for his left arm and reared back when he snapped fangs at her.

"I'll stop struggling when you release me, witch," he snarled and twisted his clenched fists, his muscles flexing beneath his dark Henley as he glared at her.

"You didn't give me much choice," she barked back at him, some stubborn part of her refusing to take all the blame for what she had done.

He snorted.

She had never met a man who could say so much with only a noise. That snort was pure disbelief, and rightly so considering she had had a choice. She could have just knocked him out with the spell and left.

Instead, she had plunged him back into his worst nightmare.

Although he seemed to be handling it a lot better than the last time.

Because he was angry?

Golden fire blazed in the centre of his irises, flaring around his narrowed pupils. Those striking eyes held an accusation, one she didn't want to see so she looked at her feet, which was a mistake because his left leg still dangled over the edge of the bed and she couldn't help but notice how small her feet were compared with his.

Or how close they were to touching.

As if he knew her secret desire, he shifted his foot so the sides of their boots touched, and she pulled down a steadying breath as the muted contact only made her ache even more to be skin on skin with him. Her gaze drifted to his hand. Another mistake.

She looked away when she saw all the blood on his hand and the cuts around his wrist, shame eating her from the inside.

"Have ye been off snogging that incubus? And what was all that talk about sex?" he growled and her eyes darted to his face and collided with his just as they turned pure gold. "You're no' so prim and proper it seems."

Hella planted her hands against her hips and glared at him, because who was he to question her life choices? She decided what she did with her life. Not anyone else. Definitely not him. She didn't need his judgement. She certainly didn't care what he thought about her.

She ignored the sting in her chest and tipped her chin up, stoking her anger so he would see it in her eyes as well as sense it. "You're right. I'm not. But I choose who I kiss and who comes to my bed. I don't need men making decisions for me."

He snarled, "I'm no' just any man. I'm your fated male. You're my mate."

Hella took a sharp step towards him as her anger got the better of her, the handful of words he had tossed at her like fuel on the fire in her blood, making her want to explode.

"You always say *mate* like it means slave. Yours to do with as you please," she bit out, her heart racing so fast she felt sick and her fingers tingling with magic as it came to the fore, apparently feeling she needed protection. "In your world—in your eyes—do I only exist to please you?"

Some small part of her quietly begged him to say the right thing, to change her mind about him and show her that he wasn't like every other shifter out there, thinking he owned her because she was apparently his fated one. Even if she was, that didn't give him a right to her, that didn't automatically make her his, and it certainly didn't make her belong to him like a possession.

He went terribly quiet, watching her with wary eyes. The fact he had to pause to figure out what she wanted to hear was infuriating and hurt like a bitch. Deep in her heart, she knew it was hopeless. MacKinnon might be handsome and she might be attracted to him, but he was like every other shifter out there. He viewed her as a possession purely because his instincts said she was his destined mate.

And that was something she would never tolerate.

Not even for a man she was beginning to like.

Might have even come to love in time.

"I won't release you." She stepped back and held her nerve when he growled at her, flashing his fangs, a look of disbelief and fear crossing his face. "You're another threat to me."

He lunged towards her, grunted when his chains tightened and sagged back onto the bed.

His deep voice rumbled through her as he snapped, "I'm no' a threat to you."

She wished she could believe that.

"You are," she countered and shook her head. "You brought nymphs to my door, forced me to move again, and you keep trying to kiss me."

His expression soured and he muttered, "No' like you didn't like it when we kissed."

She couldn't deny that.

His golden eyes brightened again as they narrowed on her, a calculating edge to them. "I did save your life."

"When?" She shot for coy, even went as far as thoughtfully pressing her index finger to her mouth and turning a puzzled look at the ceiling.

Which made him growl in the most deliciously frustrated way.

"The river," he snarled.

He had a point.

She shrugged anyway. "I might have made it without your help."

MacKinnon sat up as best he could again, levelling a dark look on her that made her feel he wanted to put her over his knee for being so sassy with him, but there was a glimmer of something in his eyes, there among the irritation and anger. Did he like her teasing him?

"You were chained." He smoothed the hard edge from his tone, removing the bite from it, and looked her over, from her face to her hands. His voice softened further, a teasing note to it now. "Couldn't use your wee hands to swim. You would've drowned without me, lass."

She rolled her eyes.

Enjoying herself and the way they were falling into an easy kind of banter that made her forget her anger and what a dick he could be at times.

He reminded her.

"What made you jump from a tower anyway? Was a reckless move. You could have drowned."

"What made me jump from a tower?" She glared at him, making sure he saw how angry she was again as she thought about that day, as she replayed making the hardest and most terrifying decision of her life. "An overbearing bastard thinking he could do as he pleased with me. The alternative to jumping was being the whore queen to a nymph king, and I would sooner die!"

MacKinnon went quiet again as he stared at her, his eyes bright gold and his mouth set in a hard line. Piercing. Calculating. Rage simmering. She had hit a nerve.

His whole torso flexed as he clenched his fists.

"Explain yourself," he growled as his expression darkened, his eyebrows knitting hard to narrow his eyes as he flashed fangs with each word he pushed from his lips. "The nymphs who are after you—"

"Are sent by their king. My ex. He got clingy, and I got bored of kissing his arse and petting his ego, so I kicked him to the curb. I didn't know he was a king." Although she should have spotted the warning signs, but she had been too swept up in good sex.

MacKinnon bit out, "Kings always think they can take what they want. Well, he cannae have you. You're mine."

Hella's jaw dropped.

She snapped her mouth closed and backed off another step, earning herself a furious look from the wolf. "Spoken like a true king."

He frowned at her.

Her heart raced, adrenaline surging as she pushed the question to the tip of her tongue, needing to know the answer to it even as she feared it. Her instincts about him couldn't be wrong. She needed to know they were right. She needed to know how much trouble she was in. Shifter males were notoriously possessive, but nothing compared with the tales she had heard about their pack leaders.

"You're an alpha, aren't you?"

The air seemed to seep from the room as he sat there in silence, confirming her suspicion.

Hella backed off another step. "I figured as much. You have all the hallmarks of an alpha. Demanding. Ordering people around. Thinking you have a right to control anyone and anything. To *own* anyone."

He reared back against the pillow, as if she had physically struck him with that last one, and glared at her. "I'm no' like that, lass. I'd never own anyone."

She had struck another nerve.

Her gaze dropped to his chest. A chest that bore so many scars.

Something clicked into place and weighed her heart down, instantly vanquishing her anger and destroying every shred of hostility she felt towards him, replacing them with another emotion.

Pity.

She whispered, "Because someone owned you once."

MacKinnon exploded in a rage so fierce the bed didn't stand a chance even with her spell reinforcing it. The two posts cracked under the force of his anger as he moved to his knees and surged towards her, his arms at his sides. His hands flew forwards as the wooden beams broke, the other ends of his shackles swinging wildly in front of him, and she tensed as he lunged to his feet.

Fearing he would come at her and do something they would both regret.

But rather than seizing hold of her, he pushed her aside and barrelled down the stairs, and she flinched as she heard the door break.

As she felt him pass beyond the sphere of her spell.

Hella roused herself and hurried down the stairs and out into the street, an apology on the tip of her tongue.

Only MacKinnon was gone.

She sank to her knees on the cobbles, her heart heavier than ever as she thought about what she had said and how she had sounded. She pressed her hands to her chest, guilt whirling through her as she considered how she would have felt if their positions had been reversed and she had been owned by someone, how ashamed she would have been, and how much it would have hurt her to have someone else point it out in the way she had.

She stared into the distance.

Feeling empty, as if someone had just torn something out of her.

Sure she would never see him again.

And hoping that she would.

CHAPTER 18

MacKinnon was done with witches.

He leaned forwards on his seat, rested his chin on his upturned palm and watched the fire hungrily devouring the logs Gregor and the others had stacked in the centre of the clearing. He rested his left forearm on his knee and let his whisky dangle from his fingertips, lost in the dance of the flames.

Feeling as if they were devouring him too.

How many weeks had it been since he had last seen Hella? The answer to that was too many and every day was a battle against himself, against his need to see her. He cast his gaze down at his drink and stared at it, memories of her dancing through his mind to torment him. His eyes shifted to his wrist, to the faint scars that encircled it beyond the sleeve of his black Henley, and he sighed.

A few days after he had returned home, the shackles he had been trying to remove through a variety of means had simply fallen off.

It had startled him and he had stilled in the clearing, halfway between his cottage and the tool shed where Gregor had been waiting for him with the method of their next attempt to remove the restraints—a circular saw.

Kin had found himself staring at the silver cuffs where they had rested on the grass.

And a heavy feeling had grown in the pit of his stomach.

A reason they had fallen off his wrists.

Hella was done with him.

She no longer viewed him as a threat to her, no longer believed he would return to her, and had moved on with her life.

The fallen shackles at his feet had felt like a symbol of their bond, one she had set him free from, severing it and leaving him adrift.

Without her.

It had felt as if someone had taken hold of something inside him and broken it.

Kin had howled so long and so loud that everyone had come out to see what was happening, and Gregor and his little mate had ushered everyone back inside when Kin had slumped forwards and pitifully grabbed the shackles and clutched them to his chest.

A moment of weakness. That was all it had been. In that instant, it had felt as if a bond they had shared had been shattered and his only tie to Hella had been ripped from him, and his wolf had responded badly.

Was still responding badly.

He stared at the whisky, swirling it around, not interested in drinking it. He wasn't interested in anything anymore. He had forgotten how to laugh. Couldn't remember the last time he had smiled. Vaguely recalled saying something to Gregor a few days ago, but was sure he hadn't spoken a word since then.

His wolf kept him quiet, lost in thoughts of Hella even when they tormented him. Was she out there, enjoying her life? With another male? Did she ever think of him? Did she feel this same choking emptiness that filled him? Or was she filled with joy because she was free of him?

Kin dropped his head to his palm and covered his eyes as despair engulfed him and had his wolf side howling, calling for his mate. Did she miss him as badly as he missed her?

The voices that had been filling the silence of the glen gradually quietened and he grew aware of everyone looking at him. He pulled down a breath and reminded himself that tonight was a celebration. Ewan was coming of age and it was a time for happiness, not misery. The young wolf had his whole life ahead of him, had reached maturity at a tender ninety-seven, ten years before Kin himself had become an adult. As his alpha, he should be the one making all the noise, turning this into the celebration it should be and teasing the wolf about his newfound desires, maybe even offering to take him to the fae town for a night to see if he could find a female to bed.

But instead, all he could do was wallow and think of Hella.

What had she done to him?

Gregor grunted as he sat down beside him, close enough that his arm brushed against Kin's, and said, "Play the fiddle, love."

The joyful sound of it filled the tense silence and Kin felt everyone's gaze leaving him. Except for Gregor's. The big blond male slapped a hand down on Kin's back, jerking him forwards.

"You need to eat something."

"What's the point?" Kin grumbled, because he had no appetite for anything now. The meat on the grill would have tempted him once, and he would have been there with Donald, tending to it and salivating while waiting for it to cook, sharing a laugh and a whisky. He huffed and stared at his untouched drink. "I'm no' hungry."

"Aye, you are hungry, just no' for meat." Gregor's voice gained an amused note that sounded forced and didn't cover the worry Kin could hear in his words. "Or maybe it is meat ye be hungry for, but the tender flesh of a certain witch."

"She's no' meat," he growled and rolled his shoulder to shirk Gregor's touch.

He angled his head towards the male and glared into his blue eyes. His anger deflated when he saw the concern shining in them, and the despair, and he looked away from his second in command as his stomach churned. Gregor had been working hard to hold him together over the weeks, had gone several times to the fae town when that desperation to take care of his alpha had become too strong, and Kin knew he had tried to find the one who had cursed him.

The last time he had tried and failed, he had returned and asked Kin to tell him where Hella lived.

Kin had turned on him and driven him out of his home, and had put him in his place, much to the horror of his pack.

It was the first time he had noticed he was no longer the same male.

He was darker without Hella, quick to anger and lash out at anyone, even those who only meant to help him. He was lost. His wolf side constantly howled for his mate, clawed at his insides and left him feeling hollow and raw, a shadow of his former self. He couldn't think. Couldn't sleep. He was wasting away.

Just as the redhead had told him he would.

Only he wasn't sure whether it was because of the curse.

Or because he had realised something over the few days between leaving Hella and his shackles falling off.

He had feelings for her.

Strong feelings.

The thing that had broken when the restraints had dropped off his wrists was somewhere in the region of his chest.

And it hurt. It burned. It howled for her as fiercely as his wolf did. It ached for her to forgive him.

To come to him.

"Impossible," he muttered, ignoring the look Gregor gave him, the one that his friend often wore these days.

It questioned his sanity.

Kin wasn't sure he was sane anymore. He hadn't been sane from the moment he had set eyes on Hella, and the madness was only spreading. It wouldn't stop until he saw her again, but what good would come of that?

She didn't want him.

She truly believed he wanted to own her.

Own.

He buried his head in his hand again as he saw a flash of how she had looked at him when she had hit a very painful nail on its head and driven it right into his chest. Pity. She had pitied him because he had been owned once.

She saw it as a weakness, a point in his life that had defined him, when she was wrong.

It had been his beginning.

A fiery birth that had forged him into a strong wolf.

One able to do whatever was necessary for the sake of his pack.

"You need to return to this witch in Geneva and take her to the other one by force."

Except for that.

Kin grimaced at Gregor's words, just the thought that he had meant to do that to Hella once making him feel sick to his stomach.

He sensed everyone's eyes on him again, felt their anticipation and sighed. He couldn't take Hella to the other witch by force, but he could do something to set his pack's minds at ease.

He sat up and looked at each of them in turn, pulled down a breath and settled his gaze on Gregor's.

"I'll speak with the redhead who cursed me. I'll make her lift the curse." He placed his hand on his second in command's shoulder, gripping it tightly through his thick navy shirt.

Gregor nodded and relaxed, his shoulders sagging beneath Kin's hand.

The other dozen wolves who watched him followed suit, the tension leaving the air as they went back to the celebration. It was louder than before, far more jovial as Gregor's little mate, Siobhan, played the fiddle and Ewan and Donald danced with Magda and Shona.

Gregor palmed his shoulder and then stood. Kin looked up at him, catching his wide smile as he looked at his mate and she silently beckoned him with a glance in his direction. He watched the male drifting towards her. There was love in her eyes as she watched his approach, a warmth that grew as the distance between them closed and she smiled coyly at him.

Kin wanted that kind of love.

And for a moment, he had thought he had found it.

And then he had ruined it.

Gregor glanced back at him, frowned and stilled, and pivoted towards him. Kin frowned right back at him as the blond strode towards him instead of his mate, and tilted his head back when Gregor reached him. He arched an eyebrow when the male gripped his nape.

"It's no' my place, but... I know ye be going to see your wee fated one. The redhead won't give you what you want... so ye be needing the advice my pa gave me. The key to winning a mate." Gregor brought his head down, moving his mouth close to Kin's ear, and Kin listened intently because his friend was right. He could petition the redhead until he was blue in the face, but she wouldn't care. The only one who could help him now was Hella. Gregor palmed his nape and sighed. "When ye see the lass, tell your wolf how much ye need her. Be honest with ye'self, and your wolf will listen... be firm with the unruly bastard... and then stand by her, not on her."

Kin frowned as Gregor straightened and released him, stared at his back as he crossed the clearing to his mate and swept her into his arms, making her laugh as her bow slid sharply across the strings of her fiddle. Gregor laughed with her, his whole face lighting up, and Kin ached to hold Hella like that, to laugh with her and have her laugh in return, to see her smiling in the way Siobhan was as she gazed up at her mate.

He mulled over Gregor's advice, a feeling building inside him.

It couldn't be that simple.

But he had nothing left to lose.

He would try to do as his friend had advised and if his wolf instincts wouldn't be cowed, he would give Hella space until he had tamed them. He had one last shot at this. He could feel it in his soul. His time was nearly up. Death was coming for him.

He chuckled mirthlessly as he imagined how Hella would react to him showing up on her doorstep.

Death was probably coming for him either way.

But he would sooner die by her hand than by some damned curse.

Either he would be victorious or it would all be over and he would go to the grave in the way he had always expected—as an unmated male.

MacKinnon pushed to his feet.

Prepared for one last fight.

CHAPTER 19

MacKinnon's head spun as if he had downed a bottle or two of whisky as he stumbled his way through the streets of the Geneva fae town, drawing gazes again. He paid them no heed, focused instead on remaining on his feet and finding Hella. He had left for the fae town in Fort William as soon as possible, heading to the portal there, but his condition had worsened every second of the journey, so much so that Gregor hadn't wanted to let him go alone.

Kin had refused his offer to come with him, because he damned well didn't need an escort. He was fine. He swayed sideways, hit a wall and grazed his cheek as he slid along it, his feet still carrying him forwards. He *would* be fine.

"Jus'need to find Hella," he muttered to himself and blinked to clear his vision. He sniffed, desperately trying to catch her scent. "Have to be close now."

He felt eyes on him and wobbled away from the wall to glare at their owner, a little witch with violet and black hair. She was quick to hurry away from him, heading down the cobbled road at speed.

He glanced over his shoulder at her, lost his balance and landed on the cobbles with a grunt. Odd that a witch was in this district. Had she come to see Hella?

Hope surged, the fear that she would have moved falling away as he pushed back onto his feet, straightened and held his arms out at his side to steady himself before risking moving forwards.

"Hella," he murmured, scenting the air for her.

Aching for her.

His wolf was restless, so he told it the same damned thing he had been telling it from the moment he had reached the fae town in Fort William. They were doing things his way. Logic and not instinct was in control this time. He needed Hella, more than air, more than anything. He needed her. It didn't have the effect Gregor had promised. His wolf wasn't cowed by his words.

Why?

He spotted the familiar house ahead of him and finally caught her scent, and his wolf went haywire, had him close to shifting and running there. He clenched his fists and reined in the desire to use his wolf form. Logic, not instinct. He needed to be careful. He needed to approach her with caution. There was no predicting how the witch would react to his presence.

Actually, there was.

She was probably going to shackle him again.

Possibly kill him herself.

MacKinnon breathed through the momentary spike in panic. He could do this. He squeezed his eyes shut and fought a wave of dizziness, wobbling on the spot. He wasn't sure he had the strength to do this, but gods, he needed to try. If he messed up with her now, there was no leaving her alone for a while to cool off and then trying again.

This was it.

Last chance.

His wolf side battered his soul, wild with a need to reach Hella and stake a claim on her.

He *needed* her.

It had no effect.

He huffed and trudged forwards, sure now that Gregor had been talking shit. There was no taming his instincts so he could do this right, so he could be gentle and charming, not dominant and rough.

He chuckled and it grew into hysterics that had half the street coming out to stare at him as he drifted towards Hella's home. His laughter ended abruptly and he glared at all of them, flashing his fangs as a hunger to rip them all to shreds rolled through him. Several of them were quick to make an exit. A few lingered, their gazes curious.

Understandable.

He glanced at himself in a window he passed, barely recognising the savage, wild-eyed gaunt male reflected back at him.

He wasn't going to be sweeping Hella off her feet with his good looks anymore, that was for sure.

Kin reached her door and banged on it, hoping she was on the other side as his body grew weaker still and he had to brace his left hand against the wall to keep himself upright.

The wooden door opened.

"MacKinnon!" Her soft voice was his undoing.

Roused a fire in him that warmed him right to his bones as she spoke his name with surprise and a hint of relief, and his eyes slipped shut as he sank into the feeling that blazed through him. Home. He was home.

He opened his eyes and looked at his beautiful, blue-haired bonnie witch, right into her bewitching green eyes that shone with a warmth he didn't deserve and in that moment he knew.

He *needed* her, not because fate had made her for him, but because he felt right down to his soul that fate had made him for her.

That there was one woman in this world he had been born to love, and he was looking right at her.

And gods help him, but he had fallen for her.

The other half of his broken, blackened soul.

The light to his darkness.

The beauty to his beast.

And just like that his wolf calmed, lowering its head in pure reverence of the female before him.

Hella stepped towards him, her right hand coming up.

Kin caught it and pulled her to him, and she angled her head back, her gaze instantly dropping to his mouth, an invitation he couldn't turn down. He swooped on her lips, claiming them in a soft kiss this time, one that added to that warmth she roused in him and had his head fogging as his heart healed. Her lips were like nectar of the gods as she opened to him and he drank deep, couldn't get enough of her as strength poured back into his tired body. Her little hands fisted his shirt as she kissed him back, her soft curves inflaming him as she pressed them against the length of his body, bringing them into sweet but tormenting contact. He needed more than this. He needed her bare skin against his.

He wanted to growl when she pressed her hands to his chest and stole her lips away from his, but she stopped him with one word.

"MacKinnon," she whispered, a balm to his soul, and he wanted to tell her to say it again, to keep saying his name in that breathless way and never stop, because he couldn't get enough of it. She swallowed hard and her brow furrowed as she gazed up at him, the concern in her green gaze unravelling his strength. Never had he thought it possible for her to look at him like that—as if she felt something for him. Something as deep and powerful as he felt for her. Her head shook slightly as she took him in. "I haven't seen you in weeks and… mother earth… what happened to you?"

"The curse," he snapped as unwanted anger surged to the surface and he rubbed his sore eyes, fighting the urge to lash out at her because she was responsible for his condition. No. She wasn't. The redheaded witch was. Hella was just another victim of this curse, and he was sure she could break it, or at the very least she could help him grow strong enough to break it himself. He lowered his hand and reached for her. "Another kiss, lass."

She stepped back, evading him.

He growled, furious that she was still fighting the attraction he knew she felt towards him, the need that he had tasted in that kiss and felt right the way to his bones. He couldn't mistake the scent of desire on her or how she had responded to him, and he certainly couldn't miss the hunger that still shone in her eyes as she gazed at him.

His wee witch was pleased to see him.

She had missed him.

He reached for her again, determined to have her back in his arms, to steal a little more strength from her lips.

"I'll help you," she said and his heart soared.

And then plummeted when she turned away and went to the books spread across the thick wooden bench table and began leafing through them and he realised she wasn't talking about bedding him.

"There has to be a way to lift the curse," she muttered as she set one book aside and started on another. "I was looking into curses in general while you were gone, but they're so specific and I had no one to ask about the details of your one in particular."

"Really?" he bit out, his mood taking a dangerous turn as he stepped into the room and slammed the door behind him. "Couldn't think of anyone at all? No' like… say… *me*… oh… or maybe the *hackit bint* who cursed me to get back at you? Why didn't you try asking her?"

Her shoulders tensed but she said nothing, didn't even do him the courtesy of looking at him. He resisted the urge to palm the steel-hard bulge in his black jeans and stomped towards her, determined to have her look at him because he wanted to see in her eyes that she felt guilty about not coming to him.

He needed to know she had missed him as badly as he had missed her.

She glanced at him when he drew level with her, a quick one that barely had her eyes landing on his chest before she returned them to her book and began leafing through it with renewed vigour as she muttered, "There's no need to shout."

MacKinnon huffed. There was every need to shout. He was angry, hurt that she had been trying to work on his curse but hadn't even considered coming to see him.

And gods... had he stayed away all that time because he had wanted her to come to him?

He pressed his left palm to the top of the table as he considered that, as he realised that it was the truth. All those weeks, all that suffering, and all because some foolish, pathetic part of him had wanted her to come to him for once. He cursed his heart, aware it was responsible for his ridiculous actions.

"Tell me again how you came to be cursed." Her voice was small, weak, and he sensed her nerves as she kept her eyes on her books, hiding in them.

It wasn't fear that made her act in such a way. No. His wee witch responded to fear in a very different way, would have put him in his place rather than withdrawing into herself. Or perhaps it was fear, but not of him. She feared what she might do if she looked at him.

Because she wanted him.

She could pretend all she wanted that she didn't, but he could feel it in her, smell it on her. She desired him, was battling her attraction to him right that second, as her eyes kept trying to shift to him and she diligently kept her profile to him. He edged closer to her and her breath hitched, her slender shoulders tensing for a split-second to give away the effect he had on her.

She liked him close. She liked it as much as he did.

"Not going to tell me?" she whispered, her voice faint, and she swallowed hard. Almost looked at him.

He stepped back and rubbed his tired eyes as he tried to focus on remembering the details of what had happened when the witch had cursed him. When the fog in his head only thickened in response, he began pacing. Every step was a chore but he couldn't keep still, even when he felt ready to drop. Her scent had him wired, aching for her, and there was no way he was going to be able to think straight when she was in the room with him and he could still taste her on his lips.

Could see the blush on her cheeks that told him she had liked that kiss.

"Another kiss, lass," he husked and stepped towards her, keeping his voice gentle and his movements predictable, calm, so he didn't scare her off. "I felt better when you kissed me."

She frowned at him. "You sound like an incubus now... feeding off pleasure."

Something crossed her eyes, something she wouldn't say, and he didn't like that she had compared him to that nymph king in her mind.

"I'm no nymph. I'm no incubus," he barked and swept his hand out, sending one of the books flying and ripping a gasp from her. She hurried around the bench table to retrieve it and he didn't miss how she chose to go the long way around, avoiding coming closer to him. He growled as his fangs punched long from his gums and dug his claws into the wooden slab that separated them as he turned on her. "This wasn't my choice. This is your fault. You did something to piss off that witch and I'm paying for it."

She flinched and tucked the book to her chest, averted her eyes and kept them away from him. Her shoulders sagged beneath her very plain black dress, the kind he had never imagined seeing on her. It wasn't corseted, or stylish, or short. No silk or ribbons or that sheer stuff the first dress he had seen her in had on it. It was one drab piece of cotton that reached all the way to her ankles and covered her arms too, and it struck him that it was a disguise—a desperate attempt to remain hidden from the nymph.

And yet she hadn't changed the colour of her hair.

Because she hadn't found the courage to actually leave this place.

He looked around at the small lodgings, at the brown paper bags in the corner that had little white tickets stapled to them and the black sack next to them, and the paper plates and plastic cutlery on the ancient woodworm-eaten sideboard. He recalled the witch he had seen in the street and the pieces fell into place. Hella hadn't left this place since he had left her. Witches had been bringing her food and things she needed. She had spent weeks in these cramped conditions, staring at the same four walls, while he had been running through glens and swimming in lochs and doing his best to forget her.

"Why didn't you come to me, lass?" He carefully edged towards her, his tone softer than he had ever heard it as he held her gaze and saw in her eyes that things had been hard for her here, that he wasn't the only person who had been suffering. "I can protect you. You know that."

The softness that had been in her eyes was gone in an instant as they narrowed on him. "For what price? A set of fangs in my neck and a mating mark? The invisible shackle of a bond?"

He reared back and glared at her, but no denial bubbled up from his heart and it pissed him off. He tried to tell himself that he wouldn't have made such a demand, he wouldn't have set such a high price for his protection, but it was a lie. If she had come to him before he had reached his lowest point and Gregor had advised him on how to win a mate, he would have tried to force a bond on her. He would have made the same mistake many wolves did with their fated ones.

"Hella," he whispered and held his hand out to her, trying to be soft and show her that she was wrong and he had changed. "I'm not the same as I was. Come with me now. Let me protect you."

She shook her head. "I can protect myself."

He cast a pointed look at her home. "Is that why you're still hiding from the nymphs? I dinnae see you parading around town as you were when I met you. You're a shadow of the female I saw that day."

She glared at him, her lips settling in a mulish line, and slammed the book down on the table. "And you're a shadow of the male who came to my aid. How are you meant to protect me when you're so weak?"

He stepped back, bracing his left foot behind him as she delivered that blow to his pride. Weak? He was an alpha. He wasn't weak.

His head turned, the entire room spinning with it. Fine, maybe he was a little weak right now, but there was a way to fix that. He palmed his forehead, easing the pain there, and tried to think of a way to convince Hella to do what he needed her to do—surrender to her attraction to him.

She must have taken his silence for anger or hurt, because she whispered, "I'm sorry. I've been trying to find a way to help you."

"You know how to help me," he growled and her cheeks flushed, her pupils dilating and telling him she was well aware of the one way she could save him. He rounded the table, surprise rolling through him when she didn't move away this time. She didn't look at him either. She kept her head bent, her eyes on her hands where they rested on top of the tome she had slammed into the table. He lifted his left hand and reached for her, gently laying his fingers on the other side of her jaw. "I need you, Hella."

She angled her head away from him.

He let his hand drop from her face and huffed. "You'll let every male in this town between your thighs, but no' me. You dinnae need a king to be a whore queen."

She flew at him, striking him hard on his right cheek, the sharp slap making his ear ring.

"I deserved that." Kin sighed and closed his eyes, all the fight leaving him and despair sweeping into his soul to replace it. "This… this isn't like me. I'm tired, Hella. Afraid. The gods only know how many hours I have left."

He remembered what Gregor had told him. He couldn't stand on her. Meaning, he couldn't order her around and trample her, forcing her to do what he wanted. He needed to stand beside her instead, supporting her and taking care of her without caging her. He wanted to do that, but time was against him. If he had all the time in the world, he would use it to court her properly, to take her on dates and take things slow, and would probably stumble every damned step of the way, but he would do it.

If he had time.

Her hand dropped to his chest and he looked at her, into eyes that glittered with a look he couldn't name but one that gave him hope. He had never felt as exposed as he did in that moment, as if his words had stripped him bare and revealed him to her. An alpha shouldn't fear anything, but he did.

He was soul-deep afraid of dying without ever knowing if this beautiful witch was his fated one.

The one he had been waiting for all his life.

His brow furrowed as he gazed down at her, feeling as if he was standing on a dangerous precipice as he waited to see what she would do. Spurn him again or accept him? One meant death and the other salvation.

Her hesitation cut at him, cleaving a hole in his heart, and all the hope he had mustered bled from him as he realised this was a fight he couldn't win. Resignation swept through him, acceptance on its heels, and he nodded slightly, silently letting her know that he understood when he didn't.

He stepped back from her and it was the hardest thing he had ever done.

Because he was letting her go.

He tried to smile at how much he had changed, how dancing with death had moulded him into a better male and opened his eyes, and how it was all for nothing. He still wasn't going to get what he wanted, and part of him was fine with that now.

Because he would sooner die than force her to do something she didn't want.

"I'm sorry," he whispered, his throat tight, and his eyes misted. "For everything."

He blew out his breath and turned away.

Hella's little hand fisted his shirt, gripping it so tightly he couldn't move another inch.

"MacKinnon," she murmured.

He looked at her, sure she only wanted to bid him goodbye.

She pulled him down, cupped his nape with her other hand, and kissed him.

CHAPTER 20

Hella was sure this was a mistake, but if it was, she would own it, because she was damned if she was going to let MacKinnon walk out of the door and to his doom. She liked him. Fine, she more than liked him. And yes, it might have taken the sight of him so worn down and close to the edge, and the thought of never seeing him again to open her eyes, but they were open now.

Better late than never.

He angled his head and kissed her back, seizing control of it as he pressed closer to her, distracting her with how good the heat of his body felt against hers. She clutched his shirt in both hands, clinging to his shoulders as she kissed him, as their tongues duelled and she fought him for dominance. Something he apparently liked because he grabbed her waist and dragged her against him, a low groan escaping his lips as they battled hers.

On a toe-curling growl, he banded his arms around her and lifted her, twisting with her at the same time. Her backside hit the tabletop and his hands dropped to her skirts, and she gasped as the sound of material ripping filled the thick silence. Cool air washed across her overheating skin from her ankle to her hip and she shoved her hands against his chest, pushing him back and breaking the kiss.

"This is my one boring dress." Her eyes widened when she saw it wasn't one tear in the black cotton either.

It was in tatters, shredded by his claws.

He flicked her an apologetic look, but hunger soon overwhelmed it, darkening his eyes again, and it was like looking at a different person. He breathed harder as his irises turned golden, his handsome features sharpening as he raked a look over her and flexed his claws, the wicked heat in his gaze telling her he was considering ripping the rest of the dress off her to get to what he wanted.

What he needed.

"MacKinnon," she whispered, hoping the sound of his name calmed him as it had before.

This time, he growled and bared his fangs and grabbed her hips, pressing the tips of his claws into her flesh in a way that was far too possessive. He swooped on her mouth, seizing it in a kiss that was rough and demanding as he pressed her backwards.

Hella turned her head away from him and he snapped fangs close to her cheek.

Admonishing her.

"MacKinnon," she snapped back at him and grabbed his wrists, funnelling a little spell into him through them.

He jerked backwards, swift to release her as he got a taste of lightning in his veins. He cast her a furious look and came to tower over her, his back rod-straight and his eyes darker than she had ever seen them. He looked awfully as if he was considering how to punish her for denying him.

He was right. This wasn't like him. This was the curse. It was driving him to this, making him so desperate to survive and to regain his strength that he would do anything, and deep in her heart she knew he would hate himself if he let it control him and he ended up hurting her.

"Hold still." She lifted her hands and when he went to grab them, she clucked her tongue. "Do not move or this spell will go haywire and you'll probably die."

An exaggeration, but it certainly worked. He went deathly still, barely breathing.

Apparently, his survival instincts ran deep, were powerful enough that he could curb his desires. She made a mental note of that and considered what she was going to do.

Hella hesitated. The best way to get a spell into someone was skin contact, but asking him to remove his top would probably come across as a signal she wanted him to get all frisky again. Rather than risking that, she eased her hands under his Henley. His stomach flexed when she made contact, and mother earth, he had lost muscle. He wasn't scrawny, not by a long shot, but he was noticeably less muscular than before.

His low growl heated her blood.

She resisted looking up at him, but couldn't resist gently stroking her palms over his torso as she edged them upwards towards his chest. Or looking at the toned strip of stomach she revealed as his top caught on her forearms and lifted. She wanted to let her fingers follow that dark treasure trail that led downwards to the waist of his jeans as she swirled her tongue around the sensual dip of his navel.

This time, his growl was deeper and she shook herself out of her reverie as she realised it was because he could feel her rising desire and wanted to act on it. He had made it clear countless times that he could sense her need and felt driven to satisfy her, and she was probably throwing off strong signals that were making him even crazier.

Soon. He could take all he wanted from her and give her everything she needed soon. She just needed a moment to check something.

"Mind on business, Hella," she murmured to herself, denying the urge to keep soaking up the delicious sight of his body.

Her palms met his chest and she spaced them a few inches apart on either side of his racing heart, closed her eyes and used a spell to form a connection between them, one that would allow her to do a little probing.

Her eyes shot wide.

She had barely scratched the surface when the truth hit her like a bomb, shaking her.

"Mother earth," she breathed and looked up at him, her gaze colliding with his as shock rolled through her.

The curse really was killing him. She could feel it like a creeping rot in his body, spreading outwards from his heart, and it wasn't only stealing his strength. It was affecting his mind too, twisting his thoughts towards one thing—the pursuit of the only thing that could bring him relief.

Her.

When she found the witch who had done this to him, she was going to kill them. They would pay for hurting MacKinnon. They would pay for using him to get to her, involving him when they should have had the balls to come at her themselves instead.

"We're doing this," she said and kept her hands against his chest, locking her elbows when he tried to move towards her again. "But I have a condition, and you're not going to like it."

His expression darkened and his heart thundered against her palms, and she swore she could feel his panic.

She stared into his eyes, keeping her with him. "You're not the only one afraid, MacKinnon. You're not yourself. If there was any other way to make sure you didn't go too far or get too rough—"

"Do it." He held his wrists out to her, his deep voice gravelly, the earnest edge to it far too sexy. "I don't want you to fear me, Hella. I don't want to hurt you."

His eyes told her something else as they darted between hers, something that resonated within her.

He wanted this to be the start of something, not the end.

Gods help her but she wanted that too.

She also wanted something else.

"Take your top off." She pushed her hands upwards towards his shoulders as he growled low, his eyes narrowing on hers.

He whipped it off, revealing his body to her, and she masked the horror that rolled through her as she saw just how much the curse had ravaged him. She could probably fit her hands around his biceps now. She ached for the old MacKinnon, the one who had been healthy in mind and body. She could bring that man back to her. All she had to do was take things to the next level with him and that was hardly a chore.

He tossed his shirt on the floor, his gaze still riveted on her, as if he couldn't look away, and she liked that. She liked that he was always so transfixed by her, as if she was the only other person in this world. A woman could get used to having such a handsome, powerful man doting on her and satisfying her every need.

While still retaining her independence, of course.

She wasn't sure how she was going to wrangle that, knew in her gut he would have ideas about them that she wasn't going to agree with, but she would figure it out once MacKinnon was back to his normal self.

Hella said the incantation in her mind as she reached up and skimmed her hands down his arms in one fluid motion, keeping her eyes locked with his, distracting him. When her fingers met his wrists, she funnelled the spell to their tips and completed it. Cold metal replaced the warmth of his skin and she held her breath, bracing herself for his reaction when chains unravelled from the twin thick cuffs and snapped to a point on the floor behind him.

He sucked down a breath, and then another, swallowed hard and glanced at his wrists.

And frowned.

"Silk? Silk isn't strong enough to hold me, Hella." His golden gaze leaped to meet hers and then dropped back to his wrists.

Her secondary spell had worked then. She had hoped that if she tricked his eyes into seeing violet silk wrapped tightly around his wrists and his body into feeling the softness and warmth of that material, that he wouldn't panic and go to that dark place he did whenever he was chained.

"It's plenty strong." She stroked her fingers over the silver manacles she could see.

MacKinnon tugged at his right restraint, testing it and finding it satisfactory judging by how his eyes darkened with desire again, hunger lighting them as he shifted them back to her.

He raked his gaze over her, heat following in its wake, sending her temperature soaring together with the fact she had chained him facing her on the desk. Wicked images of him taking her on it filled her mind. He sniffed and then growled, baring fangs that only made her feel hotter now that he was chained and he wouldn't be able to easily reach her neck.

His claws flexed as she paid him back, leisurely taking in every inch of his torso as her fingers drifted to it. She stroked them over his pectorals and then down the ropes of his stomach, the short dark hairs that covered him teasing her fingertips as much as the feel of his muscles as he tensed.

Her left hand drifted lower as she tilted her head back and lifted her eyes to lock with his again, and his eyelids drooped as she stroked her palm over the impressive bulge in his jeans. Her blood heated another few degrees, scorching her as she remembered how he had looked naked, how big he had been when she had watched him dreaming of her.

He pressed his cock against her hand and lunged for her, trying to seize hold of her ruined dress as he aimed fangs at her shoulder. She leaned back, evading him, and he growled and flashed his fangs as the chains holding him shortened, pulling him away from her and placing her beyond his reach.

Hella huffed as she hopped down from the desk and moved around it, putting it between them. "You're being too much of an alpha with me. You want this to happen, then it's happening on my terms. You play by my rules."

That didn't go down well.

He snarled and yanked at his restraints, his expression darkening as they refused to give and he couldn't reach her.

She risked it and went back to him, moving around behind him. She reached under his arm and pressed her right palm to his chest, right over his heart, and leaned her cheek on his biceps.

He stilled and his gaze flicked to hers.

"You know, I've done my research and I've gathered proof of something you won't like. Your instincts are telling you a lie, MacKinnon. The same lie they tell every male who finds his fated one. I've seen it countless times in this town. Enough times to know you have this whole thing about fated mates wrong." She feathered her fingers over his chest, teasing the crisp hairs, following the line of one of his scars from one pectoral to another. Her eyes drifted up to meet his and she licked her lips, teasing him and savouring the way his gaze grew hooded again, his eyes locking on her mouth. "You don't own me. I own you."

He stared at her, breathing so hard that he shifted her hand with each one.

No denial?

She had expected him to rail at her, to let his alpha side loose and listen to his instincts rather than her. Or were his instincts now in line with what she had told him? Had he realised that the tables had turned and he was hers now, born to serve her?

Her hand slipped from his chest as she stepped away from him, savouring the way his eyes tracked her, keeping her desire at a boil. She stopped once he could see her, made sure he was watching and then removed the remains of her dress, revealing her body to him.

His growl thrilled her, the feel of his eyes raking over her heightening her desire, making her ache for him.

She reached around behind herself and unhooked her plain black bra and cast it aside.

His throat worked on a hard swallow and his lips parted, the hunger lighting his eyes growing stronger as he lowered them to her breasts. She stroked her fingers around her nipples, so they tightened into tempting beads.

This time, he snarled and fought his bonds, straining with both hands to reach her.

Hella sashayed back to him, still teasing her breasts.

The moment she was close to his side, she let the chains loosen enough that he could move more freely and he twisted and knocked her hands aside. She shivered as he made contact, his calloused hands cupping her breasts and his thumbs brushing her nipples. His chains were cold against her overheating flesh, adding to the thrill coursing through her like a drug.

She ran an appraising look over him. Where to start? The answer to that question was easy.

She removed his hands from her and kept hold of his right arm, eased under it and came to stand before him with her back to the table. His rumbling growl and the hungry look in his eyes, one that made her feel as if he wanted to eat her whole, were thrilling, had heat sweeping through her from her toes to her cheeks.

He palmed her breasts again, his large hands covering them, and she savoured the feel of his rough skin against their sensitive tips as she trailed her fingers down his stomach, heading for the waist of his jeans.

"Let me get a good look at you." She made fast work of the buttons and bit her lip as his fly parted and his cock sprang free.

Heat pooled lower as she took hold of it, the heaviness of it in her hand sending another sharp thrill chasing through her. He was bigger than she recalled, and bigger than any man she'd had before. Her cheeks flushed deeper as she stroked him, wringing a drop from the broad head, and an urge to taste that bead of moisture struck her.

Hella bent over and dropped her head, wrapped her lips around him and moaned in time with him as she explored him with her tongue. He growled and fisted her hair. When he began pumping his hips, trying to fuck her mouth, she gripped his hips and pushed him back, earning a feral snarl from him.

"I'm in control here. Not you." She narrowed her eyes on him, trying to be firm when all she really wanted to do was suck him until his legs gave out and he bellowed in pleasure. She stroked her hands down his arms to his wrists. "I own you."

He really didn't like that.

He turned savage in a heartbeat, his expression twisting in vicious lines as his eyes glowed gold, and she flicked a worried glance at his chest, aware she had gone too far even when she had only been trying to amp up the wickedness of the moment with some sexy talk. He grabbed her before she could focus on the spell that held him so the chains would shorten, his mouth descending on hers. His kiss was rough, his grip on her too tight, and she swore she could feel him slipping, surrendering to his instincts.

Not good.

She desperately placed her hands against his chest, over his thundering heart, and tried to break free so she could call his name and bring him back to her.

Only her touch was enough to do that this time, had him wrenching away from her mouth to gaze down at his chest.

Hella stroked her palms over it and then lifted her right hand and pushed her fingers through his wild dark hair. Not petting him. She wasn't petting the big, bad wolf. He liked it though, his gaze growing hooded again, his features relaxing as he leaned into her touch. Apparently, her wolf enjoyed being petted.

She smiled wickedly and lowered her other hand to pet him elsewhere. He groaned as her palm brushed his hard shaft and it kicked, eager for her touch.

Eager for her. She wanted it too, was on fire for this male. She stroked him a few more times, distracting him with the pleasure and sedating him, and then released him and hopped up onto the bench table.

His growl of displeasure died before it fully left his lips as she shimmied out of her panties and spread her legs, baring herself to him. He swallowed and seized her thighs, trying to pull her to him as he stepped towards her. A hand on his cock stopped him this time, and he stilled as she stroked it and touched herself. He stared at her hand as she teased her own flesh, his rumbling growls and little grunts filling the thick silence.

He grabbed his shaft.

Hella stroked the head, smearing moisture into it. "I know you need me, but I need to be ready for you."

He stilled and frowned at her, released his breath and dropped his gaze back to her hands. She rewarded him for his patience by stroking him, giving him some relief. Which only made her burn hotter. She couldn't tear her gaze away from him as she touched herself, imagining him filling her, growing wetter by the second.

Aching for him.

Too much.

She leaned back slightly and drew him towards her, desperate to feel him inside her and live out her fantasies.

MacKinnon growled and grabbed her hips, and before she could catch up, she was face down on the table and he was inching into her from behind. She gripped the edge of the table as he slowly filled her, stretching her to the point of pain, and whispered a spell, one designed to take that pain away, because she wanted only pleasure from this moment. She moaned as he nudged deeper and grunted, his breaths sawing from him as he struggled to join them slowly. It touched her. Even this far gone, this desperate and wild for her, he didn't want to hurt her.

"MacKinnon," she breathed and he slid deeper still, and gods, she needed him all the way inside her, needed to know the feeling of being one with him. She didn't want slow. She wanted fierce. She wanted to *feel* him. She looked over her shoulder at him. Tight lines bracketed his mouth as he focused on where they joined. His gaze lifted to hers. She pushed back onto him a little, trying to show him that she needed him. Now. She whispered, "Kin."

His expression shifted, delight in his eyes one moment and hunger the next, and she cried out as he thrust deep into her, filling her all the way.

He leaned over her, fisting her hair with one hand to pull her head back and gripping the bench with the other as he pounded into her, punishing and powerful thrusts that would have moved the bench if he hadn't been holding it in place.

Mother earth.

She breathed hard as he took her, lost in how wicked it was as he bent her to his will, making her a slave to him and her desires. Delicious. He pumped her harder, each brutal thrust striking her deep in her core, and she loved it. He groaned and grunted against her back, his breath washing her bare skin as he drove into her, pushing her towards what she knew was going to be an earth-shattering—no, life-altering—release.

He moved back, releasing the bench, and she gripped it instead, trying to hold it in place as he deepened his thrusts and palmed her backside, his grip on her hair forcing her head up and her spine to arch. Her nipples brushed the wooden top with each thrust, adding to her pleasure, and his balls slapped her sensitive bead. He massaged her buttock and she was close, soaring and desperate for one final push.

MacKinnon stroked his thumb down the cleft of her buttocks and pressed it into her, digging his fingers into the fleshy cheek at the same time, holding her firmly in place. A cry burst from her as pleasure detonated inside her, so intense that everything went hazy for a moment before it came back and she could breathe again. He pressed his thumb deeper as he continued to take her, rougher now, riding her climax and driving her towards another. His chains rattled against her hips, cool against her flesh as he pumped her deeper, faster, more desperately.

She was close again.

The door in front of her opened and she almost screamed in horror as Fenix filled the doorframe. The tawny-haired incubus stared at her, his green eyes wide as he got one hell of a view of her and MacKinnon.

MacKinnon growled and took her harder, the dominant way he responded to the presence of another male thrilling her and sending her soaring higher.

Fenix swiftly backed out of the door and closed it, and her momentary horror was quick to disappear as MacKinnon kept thrusting, his grip on her tightening as he pushed her right to the edge again.

He plunged deep inside her and howled, his entire body shuddering as he spilled, powerful hot jets that had her thighs quivering and body shaking against the table as she followed him. He eased out and back into her, slowly this time, thrusting gently as he came. Each one was slower than the last as he throbbed and she pulsed around him, coming down with him as she caught her breath.

She mourned the absence of him as he pulled out of her and she turned in time to see him sag against the wall, his chest rising and falling on hard breaths and his silver gaze hazy.

Hella locked gazes with him, awareness sweeping through her.

She had just ruined everything.

She would never want another male now.

MacKinnon only made that feeling stronger by finding a clean rag and carefully wiping her, gently stroking her trembling backside with his free hand as he growled low, an air of possession in it that excited her this time.

When he was done, she turned to face him and undid the spell holding his wrists. He rubbed them and she blushed as he stooped and picked up her underwear. He held it out to her. She quickly donned it, her legs still shaking, feeling weak beneath her, and searched for a dress that wasn't in tatters. She found one over the back of her armchair and pulled it on, stumbled a few steps towards the door and looked back at him.

Needing to know he was all right.

MacKinnon nodded and closed his eyes, and slumped into the chair.

While she didn't need his permission to go and speak with Fenix, she appreciated that he wasn't going to go off the rails about it, and silently swore she would make it quick.

Because she already wanted an encore.

CHAPTER 21

The moment the incubus left them alone in the well-appointed pale blue bedroom he had teleported them to, MacKinnon turned on Hella.

"I don't like this," he growled and began pacing, his eyes locked on the door as his senses stretched outwards, charting everything.

Including the fact there were three incubi on the floor below him and the one called Fenix appeared to be heading towards them.

His beautiful fated female was in a house with four sex demons and why? Because she apparently felt compelled to help one of them.

The same one who had come to her all those weeks ago and had talked about her private life as if he knew every juicy detail of it. How close were they? Kin didn't want to know the answer to that question, so he pushed it out of his head.

"It's only temporary. I'll help Fenix with his problem and at the same time I don't have to worry about the nymph." She touched her messy blue hair and pulled a face.

MacKinnon rounded on her. "I offered you protection from the nymph. You don't need this male."

She arched an eyebrow at him. "Here I thought you would be different after sex, but apparently not. You're still growling and snarling and snapping your fangs at me."

She twisted away from him and he grabbed her arm, tugging her back to face him.

"I'll no' have you cavorting with sex demons." He came to stand over her, every instinct he possessed howling at him to make it a demand—an order.

She wrenched her arm free of his grip.

"I'm sorry? Cavorting? Why don't you just say it straight, MacKinnon?" She stepped up to him and prodded him hard in the chest, and he didn't like the way she had returned to calling him by that version of his name when she had shown him the bliss of hearing her call him Kin. Her jabs punctuated each word that lashed from her lips as she glared up at him, silver and gold stars sparking in her emerald irises. "You think I'm going to fuck them. That I have no control over myself and will be spreading my legs for them the second I'm within screwing distance."

She dug the tip of her finger into his chest and twisted it with those last two words, and then pivoted away from him on a huff.

He curled his hands into fists at his sides and clenched them, reining in his urge to follow his instincts, aware it would only make things worse. He and his wolf side were at odds again, that part of him snarling and wild, sure that one of the males was going to steal her from him, and it was making it hard to think straight.

Making love to Hella had given him back his strength and returned his body to what it had been before the curse had ravaged it, but it had done a number on his instincts. They were stronger now, constantly pressing him to dominate her and make her belong to him, and he was already growing tired of fighting them every step of the way so he didn't mess things up with her.

Not that he was doing a good job of that.

"No," he grumbled and scrubbed a hand down his face. "I didn't mean it like that."

She sighed and rolled her eyes in that way that screamed she didn't believe a word that left his lips.

"I didn't," he barked and his hand fell to his side. "I just… I…"

She gave him an expectant look, one that morphed into disappointment when words failed him. "Let me finish for you. You just think I'll give myself to you and in the next heartbeat I'd give myself to another male, because I'm a whore queen."

"No!" This wasn't going well. He reached for her and she backed away from him, moving her arm behind her so he couldn't grab it, and he wanted to growl but tamped it down and exhaled hard instead. He paced away from her, fearing that if he stayed near her that he would do something wrong. Or more wrong. He rubbed his eyes with the heels of his hands and stilled with his back to her. "My instincts… I don't think you're a whore queen."

He grimaced as she gasped and he felt her horror trickling through their fragile blooming bond.

He spun to face her, lowering his hands at the same time. "I didn't mean it like that. Hella... lass... love..."

Words failed him again as she stared at him, mouth agape and hurt shining in her eyes.

He sighed and gave her his back again, because for some bloody reason it was easier to talk to her when he wasn't looking at her, her beauty addling his mind and rousing his possessiveness.

"The incubus is verra handsome," he muttered, hating how bleak and defeated he sounded, as if it was already settled and he had lost her.

He waited for her retort, or for her to leave and never come back.

She surprised him by coming to him instead of walking out of the door and he breathed a little easier, his mind growing a little calmer, as she laid her left hand on his back between his shoulders. Her sigh teased his ears, a soft sound that had him casting a glance at her as his brow furrowed.

"I would never sleep with an incubus. They're a demon. If I take demon seed into my body, I lose my powers... or so the story goes. I heard rumours—"

He cut her off with a growl. "So the only reason you haven't slept with him is because you fear losing your magic?"

Her eyes widened and then narrowed, the stars emerging in them again as the tinny scent of magic swirled around her, tainting her delicate scent of rain-soaked heather and spice.

"No," she bit out and glared at him. "Fenix is just a friend."

Relief swept through him, but she dashed it against the rocks.

"But who I sleep with is none of your business."

It was his business. She was his now. He knew it deep in his heart. Something fundamental had changed between them and neither of them would ever be the same, and if he had his way, they would never be apart either.

"Because I was a *pity fuck*." He hurled the words at her, ones she had said to the incubus when she had been talking to him outside her small home after making love to Kin.

Her mouth dropped open, shock rolling across her delicate features, and then all the tension bled from her and her look turned soft and understanding.

"That's why you're lashing out at me." She sighed and reached for him, but this time he moved his arm beyond her reach. She cast him a hurt look and then lowered her hand and gazed at it, her voice dropping. "I shouldn't have said that. I panicked and... I'm sorry."

He hadn't realised how much it had annoyed him until he had thrown it at her, had thought the incubus was the reason he was angry with her, but now that it was out there, he couldn't deny that it had hurt him. He had thought they had shared something, and she had treated it as if she had only done it to help him.

Which had left him feeling as if she didn't want him.

When he was mad for her.

"MacKinnon," she whispered, stepped up to him and placed her hand on his chest. "I… when I had to go speak with Fenix… my plans were very different to what just happened. I intended to deal with him and then come back to you and see if you were up for round two."

"Round two?" His eyebrows rose and his shaft stiffened. He grimaced as his jeans pinched and tried to subtly adjust himself, but Hella noticed, her luminous eyes dropping to his crotch and her cheeks pinkening. Desire laced her scent and had him reaching for her. "If my lass wants another go—"

"Later," she interjected.

He growled and his fangs dropped when she moved back a step, making it clear she meant it and was going to make him wait when he was already in agony, aching for her. This time, he wanted to make love to her face to face, wanted to drown in her eyes as they found release together. He wanted to show her that he could be gentle, and sweet, and whatever she needed in order for her to fall for him.

"I really should get changed and go help." She hurried away from him and he tracked her with his gaze, his mood darkening as he realised something.

She meant to go and help the incubi without him at her side.

Over his dead body.

"I'm coming with you."

She cast him a look of wide-eyed surprise that rapidly turned into her shaking her head. "No. You need to rest. I have this. Just have a nap and regain your strength."

He stepped up to her. "I'm as strong as an ox and I don't need to rest. What I need to do is go with you."

"Why?" Her look turned cautious. Curious. Far too wary. All the warmth left her eyes as she gazed up at him. "Because you know fae and can read magical texts and help out, or because you want to stand guard over me? Which is it, MacKinnon?"

The cold edge to her eyes and the barriers he could see coming up between them said she knew which one it was, and she didn't like it.

She backed off two steps, her face an icy mask that chilled him. "I don't need a guard dog, wolf. I don't need someone trying to control me or thinking they own me. I certainly don't need someone who believes they need to shadow my every step because they can't trust me."

"Hella." He reached for her and she glared at his hand, making it clear she wasn't going to be taking it this time. The wounded look she gave him as she turned away from him told him to give her space, to give her time to cool down and use it wisely to figure out what he could say to make things better and make her see that he did trust her.

He just didn't trust the incubi.

She muttered things beneath her breath as she grabbed her carpet bag and set it down on the dressing table on the other side of the large room.

He remained where he was even though the small distance between them pained him and he wanted her close to him again, wanted to rip down the barrier he had made her put up and show her that he could be the man she needed him to be.

For what felt like the hundredth time since he had met her, he cursed his wolf instincts.

He also cursed his inability to keep his big mouth shut until he had filtered his thoughts when he said, "It will be different when we mate."

She whipped to face him, clutching a dress in her hands, shock written in every line of her face and in her scent too.

"That's it. That right there is the final straw. You don't get to make decisions for me, Grant MacKinnon!" She threw her dress back into her bag and grabbed it. "You most certainly don't get any say in whether I become your mate or not. I won't stand for it. I don't want another overbearing, narcissistic control freak in my life. I don't want someone who doesn't treat me like an equal. I don't need someone who wants to control my every move. I'm going down to help my friend and I'm going to request another room, and you're staying the hell away from me unless you want to find out how true the whole *'woman scorned'* saying is. I'll fry your balls right off your body if you come near me again."

She hurried through a door into an adjoining room.

Kin sank onto his backside on the navy bedclothes on the king-sized bed and stared at the wooden door she slammed closed behind her.

"Way to balls everything up," he muttered to himself and leaned forwards, resting his elbows on his knees.

He placed his head in his hands and sighed, trying to figure out a way to make Hella forgive him and to make her see he hadn't meant it like it had sounded. He hadn't just decided they would mate and that was that. He had meant it more like *if* they mated. Only it hadn't come out that way, because his wolf side couldn't bear the thought of her not being his, so it had twisted his words into something more definite.

And demanding.

He groaned and palmed his forehead, desperately seeking a solution before Hella came out of the room. *If* she came out of the room. For all he knew, it had another exit. He focused his senses on her and found her there on the other side, moving around. Not gone yet. He needed to find the right thing to say to her, so she wouldn't ask her friend for another room and end up leaving him.

Or seek to fry his balls off as punishment.

The door opened and he lifted his head enough that he could look at her.

Although, she had found another way to punish him for trying to control her.

She dropped her carpet bag by her pointed black stiletto boots and his gaze tracked her stripy black and white stockings upwards to the ruffled skirt of her corseted black dress.

He growled at how short it was and how it flashed a strip of creamy thigh between the top of her stockings and the hem of her skirt, and pushed to his feet.

She gave him a disinterested look as she finished pinning her blue hair in a tangled mass at the back of her head and strode past him, her bare shoulders tipped back.

MacKinnon was going to put her in her place.

But then his gaze caught on her unmarked nape.

He stilled and stared at it, the sight making him ache for another reason as she drifted away from him, heading for the door. Gods, he wanted to sink his fangs into that spot and hold her with them as he claimed her.

He wanted his mark on her.

He needed the bond with her.

Something he wasn't going to get if he continued messing everything up by letting his instincts take the reins. She would leave him, and she would take his heart with her, and he would be a hollow shell for the rest of his days.

She reached the door and he roused himself, because he was damned if she was going down to help the incubi while dressed in such a provocative manner. If she wanted to punish him, she could stay here and pummel him with words and fists and magic for all he cared. Anything she wanted to throw at him, he would take.

But he couldn't take this.

He couldn't bear the thought of her parading around in front of sex demons dressed in such a fashion.

This punishment was too much.

Or maybe it wasn't enough.

He had done everything wrong again, had let his instincts control him, and had driven her to do this. He had behaved exactly as she expected of an alpha wolf, acting in a domineering manner that he knew she hated. He fought to find the right words, selecting them carefully, desperate to show her that he was sorry and that he would do better, and that he didn't want to control her.

Before he could find the words, she looked over her shoulder at him. "Don't wait up."

And slammed the door in his face.

Kin grabbed the handle and twisted it, determined to follow her.

Only the door wouldn't open.

He tried again, frantically turning the knob, and then struck the door. His fist bounced right off it and hit him in the face, and he growled as light shimmered over the door. He growled and hurried to the other door, the one that led to the room where Hella had changed, only to find he couldn't open it either. The sash windows on either side of the bed wouldn't even let him near them.

Trapped.

His wily wee witch had used magic to trap him in this room.

And by the gods, he deserved it for how he had acted. He was no better than the nymph, believing he could just take what he wanted from Hella without any consideration for how she felt or what she wanted. No, that wasn't true. His instincts as an alpha wolf wanted that. Not him. He pressed his hand to his chest, to the heart that ached for her to come back to him and give him another chance. This time, he would hold his tongue until he had mastered his instincts and knew the words that were going to leave his lips were ones that came from his heart.

He didn't want to control her or make decisions for her. He wanted her to stand by his side, as his equal, exactly as she wanted. Gods, he wished he hadn't been born a wolf or a shifter of any kind. He looked at the window to his right, making another wish—that he could speak with Gregor. Gregor would know what to do. The wolf was wise, had given him good advice, but Kin hadn't been prepared for how strong his instincts had become the second he had joined with Hella. The urge to bite her in that moment had been strong, almost overwhelming, and it had been a constant battle to deny his instincts and focus on pleasing his female instead. It was still a constant battle to deny them.

He had to master this.

It was just another fight and he would be the victor this time too. He would tame his instincts again, as he had before, and make her see that he could be a good man. His gaze drifted around the room, moving from one magically sealed exit to the next, gaining pace as he cycled through them. He idly rubbed his chest, following the line of one scar, and breathed harder as memories surfaced. A small, weedy voice echoed in his head and he couldn't hold back the words as his gaze settled on the door Hella had slammed in his face.

"I swear I'll be good if you let me out, Master," he whispered, his voice cracking as pain lanced his heart. "I'll do better. I'll do whatever you want. Please don't punish me again."

He backed towards the bed and slumped onto the end of it, all his strength leaving him as emotions whirled inside him, anger swift to rise as he realised what he had said and how desperate he felt.

How weak he was being.

Kin glared at the door, dug his claws into his knees and focused his mind, shutting out hissed words about cages and battling the tide of his memories, determined to remain lucid.

Willing his mate to return.

CHAPTER 22

MacKinnon had pushed her buttons and before she had known what she was doing, Hella had changed into her sexiest dress and used a spell to trap him in their room. She was going to regret that.

Already was, if she was being honest with herself.

She trudged downstairs, denying the urge to turn on her heel and go back to MacKinnon and apologise. He was the one who should be apologising to her. She pressed her lips together. Not that he could do that when he was trapped in their room.

Her steps slowed and she glanced back up the elegant staircase. Why did he have to go back to his old ways? For a moment, she had felt something had changed for the better between them, but now she could see she was mistaken. Nothing had changed. MacKinnon still had the attitude of a king, expecting her to bend to his will and do what he wanted without question, and worse, he had revealed he didn't trust her.

She tightened her grip on the railing and sighed. Or maybe he did trust her, but his instincts didn't. She wished she knew a shifter well enough that she could ask them about this because she needed some perspective, or at least a rough guide to dating a werewolf. A what to expect when he finds his fated female in you type thing. Someone really should have written a book about it by now. She could only imagine how many women out there were going through the same thing she was, being thrown around on a turbulent sea of emotions and not knowing whether the next wave was going to lift her up or pull her under and drown her.

His behaviour was far too unpredictable and she didn't like it.

But then, she got the impression he didn't like it either.

She sank to her backside on the step and hugged her knees. Maybe if they talked. She huffed. If they talked right now, he would probably say everything wrong, inciting her wrath and forcing her to keep her promise to remove his balls. She needed to do something though. She couldn't go on like this, not really knowing where she stood or what was happening from one moment to the next. She hated the feeling that she was spinning out of control and in danger of things going badly wrong. By badly, she meant ending up with a mating mark on her neck that she didn't want.

Hella propped her chin up on her palm and gazed at the foyer of Fenix's elegant Scottish mansion.

Although... if MacKinnon played his cards right, she might want that mark.

But he had a lot of work to do to make that happen.

Starting with improving his behaviour.

She glanced back up the stairs. Not that his jail time was going to make that happen. When she went back to him—and it was *when* not if and not only because she had left her precious bag in the room—he was going to be angry with her.

She would use their time apart to figure out a way to quickly calm him.

Easier said than done.

Voices drifted along a corridor and she heaved another sigh and pushed to her feet, aware she couldn't keep Fenix waiting. If she did, he would probably come looking for her and she didn't want him to find her sitting on his stairs moping over MacKinnon and nursing her aching heart. She would never hear the end of it.

Hella frowned as she approached the door to the library and Fenix's voice came through it.

"Besides, she isn't alone. I'm only going to warn you once that there'll be no flirting, no attempted seductions, not even *innocent* looks at her." It was just like Fenix to be protective of her and to lay down the law with his family, making sure she felt safe. A smile curled her lips, but it faltered as he continued, "Break the rules and the wolf with her will probably break every bone in your body."

She glanced up at the ceiling in the direction of their room, fighting the urge to go back to him, and then sucked down a breath and pushed the door open.

Fenix glanced her way, his green eyes warm with a silent greeting. His tawny hair was wild, as if he had been running his fingers through it. He probably had been. He had confessed once that his family were hard work, constantly in need of subtle and not-so-subtle corrections to their behaviour. Of the four incubi he had taken under his wing, two were good and two were pure evil judging by the things Fenix complained about to her.

Although she always saw love in his eyes even when he was ranting about whatever rule they had broken or the state he had found his home in.

She strolled into the room, aware of all their eyes on her and noticing that Des was missing. Tiny, a sweet young incubus with scruffy sandy hair and blue eyes currently holding flares of gold and cerulean as he gazed at her stockings and blushed, stood beside Fenix, his loose charcoal T-shirt and dark blue jeans a contrast to Fenix's more formal fitted black shirt and tight black jeans. She doubted Tiny had been the one to earn a warning from Fenix.

Hella glanced at the brunet, Rane, where he stood off to one side like a shadow in his black T-shirt and matching jeans, keeping his distance from everyone. He flicked her a disinterested look and went back to his work. Not him either then.

Which left Mort.

The troublemaker.

The tall blond's hazel eyes were bright with sparks of gold and cerulean as he stared at the top of the long wooden table that occupied the centre of the room, diligently keeping his eyes off her. Which meant he was the one Fenix had warned. He looked ready to run from the room rather than face her, something she found amusing as she approached him.

Hella stopped beside him, leaned in close, bringing her lips to his ear, and breathed into it. "Oh, he'll rip you apart like a chew toy, incubus."

Mort's throat worked on a hard swallow and he blanched a little, and maybe having an alpha wolf for a man wasn't such a bad thing. It certainly made her feel safer when she was around incubi. The last time she had come to this house, she had felt as if she was in constant danger. Both Mort and Rane had been more than a little forward with her.

Either they had grown up a lot since then, or the threat of a wolf was enough to keep them on their best behaviour.

"Hella," Fenix chided and she sighed and sashayed her way along the length of the table on the opposite side to him. She pretended not to notice the questioning look he gave her as he took in her outfit and clung to her confidence, refusing to let him rattle it. His tawny eyebrows knitted hard and he shook his head slightly, and she had the feeling he knew why she was dressed the way she was. His tone brooked no argument as he said, "I have rules for you too. No teasing my family."

Lightning shook the building, making the lights flicker, and Hella cast him a questioning look.

"Pest problem," he muttered and she gave him a look that told him she knew what he was doing, using her own words on her to try to make her not poke her nose into who was outside casting powerful thunder magic. He pushed a stack of books towards her. The leather-bound tomes had seen better days and there were papers sticking out from the pages, making them even thicker. "Anything you think might be useful, flag it for us. We can all speak fae and Mort knows his way around runes."

Hella's eyebrows shot up as she looked at Mort, surprise sweeping through her.

Mort scrubbed the back of his blond hair and refused to look at her.

Interesting.

Outside of witches and other magic users, it was rare for someone to know runes. Had the incubus been involved with a witch at some point? Or did magic run in his family? Incubi didn't just appear. They had mothers, although most of them never knew them. It was common for women to give up any baby sired by an incubus. Incubi were still viewed as parasites by most in the immortal realms and there was still a stigma attached to bearing the offspring of one.

Fenix rolled the sleeves of his black shirt up.

Hella frowned, her focus stolen away from Mort by the sight of a marking on her friend's right forearm, one that was new. It was a circular design with symbols and what looked like a dragon and a stag in it. It wasn't like Fenix to get ink. He didn't particularly like the fae markings that tracked up his forearms and over his shoulders to reveal his lineage, so she couldn't imagine him choosing to get more markings on his skin.

Without looking at her, he muttered, "Don't ask. Unless you know ancient fae?"

When he glanced at her, she shook her head, wishing she did now because she was curious about the mark. Who had given it to him?

"There are probably a few in Lucia you could ask about that mark though." She leafed through the first book, a particularly boring one containing very basic spells. She tossed some of the loose pages into an empty cardboard box and set the ones that warranted a closer look in a pile beside her.

She also dog-eared pages in the book, which surprisingly earned her a glare from Mort. He wasn't a fan of folding the top corners of pages in books? She had never figured him for that sort of man. In fact, she had figured he had never read a book in his life. Was there more to Mort than met the eye?

"Lucia? That where your nymph boyfriend is? Does he know the language?" Fenix's lips wobbled as he fought a smile and she scowled at him and added an eye roll when he tacked on, "Oops, forgot you traded up. Furry is more your thing now."

"MacKinnon isn't my boyfriend, and neither is the nymph." She grabbed the next book, not wanting to talk about either the nymph or the wolf, and searched for a subject change. "And nymphs aren't the only breed in Lucia."

"I know. Sirens live there too." Fenix pushed aside a stack of papers.

Hella jerked her chin towards the mark on his arm. "Sirens won't be able to help with translating that mark, but the seelie might."

"The seelie?" His gaze snapped to her and he bit out a ripe curse. "I've been trying to track an unseelie. I didn't go to Lucia because I thought it was only home to—damn it."

"Why do you think few people who go there come back?" She scoffed. "It's not the nymphs and the sirens killing or capturing them." Her mood took a sharp downwards turn as Ethyrian popped into her head, together with all the disgusting things he had said to her. She muttered, "Although the bastard nymphs do love taking captives."

"You're staying here until some of the heat you're feeling in that fae town dies down, got it?" Fenix planted his right hand against the polished top of the table and leaned on it as he stared at her, his tone hard and unyielding.

Demanding.

Her lips flattened as her mood shifted again, darkening as she glared across the table at him, making sure he knew how little she liked the fact he had just issued an order to her. What was it with the men in her life these days? When had everyone started thinking they could boss her around and she would do as they wanted? She was getting tired of it.

But Fenix did have a point.

She was safer here.

She tried to think objectively, pushing aside her dislike of being told what to do. Rebelling against Fenix just because he had made an offer sound like an order was a sure-fire way of getting herself captured by Ethyrian again. Just like rebelling against MacKinnon had made her come storming down into a room filled with incubi in a far too sexy outfit.

Maybe she had overreacted. Just a little.

She pulled down a breath and denied her first reaction, the initial instinct to push back against Fenix, and huffed as she looked back at her book, and nodded.

He added, "Your boyfriend can stay too."

That earned him another glare.

And the bolt of electricity that shot across the table to zap his hand as she pressed hers to the other side of it.

She smiled wickedly when he glared back at her and went back to her work, but it wasn't long before she found her thoughts drifting to MacKinnon again. Fenix kept calling him her boyfriend, and although she knew he was only doing it to tease her, it was filling her head with questions she didn't have answers to and she didn't like it.

Like, what kind of boyfriend would the wolf make?

Was it even possible for them to date or would his wolf instincts keep driving him to take the next step with her?

Was she really his fated female?

That one stuck in her head, tormenting her by degrees, keeping her focus away from her work as she idly flicked through the book in front of her, not really noticing what was on the pages. What if it was all just a spell? How was she going to feel if whoever had cursed him lifted it and he discovered she wasn't his fated one and no longer wanted anything to do with her?

There was no spell on her.

Meaning her feelings for him, whatever they were, were real.

Meaning she would get her heart broken if he left her.

Hella carried the book to the armchair by the fire and sat sideways on it, dangling her legs over one of the arms and resting her back against the other. She glanced up to her left, towards their room. Surprise trickled through her, mingling with worry. Why wasn't MacKinnon trying to bash his way out of his current prison? She had expected him to kick up a fuss, enough that she would have to excuse herself and go to him.

But he was silent.

Was he all right?

Her stomach twisted as a possible reason for his silence hit her.

What if his captivity had involved more than chains?

She tensed and Fenix glanced at her, and she buried her face back in her book, hiding from his inquisitive gaze. She wanted to go and check on MacKinnon, maybe even talk to him and get some things out in the open so things between them could be better, but she couldn't. She had promised to help Fenix.

And she knew there would be comments that would hit too close to the mark if she left now.

Fenix was watching her closely.

Too closely.

The last thing she needed when her feelings were in a muddle and she wasn't sure what to do was Fenix teasing her about the wolf, saying things that made her want something she was starting to feel was impossible.

Like MacKinnon being her boyfriend.

She couldn't remember the last time she had been in a serious and committed long-term relationship with someone.

But mother earth, part of her wanted that with MacKinnon.

Why couldn't he just do things right? Why did he have to keep pushing her buttons? She glanced at Fenix, feeling worn down and sure he could see it as his gaze softened and he looked as if he wanted to ask her if she was all right. A thought struck her. Fenix was mated. She wasn't sure incubi suffered the same overpowering mating instincts as shifters did, but maybe talking to him would still help her gain some perspective and help her forgive MacKinnon whenever he did something that riled her.

At the very least, it might help her cut him some slack.

Lightning struck, casting bright light into the room from the sash windows to her right and she glanced there, tempted to go and deal with the witch that was currently intent on rattling the house and everyone in it.

Fenix glanced at Rane where he stood sentinel by the window.

The dark-haired incubus kept his focus on the world outside, his back to Hella. Was he the cause of the current pest problem Fenix was facing?

"No point standing there staring out of the window." Fenix walked around the table, heading for the younger incubus.

Rane glanced at him and quietly asked, "Will the barrier hold?"

"It will hold." Hella looked up from her book.

Rane tensed and wasn't that charming, and telling? He was on his guard around her, a witch, and another one was having fun with thunderbolts just a short distance away. It didn't take a genius to see the incubus had upset a witch and the one guaranteed way of doing that was tainting her connection to nature and her magic.

Although apparently the rumours were true and a witch could retain her power after accepting demon seed into her body.

She curled her lip as Mort cast her a heated look. Not that she had any interest in finding that out for herself.

Mort had clearly forgotten Fenix's warning or perhaps the hours they had passed in this room together and her stupid choice of outfit had finally taken their toll on him, stoking his incubus hunger and bringing it to the fore, because the blond incubus abandoned his work to casually lean against the armchair opposite her, his left elbow resting on top of the tall back.

He purred, "I bet you could reinforce it for us. You look as if you could cast spells that would make the witch who had cast this one look like an amateur."

Hella rolled her eyes for effect and returned her focus to her book as she sighed. "Shoo. You can't charm your way into my panties."

Mort looked at Fenix, his tension a palpable thing in the air, drawing her gaze back to him. She held back a smile as he paled and she could practically see his mind churning, running over the reasons he might not be able to charm her.

Judging by how terrified he looked, she figured he hit on the one about mates. An incubus couldn't use his charms on his mate. According to Fenix, an incubus's fated one was immune to them, meaning they had to win her over the old-fashioned way rather than manipulating her emotions to suit him.

Fenix shook his head. "It's not that. She takes precautions. A spell that makes her impervious to our powers."

Relief washed across Mort's face as he raked long fingers through his blond hair.

Hella was bored and couldn't resist rattling him a little more. She ran a slow, leisurely look over him from head to toe, and purred, "It is a shame you're an incubus and off the menu. You're almost as handsome as Fenix." She looked at Rane and then Fenix, and finally settled her gaze on Tiny. "This would have been a dream come true once if you all weren't incubi."

Fenix did a perfect imitation of her and rolled his eyes. Mort and Tiny tensed as one, their eyes gaining gold and blue swirling flakes as they both stared at her. A blush climbed Tiny's cheeks and he quickly sat down, covering his lap with a book.

Rane just sighed and continued to stare out of the window.

Until a feral, booming howl of rage shook the house, causing all three of the younger incubi to tense and whip around to face the door.

Hella tensed with them, her heart lodging in her throat as she cursed herself for teasing Mort and the others. She should have known MacKinnon was listening, that he hadn't dozed off as part of her had expected and would be angry if he heard her flirting with other men. Not only that, but her careless words had probably just given him ammunition to use against her. He had presumed she was going to come down and fraternise with the incubi and now she had openly talked about bedding them.

Fenix flicked her a very unimpressed look and muttered, "I think he heard you."

She tried to shrug it off, but her shoulders were too stiff and she couldn't relax enough to pull off the calm, uncaring look. Fenix's green eyes narrowed on her and she had that feeling again, the one that said he wanted to pull her aside and talk to her about MacKinnon.

That he knew she had feelings for the wolf and was having a hard time dealing with them.

Banging and creaking came from upstairs, drawing everyone's gazes there, and she grimaced as something smashed and wood snapped. This was the reaction she had expected from MacKinnon when she had locked him in the room, and now that he was on a rampage, destroying everything in sight, she felt as terrible as she had imagined she would.

Fenix gave her a pointed look, one that ordered her to go and deal with her wolf.

Hella shot to her feet as something slammed into the floor above her and dropped her book on the seat of her armchair.

She flinched as glass smashed, her heart rushing in her ears, and fidgeted with smoothing her skirt down, trying to look calm and fooling no one judging by how Fenix looked at her.

She waggled her finger towards the door. "I'll... um... I'll just go and calm him down."

She hurried to it and pulled it open.

And just as it closed behind her, she heard Mort speaking.

"Is she going to fuck him? Because you said no sex in the den."

No. She wasn't going to screw MacKinnon.

A vicious howl echoed around her and she shivered as she felt the possession in it.

Her blood heated against her will.

Her body came alive.

Fine. If he kept howling like that, she might have trouble resisting the urge to climb him like a tree and make him howl for a different reason.

She raced up the stairs, trying to gather her confidence so she could use it as a shield, making sure he didn't see how flustered she was and how sorry she was about what she had done.

Or how badly she needed him.

She didn't care that he was furious. She didn't care that he was throwing a tantrum. She didn't care that he was all growly because she had teased another male within earshot of him. She didn't care that she had turned him into a beast again, howling and snarling in a possessive way. She didn't like that he was possessive.

Not at all.

She stopped in front of their room and schooled her features.

Pushed the door open.

MacKinnon swung towards her, his dark hair wild and his broad chest heaving, his lips pulled back off his enormous fangs as he breathed hard. His eyes were pure gold as they landed on her.

Pure possession.

Good gods.

She felt like the prey to his predator as he stared at her, his big body straining with each breath he pulled down, muscles flexing and stretching as he curled and uncurled his hands.

His fingertips were bloodied.

She looked at the destruction he had wrought, at the evidence of his rage, and a knot formed in her stomach. This was her fault. He made mistakes, but so did she. They were as bad as each other. She felt that right down to her soul.

Together with something else.

Maybe fate had made them for each other.

Maybe it was time she stopped fighting her feelings.

And stopped fearing them.

She was strong, powerful, and she could handle this wolf and anything he could throw at her. He wouldn't decide her fate for her. She would decide his.

She was taking control.

MacKinnon slowly eased to face her, his eyes never leaving her face, cutting an imposing figure as he towered in the middle of the room with the bed at his back. The one piece of furniture he hadn't turned into firewood, she noted. He stared at her, that possession that lit his eyes thrilling her as much as his howl had, igniting a fire in her veins that only he could sate.

Or maybe she could let him have the reins a little.

Like a treat.

"Kin," she started.

And didn't get to finish her apology.

He sprang at her, gathered her into his arms and pinned her to the wall.

And claimed more than her lips with another toe-curling kiss.

CHAPTER 23

MacKinnon tried to shut out the images in his head as he sat on the end of the bed, fending off sleep. It wasn't images of his past that tormented him now. It was images of Hella with the incubi. She had been gone hours, and his imagination had been running wild. Were the other three incubi he could sense in a room somewhere below him as handsome as the one called Fenix?

He pushed to his feet, paced to the dressing table, and stared at his reflection. Compared with the incubus, his looks were lacking. Fenix had an elegant bone structure and was classically handsome, possessed the sort of looks many women desired in a male and Hollywood would turn into a star.

MacKinnon, however, was a little too harsh in the brow and jaw, and his nose had a kink in it from a brawl as a pup. Even his eyebrows weren't as refined as the incubus's.

Lightning struck, making the lamps flicker again and casting bright light across his face that threw half of it into shadow and made him look like a monster as his eyes glowed gold.

He dreaded to think how handsome the others in the house were. What if they were more handsome than Fenix?

Images popped into his head of Hella in compromising positions with the males, the cries that left her lips as wild and sweet as the sounds she had made when he had been inside her.

He scrubbed a hand down his face and banished them, before his mood took a darker turn and he surrendered to it.

He heaved a long sigh, went to the bed, and sank back onto the end of it.

Being able to hear them talking wasn't helping his mood. He had tried tuning them out, but had ended up tuning into them instead, curious as to what they were saying to each other. Apparently, the answer to that was things he didn't want to hear.

The sensible part of him knew she was only teasing because she had that tone to her voice, the one he had heard her use a few times now, occasionally to his delight, but the rest of him grew agitated as he caught her words.

"You're almost as handsome as Fenix. This would have been a dream come true once if you all weren't incubi."

Kin launched to his feet and growled at the wooden floor, rage blasting through his veins to have a red veil descending. His heart thundered as his wolf side snarled and bashed against the cage of his human form, wanting out, and for once he and his instincts were on the same page.

Violence.

He craved violence.

If Hella wanted to keep him locked in this room, if she wanted to flirt with other men, then she would just have to deal with the consequences of her actions. He stormed to the dresser, gripped it with both hands and hefted it into the air on a howl. He twisted and hurled it clear across the room, making a huge dent in the pale blue plaster. The drawers fell out as it dropped to the floor and he kicked off, was across the room in a heartbeat to snag one and smash it on his knee. He tore another two apart with his bare hands, saliva rolling down his fangs as he growled and unleashed his fury on it. When it was nothing more than tinder fit for the fireplace, he grabbed a wardrobe and gave it the same treatment.

His fingers stung, the scent of blood heavy in the air as he panted and stalked across the room to rip into another set of drawers. He grabbed the mirror from the top of them and pivoted, smashing it into the wall, and grunted as some of the glass bounced back and hit him, cutting into his hands. He didn't care.

Black fur rippled over his skin as he snarled and destroyed a second wardrobe and a chair, hurling both at the window. They bounced back off the spell Hella had placed on the room, denying him the satisfying sound of glass smashing, and his gaze flicked to her carpet bag.

It had glass in it.

It contained everything she loved.

MacKinnon stalked towards it.

Stilled when he sensed Hella close to him and her intoxicating scent filled his lungs. His wolf calmed and he focused on her, narrowing the world down to her where she stood on the other side of the door.

It opened to reveal her.

Her pretty mask of indifference fell away the moment she looked at him, her green eyes widening as they took him in and then the room. He breathed hard, pulling her scent deep into his lungs, savouring it and the fire it lit in his veins, the need that built with each second that ticked past. Her eyes revealed everything to him, told him a thousand things.

Told him that he wasn't alone.

He stared at her, silently stalking his prey as a need rolled through him.

A hunger to possess her.

She was his.

Every fibre of his being howled that at him.

She tipped her chin up. The action was slight, but he noticed it, together with the hardening of her eyes that warned him she wanted to be in control again. Not this time. He wouldn't hurt her, but he would have her. He could feel her need, knew her desires better than she did in that moment as his instincts whispered what she wanted.

She wanted to be possessed by him.

The destruction he had wrought because she had dared to flirt with another man had excited her, had brought her running back to him, and try as she might to pretend she didn't desire him, it was right there in her eyes for him to see.

He turned to face her, moving slowly so he didn't spook his prey, and hid nothing from her as he stared into her eyes. He wanted her. Plain and simple. He needed her and he was going to have her. He was going to satisfy her needs and please his female. His fated one.

And once she was sated, they would be having a talk about her bad habit of restraining him.

Her pulse drummed a fast rhythm in the side of her neck, attempting to lure his gaze there. He kept it locked with hers instead, waiting to see how she would react to the possessiveness of his gaze.

Her pupils dilated, devouring the emerald of her irises.

Rose climbed her cheeks.

"Kin—"

She didn't get to say whatever it was she had wanted to tell him. The sound of her saying his name, the one he wanted to hear on her lips, broke the tether on his restraint and he sprang at her.

He gathered her into his arms, banding them tightly around her, and pinned her to the wall near the door as he claimed her lips, swallowing her shocked gasp, and the moan that followed it.

Her hands flew to his shoulders and rather than shoving him away, she frantically clutched at his muscles, dragging him closer. His wicked wee witch. She was wild as she tore at his shirt, pulling it up over his head, breaking the kiss for just long enough for the material to pass between them. The moment his chest was bare, her hands were roaming all over it, making him as crazed as she was.

Or maybe not even close.

She raked nails down his stomach and tackled his jeans, had his shaft freed in less than a few seconds. She worked it with her hand, maddening him, and he kissed her harder, his pulse skyrocketing.

On a low growl, Kin reached between them and tore her panties away.

She tensed against him, another gasp bursting from her lips, one that he turned into a moan again as he stroked her plush petals. He joined her, groaning as he felt how wet she was, how ready she was to accept him.

Her left hand gripped his bare shoulder and she pulled herself up, wrapped her legs around his hips and eagerly drew him to her. He fisted his cock again and then gave her what she wanted, sliding the broad head down through her folds to breach her. Gods. His breath hitched as he nudged inside her, his heart going wild as her heat scorched him and his instincts roared up on him, attempting to steal control and make him assert his dominance.

He denied them, easing into her instead, making her take every inch of him and showing her what she did to him. He was crazed for her, craved her like he had no other, and couldn't get enough of her. She tunnelled her fingers into his hair, twisting the dark lengths around them, and dragged his head down to hers. Her lips claimed his, her kiss fierce and demanding, and he groaned as he heard the silent order in it.

She didn't want gentle.

She didn't need him to be soft and tender.

She wanted wild and passionate, and gods, he could do that.

Kin held her hips in a fierce grip, unable to resist digging his short claws in to anchor himself to her as he withdrew and plunged back in. A moan burst from her lips, washing over his, and she pressed her fingertips into his flesh, scoring his scalp and clinging to his shoulder as she began to work her body against him.

Riding him.

He growled and pinned her to the wall, let go of the reins and let his desire take the helm. He wanted to possess this female. He wanted to stamp his mark on her and ruin her to all others, so she would only ever want him. No other male would ever satisfy her in the way he could.

On a wicked snarl, he pressed his claws deep into her hips and pumped her harder, faster, curling his hips as he held her in place, taking her mouth with the same ferocity as he took her body.

"Kin," she cried and arched towards him, desperately clutched at his head and his shoulder, a frantic little thing as she rocked on him.

His female needed more.

He gave it to her, driving her into the wall, rattling it with the force of his thrusts, a slave to how good she made him feel and his desire to please her. He dropped his head to her shoulder and pressed his forehead against it as he bent his knees so he could go deeper, leaving no part of her untouched. She murmured his name in his ear, chanting it like a prayer, urging him on. The need to possess her rose within him, had him turning his face towards her throat and his gaze locking onto her nape. His fangs ached and he fought his instincts, struggled to focus on satisfying her and himself.

One day.

One day she would be so crazy about him, so in love with him, that she wouldn't deny his claiming bite.

He fantasised about it as he rocked into her, his breaths coming faster, his shaft thickening as release coiled at the base of it.

Hella threw her head back and yelled his name as her body kicked against his, as she clenched and unclenched him, her bliss trickling into him through their growing bond. He groaned and buried his face in her shoulder again, pressing his forehead hard against her as his balls tightened. He tried to keep going, wanted to give her another release before he found his own, but the way she had called his name and how she clung to him as she trembled pulled him over the edge with her. He loosed a possessive growl and bit down on his lower lip as he plunged into her, thrusting to the hilt, and spilled, his cock throbbing and kicking with each jet that rocked him.

Kin clung to her, tasting his own blood, lost in a haze as he continued to spill, as his climax stretched out into the longest one he had ever experienced. She slowly relaxed against him, her body going lax as she exhaled softly. He held her on him, still pulsing, each one sending an aftershock of pleasure through him.

When she gently stroked the back of his head, teasing his hair with her fingertips, he sighed and closed his eyes, wrapped his arms around her and held her.

And realised he needed more of this.

He needed more of this calm and this tenderness, wanted to savour it because it was new to him. A lover had never stroked and petted him the way

Hella did, her touch like magic, soothing his ragged emotions and centring him.

"Kin," she whispered, breath teasing his ear. "I'm sorry."

He released his lower lip and his fangs receded. "What for?"

"Everything," she murmured.

And stole his heart.

"I'm not good at this." She chuckled. "Which is an understatement. This is… this is a bit new."

He heard something else. It was a bit frightening. She was used to being in control of her life and he kept trying to take it from her. No more. She was right and she owned him. She owned all of him. He would do anything for her.

Almost anything.

He would never let her go.

He turned with her and she tensed.

"Where are we going?" She pressed her hands to his shoulders and pushed him back.

He lifted his gaze to meet hers and loved how her eyes sparkled with stars. He had done that.

"To the bed. To rest. I need to hold you." He half-expected her to deny him, but she relaxed and didn't protest. Because she wanted to be held by him?

Her left hand lifted from his shoulder and she stroked it across his lower lip, her gaze growing concerned. "What happened here?"

He looked away from her, purely because he needed to be focused on not tripping over the broken furniture on his way to the bed. It had nothing to do with how awkward he felt as he grumbled the answer to her question.

"I needed to bite you, so I bit myself instead." And it hadn't been at all satisfying, but it had kept his fangs busy and had stopped him from crossing a line.

"Oh." Her eyebrows rose as he flicked a glance at her and he noted that she kept stroking his lower lip.

Maddening him.

He drew the covers back on the bed, set her down on her feet on the mattress, and stepped back from her. Even standing on the mattress she was only a head taller than him. His petite witch.

He reached for the ribbons on her corset.

She tensed and both hands came up as her gaze dropped to her chest. "What are you doing?"

"Undressing you. I want you to be comfortable." He wanted her naked.

She didn't seem to mind, lowered her hands and let him have his way. Or maybe she wanted to watch him suffer. His fingers were too big for the delicate lacing and he ended up getting one of the fine ribbons tangled with another.

He huffed and his claws extended.

Hella snatched his wrist. Not to stop him, but to guide his hand to her side.

Where there was a damned zipper.

She smiled wickedly at him and he mock-scowled at her, even as he savoured her amusement.

"How long were you going to let me struggle to get you out of this damned thing?" He eased the zipper down, anticipation curling through him to heat his blood as his gaze locked on the strip of creamy flesh he slowly exposed.

She shrugged. "About as long as I did. I don't take violence towards my possessions very well. The moment the claws came out, it was game over."

It was a good job she had arrived before he had gone to town on her carpet bag then. He could only imagine how furious she would have been had she found all her possessions destroyed.

He was tempted to quip about how he didn't take violence towards his possessions very well either, but the filter he had been working on caught it before it left his lips. Another good thing. At least he was learning to watch his mouth. Speaking of her as a possession, even in a playful way as it would have been, would end with him castrated and alone.

He bit back a groan as he peeled her corset away to reveal her breasts. She must have noticed his pained expression, because another smile lit up her face and she tormented him further by bending to shimmy her skirt down her legs. She reached out and gripped his right forearm as she tackled her boots, steadying herself.

And warming him.

He gazed at her hand on his arm, a sign of trust and maybe a little dependence that he enjoyed.

When she cast her boots aside and reached for her stockings, he snared her hands and stopped her.

"Leave them." His voice had gone low, gravelly, and his blood burned as he gazed at her, the thought of her silky stockings brushing his bare legs as she lay with him rousing his desire.

She rolled her eyes and straightened to stand before him in all her glory, a temptress that beckoned him to her, had him wanting to gather her in his arms and make love to her this time.

And then she flopped onto the bed, pulled the covers over herself to steal herself from view, and patted the spot beside her when he didn't move.

"Come on. Strip and hop in." She made it sound as if this wasn't a big moment for them.

It felt monumental to him.

He hadn't slept beside a female since becoming alpha of his pack. Before then, his relationships had been few and far between, and had never lasted long. He couldn't remember the last time he had slept with a female.

Kin rounded the bed to the other side and stripped off, tackling the easy part. Or what should have been easy.

The way Hella's gaze tracked his hands, following their every move, and her little gasp when he shoved his trousers down his hips and his length sprang free, had his blood heating further, until his veins were an inferno and he couldn't keep his mind off her curves and how she was almost bare beneath the covers.

He kicked off his boots and his jeans, and climbed into bed beside her, settling on his back.

Finding it strangely comforting to be beside her like this.

Hella made it even better by shuffling towards him and slinging her right leg over his, teasing him with the softness of her stockings. Her fingers traversed his chest and she angled her head back, her eyes coming up to lock on his face.

He slid his gaze to meet hers.

And gods, this was comfortable.

His wolf settled down, curling up in a contented way as she feathered her fingers across his flesh and gazed at him, a sparkle in her eyes that bewitched him. Her touch was like magic, calmed and eased the tension from him, until he felt more relaxed than he had ever been.

A moment had never been so perfect.

She proved him wrong about that by resting her cheek on his chest.

Now it was perfect.

He eased his arm around her and she didn't protest. In fact, she snuggled closer as he stroked his fingers up and down her arm.

When she continued running her fingers over his chest, he looked down at it, curious about what she was doing. Her delicate fingertips stroked the line of a scar that cut from his left shoulder to where her chin rested on his right pectoral.

She tilted her head back again, her eyes soft but laced with curiosity, and a dash of hope.

Her finger unerringly followed the silvery streak across his chest again.

And her voice was softer, gentler than he had ever heard it, telling him how much she wanted to know the answer to her question and how she feared he would be upset about her asking it.

"How did you get these scars?"

CHAPTER 24

MacKinnon didn't like to talk about his past, but as he gazed down into Hella's beguiling green eyes, he knew it was something he had to do. His past felt like a barrier between them, one he needed to overcome if he was going to have the future he wanted with all his heart, and he didn't like the thought of her coming up with her own answers about his scars and his time in captivity.

He would rather he put it all out there, as shameful as it was, and have her know the truth.

Even when it might mar her opinion of him.

He watched his fingers as he stroked her arm, relishing the fact she let him touch her like this, was in his arms and not fighting him for once. He shifted his gaze to hers and saw in it that she wanted to know about him, even the ugly parts. It was important to her. He felt that in his soul, and it made him think about the years that had come before his captivity, when he had been with his pack and his mother.

She had told him once that it was always better to speak the truth than tell a lie, even if the truth hurt.

It had taken him too long to understand what she had meant by that.

In fact, he had lost her before he had discovered the truth about her.

"The alpha of my pack gave me this one." He stroked the start of the scar, remembering that day. "I returned to the pack having escaped my captivity thanks to a group who came to rescue someone else and discovered my mother had died. Mortal hunters had come and she had been left undefended in the cottage by the borders of the territory. She hadn't stood a chance."

Hella frowned but her voice was soft as she asked, "Why was she alone?"

He cleared his throat as it tightened and pushed the words out. "My mother was meant for the alpha of the MacKinnon pack, but she fell for his brother and gave herself to him. I was the result. When Ma told the alpha what had happened and confessed her love to the brother... it didn't go the way she wished."

When Kin had learned of what had happened to her, he had felt she was a fool for admitting how he had come to be, that she should have kept her mouth shut and made the alpha believe he was the sire of her pup. Now, he wasn't so sure. He could see why she had chosen to speak the truth, even though it hadn't worked out for her.

Love.

She had been in love with a male and had thought they would have a life together.

She had risked it all for love.

Kin gazed down at Hella, lost himself in her eyes and hoped that she would prove him wrong and show him that sometimes it was worth risking being hurt.

Sometimes, it paid off.

"Bastards," Hella growled, sounding as vicious as any wolf female, and then her expression softened again, her eyebrows furrowing as she gazed up at him. "Did they banish her because of you? Is that why she was living at the edge of your pack's territory?"

"Aye." He nodded, glad that he didn't have to try to tell her everything. "We were happy. I never knew of her banishment. I thought she chose to live apart from the pack and I was schooled with the other pups. I was always so eager to return to her that I never noticed I was treated differently."

"Did you give the alpha hell?" Her look soured. "I hope you beat him black and blue."

Kin smiled. "I didn't let him off lightly. I left the pack for a while after that and took my time growing stronger, learning all there was about fighting. I intended to come back and claim his head, and the position of alpha. Only he died before I could. Instead, I won the position of alpha by defeating all challengers for the position."

"Are you a good alpha?" She circled his left nipple.

"The best."

That earned him a slap and a scowl from her. "Be serious."

He sighed and looked at the ceiling as he thought about it. "I've never had any complaints. I'm just, and take care of my people, and never place them in unnecessary danger. Too many alphas out there want to make their mark or prove their pack's strength by participating in battles. I'd rather we all lived peaceful, fulfilling and long lives."

She looked satisfied by that answer as she snuggled closer.

"Kin." Her expression sobered and he knew what was coming. He braced himself for it, but it didn't stop him from flinching as she quietly asked, "How did you come to be someone's captive? Was it because of your alpha? Or did the mortals who killed your mother take you?"

He swallowed hard. "Nay. Nothing like that. I was a pup, looked no older than nine or ten to human eyes, but was more like forty or so. I was out in the glen running and had always wanted to see the other side of the mountains that enclose the valley. I had been told countless times not to cross the border and to remain in the glen. Even the alpha had told me."

"The rebellious years, huh? I know those well." She laid her palm on his chest, soothing him and calming his wolf side.

He made a mental note to ask her about her so-called rebellious years later. She wasn't the only one who wanted to know more about the other.

"I should have stopped once I could see the other side of the mountain, but evening was falling and it looked so magical, and I saw moving lights below me. I was an idiot."

She frowned now and petted his chest. "You were curious."

"Same thing," he muttered and huffed, wishing he could turn back the clock and change his past, even when he knew it was impossible. "The lights were from a caravan led by immortals. I drew too close and they spotted me, and I wasn't fast enough. The next thing I knew I was in a cage and then I was in an arena and being sold to fae nobles."

She gasped, her wide eyes bewitching him together with the shock and anger he could read in them. His wee witch didn't like that he had been treated so miserably, and they had only just scratched the surface. How furious would she be once she knew the truth?

"I can't believe immortals would treat other immortals like that." She shook her head.

Kin lifted his hand and brushed his knuckles across her cheek. "They do. It happened back then, and it still happens now. Immortals are always buying other immortals, pushing them into slavery or worse."

"What was it like?" She lowered her gaze, avoiding his, and he smoothed his fingers down to her jaw, silently telling her that she didn't need to fear asking him questions. He wanted the truth out there. He wanted her to know him, despite how much it hurt to remember his past.

"I did things I'm not proud of, Hella. I lived in a constant state of fear. I wasn't the only one the fae nobles held in the cages. There were others too. Shifters of every breed. Most nights they would make us perform in one way or another, whether it was innocent entertainment in our animal forms… like a circus… or something more—" He couldn't bring himself to say it, not when he could feel her looking at him.

"The scars I saw when you shifted into your wolf form…" She trailed off, and the fact she couldn't bring herself to talk about them led him to suspect she knew how he had gotten them.

"If I disobeyed my owners or displeased them, I was punished." He closed his eyes and lifted his free hand to pinch the bridge of his nose as the past roared up on him. Rather than seeking to subdue it this time, he let it come. He let the memories roll over him. "They would whip me raw most of the time, but… sometimes… sometimes they punished me in other ways. The master preferred young boys and—"

Hella placed her fingers against his lips. They were trembling.

He opened his eyes and angled his head towards her.

The tears that lined her dark lashes stripped his strength from him, and the way she shook her head, her gaze imploring him not to continue, had him falling silent. Apparently, sometimes the truth hurt others too.

She gripped his shoulder, pulled herself up his body and kissed him, her breasts pressing against his chest. Her lips moved gently over his, the softest kiss he had ever received, and he felt her pain, her sorrow, and her anger.

Tasted it in the salt of her tears.

She lowered her head and pressed her forehead to his as she whispered, "I'm sorry."

"What for? You didn't do all those things to me." He caught her waist and tried to ease her back so he could see her face, but she gripped his shoulders and refused to budge.

Her voice cracked. "I'm sorry I chained you… that I trapped you in here. I'm sorry I hurt you. It was wrong of me, Kin. It was so wrong of me."

"I was being a dick," he muttered, trying to lighten the mood and failing judging by how she shook her head and her tears splashed onto his cheeks. He sighed and wrapped his arms around her, palmed the back of her head with his right hand and held her to him. "All forgiven, love."

When she remained silent, he tried to find a way to get her talking again, because he needed to hear her voice.

"So… you were rebellious when you were a bairn too?" He eased his hold on her, reluctant to let her go but wanting to see her face to make sure her tears had dried up.

She shuffled down him a little, almost shattering his focus as her body slid down his and her thigh brushed his crotch.

"Rebellious is and always has been my thing." Her smile wobbled on her lips but her tears were gone and she looked brighter.

He lifted his hand and stroked a rogue strand of blue hair back behind her ear, loving the fact she let him do such a thing.

"I never knew my father... so you have that over me, but then I guess yours wasn't exactly claiming the Father of the Year title." She drew little circles on his chest, her gaze tracking her fingers. "My mother died soon after I was born... in a war... and I was too wild... too like her... so my aunt handed me over to the coven to raise. I don't hate her for that."

"But you don't like your coven either," he said and she frowned at him, her gaze curious and intense. He stroked her cheek. "You spat the word coven like it was a curse. I have the feeling that they were a little too controlling for my hellion."

She arched an eyebrow at him. "Don't even think about trying to make that my nickname. People have tried."

"People, I presume, who now have terrible disfigurements." He smiled when the corners of her lips twitched, giving her away. She liked it when he was playful with her, letting her see the side of himself that he often kept hidden.

"You presume correctly." She flattened her palms on his chest and rested her chin on them, and her lower legs came up. The covers fell off them and she rocked her feet back and forth as she pulled a thoughtful face. "My upbringing was... eventful."

"An understatement, I imagine." His smile widened as he tried to picture how much destruction she had caused, and how difficult she had been to tame.

"What makes you say that?" Her eyebrows knitted and her gaze seared him again.

"You don't like authority or being ordered around, and the image in my head of a coven is akin to a boarding school, where the teachers are verra strict. All witches wear the same black dress when they are working, but you do not. This leads me to believe you didn't enjoy your time at the coven and you don't like conforming."

She pouted. "Far too close to the mark. Irritating, perceptive, wolf. I think I'll punish you for that."

He tensed, his wolf side perking up and ready to snap fangs at her, but her punishment was far from what he expected.

She kissed him again.

Slow. Leisurely. Addling his mind.

He grinned when she eased back and settled on his chest again. "You'll only encourage my behaviour with that kind of punishment."

She shrugged, a wicked light in her eyes. "Covens are… You're very right about them. I really didn't fit in. Too many rules for my taste. It didn't take them long to point out my flaws and try to correct them."

"Flaws?" His female had no flaws, not in his eyes.

"You must have noticed my indomitable spirit and tendency to talk my mind."

"Neither of which are flaws," he countered.

Her smile grew a little and she tapped his chest with her fingers. "Flattery will get you everywhere… but I know for a fact these non-flaws have irritated you plenty of times, and they irritated my teachers and superiors at the coven far more than that."

A sigh escaped her lips, drawing his gaze to them and his thoughts to kissing her again.

"I was a fast learner. I mastered spells beyond my years, impressing them in that way at least… but my attitude didn't impress them as much. I had no interest in doing as I was told and preferred to do what I wanted. When they tried to train me to be more like them… to be different… I acted out. The more they tried to control me… the wilder I became."

"You don't like people trying to change you." He didn't want to count the number of times he had tried to do such a thing to her. He regretted them all now and vowed he wouldn't try to change her again or impose his will upon her in any way.

He was done with that kind of behaviour.

He would rather things continued like this, with them both enjoying each other's company and growing closer.

She pulled a thoughtful face and then her features relaxed. "Would you like it?"

He shook his head.

"Everyone at the coven kept trying to change me, and it made me feel like I wasn't good enough." She brushed her fingers through the short hair on his chest, her gaze growing distant, and he cursed himself for his part in trying to change her. "I couldn't wait to get out of there. As soon as I was old enough, I left, and I never looked back. I have my business now and my independence, and I've made something of myself."

She made them sound like kindred spirits. Both of them had fought to free themselves of what had been a prison to them. Both of them had been determined to be strong and make their mark on the world, proving their worth even if it was only to themselves.

Both of them had overcome a difficult childhood, but it had shaped them. It had hardened him and made him aggressive towards anyone who would seek to chain him and control him.

And gods, it had done the same to her.

The bonds she feared weren't physical though. They were emotional. She feared letting someone get too close to her, afraid they would try to change her or perhaps that they would leave her alone in this world.

And she feared him placing a claim on her because she viewed it as a shackle, a way of controlling her.

Changing her.

"I would never change you, lass." He let the words tumble from his lips, sure they were a mistake but he needed her to know where he stood and that she was wrong about him. "Anyone who tries to change you is wrong. I'd never change a thing about you."

Her cheeks pinkened and then she got that look in her eyes, the one that said she wanted to call him on something and he knew what it was, so he pressed a finger to her lips to silence her.

"A mating mark isn't a way of controlling you, Hella. It's far from it." He tipped his head back into the pillow and sought the right words, the ones that would convey how he felt whenever he thought about his mark on her nape or about fated mates. "If you consented to be my mate, the mark would signify that we were bound... aye... but more than that, it would show the world that I'm taken. Wolves would know the mark is mine."

"And that I'm yours." She sounded upset, so he lowered his gaze to her. Only there wasn't anger in her eyes. There was a softness that warmed his soul.

He sighed. "Aye, they would know you're my mate, but they would know *I'm yours*. What you said, lass... about owning... I think you're right. I might be the one to mark you, but you'll be the one to own me."

She already did.

She owned him. Heart, soul and body.

"Why don't the men end up with marks on their napes?" She looked irritated by the thought the marking was one-sided.

He took pleasure in correcting her. "They do. Gregor, my second in command, bears his mate's mark on his nape. When they mated, she bit him so hard he needed stitches. I'd never seen Siobhan so terrified or Gregor so embarrassed when she came screaming into my home to get me."

Hella cast a look he could only describe as pure longing at the side of his neck and the hairs on his nape rose, making it tingle with awareness and causing an ache to bloom deep in his chest.

For a heartbeat, he thought she would say something, perhaps admit that she wished she had fangs so she could mark him too, but then she closed her eyes and turned her head and rested it on his chest.

MacKinnon sighed and wrapped his arms around her, holding her tucked against his side and listening to her breathing as it changed, growing softer. When she had been still for some time, he angled his head away from her and looked down at her face.

Her beauty hit him hard.

Together with the fact she was sleeping in his arms.

Trusting him.

How things had changed.

Kin watched over her, aware that more than their situation had changed. He had changed too.

He had fallen in love with her.

And he hoped she loved him too.

Lightning struck outside and it felt as if that thunderbolt had hit him in the heart as something dawned on him.

He didn't care whether she was his fated one or not. He loved her. She made him crazy in a good way, and calmed him too. His wolf side was a testament to the power she had over him. He had never felt so content—so at peace—so complete. He had never felt so still. So perfectly still.

As if he was exactly where he was meant to be at last.

That feeling and the warmth that filled him whenever he gazed at Hella made something else hit home.

He couldn't betray her.

His plan was shot.

Hella believed she could help him with the curse, and it was sweet of her, but already he could feel it eating away at his strength again. The curse was affecting him more quickly. If he let things go on, the time he could go between making love with Hella to strengthen him would grow shorter and shorter, until what? It was no longer effective at all? As much as he wanted to stay with her and was enjoying his time with her, he couldn't go on like this.

Because he didn't want to cause her pain.

He had seen the hurt in her eyes when she had seen the state of him and how the curse had ravaged him, and had felt her desperate need to help him. If he stayed with her, she would be forced to watch him fade like that every time they made love, and if she couldn't find a way to break the curse, she would grow more and more desperate, and more and more upset with herself. Her inability to help him would destroy her.

He couldn't let that happen.

He needed to find a way to break this curse without hurting her.

But what if he broke it and it changed things between them? What if everything he felt for her was just the spell manipulating his feelings?

It couldn't be.

He didn't want it to be.

He needed to know if this feeling was real and there was only one way to find out.

His senses reached outwards, to the world outside the house, and the familiar rain-soaked green mountains that enclosed it. He had known the moment the incubus had landed with him and Hella in this room that he was close to home.

Close to the fae town in Fort William where the redheaded witch lived.

His gut said that she wouldn't be kind enough to lift the curse and free him from it if he asked her.

Which left him with one option.

Kill the witch and hope it broke the curse.

CHAPTER 25

Hella stretched and grinned, feeling wonderful from head to toe. It was amazing how fantastic sex could improve your mood. She rolled onto her left side and frowned when she found the spot beside her empty.

Where was Kin?

Maybe he was taking a shower.

Her blood warmed at the thought of joining him and she tossed the dark covers off her, rolled to her other side and out of bed. She padded barefoot around it, picking her way through the pieces of wood and glass that were still scattered around the floor, her smile growing a little wider as she spotted one of her stockings draped over the remains of a drawer.

Kin had removed them in the most delicious way when she had woken him in the early hours, unable to resist the need that had built inside her as she had watched him sleeping. He had smoothed her stockings down her legs, kissing the skin he revealed as he went, sensitising it and bringing her entire body alive. He had tortured her mercilessly with his tongue for what had felt like hours before he had finally listened to her plea to give her what she really needed from him.

They had worn each other out, fooling around until dawn, and she had drifted off in his arms again.

She had never experienced such an incredible, blissful night with a man, and she didn't want to experience anything like it again if Kin wasn't the one sharing it with her.

Mother earth, she was smitten with him.

More than smitten.

She pushed the bathroom door open and frowned when she saw it was empty. Where was he?

Had he gone down for breakfast?

She found her carpet bag, pulled out a black empire-line dress and fresh underwear. She dressed quickly, shoved her feet back into her boots and hurried to the door, finger-combing her blue hair as she went. She paused and looked back at her bag. Rushed back to it and sifted through the contents, looking for a potion.

When she found the small, violet teardrop-shaped glass vial, she checked the label she always liked to put on the potion to make sure it was the right one.

Drink me.

She intended to do just that, using the spell to transport not just her this time. She wanted to take Kin to the nearby fae town to see if they could find the witch who had cursed him and get her to remove it. Travelling via the potion was faster than taking a taxi.

Hella slipped it into the pocket in her dress and left the room, all but ran downstairs to the dining room. She was sure Kin would be there, filling his stomach and replacing the calories they had burned last night. Maybe she could refuel him in another, more wicked way before they hit the fae town. He did need to keep his strength up after all and she worried the curse was probably already draining him again.

She stopped at the entrance to the dining room and stared at the occupants seated around the table.

Tiny stood and ran a trembling hand over his scruffy sandy hair. "Would you like some breakfast?"

She waved him away. "Have you seen Kin?"

He shook his head.

Deep voices rolled along the corridor behind her and she looked over her shoulder at Mort and Rane.

"Where should we start with the research now Fenix has gone back to stalking his mate?" Mort said and Rane shrugged, rolling his shoulders beneath his black T-shirt. "He's going to want leads or at least some answers when he gets back."

"Have you seen Kin?" she said.

Rane muttered, "No."

Mort glanced at the wall to his left. "Saw the wolf running this morning."

"Around the grounds?" She supposed she had kept him cooped up most of yesterday.

The blond incubus shook his head, his hazel eyes serious as he pointed to a spot behind her. "Over the mountain."

Her stomach dropped, an uneasy feeling flowing through her as her heart stung. "He's gone?"

Mort gave her a disinterested look and pushed past her. "Guess so."

"And you didn't think to... I don't know... maybe wake me up and tell me?" she snapped as she turned to keep her eyes locked on his back, anger spiking her blood to chase out the hurt. Her fingertips tingled as her magic raced to them, clearly feeling she needed protection.

She wasn't the one who needed protection right now.

"You limp dicked bastard," she bit out as she glared at Mort, aware he hadn't told her on purpose, that he had wanted MacKinnon gone for some reason. Because he fancied his chances with her if her wolf was out of the picture? Like hell she would ever stoop to sleeping with Mort. Kin was the only one she wanted. She spat, "Enjoy the next two weeks of not being able to get it up!"

Mort pivoted towards her, his eyes wide as horror flashed across his face. She didn't hang around to hear his complaints or pointless pleas for her to undo the spell she had cast on him. She raced from the mansion, not even slowing when she reached the gravel that covered the driveway, her eyes fixed on the mountains that surrounded the grey granite house.

She knew where Kin was going.

He wasn't going home.

He was heading to the fae town. He was going to find the witch, and gods, Hella hoped she was wrong about the reason he was looking for her. Her heart ached, cold at the thought she might not be, that everything that had happened over the last few days might have been a lie.

That it all might have been a lie.

She reached the perimeter stone wall and scrambled over it, and stilled on the other side, awareness drumming inside her. Running would get her nowhere. Kin was faster than she was. She would never catch up with him before he reached the fae town. Her only hope was beating him there and stopping him, and she wasn't sure she wanted to do that.

Part of her wanted to know the truth and see what his plan had been.

The rest of her couldn't bear the thought of discovering none of it had been real for him.

Hella pulled the potion from her pocket, her hand shaking and heart swaying back and forth as she stared at it. It couldn't be a lie. Everything they had shared last night had to have been real. She had never opened up to anyone like that, and deep in her heart she felt Kin was the same. He had never opened up to someone like he had with her. This thing happening between them had to be real.

It had to mean something.

She flicked the lid off the vial and swallowed the contents, and focused on a spot in the fae town where she had always lingered during her visits to take everything in.

Someone gasped as she appeared next to the best café in the town, one at the start of the witches' district. She glanced at the black-clad women and scattering of men who occupied the circular tables that spilled out onto the cobbled road, singling out the one who had been shocked by her arrival.

"Have you seen a wolf shifter come through here? About this tall. Dark hair. Silver eyes. Possibly wearing a long-sleeved top and black jeans and looking a bit frantic?" She willed the witch to say that she had, but the mousy-haired woman shook her head.

Damn.

Hella looked both ways along the wide curving street, unsure where to start. Kin could be in any one of the white buildings that hugged the road, their jewel-coloured canopies reaching towards the middle of it and complementing the shiny green, violet and blue tiles that formed the undulating roofs that had always reminded her of dragons. She looked at the upper floors of several of the buildings, wondering if he was up there.

Maybe she had gotten lucky and he hadn't arrived yet.

She cast a glance over her right shoulder, up at the ochre wall of the cavern where the tunnel to the surface exited and met the stairs that wound down into the town.

"I saw someone matching that description."

She whipped back around to face the owner of that voice, a witch with short violet hair and a white pinafore over her black dress. The woman removed several cups of coffee from her tray and placed them on the table occupied by three men, not noticing the way one of them gazed at her.

Kin had looked at her like that once, with a mixture of desire and adoration in his eyes.

"Which way did he go?" Hella looked both ways along the street again, unable to focus on the witch in case she missed catching a glimpse of Kin in the crowd. The witches' district was busy as always, the road packed with people out for a stroll or looking for a potion.

"That way." She pointed to a narrow alley between two buildings on the other side of the road. "He was hauling arse."

"Thank you." Hella turned in that direction and chanted an incantation in her mind as magic swirled down to her fingertips. Now that she knew where he had gone, it was easier for her to track him with a spell. She wouldn't need to cast one that could split and search in several directions, saving her strength.

She had the feeling she was going to need it.

She turned her right hand upwards and brought it before her as she neared the end of the incantation and a small golden orb formed above her palm.

The second she had finished the spell, the orb flashed and shot away from her.

Hella hurried after it, her boots pounding the cobbles as she sprinted down the alley. The orb shot right and she skidded as she turned to follow it, and ran faster as it began to accelerate, moving away from her. Not good. She tracked it down another alley and then another, watching it get further and further away from her no matter how fast she ran, and just as she was sure she was going to lose it, it stopped.

Hovered in the air in front of a door.

Kin was in there?

She looked up at the height of the grey three-storey building, an unusual choice for a witch. Normally fae and other immortals lived in these houses in the centre of the town, and the shifters, witches and demons stuck to their districts.

Hella gathered her strength and approached the door. The golden orb fizzled and disappeared as she reached it and she blew out her breath as she stared at the black wooden door. To knock or not to knock?

She went with not knocking, even when her stomach squirmed at the thought of her sneaking inside and seeing something she didn't want to witness. She held her nerve, telling herself that what she had with Kin was real and that he wouldn't betray her with another.

She was his fated one after all.

Or at least he thought she was.

The jury was still out on that one.

The door wasn't locked. It eased open as she twisted the knob and she stepped inside, refusing to creep or move with stealth. Not because she feared seeing something she didn't want to see and wanted to disturb them, but because she wasn't the kind of witch to pussyfoot.

She tipped her chin up and squared her shoulders, but no one was in any of the downstairs rooms she checked and she began to wonder whether her spell was wrong and Kin wasn't here.

And then someone moved upstairs.

Hella hurried up the twisting wooden staircase to the first floor and spotted an open door at the end of the hall. She gathered her confidence, and her magic, as she strode towards it, sure that Kin was there.

And he wasn't alone.

"We had a bargain, Grant MacKinnon of clan MacKinnon, and you swore you would fulfil it."

Hella frowned as that high, feminine voice echoed along the corridor, trying to place it and sure that she knew it.

What kind of deal had Kin struck with this female? He had said the witch had cursed him. That didn't sound like a deal to her.

"Come, wolf."

He growled, the sound pure malevolence.

Or hunger.

She rushed into the room, needing to see what was happening.

His broad shoulders tensed beneath his dark Henley as she entered behind him and pain lanced her heart when she spotted the feminine hand on his right shoulder. Polished black nails pressed into his flesh, clutching him as his head bent towards the female before him.

That female leaned to one side, peering past his arm to her.

"Godiva," Hella breathed as she set eyes on the tall, beautiful redhead.

The witch stepped into view, her hand remaining on Kin's shoulder, and Hella wanted to rush to him and tear Godiva's hand away from him. She really wanted to separate them when she noticed the slinky, long black dress Godiva wore, one that had a slit up the right side to flash a lot of leg.

Godiva's dark eyes brightened as her burgundy lips curled into a smile. Something was different about her. Hella couldn't quite place it as she stared the witch down, and forgot all about it when she spoke.

"Ah, you did bring her to me as promised!" Godiva cast an adoring look at MacKinnon and then shot Hella a sly smile.

Hella's ears rang, realisation hitting her like a wrecking ball to shatter her confidence.

And her heart.

It fractured into a thousand pieces, any warmth she had felt and all her feelings for Kin pouring from it to churn in her chest into something raw and hot that had magic racing to her fingertips and set her blood on fire.

The wolf had known how to lift his curse and free himself of it.

And here she was.

Just as he had planned.

She cast a disappointed look at him and knew it came off wounded when Godiva grinned and stroked his shoulder. MacKinnon angled his head towards her, but he didn't look at her. He kept looking at Godiva.

Hella stepped back from him as anger built inside her, destroying all her softer emotions.

"Was this the plan all along?" she spat and glared at him. "She cursed you so I would see it and would end up trying to help you, and you would get close enough to me to betray me by bringing me here to her? If I had known, I would have slammed the door in your face that day as I damned well should have!"

Instead, she had surrendered to her desire and it had deepened her feelings for him, transforming them from like into something that was now tearing her apart, just as she had feared.

She swore hurt glittered in his eyes but he still didn't look at her.

She tried to calm her magic, wanting to use it to see whether Godiva was manipulating him, but it refused to settle while her feelings were in disarray, her mind churning at a rapid pace and her heart aching as if he had plunged a knife into her chest.

"Since you have fulfilled your end of the bargain by luring the witch to me as you promised, you may wait for me in the adjoining room for your reward," Godiva said, her imperious air making Hella want to fly at the bitch and rip her red hair from her head.

But she was too busy staring at the wolf as his eyes changed, the sharp edge of anger they had held melting away into something akin to regret.

Or perhaps relief.

"Yes, wolf, you fulfilled your end of the *bargain*," Hella bit out and he frowned at her now, coming to face her, but he still didn't step away from Godiva. She knew she was being unreasonable but the thought that he really had betrayed her, that he had orchestrated this whole thing, making her fall for him, hurt so badly that she couldn't breathe and couldn't bear the sight of him. "You may leave."

He growled at her, flashing fangs, and got that look in his eyes, the one that always made her feel as if he was considering putting her over his knee.

She focused on Godiva, shutting him out as she tried to pull herself together and put things into perspective, something that was hard as his presence sucked the air from the room and made her ache with a need to fall into his arms and beg him to tell her that Godiva was lying.

What she really needed to do was beat the living hell out of Godiva.

"You spineless bitch," she spat and Godiva's dark eyes widened, and Hella wasn't buying her apparent shock because she was sure plenty of people had called the witch worse things over the years. "You cursed him to get to me because of Ethyrian and you should have just come at me instead."

"Oh, but this was more fun. You took something of mine, and I took something of yours." Godiva smiled slowly and stepped up behind MacKinnon. She stroked her hand over his chest and he didn't push her away. Hella hated that the witch knew the pain she had caused, that she knew that Hella had recklessly fallen for MacKinnon and now she was paying for it. Godiva slid him a heated look. "You should wait in the other room. I'll be done in a moment and then we can catch up."

Hella glared at her, magic swirling around her fingertips now, a maelstrom that lacked direction as she struggled to focus on something other than the way Godiva was running her hands over MacKinnon's chest and how he was slowly turning his face towards her as his eyes began to glow gold.

She couldn't watch this. Even if it was a spell making him do this, this betrayal was too real.

Hurt too much.

She raised her hand and unfiltered magic shot from her fingertips as she screamed, struck the air between Godiva and MacKinnon and hurled them apart. Godiva slammed into the wall between two windows and landed with a grunt on the wooden floor. MacKinnon hit a partition wall with such force that he went straight through it.

"I never took anything from you!" Hella barked and tasted the lie on her tongue. She clenched her jaw and reined in her anger, trying to focus her turbulent thoughts and stop her magic from reacting again. "Look, if I had known Ethyrian had gone to that masquerade ball with someone, I would never have left with him. I saw you dance with him a couple of times, but he gave me no indication that you had come together and he never mentioned you once in the time we were together."

The tips of Godiva's long red hair fluttered as she picked herself up, her expression blackening as stars lit her dark eyes, and Hella felt like a bitch, which was wrong on so many levels given how much Godiva had just hurt her.

Hella held her hands up by her sides. "But you know what... you win. You can have Ethyrian. Please... take him."

She hesitated as MacKinnon stepped through the hole in the wall.

Only he looked not at her, but at Godiva.

She focused on him, running through an incantation in her mind, devoting all of her attention to it and shunning her hurt and anger. When she managed to complete it without a hitch, which surprised her given how the wolf was staring at the other witch with heat in his eyes, she waggled her finger in his direction.

And felt nothing.

If he had been under a spell, she would have sensed it.

Which meant his actions were done of his own free will. She kept telling herself that it was possible she was mistaken, but it wouldn't stick, and in the end the pain became too much and she needed air, needed to get away from him for a moment at the very least.

Forever at most.

This was for the best.

She sucked down a breath, gathered the pieces of her broken heart, and looked into Godiva's eyes, shutting out the wolf.

"You can have both of them," Hella growled. "I want nothing to do with either the nymph or this wolf."

Hella wasn't sure what she had expected in response to that. Some wild attempt to stop her from MacKinnon? A growl? A howl of rage? A sign that he wasn't himself. That was what she had wanted. A powerful enough reaction would come to the surface regardless of any spell he was under. The fact that he just stood there, not even looking at her cut her to her soul and told her what he wouldn't.

It was over.

CHAPTER 26

MacKinnon internally howled in rage as Hella walked out of the door, his body refusing to obey his commands to intercept and stop her. He continued to stare at the witch, Godiva, fury mounting inside him as his wolf side continued to howl and savagely attack his mortal form, desperate to go after Hella.

Godiva sauntered towards him, sighed and leisurely dusted plaster from his shoulders, her touch revolting him. He wanted to growl at her, but his damned lips wouldn't move and his voice wouldn't work. All he could do was glare.

"That wasn't very nice of her, was it?" she said, her voice light, with no trace of the guilt she deserved to be feeling in it. She had just ruined everything.

Had that been her plan all along?

Bringing Hella to her had never been the way to break his curse. This was what the witch had really wanted. She had wanted to hurt Hella in the way she had been hurt. In the end, she had hurt both Hella and him. She had destroyed everything.

His wolf howled, but not in rage this time. It bayed, the sound mournful as it called for Hella, as he ached to have his wee witch back in his arms and make her see the truth.

He had come here to fight the witch and make her release him from the curse in exchange for not killing her, and if she had refused, he had intended to take her life and hope it would shatter the spell on him.

Only the moment he had confronted her, she had cast another spell on him, one that had stolen control of his body and turned him into her puppet.

And he realised now it was because she had known Hella was coming.

Godiva had wanted her to witness him apparently enthralled with her, unable to take his eyes off her, and he was going to kill the witch for how deeply she had hurt Hella with that trick.

But first, he needed to escape this spell somehow.

He needed to go after Hella.

Godiva paled and pressed a hand to her head, and for a moment he thought she would pass out, but then she rallied, pretending she was only brushing dirt from her forehead.

What was wrong with her? She wasn't well, he could tell that much. She looked different to before, as if the curse had been ravaging her strength too, wearing her down. The moment he had seen her, he had noticed she was thinner and her eyes were no longer as bright.

Or maybe it wasn't the curse that had done this to her.

He thought about what Abigail had said about dark magic—that it often demanded a high price from the caster.

Was it possible Godiva really had used a spell to discover who Hella's fated mate was so she could send them after her?

If she had, then Hella was his fated one and he had just lost her.

"You look… upset." Godiva ran her black painted fingertips over his cheeks, gently angling his head towards her. "I could kiss it better."

He bared fangs at her.

A start.

"I take that as a no." Godiva twisted away from him and moved beyond his reach, giving him the impression she knew her hold over him was waning. She thought such a paltry distance would stop him from removing her head. She was mistaken. She smiled over her shoulder at him. "I suppose you did hold up your end of the deal."

He tried to speak and managed to move his lips.

Kin pushed words out of them. "Never… had… deal. Cursed. Break."

It would do.

Godiva clearly got the message because she pulled a face. "Only if you vow not to kill me."

He glared at her. He wanted to rip her apart with his fangs, but he managed to force a nod. He would track her down and kill her later, after he had found Hella and made her see the truth—that he loved her and had only come here to make the witch lift his curse, but she had manipulated him.

Although part of him was sure that once Hella gave him a chance to explain himself that she would be the one coming to kill the witch.

He hoped.

Gods, it was wrong of him, but he hoped she was so angry that she came after Godiva, because it would show him how deep her feelings for him ran. He needed to see that now more than ever.

"Vow it." Godiva swept her hand through the air.

MacKinnon's body suddenly felt heavier and he stumbled a step forwards, placing his right foot out in front of him to stop himself from falling, and shook his head. He narrowed his eyes on Godiva, battling the urge to tear her apart now.

"I vow it," he grumbled, reminding himself that now was not the time for his revenge.

Hella was out there, hurting and angry with him, and he needed to find her. The quicker he set about doing that, the easier it would be to track her down.

"Lift this curse," he growled and took a step towards Godiva.

"I can't." She stared into his eyes, her face a cool mask even as he flashed fangs at her.

"What do you mean, you can't?" he barked and took another hard step towards her. "Listen to me, you vile bint, and listen well—"

"It's a curse, dummy," she interjected as she eased down onto a chair and again looked ready to pass out. "It broke the moment you brought her to me."

So he had vowed not to kill her for no reason. Godsdammit. He growled at himself now, feeling like an idiot for not putting two and two together, but then he had never been cursed before. His growl became a snarl of frustration as he realised that if he had told Hella about the way to break his curse rather than keeping it secret from her, she probably would have pointed out that he only had to bring her to Godiva in order to break it. He didn't actually have to betray her or do anything sinister.

Hell, his wee witch probably would have insisted they visit Godiva together, thus freeing him of the curse.

"Hear me well, witch." He flashed fangs with each word, driving his point home. "You come near me, my clan or Hella again and I will end you."

Godiva merely waved him away, a disinterested look on her face. "Be gone. I have important matters to attend to."

Kin snorted. "If you think to win the nymph back, think again. He wants Hella as his bride."

Her dark eyes widened. "He what?"

He relished how horrified she looked, how he had rattled her with only a handful of words, but then his smile faded. Ethyrian did want Hella, and now she was alone, no doubt returned to her home in Geneva.

Vulnerable.

Everything inside him howled at him to move and he was out of the door in a flash, his heart thundering as he bounded down the stairs and out into the street.

Because his fated female was in danger.

Kin skidded to a halt at the end of an alley, breathing hard.

His fated female.

He pressed a hand to his chest, feeling his heart drumming hard, and focused on himself, shutting the world out. A feeling grew inside him, becoming more powerful by the second as he thought about Hella. Need rolled through him, an urge so strong that it overwhelmed all reason, had him running again, frantically following the warren of alleyways towards the main street.

He growled as he hit it and barrelled through the crowd, wild with a need to reach his destination, because his female was in danger.

His fated female.

He felt it all the way to his bones—to his soul.

Hella was the other half of that soul, the one female in this world who had been made for him to love, to cherish and protect. Hella was his true mate and Godiva had discovered it at great cost to her health and had brought them together. He growled, far from happy about that, torn in two by it. He despised the witch and her curse, but at the same time, he owed the bitch. He might have never found Hella without her.

Kin made it to Abigail's shop. The bell above the door tinkled and he tried to slow as a brunet male dressed in a long fitted black coat stepped out of the store, but he was going too fast. He bumped into him, knocking him back into the door as it closed behind him. The male turned cold dark eyes on him and the air charged in a way Kin had never felt before.

He didn't smell the tinny scent of magic or feel the familiar electrical spark.

The air chilled as if the temperature had plummeted to an Artic level and a weight pressed down on him as the male witch's eyes narrowed on his, his lips thinning as his jaw clenched.

And then the son of a bitch looked over his shoulder, through the glass in the door, pushed his black-rimmed glasses up his nose with his index finger and relaxed as he stepped towards Kin.

The brunet's touch was light on Kin's chest, but the force of it was enough to have him almost falling into a stack of copper cauldrons. He fought for balance as the male casually walked past him and breathed a sigh of relief when the bastard disappeared into the crowd.

Kin frowned and huffed again.

His breath fogged in the air.

He shuddered and rubbed his arms. He never wanted to see that man again, that was for sure.

Kin pushed the shop door open, his gaze seeking Abigail, a need to make sure she was all right flooding him. She looked up from a book she had open on the counter.

"Kin!" Her bright smile hit him hard and he was glad she was fine.

"Lovely customers you have, little witch." He stepped deeper into the shop. "Never met a witch who could chill the air with a look like that."

Her delicate features grew guarded. "Don't mess with that one."

A chill skated down his spine. It wasn't often Abigail issued warnings. In fact, he swore it was the first time he had seen her looking and sounding so serious. How dangerous was the male he had almost sent crashing through the door? How badly would things have gone for him if that had happened?

He looked over his shoulder at the door.

"Leave it," she said, drawing his focus back to her. She smiled again, but it wobbled a little and fell from her lips. "Seriously, Kin. Don't."

For a moment, he thought she wanted to protect him, and he was going to tell her he wasn't the sort to provoke a powerful witch, which given his current situation would have been a lie.

But she silenced him by gazing out of the window and whispering, "He has enough problems."

Kin looked there too and then back at her, not missing the soft look in her eyes before she plastered another breezy smile on her face. Abigail felt protective of the man he had almost mown down, which was interesting given the fact that he had seemed more than capable of taking care of himself and any threat to his well-being.

He wanted to probe more about the male, but added it to the list of things to do once he had found Hella and set things straight with her.

"I need a token. Good for... maybe a dozen trips." He didn't hide how badly he needed it when she shot him a curious look, let her see how torn up he was by what had happened and how afraid he was too. "I found the witch who cursed me and went to make her lift it, and my wee witch... Hella... she found me there. The hackit bint Godiva cast a spell on me to make me do her bidding and now... my mate... she thinks I betrayed her and she's madder than hell at me and I need to talk to her... but she's a witch. I'm getting the feeling she'll be teleporting my arse back home every time I try to make her see she's wrong about me... at least the first few times."

Hopefully, if he kept showing up on her doorstep, he would eventually wear her down enough that she would give him a chance to explain things.

And confess some things too.

Like the fact he was madly in love with her.

And that she was his fated one.

Gods, the way she had looked at him still cut him to his soul, had him bleeding inside and losing hope. He wasn't sure he could make her believe him, but he had to try. She could use her teleportation trick on him as many times as she wanted—she wasn't going to get rid of him that easily.

Even if he had to move to her fae town so his home was there and she couldn't teleport him far away from her, slowing him down, he would keep trying until she finally listened to him.

"Here." Abigail dumped a cardboard box on the counter and the wooden tokens it contained rattled. "You might need the whole lot if you've upset a witch who can use teleportation spells."

Kin glared at her, but grabbed a handful, enough for at least two dozen teleports. He removed one and shoved the rest in the pocket of his black jeans. "Put it on my tab."

"Good luck!" Abigail called as he raced out of the door, heading for the nearest portal, and he frowned as she muttered, "You're so going to need it."

He was well aware of that.

Kin hit the point where the portal was and palmed his token as he ran through the necessary words, faster than usual, and tacked on his destination. The second he touched down in the Geneva fae town, he was sprinting towards Hella's house, weaving through the promenade crowd.

He ran through what he was going to say as the flagstones gave way to cobbles and he left the townhouses and elegantly dressed immortals behind. He was sure she was going to teleport him the moment she saw him, but he would use the time to instruct Gregor to have the car ready and be prepared to drive him back to Fort William.

For at least the next few days.

If he couldn't make Hella see sense by then, he would temporarily relocate to this town as a last resort. He hated the thought of leaving his pack undefended and without their alpha, but Gregor would take care of them in his stead while he smoothed things over with his witch. Gregor would understand, and he was sure his pack would too. He was sure they all wanted to see him happy.

His strides slowed as he approached the small rundown white house and he saw the door was open. His senses stretched outwards, sharpening until he could hear and smell everything.

And his stomach dropped.

He could smell Hella but the scent was faint.

Tinged with an acrid note.

Fear.

He hurried to the door and growled when he saw it wasn't just open, it was hanging off its hinges. Ice skittered down his spine as he stepped into the room—a room that looked as if he had gone at it in a rage. He didn't think the place was a mess because she had packed up and left in a hurry to avoid him, because she kept everything of value in her precious carpet bag. Not only that, but books and broken glass littered the floor. She wouldn't have left those tomes behind or broken so much of her vital equipment and ingredients bottles if she had been packing to leave. She would have been careful with them.

The table had been tipped over too, so the top faced him, and the armchair had been toppled and dragged closer to the door.

She hadn't left by choice.

He drew down a deeper breath, catching her scent and a hint of masculine musk that was familiar.

Nymph.

He growled low as rage curled through his veins.

The king had found her.

CHAPTER 27

Hella was in the deepest sort of shit. She had been so hurt and angry when she had been walking through the Geneva fae town after exiting the portal that she hadn't been paying attention to her surroundings.

And she had walked right into a trap.

She hadn't noticed the nymphs in her temporary home until it had been too late. This time, Ethyrian wasn't playing around either. The second she had stepped into her home, a spell had activated, freezing her in place. Meaning the nymph had hired a witch to do his dirty work. Guards had rushed in before she could figure out the counter-spell and she had ended up with a very fancy new pair of bracelets.

The kind that stripped her magic from her.

Not only that, but she was no longer a guest in the ivory tower of Ethyrian's castle.

She was now a certified prisoner, slumming it in a dank cell that was more than a little smelly. Water dripped somewhere in the distance, the constant plip-plip-plip driving her insane, and something kept skittering around in the dark and she hoped it didn't try to eat her, because she had no way to defend herself.

She cursed the silver cuffs that were tight around her wrists, not the one-size-fits-all that the nymphs had used on her before. They had been tailored specifically for her.

She cursed Kin too.

Hella rubbed her bare knees and hugged them as she sat on the damp, thin mattress someone had slung on the stone floor for her. She had never had her heart broken before, but she figured this was what it felt like. She couldn't even muster the energy to yell and scream until the guards got annoyed enough that they came to shut her up.

For a moment there, everything had been perfect.

Or as close to perfect as it had ever been.

She'd had a good, somewhat growly and possessive, guy she could have probably smoothed the rough edges off to upgrade him to great. She had been having mind-blowing and earth-shattering sex. And for the first time she had signed up as the small spoon in a cuddle-fest that had given her the best sleep of her life.

And she had felt loved.

And that was the real kick in the lady balls.

She didn't remember ever feeling so loved.

Her family had pushed her off onto the coven as soon as they were able and had never wanted her back for the holidays, and it had made her feel as if she didn't deserve love, as if she was going to go through her life without finding someone she loved who loved her in return.

And then Kin had come along.

And part of her had foolishly believed he loved her in the way she loved him.

Hella huffed, aiming it at herself and not him. She knew she was being mopey when she should be being kickass and escaping, but she was tired and needed a moment to lick her wounds.

She didn't have any proof that MacKinnon really had been pulling the wool over her eyes the whole time. She also didn't have any proof that he had been under the influence of magic when she had found him with Godiva. And she had no chance of following through with her plan to get to the bottom of things and find out the truth now anyway.

Ethyrian wasn't exactly going to let her go back to the fae town and continue her work, and he definitely wouldn't let her out of his sight—or out of whatever gilded cage he constructed for her—if he knew about the wolf. MacKinnon was possessive of her, but he wouldn't hold a candle to Ethyrian if the nymph knew she had feelings for another male.

She needed to be careful not to mention the wolf.

She frowned and sighed. Apparently, some part of her was already on the way to forgiving MacKinnon and still believed in him. The rest of her was convinced he was a no-good lying bastard. She clasped her knees and stared at the wall opposite her, going in circles as she thought about him and what had happened, trying to get to the truth, even if it was one that hurt her.

She replayed everything that had happened in that room with Godiva and MacKinnon, and something dawned on her—Godiva *had* looked different. The dark circles beneath her eyes and the sallowness of her skin had been subtle, but when Hella compared how she had looked then to how she had looked at the ball in Paris, it was clear as day. Godiva was sick.

Hella frowned at her knees.

Or maybe sick wasn't quite right.

Back at her coven, there had been a cage in the library, a place where they kept dangerous tomes that contained dark magic. The books had been there so the teachers could show students what dark spells looked like and lecture them on the dangers of using such magic. A group of girls had broken into the cage one night and convinced a young witch to do one of the spells, telling her it was the only way she could join their group.

The witch had ended up in the infirmary, a hollowed-out shell of herself.

Hella had seen her through the window and had felt bad for her. She had looked so gaunt and vacant, and although she had returned to something akin to her normal self after months of recuperation, she had never been the same. The spell had ravaged her strength, stealing years of her life according to the teachers who had used her as an example and a warning to avoid dark magic.

Had Godiva used dark magic? The more Hella considered all the possible spells the witch could have used to fool MacKinnon into feeling Hella was his mate, the more she began to feel he hadn't been fooled. Such spells wouldn't have lasted as long as MacKinnon had been after Hella. They would have faded and lost their hold on him, and Godiva would have been forced to renew the spell on him to keep him convinced that Hella was his mate.

Godiva hadn't used light magic to trick the wolf into thinking Hella was his fated one.

The foolish witch had employed dark magic to find out who Hella's fated one was and then she had tracked down MacKinnon and cursed him to make sure he did as she wanted.

Which meant he really was her fated one.

She didn't have time to process that. The iron door of her cell creaked open.

"Up," the guard grunted and she flicked him a bored look. "The king wishes to speak with you."

He said that as if she should be honoured by it, so she rolled her eyes.

"You can deliver a message to your king," she said and flipped the guard off.

The blond male stomped into her cell, seized hold of her and dragged her onto her feet, his grip bruising as he pressed his fingers into her flesh. She struggled and scratched at his hand, scoring red marks across his perfect pale skin, and he didn't even flinch. He just dragged her from the cell and along the corridor, moving quicker than she could manage. She grimaced as she trod in a puddle and something squished between her bare toes, silently cursed the guard who had taken her boots from her, declaring their heels could be used as a weapon.

She stubbed a toe on the first stone step of the staircase and took her anger out on the guard, punching his hand to make herself feel better and hoping it hurt more than her throbbing toe did.

He carried on up the spiral staircase as if she wasn't even there, pulling her along with him. It grew lighter as they left the dungeon behind, the air becoming fresh enough that she could breathe without gagging. She sucked down deep breaths, savouring each one that purged the smell and taste of rotting flesh and bodily functions from her lungs, mouth and nose.

When they reached the top of the stairs, the guard shoved her in front of him, almost slamming her into the wall.

She scowled over her shoulder at him. "You really should work on your manners."

He didn't even bother looking at her. He kept his eyes forward, fixed on a point beyond her as he marched her towards what felt like her doom.

Female servants scurried around, those who were moving along the corridor rather than crossing it pausing to bow their heads as the guard approached them. Nymphs. Even the lowest among them expected women to be subservient.

Which was so not her style.

So, while Ethyrian's castle might be rather impressive, with the solid gold detailing that covered the ivory walls and ceilings of the wide corridor and ribbons of that precious metal coursing through the pale marble floors, and might have swayed a weaker woman with the promise of riches and a life of luxury, she was going to have to escape again.

She just needed to figure out how.

And soon.

The clock was ticking.

She felt that deep in her gut as they finished navigating the corridors, passing elegant drawing rooms and even a gallery that had paintings and sculptures of past kings, and entered an enormous double-height room.

Ethyrian sat on a throne on a dais of turquoise stone and gold at the far end of it, dressed in a fine white silk shirt and rich green leathers that hugged his thighs as he spread his knees and gazed at her.

Her guard pushed her in the back when she instinctively stopped, feeling like a prey animal that was about to get served up to the worst sort of predator.

She tipped her chin up and her shoulders back, refusing to let Ethyrian see her fear as she strode towards him along the rich turquoise strip of carpet that lined the centre of the impressive room. The arched ceiling was pure glass, with only narrow beams of solid gold supporting it, revealing the strange twilight sky of Lucia. Aurora chased across the faint stars, and it would have been beautiful had her current company not been so terrifying or her fate so dire.

The guard shoved her again and she scowled over her shoulder at him. He glared at her this time. If she'd had her boots, she would have driven her heel into his toe. If she'd had her magic, she would have brought the glass ceiling down on him and Ethyrian. Too many ifs. She needed to focus on what she could do in her current state.

She considered her options as she marched towards Ethyrian.

It didn't take long.

Her magic was bound—meaning she was as strong as a mortal—and no one knew where she was. Essentially, she was screwed.

But if she was going down, she was going down fighting.

With words at least.

"Your royal douchebag." She dipped in a curtsey as the guard pulled her to a stop twenty feet from his king.

Ethyrian's broad mouth flattened and his blue eyes flashed dangerously. "Your misbehaviour will not gain you what you want. I have learned your tricks. You escaped my tower. You cannot escape a cell. You fled from my men. You could not flee from a trap."

He had her there.

She shrugged.

He drummed the fingers of his left hand against the golden arm of his throne and it was nice to see that she was already getting to him.

"When you are queen, you will act appropriately or you will be punished." His tone brooked no argument.

So Hella decided to argue with him.

"If you want a queen, that witch you dumped to pursue me is open to the position. She even sent someone to take me out of the picture. Godiva honestly thought I was still with you and wanted a crown on my head!" She rolled her eyes. "I want neither of those things and I told her as much, so she'll probably be swinging by soon to see you. I'm sure she'll fawn over you all you want, so you have no need of me… now if you'd be a dear, I'll be on my way."

She lifted her hands before her and looked at her restraints.

"Silence!" Ethyrian pushed to his feet.

"No," she bit out and tilted her chin up. "Let me go. I'll make a terrible queen. You'll be lucky to make it through our wedding night with your manhood still in place."

He raised his left hand.

The guard behind her kicked her in the back of her knees.

She grunted as her legs buckled and she landed hard on the carpet.

Ethyrian smiled wickedly, far too much pleasure and amusement in his eyes for her liking. He knew he had the power here, that all she could do was bark and snap her fangs at him. She was beginning to see how Kin had felt all the times she had chained him, and regret was swift to flare again, worse this time. It chipped away at her strength as she thought about the wolf.

"Crawl to me," he drawled.

Hella glared at him and mustered her strength, clinging to it. "Go to hell."

Ethyrian stepped down from the dais and pointed to the toes of his dark green knee-high boots. "Crawl to me and beg me for mercy."

"Mercy?" She scoffed. "You don't know the meaning of the word. You're going to wed me without my permission. Where's the mercy in that?"

His slow smile chilled her blood and her instincts screamed that he was up to something, that she was playing a dangerous game by denying him what he wanted.

"I was not asking you to beg for mercy for yourself. Your fate is sealed." He took another step towards her, the action stealing her breath as she looked up at him, into eyes that were glacial now. "I speak of the wolf."

"MacKinnon?" she breathed, a chill sweeping down her arms and spine. "You know about him?"

"The male seeks to take what is mine and must be dealt with—"

"What is with ego-tripping men thinking they own me all the time?" She shot to her feet, cutting him off as anger blasted through her, obliterating the momentary spike in her fear.

Ethyrian continued without missing a beat. "And you get to decide his fate. If you do not beg for mercy, my guards will capture and kill him. If you do, the borders of my realm will be closed to the wolf and he will live."

The cold look in his eyes told her that he was serious.

What choice did she have? As angry as she was about what Kin had done to her, as hurt as she was, she couldn't let him die.

Because she still loved him.

Hella swallowed her pride and dropped to her knees, hesitated for only a heartbeat before she crawled to Ethyrian as he wanted and sat back on her heels by his boots. She gazed up at him, hating herself and hating him too, and hating Kin a little for making her love him enough that she would do anything for him.

Even this.

"Mercy, Ethyrian. I… I beg of you, my king. Grant mercy to the wolf." Her hope bled from her as his eyes darkened, his face twisting in harsh lines as if he hated each word that left her lips a little more than the last.

Because they revealed she cared about MacKinnon.

Ethyrian leaned over and caught her chin between his fingers and thumb.

His mouth covered hers and she somehow managed not to squirm as he kissed her, sealing her fate.

His blue eyes were hooded, shining with a hunger that repulsed her as he released her and straightened. He clapped his hands and several females rushed into the room, coming to flank her. Hella wasn't surprised to find them dressed in gold bikini tops and bottoms, with a sheer turquoise sarong around their waists. How long would it be before she got her own matching outfit?

"Prepare my bride," he said with a glance at one of the scantily clad women, and then lowered his eyes to lock with hers again as he smiled—one of victory. "I will consummate this marriage before the sun rises on a new day."

Two of the females pulled her onto her feet.

She turned with them, her mood growing darker by the second, one thought spinning around it.

A new plan.

Ethyrian would be dead before dawn.

CHAPTER 28

MacKinnon slipped through the trees that bordered the pale stone wall, wary of the shadows but willing to use them to cover his approach. He froze against the thick trunk of one as he sensed guards approaching, pressed his back to it and listened. Like the other dozen or so guards he had passed, these ones didn't utter a word.

Beyond the wall however, the castle was abuzz.

Something was happening.

He looked to his right, towards a road he had followed to the castle walls, and spied another opulent white carriage approaching, drawn by four horses.

That was the twelfth one to arrive.

Was a celebration taking place tonight?

Kin had to bite back a howl of rage and barely stopped himself from bursting from the bushes to butcher everyone as he realised what was happening.

The nymph king had his bride and intended to wed her as soon as possible.

He held himself back, denying his need to tear the world apart, because not everything was in place yet. People were still arriving, meaning there was still time for him to find Hella and save her.

Another coach rolled along the road, the driver looking impatient. A blond male, clearly a nymph, poked his head out of the window in the door and glared at his servant, and then at the route ahead of them. Whatever angry words he had been about to let fly at the people responsible for holding him up died on his lips and he slunk back into his carriage.

Kin couldn't blame him.

The hold-up was an elegant couple on foot, accompanied by a dozen guards dressed in white armour that covered them from head to toe, leaving only a slit across their eyes open. Several of the guards flexed talons around the staffs of their white and silver spears as the horses behind them whinnied.

They weren't nymphs.

The guards' armour concealed their appearances, but the couple wore fine clothing—a silver-edged white robe for the male and a white dress with a delicate silver scrollwork corset for the female.

Both of them had pointed ears.

Fae.

Their white hair and alabaster skin made him think of the ones his mother had told him about as a pup—the benevolent faeries.

The seelie.

It would explain why the driver of the carriage was so reluctant to force them to move faster. Here in Lucia, the seelie were one of the two great powers. The other was their dark cousins, the unseelie.

Kin noted there were none of those dark fae present.

The nymph king probably didn't want a war breaking out during his wedding.

The seelie and their entourage entered the walls and Kin looked over his left shoulder, gazing up at the castle that towered beyond them. He needed to get in there, and to do that, he needed to blend in with the attendees.

Rather than heading further along the wall, he backtracked, moving from tree to tree, placing some distance between him and the gatehouse. He studied everyone who passed him, cataloguing their size compared with his, and was beginning to think he might have to attempt to slip in unnoticed as he was when he finally spotted a male close to his six-ten and build.

The male's dark blue knee-length tunic and trousers were going to be a bit of a squeeze, but he would manage it.

Kin tracked the male, tailing him and waiting for an opening. When none presented itself and the male was dangerously close to the gate, he lunged from cover, slapped his hand over the male's mouth and dragged him back into the trees. He viciously twisted the fae's neck, snapping his spine, and lowered him to the ground.

And waited.

Sure someone would have spotted him.

When a few painful minutes had ticked past and no guard came to fight him, he stripped the male down to his underwear and shirked his own clothing. As predicted, the trousers were a tight fit, but the material was stretchy enough that they weren't too uncomfortable. The tunic had a little more room in it than he had thought. He finished fastening the silver buttons and picked up the sword belt. An added bonus.

It had been some time since he had fought using a sword, but he was sure he would remember how if he was forced to use it. He tightened the belt around his waist so it cinched in his tunic and the weapon sat snug against his left hip, smoothed his appearance and neatened his hair, and then blew out his breath.

"This is such a stupid idea," he muttered as he approached the road, his nerves rising.

But apparently love made wolves do crazy things.

He held his nerve and stepped out onto the road, quickly moving to blend with a mixed group of immortals who were moving at pace towards the gatehouse. None of the males seemed bothered by his presence as they continued to talk about the honour of being invited to the wedding.

He glanced behind him and frowned as he saw the road was empty, and then looked ahead of him at the castle. The guards had already closed one half of the tall golden arched doors.

Kin stared at the open side, feeling twitchy now as he battled the urge to make a break for it and run through before the guards could shut him out. He pulled down a steadying breath and focused on the castle, on scenting the air and seeking a sign of Hella.

He caught the faintest note of heather.

His heart steadied, his mind calming, and he settled his left hand on the hilt of his sword as he willed her to be strong, to be the same stubborn and wily witch he had come to love.

He was coming for her.

He kept his head down as his group passed the guards and didn't look up until he was deep inside the palace. White stone walls threaded with pure gold and turquoise lined the wide hallway, and there were alcoves at intervals with solid gold statues of nymphs in them. Former kings, he presumed.

The excited chatter grew louder as the movement of the crowd slowed where it reached a towering set of gold doors.

Kin found himself taking in what he could see of the palace, including the painted ceiling that depicted nymphs and females in very compromising positions, all of them in the throes of ecstasy. Gold columns stretched down from it and he was tempted to touch one to see if it was paint or the real deal. He bet it was the real thing. Probably solid too.

Everything about this place screamed wealth.

It made his cottage look like a shithole.

He wasn't sure Hella was going to want to trade this for his home, but then she wasn't here by choice.

This king wanted to own her.

Enslave her.

Kin couldn't let that happen. His blood boiled at the thought of her being treated like that—treated as he had been.

A murmur swept through the crowd, rolling towards him, and he looked at the doors in time to see them open. The room beyond them was vast, with a curving glass ceiling. He followed the crowd as they slowly filed into the room, his gaze darting over what he could see of it as he ventured closer. White walls with golden columns ran the length of the room, and a strip of turquoise carpet edged with gold led the eye to the raised blue stone dais at the far end.

He grew twitchy again as he stepped into the room, his eyes fixed on the golden throne.

The only seat in the house.

The places for guests were marked by gold railings and everyone was standing.

A power play on the nymph's part.

The king wanted to be different to those he viewed as beneath him.

A female dressed in very little held her hand out to Kin's right, her head bent, and he filed in behind several other males, close to the back of the room. He scanned the crowd. There had to be close to five hundred people. Not only that, but in front of every gold column on either side of the room stood a guard and there were a dozen of them lining the far wall, flanking the throne. He glanced back over his shoulder to see the same there. Six guards on either side of the door.

Getting Hella out of this was going to be difficult.

He faced forwards again and his gaze caught on something that threatened to ignite his anger and make him explode.

There was a gold cushion on the floor just in front and slightly to the left of the throne.

A place for Hella to kneel beside her king.

Like an animal.

Kin couldn't hold back his growl, didn't care that it drew a few curious gazes as he glared at the throne, silently making a vow he intended to keep even if it killed him.

The king's death was going to be slow and painful.

And the music started.

CHAPTER 29

It hadn't taken Hella long to realise that the women Ethyrian had summoned to take care of her weren't servants.

They were part of his harem.

And they hated her.

They hadn't said as much with words, but then actions always spoke loudest.

Hella grimaced and gritted her teeth as the one she assumed was the head mistress, a curvy and elegant white-haired female who might be a seelie, tugged the brush through her hair, yanking on her head and probably pulling great hanks out.

"You must be so excited," a pretty young brunette said as she buffed Hella's skin raw with a sponge, making her legs sting beneath the far-too-hot water in the large bathing pool.

"To be chosen to be queen. It is quite the honour." A black-haired beauty with bright blue eyes jabbed Hella beneath her fingernails with a stick.

She snatched her hand back before the woman could torture her some more. "Really, all this fuss isn't necessary."

The mistress yanked on her hair again, her voice sweet. "Oh, but it is. What the king desires, is what the king is given. His orders were very clear."

"I don't think his orders entailed torturing me." She fended off the female with the stick and nudged the brunette with her bare foot, pushing her away. "Really, I'm quite clean."

She stood, trying not to be embarrassed as she rose from the water and the suds rolled down her naked skin. None of the trio tried to make her sit back down, which was a relief. She turned towards the steps out of the huge bathing pool, and the black-haired one took hold of her arm, gripping it just tightly enough that she left red marks on Hella's skin when she had finished *helping* her up the steps and released her.

Hella was tempted to offer them a deal, but her gut said they wouldn't take it. They clearly liked their positions within Ethyrian's harem and while helping her escape would mean he didn't have a queen to replace them with, it also meant they would probably be killed by him in a fit of rage.

The mistress led her into the adjoining bedroom, to a white dressing table that had a large mirror attached to it and a lot of jewellery laid out on the top.

Hella slumped into the chair and tried to be on her best behaviour as the white-haired female came to stand beside her and worked to undo her right cuff. She focused on her fingers as the shackle opened and fell away from her wrist. Not even the faintest tingle. The spell in the single remaining cuff was strong enough to keep her magic in check. So much for escaping that way.

The mistress reached for a wide silver cuff that had a cluster of teardrop sapphires arranged in a pattern in the centre of it and snapped it around Hella's naked wrist. A weight instantly pressed down on her and she glared at the point where it fastened, watching the metal meld together into one seamless piece.

Fantastic. She now had fashionable restraints. Anyone who saw her shiny new bracelet would assume it was just jewellery and not a collar.

A way of changing who she was into something she didn't want to be.

A powerless mortal.

Hella pulled her shit together and reminded herself that she had a plan and it was going to work. While the mistress was replacing her other shackle with a matching bracelet, she idly ran her fingers over the array of jewellery, pretending to be fascinated by how beautiful they were.

Which wasn't difficult, because they were. Gold and diamond necklaces. Silver tiaras. Rings with every precious stone imaginable set into them. And hairpieces. She settled her fingers on an oval silver one and checked no one was watching before carefully slipping the long matching pin from it and tucking it into the four-inch cuff around her wrist.

The mistress finished fastening the one on Hella's left wrist and set the shackles down on the top next to all the jewellery.

"I believe the diamonds would suit you best." The woman reached for the necklace Hella had been admiring, picked it up and moved around her.

The youngest female gathered Hella's blue hair up, allowing the mistress to secure the necklace around her throat, and Hella subtly checked the pin she had stolen was secure behind her cuff.

A hidden makeshift dagger she was going to use on her unwitting husband's throat the moment he was alone with her.

She ran through her plan in her head as the women worked on styling her hair in countless curls that they then pinned high on the back of her head and affixed a silver tiara in front of the mass.

When they made her stand, she took to staring at her reflection as they dressed her, thankfully not in next to nothing like they were wearing. The sheer turquoise dress was far from something a witch should wear though. It gathered in layers over her chest, squashing her breasts together, forming a strapless corset. From her hips, the lengths of material flowed to her ankles at the front and trailed on the floor at her back, and none of them were stitched together. A stiff breeze was all it would take to flash everything at the guests.

And she meant everything.

"No underwear?" She cast a hopeful look at the mistress.

Who shook her head and continued lacing the silver filigree corset around Hella's waist, one that pushed her breasts up and accentuated them even more, and was in danger of cutting off her air supply.

She had figured as much. Ethyrian wanted easy access to the goods, was clearly eager to make sure he crossed all the Ts and dotted all the Is as soon as possible. Heaven forbid she be allowed to have a little dignity today of all days.

Her wedding day.

Her stomach twisted.

She pressed her hand to it and stared at her reflection, not recognising herself.

All these years of wanting to wear something other than a black dress and now she ached to be back in one. She had never realised how big a part of her identity her black dresses were. Everyone who saw her in one knew she was a witch. With this dress and her magic bound, what was she?

A shadow of herself.

No.

She was someone else.

Ethyrian had effectively altered her into an entirely different person by using nothing more than a change of outfit and a pair of silver cuffs.

All these years of fighting against people who wanted to change her, clinging to what made her who she was, and now her worst fears had come true. She was no longer Hella. She clenched her fists. No. She was Hella. She was just Hella having a really bad day, one she was going to change as soon as she was able and then she would be back to her old self.

Although she wasn't sure how to escape this realm, even if she did manage to escape Ethyrian.

If he had kept his promise, he had sealed the borders to MacKinnon and she suspected he had sealed them to her too. She mentally shrugged that off. One step at a time. She would deal with the problem of leaving this realm once she had dealt with Ethyrian.

"There. You are ready." The mistress stepped back and all three of the women ran envious gazes over her.

Hella rotated left and then right, relieved to see that there were enough layers at the front of her dress to conceal the fact she was sans panties.

The youngest woman bent and slipped highly impractical shoes on Hella's feet. The flat soles would have been fine if not for the fact the shoes were made of crystal and were cold as ice, and pinched like hell.

"Who am I, Cinderella?" She hitched her skirt and glared at the shoes, and realised something.

They probably weren't glass.

They shone in the same way her diamond necklace did.

Mother earth, if she did manage to escape, she was taking all of this with her. She could pawn it off and be rich beyond her imagination.

"Come." The mistress took hold of her arm and led her out of the room, through the palace and down to the ground floor.

Hella swallowed when she saw the towering gold doors ahead of her and tried to settle her racing heart. She checked her cuff again, making sure her hidden dagger was still in place. Sickness brewed in her stomach, but she had to do this.

Ethyrian would keep his word.

She hoped.

The doors opened, the classical music growing louder as they parted, and she fought the momentary urge to turn and bolt as fast as she could in the other direction as she stared at Ethyrian where he waited at the end of the aisle.

He stood in the middle of the dais, cutting a fine figure in a white tunic jacket that reached mid-thigh and had turquoise detailing on it, and matching dark teal trousers that hugged his legs, together with polished black and gold knee-high riding boots. His long blond hair had been drawn back behind his shoulders, and his crown was in place, the knotted band of gold bright in the candlelight.

He was handsome, but he was no MacKinnon.

Those striking blue eyes she had once admired were nothing compared to her wolf's silver ones that told her everything he was feeling. Had he really betrayed her? Or had Godiva somehow worked a spell on him that she hadn't been able to detect? It wasn't like her to miss something like that, not when she had worked to be the best witch there was, one not easily fooled by a spell, but then she had been an emotional wreck. Focusing through the pain had been difficult and there was a chance, albeit a slight one since she *was* the best witch out there, that she had failed to detect a concealment spell.

She sighed and told herself that there was little point regretting her actions now.

Her future stood before her and she had made her decision, one that would hopefully keep MacKinnon safe.

Heads turned towards her, murmured comments lost on her as she gathered her courage.

And took her first step forwards.

Towards her doom.

The harem left her at the doors and as little as she liked them, being left to walk the entire length of the aisle alone was so daunting that she wished at least one of them had stayed with her. Everyone gawped at her as she passed them and she tilted her head up, squared her shoulders and clung to the tattered shreds of her courage.

Trying to look like a queen.

Failing dismally judging by a few looks she received from finely dressed women.

An electric shiver chased down her spine, lighting her up inside.

Hella glanced to her right.

Was stunned as she locked gazes with Kin.

Idiot.

Panic threatened to crush her fear and slay her courage, and she wasn't sure where to look. She tried to keep her eyes away from him, but failed. His visage was dark as he tracked her, fury mounting in his molten gold eyes, and she worried part of him believed this wedding was her idea.

Even when she knew he might be an idiot, but he wasn't that much of an idiot.

He could no doubt sense the fear in her and how desperate she was to escape. She turned her cheek to him as she passed him and willed him not to do anything reckless. She made it a handful of steps before she could no longer resist glancing back at him to make sure it really was him and not some figment of her desperate imagination.

His dark eyebrows knitted hard above his glowing golden eyes and his lips turned downwards, flashing a hint of fangs.

And gods, it really was him.

Here in Lucia again to rescue her.

Risking his life for her sake.

If she had needed proof that she had been wrong about him, he had just given it to her without even uttering a word.

When he looked as if he wanted to come to her, she subtly shook her head.

If Ethyrian had closed the borders as promised, then Kin was trapped here, and the moment the nymph realised he was in Lucia, he would be after her wolf's head. She wasn't sure what to do. The safest option was sticking to her original plan, but the way Kin's gaze drilled into her back as she approached Ethyrian said that wasn't going to happen. Her wolf was a ticking bomb, and sooner rather than later, he was going to explode.

The aisle gave way to the steps of the dais and Ethyrian extended his hand to her.

She needed to come up with a new plan and fast.

Hella tried to figure out what to do as she lifted her arm and reached for Ethyrian.

MacKinnon took it all out of her hands.

On a blood-curdling howl, he came barrelling down the aisle towards her.

CHAPTER 30

Hella looked stunning. She knocked the wind from his lungs like a punch in the chest—or maybe the heart—as MacKinnon caught sight of her.

Ashy make-up surrounded her eyes, bringing out how green they were, and her lips had been painted a sultry shade of red that made him yearn to kiss her. Her azure hair had been twirled into a high knot and diamonds glittered atop her head and around her throat, and he couldn't stop his mind from imagining him following the trail of gold to her exposed nape to kiss and lick and tease it until she surrendered and pleaded him to bite her there.

But there was something wrong about her.

And he wasn't talking about the fear he could feel in her and scent on her as she bravely walked down the aisle towards him.

Towards the bastard nymph king.

It was her dress.

While it was certainly eye-catching and the style suited her, the colour was all wrong. His beautiful witch just didn't look right in turquoise. In fact, he found it hard to picture her in any colour other than black.

And not because she was a witch and that colour was traditional for them.

Hella bent the rules when it came to witch fashion, chose dresses that were very different from the typical style, but she had never veered away from black for the colour, and Kin knew the reason why. Black made it clear she was a witch. It declared it to everyone who saw her and left them all in no doubt of what she was.

What she was proud of being.

His wee witch didn't belong in bright colours. She belonged in black. It was part of who she was and he wanted to go to her and vow that he would find her a black dress, that he would place her back in a colour that meant a lot to her.

And he would go on to vow that he would never change that about her.

Just as he would never seek to shackle her magic as the nymph had.

He loved her just as she was—a wild, wily witch who took no crap from anyone.

Her fear grew as she noticed him, her emerald eyes locking with his for just long enough to warm his heart and rouse his courage before she faced forwards again. Because she was afraid the nymph waiting at the end of the aisle would notice her singling him out?

It struck him that she feared the king would go for his head.

The thought that she feared the male who was watching her approach with unabashed interest in his blue eyes, raking them over her curves and no doubt thinking wicked things Kin would never allow to happen, made his blood burn and stirred his wolf into a frenzy. He needed to get her away from that male— but how?

He was surrounded by guests and guards, and if he tried to intervene in the ceremony, it would be his head rolling and not the nymph's. He needed to be more subtle, to play things more carefully, and employ a strategy that would see he was the victor.

Easier said than done as he tracked Hella, watching her march to her doom, and felt her growing fear. He curled his fingers into fists and tried to steady himself, but remaining where he was grew harder the further she moved from him and the closer she got to that male.

She glanced at him and subtly shook her head.

Telling him to stay where he was?

It wasn't going to happen. He couldn't stand by and let Hella wed another, even when he planned to widow her as soon as possible by taking the king's head as his prize. The thought of her belonging to another even for a few minutes sent hot acid into his veins and scoured his chest until it was raw and hollow.

Hella was his.

Fate had made him to love her and he did. He loved her with all his heart and that was why he couldn't be a good wolf like she wanted him to be. He couldn't let her continue suffering as she clearly was. He had to do something.

He just wasn't sure what yet.

The king extended his hand to Hella and she lifted hers to place it into his.

To touch another male.

A red veil descended and before Kin knew what he was doing, he had exploded from his row, knocking several males out of the way, and was thundering down the aisle, heading straight for her.

She turned wide, shocked green eyes on him.

Or maybe horrified.

Several of the guests lunged for him and he growled and dodged, swiped with his claws to slash through their fancy clothes and landed blows that were hard enough to crack bone. He grabbed and shoved them out of his way once he had felled them, keeping his eyes locked on Hella.

The king grabbed her arm.

"Hella!" Kin roared, his fear jacking up as the nymph glared at her and began pulling her towards a door in the far left corner of the room.

He needed to reach her and help her now, before the king disappeared with her.

He punched a fae on the jaw, snapping his head around, and kicked another in the kneecap, sending him to the ground, his heart pounding a sickening rhythm as the need to protect his mate blasted through him. He bet his balls that the shiny silver cuffs she wore inhibited her magic, leaving her defenceless. She needed his help. He downed another male who dared to get in his way, kneeing him between the legs and following up by grabbing his blond hair as he bent over and smashing the male's face into his knee to make sure he stayed down.

"I'm coming, lass!" he yelled as he shoved the male into two more, knocking them out of his way.

Only she wasn't as defenceless as he believed.

She slashed the king across his cheek with something, causing the male to lose his hold on her as his hand flew to his face, and flashed a reluctant look at her feet before kicking off her shoes and running down the aisle towards Kin.

Kin stood there, stunned by the sight of her.

He took a hard punch to the kidney from behind, punishment for letting himself be distracted in the middle of a fight, and snarled as he twisted around and caught the young nymph who had landed the blow, seizing him by the throat. He spun with the male and slammed the side of his head into one of the heavy gold posts of the railings that had been used to separate the rows of guests.

Hella launched onto the back of a guard who was heading for him and stabbed him in the neck with something. Blood sprayed as she yanked her hand away from him and she grimaced as she dropped off him and kicked him in the back, sending him staggering towards Kin as he fumbled with his neck, trying to stem the bleeding.

She grabbed Kin's arm as soon as she was close enough, hitched her skirts up with her other arm and dragged him into the crowd.

Her anger hit him hard as she tugged him along with her, keeping her head down as the people parted, evidently not interested in fighting them or getting in their way.

"What the hell are you doing here?" she snapped without looking at him, her grip on his arm growing fiercer, her fingernails digging into his flesh.

"This the thanks I get for coming to rescue you?" he bit out, his own rage coming to the fore to match hers, the thought that she hadn't wanted to be rescued and had possibly planned to wed the nymph rousing it and blackening his mood.

She glanced back at him, fear bright in her eyes.

"You're trapped here now. I made a bargain with Ethyrian. You'd be—" She ducked beneath a blow a male aimed at her and stabbed him with what looked a lot like a small knitting needle at the same time as Kin punched him on the nose. The male went down and she pulled Kin forwards again. "You'd be spared, banished from this realm and left to live your life if I married him."

Kin growled at that, part of him touched by what she had been willing to do for his sake and the rest of him so furious that he wanted to turn back around and find Ethyrian to beat the living hell out of him right that moment.

"A life without you isn't one I want to live, Hella," he snarled and she abruptly stopped and looked at him, her blue eyebrows pinned high on her forehead as she gazed up into his eyes.

He wanted to mention that stopping in the middle of a battle when there were guards closing in on their location wasn't the wisest move, but he couldn't get enough of the way she was looking at him, didn't want her to stop.

And he needed her to know the truth.

"Back in Scotland… I went to the witch to make her break my curse. I couldn't bring myself to do what she wanted. I couldn't hurt you like that. And then when I found her, she cast a spell on me. Stole control of my bloody body. I never wanted to hurt you, lass. It was never my intent. I was trying to make everything right. And when you left me… I couldn't bear it. I had to find you. I had to explain, even if you turned me away. I vowed I wouldn't give up, no matter how many times you teleported me away from you. I need you, Hella. I'd sooner die than live a second without you, love." He lifted his hand and brushed his fingers across her cheek, tracking the approaching male with his senses. There was a better time to tell her this, he was sure, but this moment felt right. He held her gaze and swept his thumb over her lower lip. "That's why I decided I'll keep my fangs to myself. I'll never bite you, Hella. I won't shackle you with a bond like you fear. If it means I get to be with you, I'll never claim you."

Her eyes slowly widened and for a moment he thought she might kiss him, and then she grabbed a gold post and swung it at his head. He flinched away, anticipating the strike, unsure what he had done to deserve being hit. Did she want him to bite her?

To claim her?

There was a hard thump and then a male grunt sounded behind him.

Kin looked over his shoulder in time to see the nymph guard falling to the floor, out cold from Hella's blow.

She tossed the post aside and grabbed Kin's arm. "We'll discuss this later."

She dragged him forwards and he didn't miss the two words she muttered as the crowd enveloped them again.

"Over dinner."

Like a date? Kin could do that. He hadn't dated anyone in a long time, but whatever Hella wanted, he would do it.

He spied a set of glass doors ahead of them and took over, hauling her towards them. When she noticed them, she sped up, almost keeping up with him. As much as he hated running from a fight, he needed to get Hella safe. As soon as she was safe, he would figure out a way to deal with the nymph permanently.

Although, killing a king would probably turn an entire kingdom against him.

He and Hella would never know peace.

A guard stepped in front of them and Kin barrelled into him, sending him through the glass doors first and using him as a blocker. As soon as they were clear, he shoved the male aside and scanned his new surroundings. Not great. They were at the bridge that spanned the gorge.

Guards rushed towards them from the other side and he had a terrible sense of déjà vu as Hella pulled him in the direction of the balustrade to his left.

"We have to jump." She cast him a wild look, one that relayed the fear he could feel in her.

Fear that wasn't only about the king catching them now.

He peered over the edge of the bridge at the drop to the raging river far below them and his stomach flipped. They had survived the rapids once. They would survive it this time.

But just in case, Kin dragged Hella against him and kissed her hard.

When he released her, she muttered, "I hope that was for luck because we're going to need it."

He scooped her up in his arms when he sensed her hesitation and the guards got too close for his liking, leaped up onto the stone railing and stepped off the other side. Hella screamed all the way down, the shrill sound piercing his sensitive ears, and he braced her against his chest a split-second before they hit the water. She twisted his jacket into her fists and clung to him as they were spun around by the current, and he clutched her more tightly, fear pounding in his veins. Her wrists weren't bound this time, meaning she could swim more freely, but he was damned if he was risking losing his hold on her.

His boots met rock and he kicked off, propelling them back to the surface. Hella gasped for air as they broke it and spluttered as she got a mouthful of water. He fought the current, kicking hard to keep them from going under again. They bumped into a boulder and were spun around, the world whirling in a dizzying way before he managed to right their course.

With the help of another huge rock.

Hella grunted as she struck it, taking the brunt of the blow.

He palmed her ribs and stared ahead of them, towards the end of the canyon. "We should drift further downstream this time."

"Covering our tracks," she murmured, her voice tight from coughing up water. "I like it."

He glanced at her as he heard praise in her tone and she pulled a shocked face.

"What? I can't compliment you when you do something right?"

"I'm just so used to being berated," he said, holding back his smile when she scowled at him.

"I'm not all that bad." She pouted and he knew she wasn't being serious, was only teasing him, and gods, it felt good to have her back in his arms, poking fun at him.

Part of him had thought he would never experience this with her again, that he had ruined everything and it was over. Yet here she was, clinging to him, a smile in her eyes as she gazed at him with what looked a hell of a lot like love and gratitude.

She was fishing for compliments, so he smiled at her, marvelling at how her cheeks coloured when he did that.

"No better witch in this world." He adjusted his grip, lowering it to her waist.

She arched an eyebrow at him. "Don't think I missed the caveat there. *This* world. I think you meant to say no better witch in all the worlds."

"Aye, lass." He dropped a kiss on her cheek, feeling the heat of it beneath his lips. "No better witch than my one."

She moved closer to him rather than pushing him away, rested her cheek against his as they rounded a bend and he had to begin swimming to keep them moving at a pace. When they were far from the castle, he took her to the bank and helped her out of the water.

The layers of her dress clung to her and she tugged at them, muttering dark things about a lack of underwear that made him want to growl and return to the castle to deal with Ethyrian.

Her look turned sombre and her hurt lashed at him, and he knew the source of it.

"We'll get you home and back into a black dress." His eyebrows knitted hard as he tried to figure out a way to make that happen.

Her gaze lifted to his face and her brow furrowed as she stared at him. "A black dress?"

"Like a witch wears. A witch's dress… but with a wee bit more flair. That's what my lass loves."

She gave him a look that said she might love him.

"Want me to break those?" He gestured to her cuffs.

She cast another sorrowful look at them. "I don't think you'll be able to. They're sealed with another spell. The metal melded together."

She turned her hands over to show the underside of the cuffs and he took hold of her right one anyway. It was worth a shot. There was barely room to wriggle his fingers between her flesh and the metal, but he managed it. Once he had a firm grip on the cuff, he gritted his teeth and pulled his hands apart, his muscles tensing as he used all his strength on it.

And nothing happened.

He kept trying, but the metal wouldn't bend, let alone break, and every second he spent trying to free her of them was a second the nymph's army could be closing in on them. He growled as he gave up, hating the nymph and the cuffs, and himself to a degree because he wasn't strong enough to free his fated one.

To restore her beloved powers.

Her smile was small and made him ache as she looked at him.

"I'll find a way to free you, love. I swear." He smoothed his hands over hers and she nodded, the slight action lacking her usual confidence. "I'm going to kill that bastard."

He stormed past her, back in the direction of the castle, but she caught his arm and gripped it so hard that he stilled. Her fear hit him hard and he looked back at her.

"Not without me, Kin. I don't want you to fight him without me there." Her lips flattened and her gaze turned wary.

She didn't need to tell him her reasons for him to know them. She wanted to be there by his side to protect him. She felt the same powerful needs he did, was a slave to her desire to take care of him and watch his back, and ensure he survived.

He nodded reluctantly, showing her that he wouldn't go after the nymph before she was free of her cuffs and her powers had been restored. They would do this together.

"I'll figure out a way to get us home," she said.

Kin pulled several wooden tokens from his pocket. "I already have that covered. I just need to find a portal."

Her eyes lit up and then faded. "But what if Ethyrian kept his promise and he closed the borders? A portal won't get us out of here."

He wanted to tell her that he doubted the nymph had kept his promise, because the male had probably wanted Kin to show up and give him a reason to take him out of the picture.

"We'll find a portal and see what happens." He took hold of her hand, threading their fingers together, and began walking with her.

She hurried to keep up with him, taking two strides for every one of his as he led her further from the castle. He wasn't sure where he was going, but the more distance he put between him and that building, the better. There was bound to be a portal somewhere.

The clearing along the bank gave way to dense trees that were bright with glowing bugs and flowers that illuminated their way. Hella's head turned this way and that as she took them in, and he kept his focus on the path ahead of them.

The trees grew larger, rising to tower over them, their ashen branches threaded with violet veins that shone in the strange daylight of Lucia. Above them, aurora in shades of purple, red and green chased across the sky, drowning out the faint stars. Did it ever grow dark here?

Kin pulled Hella around the thick white trunk of one of the trees.

And came to a dead stop.

It was pitch black save the lights from the glowing veins of the trees.

He looked back over his shoulder and behind them was just as dark, and then jerked his gaze up to the sky. It was inky black, spotted with a million glittering stars and a large full moon.

"What the hell?" Hella said, uttering the question that had been on the tip of his tongue.

Kin backtracked with her, past the tree, and she gasped as they were in the light again. He moved forwards slowly this time, watching the trunk and when they were halfway past it, the lighting changed, putting it half in the light and half in the dark, and then as he continued, it was all in darkness.

"Shadows," he muttered as he remembered the warning he had been given. "This is the shadows."

He had foolishly thought the person had meant stay out of the shadows cast by the trees, buildings and rocks in Lucia. How wrong he had been. Hella shot him a confused look.

"I think this is the unseelie side of this world." He moved a few steps deeper into the darkness and the hairs on his nape rose as he felt the shift in power in the air.

"We can't turn back," Hella said and he shook his head and gave her a look that told her that wasn't going to happen so there was no reason for her to fear.

"We keep moving forwards… but we need to move carefully." He flexed his fingers against the back of her hand, reassuring himself that he had a tight hold on her and telling himself that nothing bad would happen to her. "There's bound to be a portal here."

She looked back at the tree. "The border. We crossed the border, Kin. Ethyrian never closed it to you."

Or to her.

Which most likely meant the nymph didn't possess the power to do such a thing and had been issuing an idle threat to force her hand and make her wed him. Another reason Kin was going to kill him.

"Come on, lass." He drew her level with him and started walking, keeping her pinned close to his side.

His ears twitched, his senses stretching as far around him as he could manage. Things moved in the darkness at the edges of them and he hoped they stayed away, because he didn't want to see what kind of beasts lived in this dark world.

Hella stuck close to him and he kept glancing at her, checking on her whenever she tensed and muttered foreign words beneath her breath. Was she trying to cast spells to protect them, despite the fact her magic was bound? He tugged her closer still, his heart going out to her, and made getting her free of those damned cuffs a priority.

As soon as they were out of this dark realm.

When they came across another shallow river, he followed it, not liking being out in the open on the banks but it was better than being in the woods where the things he could sense were closer now.

"We'll find a portal," he whispered, needing to reassure her. "We'll get out of here."

She nodded.

But on the moonlit banks of the river ahead of them stood a black-haired male.

One who reeked of danger and dark power.

An unseelie.

CHAPTER 31

Hella found it half-endearing and half-irritating that MacKinnon automatically moved in front of her, shielding her from the fae they had stumbled across.

She stepped out from behind her wolf.

The black-haired male regarded them with curious silver eyes. He turned slowly to face them, his bare torso as pale as alabaster in the moonlight and his onyx trousers as dark as the sky. Water lapped at his naked feet, the only motion in a motionless world as she held her breath and was sure Kin was doing the same. Had the fae been about to bathe? His top and boots were a few feet behind him, on the mossy edge of the pebbled shore of the river. She spotted no weapon on him either. She wasn't sure whether that was a good thing or a bad thing. Surprising an unarmed dark fae sounded dangerous to her. He might feel threatened by their presence.

Then again, he might not even have a weapon or need one to deal with them.

The pointed tips of his ears twitched as he stared at Kin, assessing him. He had to stand only a couple of inches shorter than her wolf, but his build was half that of Kin's.

Not that it made him weaker.

The power that rolled off this male was phenomenal.

Dark and malevolent.

She held her nerve and her ground, unsure what to make of him but sure she should feel he was a threat.

It was hard to feel that when he turned his side to them again and bent back towards the river, clearly not that interested in them—or threatened by their presence. He cupped his hands and scooped up water.

And would you look at that?

He was holding the moon in his hands.

The reflection of it was gone from the river, now only existed in the water he held.

This was more than any old dark fae.

This was an unseelie.

And a very ancient and powerful one at that.

He looked right at her and opened his black-tipped fingers, and the water poured like diamonds from between them, and the moon was back in the river. How did he do that? Was it a power all unseelie held or specific to him? She wanted to ask him, but she wasn't sure he would appreciate her probing into his powers. It would probably make her appear more like a threat to him.

He spoke to her.

In a language she didn't know.

Kin glanced at her.

She shook her head. "I don't speak his tongue."

The fae approached them, which had Kin tensing and trying to pull her behind him again, but she stood her ground, refusing to let him shield her. When he was within ten feet of them, the fae held his hands out and tilted his palms towards her, his fingers pointing down towards the crystalline pebbles.

The lines of markings that ran from the black top thirds of his fingers to the edge of his palm glowed like the moon.

Hella peered at them, trying to make them out from a safe distance. "They're fae. You're fae. Right? Are they your lineage? Like incubus markings?"

"Incu... bus." The fae frowned and then relaxed. "Incubus. I met. Fae."

She glanced at Kin and whispered out of the corner of her mouth, "I don't think he speaks much English. He's clearly local though. He might know of a portal. Maybe he might know the modern fae tongue?"

Kin gave her a look. "Go right ahead, lass. As you so gleefully pointed out before, I don't speak it."

She grimaced when she remembered how well that conversation had gone and wished she hadn't brought it up. She didn't want him remembering the terrible things she said or how she had acted back then. She had been hoping for a fresh start with him, one where they were both more honest about their feelings and less caustic towards each other.

"My fae isn't great... not when it comes to conversational fae anyway... and I really don't want there to be any misunderstandings between us. A spell would make this easier, but that's not going to happen." She slid a worried look at the unseelie, who was already looking impatient, his black eyebrows knitted in a frown. Was she offending him by speaking English so much? Maybe he thought she was doing it so he wouldn't understand her and was plotting against him. "But then, it's risky for us to keep speaking English."

Like, very risky.

The fae lowered his hands and his eyes brightened as he flexed his fingers.

"Um," she said and tried to think of what to say as she switched to the modern fae tongue. "Do you know of incubi?"

The male arched an eyebrow and responded in stilted English. "Succubi? No. Incubus."

He pointed to his markings and then raised his right arm before him, with his forearm across his chest, and trailed a finger along his underarm and over his biceps and shoulder.

"Incubus." He uttered that word in the fae tongue and nodded.

She nodded too and responded in the same language. "Incubus. I meant incubi."

She blew out her breath and glanced at Kin, who was looking worried now. She wasn't sure she could pull this off either.

"I wish Fenix was here," she muttered in English. "He speaks fluent fae."

"Fenix." The unseelie perked up, his silver eyes bright with interest. "Fenix of the Incubi."

It couldn't be possible.

"You know him?" She grimaced when he looked confused and repeated it in the fae tongue, hoping she got it right.

He nodded. "Fenix of the incubi. Bears my brand."

"Bears your brand?" Her eyes widened and she gripped Kin's arm as she looked up at him and switched to English. "He does. Fenix has a brand. On his arm."

She looked at the fae and pointed to the area on her right forearm where she had seen the mark on Fenix.

He nodded vigorously this time.

She couldn't believe it. Of all the dark fae to run into, they had found one who might be willing to help them. Things were looking up. All she needed to do was convince him to help them and they could be home before she knew it and she could be out of this awful dress and could find a witch to remove her cuffs.

"Fenix." She patted her chest. "My friend."

"Friend," he repeated in English and gracefully touched his own chest. "Archangel."

"Archangel are seriously not anyone's friends," she whispered to Kin and he grunted in agreement. "Why would he think they are?"

Kin didn't get a chance to answer that question because she realised she had gotten it all wrong.

"You met him there?" she said in English and then tried again in broken fae when the male only frowned at her.

When he still looked puzzled, she scowled at the silver cuffs around her wrists.

"This would be so much easier with my magic. One translation spell and I'd be able to talk to him without fear of saying something that might upset him." She cast a look up at Kin when he turned to face her and loved the soft look in his eyes as he gazed down at her, his brow furrowing. She knew that look. He wished he could free her of the cuffs. She would get free soon enough.

"Magic," the fae muttered. His black eyebrows knitted hard as his silver eyes pierced her. "Witch."

She nodded and pointed to her matching cuffs. "Bound."

He didn't look happy about that as he glared at her wrists, and part of her began to hope they had found an ally in this dark fae, one who really would help them get out of this realm.

"Fenix. Friend." He pointed to the spot on his arm where Fenix had his brand and then at himself, and then he pointed at her. "Friend."

"Friends," MacKinnon put in. "We're all friends here."

The male looked confused again and began muttering in the fae tongue.

She caught snippets of it, but not enough to follow what he was saying.

Hella sighed.

They were getting nowhere.

As dangerous as it was and as much as she didn't want there to be any misunderstandings between them, she needed to risk using his language. Ethyrian was bound to have his entire army out looking for them. They didn't have time to waste. Every second they spent with the dark fae was a second that brought them closer to danger. If the nymph caught Kin, he would kill him, and the thought of him dying ripped at her heart. She couldn't bear it. She had to get her wolf out of this realm and this fae was the key to making that happen.

She ran through all the fae she knew, dredging up things long forgotten since they were never used in magical texts. Fenix had taught her a few greetings over the years and a smattering of conversational phrases that she had never used other than to irritate him. She hoped she had enough to cobble together something that would convince the fae to help them.

Hella blew out her breath to steady her nerves and translated what she wanted to say into fae, hoping she got it right. "We're in danger."

The black-haired male changed before her eyes, growing infinitely more terrifying as his eyes turned crimson and his lips darkened towards black. She backed into Kin as the fae's skin paled further and inky markings curled around his biceps to sweep over his shoulders and down around the square slabs of his pectorals, ending in a swirl near his collarbones. Kin seized hold of her arms as the male's transformation didn't end there.

His black nails became inch-long claws and his teeth sharpened into fangs that he bared, his canines longest but the incisors next to them growing pointed too.

His scarlet eyes locked on them, the jagged silver around his elliptical pupils glowing as bright as the moon suspended in the inky sky above them.

"Something I said?" she whispered, her voice barely there as fear flooded her and she pressed her back against Kin's front.

Had she just told the fae they were a danger to him?

The words for danger and dangerous were no doubt very close and she had been feeling the pressure, was no longer sure her pronunciation had been correct.

The fae disappeared in a black mist that sparked with gold flecks.

Hella seized Kin's hand, needing to feel it in hers and know he was there with her, and braced herself for impact.

CHAPTER 32

If MacKinnon had been able to teleport, he would have swept Hella away from the realm of the unseelie the second the male transformed into something out of a nightmare. As it was, he scooped her into his arms, tearing a shocked gasp from her, and twisted to run in the direction they had come.

His entire body locked up tight as the unseelie appeared there, but it wasn't the reason he had just frozen right down to his marrow.

No, the reason stood beyond the unseelie.

The nymph king and what had to be two dozen guards.

Kin's heart thundered as he stared at Ethyrian, not liking the odds.

"How did he find us so fast?" Hella whispered, her nerves trickling into him, and the hunger for violence growing inside him intensified as he felt her trembling. His witch wouldn't be so afraid if it wasn't for the cuffs that were subduing her magic.

He glared at them. "The fuckin' cuffs."

She glanced at him and frowned.

Ethyrian slowly clapped.

"Not as dumb as you look, are you, wolf?" His blue gaze slid to Hella. "Did you honestly think I would not ensure you were unable to escape me again, my bride?"

"I'm not your bride!" she snapped and pushed out of Kin's arms.

Kin glanced at her to check on her, sure stars would be spotting her irises in response to her rage. Only they were plain green. Because of the cuffs. He cursed them and his inability to remove them, and then frowned as he shifted his gaze to the unseelie where he stood between them and the nymphs.

The male was stronger than he was, and he had looked angry when he had seen Hella's cuffs. Could he break them?

"Walk away, wolf, and whatever you desire will be yours." Ethyrian's regal tone grated on Kin's last nerve.

Hella tensed beside him, her gaze leaping to scald his face, and he glanced at her and saw the fear glittering in her eyes. He made a decision the moment he locked eyes with her, one he knew might end in his death, but gods, it would be worth it if Hella could be free.

He bared his fangs at the nymph. "Get tae fuck, ye hairy bawbag. Hella is my fated mate and I'll be taking her back with me."

Shock swept across her beautiful face and their growing bond, and it wasn't the best way to break it to her that they were really fated, but it was a fantastic way of triggering rage in the nymph king.

Exactly as planned.

"Slay the wolf!" Ethyrian drew a sword and pointed it towards him.

Six of the guards unsheathed their twin daggers.

"Unseelie." Kin grabbed Hella and shoved her to his right, towards the trees that lined the riverbank, as the black-haired male glanced over his shoulder at him. He prayed to his ancestors that he was right about the dark fae and that the male did want to help them. "Her cuffs."

"Oberon," the unseelie growled and transformed into black mist. He reappeared beside Hella as the first wave of nymphs reached Kin and casually swept his right hand out. The nymphs hit an invisible barrier and fell on their backsides and the unseelie said something in the fae tongue.

"Is that his name?" Kin barked, keeping his focus on the guards as they picked themselves up and grabbed their daggers.

"Yes," Hella said and then squeaked, "What are you doing?"

Kin glanced her way and growled as she struggled on Oberon's shoulder. The sight of another male touching his female triggered his own rage, had a red veil descending and black fur sweeping over his arms. Oberon turned and set her down on the mossy bank, and arched an eyebrow at Kin.

"Fated," he muttered, and bowed his head, closing his eyes at the same time. "Apologies."

The guards came at Kin again.

And again hit a barrier.

Kin edged towards Oberon, not taking his eyes off Ethyrian or his men. Hella gasped and he resisted the urge to look at her. The familiar tinny scent of magic laced the air and warmed him right down to his soul. He risked a glance at Hella and found her rubbing her bare wrists, relief written in every line of her face and in her feelings.

She was free.

Now all he had to do was get her out of here.

"Oberon." He locked gazes with the male, needing the fae to see how badly he needed him to do this one thing. He pointed to Hella and she shook her head, her eyes widening. "Teleport. Mortal world."

"No!" she bit out and stepped away from Oberon, who didn't look at all inclined to do as Kin wanted anyway. "This is my battle too."

She flexed her fingers and silver stars pricked her eyes, and gods, it was good to see them again and that mulish twist of her lips. He half-expected her to huff or roll her eyes.

She did something else instead.

She muttered words and swept her hands down over her dress, and in the wake of them it turned black. When every inch of it was onyx, she smiled.

"That's better." She wriggled her fingers and light glowed at their tips.

"Much better, love." He wanted to pull her into his arms and kiss her when she beamed at him, revealing how happy she was now that she felt like herself again. He held his hand out to her instead, aware this was no place for making out with her. They could spend hours doing that later, once this was over. "Come, my beautiful fated female. We have a battle to win."

"And a king to kill." She slipped her hand into his and the scent of magic in the air grew thicker.

His head tingled in a weird way, his vision blurring a little, and his wolf side went haywire in response and then he suddenly felt normal. "What did you do?"

"You do speak my tongue!" Oberon's crimson eyes narrowed as he grinned, flashing killer fangs. "Why did you not do so earlier?"

"Ah… because I don't?" He looked at Hella for an explanation.

"Magical translator spell. Whatever we say, he'll understand and vice versa. It doesn't last long though." She turned to Oberon. "We need your help. King Ethyrian is trying to force me to be his bride and MacKinnon is my fated one and I just really want to go home."

The guards bounced off the barrier again, only this time, jagged white lines glowed in the air where they had hit it.

"I will aid you, Hella of the Witches and MacKinnon of the Wolves." Oberon pressed a hand to his bare chest and turned a dark look on the nymphs. "King Ethyrian trespasses in my realm."

"Your realm?" Hella blinked. "You're a king?"

"A prince." Oberon dipped his head.

And then he was gone.

Someone screamed a split-second later and the scent of blood joined that of magic in the air.

MacKinnon stripped off, keeping his focus on the battle happening between Oberon and the nymphs, no easy feat considering Hella began staring at him the second he removed the navy tunic jacket.

"What are you doing?" she said, her gaze tracking his hands with interest as he bent over and took off his boots.

"Shifting." He wasn't sure how long he would be able to retain his wolf form given the fact pain tended to make shifters transform back into their human one, but he had spent years honing his fighting skills as a wolf, learning to use speed and his fangs to his advantage.

Her eyes widened as he shoved his trousers down and he frowned at her.

"Don't let me stop you." She waved him on, looking as if she was enjoying the show.

He sighed and pushed his trousers the rest of the way down and kicked them off his feet.

"Be careful," he said and then shifted.

The transformation from man to wolf lasted only a few seconds, but he was aware of Hella's grimace throughout every single one of them. Something told him she had never stopped to watch a shifter transform before. It wasn't pretty.

Oberon growled something in a tongue the spell Hella had used on him didn't translate, but it sounded like a suitable vicious accompaniment to the raking of his inch-long claws over the throat and stomach of one of the guards. The blond male didn't get a chance to cover either wound with his hand. They barely twitched before he had dropped to the ground, landing face-first on crimson-soaked pebbles.

Kin cast Hella one last look, needing to know she had got his message and would be careful, and then kicked off.

Setting his sights on Ethyrian.

The king had fallen back, was using his guards as a shield now as Oberon tore through them. One of the guards disappeared and every instinct Kin possessed growled that he would return soon enough.

With reinforcements.

Bright flashes of magic lit up the darkness as Hella joined the fray, her spell sending several nymphs shooting into the air in all directions. One of them hit the nearest tree, a garbled scream bursting from his lips as he hit a branch and it speared him clean through the stomach. Blood rained down, splattering Oberon's white skin as he pirouetted around two of the nymphs, slashing one across the chest with his claws. He sank his nails into the shoulder of the second one and hauled him backwards, towards him, his eyes glowing scarlet in the dim light.

Oberon ran a lone claw down the male's throat and licked the blood from it, and then whispered something into his ear.

The nymph went deathly still; his struggles ceasing. When Oberon released him, the blond turned on his own comrades, his eyes shining with a hunger for violence as he brandished his twin daggers.

The tales of the unseelie were true then. They did sow discord.

Kin swept under the blow one of the guards aimed at him, his paws skidding on the crystalline pebbles, and twisted once he was behind the male. He sprang at his back and sank his fangs into the guard's shoulder and savagely wrenched his head back, tearing a great chunk of flesh from him. He kicked off, knocking the male forwards as he bellowed, and spat it out, his golden eyes fixing on his next victim.

This one was larger and faster, expertly wielding his daggers to keep Kin at a distance. Kin hopped left and then right, seeking an opening. Hella gave it to him. She hit the male with a blast of green light that knocked his left shoulder backwards. Kin launched at his chest, clamped his fangs down on his throat and knocked him over, landing on top of him. He locked his jaws as the male struggled beneath him, growling the whole time as he monitored his pulse, listening to it slowing.

White-hot pain lanced his side and he snarled as lightning ran through his bones, making them ache as they began to transform. Godsdammit. He hadn't expected the guard to retain enough strength or sense to retaliate and had left himself wide open to attack. He bit down harder, killing the male, and released him and staggered backwards. His left hind leg gave out and he glanced back at it.

Growled when he saw the dagger still protruding from his flesh.

He bent and tried to reach it, and whimpered when it only made the pain worse and he had to cling to his wolf form to stop the shift. He couldn't shift with the dagger still inside him. There was a danger it would rip through his organs.

"Kin!" Hella came running to him, her green eyes enormous as she stared at the dagger. She fell to her knees beside him and reached for it, and he snarled at her, snapping fangs. She jerked her hands away from him and cast him a hurt look, and then her expression darkened and her eyes gained silver and gold stars as her lips set in a firm line. "I'm pulling this out, so man the fuck up."

Manning up was something he really wanted to do in that moment. Holding on to his wolf form was absolute hell, stealing strength he needed for the fight ahead. His fur swept away and then returned as he desperately held on, denying the need to shift as the pain in his side grew more intense.

Hella gripped the dagger in both hands and didn't give him a chance to brace himself.

She yanked it out.

Kin howled as pain blazed through him, his head spinning as he morphed from wolf to man in an instant, faster than he had ever managed. He breathed hard as he sagged against the pebbles, fighting to remain conscious as his vision tunnelled. Hella wobbled in front of him, her face close to his, and he thought she might look worried about him. Which was sweet of her.

But then he made sense of her garbled words.

"Just lay there and I'll handle this."

No. He tried to reach for her, but she was already gone. His hand cut through thin air and he growled again, mustered his strength and rolled onto his side. Blood pumped over his hip and stomach, and he swallowed the bile that rose into his throat. Tiny sparks of lightning skittered through him, all shooting towards his wound, and heat gathered there. He grimaced as he looked at it and went to place his hand over it to stem the bleeding.

He stilled.

Did the wound just get smaller?

He stared at it, sure that it had, and his eyes widened as it shrank a little more. A spell. He looked over his shoulder, seeking Hella. She slammed her palms into the chest of a male twice her size and sent him flying through the air into several of his comrades. She had cast a spell on Kin. One to heal him.

He reached for her, his heart seizing as she ran at Ethyrian, not noticing the two guards coming up behind her.

"Hella!" he yelled and she turned, her eyes widening as she came face to face with the guards.

Ethyrian hit her hard on the back of her head with the pommel of his sword.

Kin's eyes narrowed, a snarl pealing from his lips as the nymph king caught her as she dropped. He launched to his feet, awareness pounding in his veins. He had only a second to reach her before Ethyrian teleported with her. He sprinted towards her, long strides devouring the distance between them, the pain burning in his side keeping his wolf form in check when he needed it now more than ever. He was faster as a wolf.

Ethyrian turned with her.

Kin dropped his shoulder and slammed into the two guards who had given their king the opportunity to grab her, knocking them out of his way, sure that at any moment Ethyrian was going to disappear with her.

Only he didn't.

The nymph king turned a black look on Kin.

And then his blue gaze shifted to Kin's right.

To Oberon.

Kin guessed the unseelie prince held the power to close the borders of his realm as he pleased, unlike the nymph.

"Get your damned filthy hands off my mate!" Kin launched at Ethyrian, aiming for Hella.

Ethyrian spun her away from him, flinging her to the ground a few feet away, and swept his sword up. Kin barely managed to dodge the blow, came dangerously close to being cut from hip to heart by the tip of the blade. He rolled to his left, wishing he had gone to his right the moment he realised he had placed more distance between him and Hella when he should have narrowed it down instead.

He paid for his mistake.

The king twisted and grabbed her, hauled her over his shoulder and started running towards the woods.

"He heads for a portal. Go," Oberon barked. "I will follow."

The unseelie didn't have to tell MacKinnon twice.

He ran after Ethyrian, chasing him through the trees, a growl curling up his throat as the nymph began to gain distance. Unlike his guards, Ethyrian was faster than he was.

While Kin was in his human form at least.

He focused on his wolf, trying to shut out the pain as he stared at Hella, watching the distance between them grow. If he didn't act now, she would be gone, and he wasn't sure he would ever see her again. His wolf side bayed at that, growing agitated enough that fur rippled over his skin. His mate was being taken from him.

His beautiful Hella.

He needed to protect her—to save her—but to do that he needed to be faster.

He growled as his fangs lengthened and his nails transformed into claws. Black fur chased over his hands and the pain in his side dulled to an ache as the world around him brightened and sharpened. He could do this. A grimace tugged at his lips as his bones burned and his side blazed, and his shift faltered.

The distance between him and Ethyrian grew again.

Kin gritted his teeth and pictured all the ways he was going to hurt the nymph. He pictured how afraid Hella had been of this male and his guards. He recalled how she had been forced to hide.

Forced to walk down that aisle.

If he didn't save her now, she would be forced to do far worse.

Kin exploded forwards, a savage howl pealing from him as he shifted, pure unadulterated rage pouring through his veins as he hit the forest floor on all fours and sprinted after the nymph who was trying to take his mate from him.

The distance between them began to close.

He wove through the trees, growling and snarling as he leaped bushes and forced himself to run harder, pushing past his limit. Ahead, the forest ended in a clearing and he glimpsed black towers in the distance, their forms outlined by the silver moonlight. The portal had to be there.

Ethyrian sped up as he reached the clearing.

Kin hit a moment later and kicked off, sailing through the air at the nymph's back.

The blond male stepped to his right, evading Kin.

He landed level with the nymph and kept running, trying to tame the savage part of him that wanted to rip him apart. He would. Once Hella was safe. Rather than trying to tear into Ethyrian with his fangs, he rammed the male in his legs. Once. Twice. On the third hit, the king went down and Hella hit the grass hard with him.

Ethyrian was quick to scramble onto his feet and grab his sword, spinning to face Kin before he could attack.

Kin lowered his head and snarled, his jowls peeling back off his fangs as he stared the nymph down. He slowly circled with the male, working his way towards Hella. When Ethyrian glanced at her, Kin lunged forwards, snapping his teeth. The nymph swung the blade his way again, fending him off at the same time as he leaped backwards to place more distance between them.

His mistake.

Kin was quick to reach Hella now she was further from the nymph, sank his fangs into the gaps between the swirls of the fancy metal corset she wore and tugged her with him as he backed off. He kept his eyes on the nymph the whole time.

The male's blue eyes darkened. "She belongs to me."

Kin released her and bared his fangs as he growled, and it wasn't nearly satisfying enough. He shifted back, forcing his wolf form to recede, because he needed to do this as a man.

"Like fuck she does," he growled at the nymph. "Hella belongs to no one."

"So sweet," she murmured sleepily.

He wanted to glance at her to check on her but kept his eyes locked on the nymph instead.

"We shall see about that." Ethyrian came at him, faster than he anticipated, and he dodged to his left and swept his arm down, barely knocking the nymph's sword off course.

He slammed his fist into the side of the male's head and grabbed his arm. He wrestled with him, twisting his flesh and trying to get him to drop his sword. Ethyrian punched him in the face several times, hard enough that Kin saw stars.

He released Ethyrian and staggered backwards, shaking off the blow in time to ready his claws as the nymph came at him again. He leaped right at the final moment, came around the nymph and slashed down his back, cutting long gashes in his white tunic jacket and staining it crimson. Ethyrian twisted on a snarl and smashed the pommel of his sword into Kin's temple.

Everything went black for a moment and then came back, and he growled as he found himself on the grass near Hella. She screamed and raised her hands, and fire shot from her palms, driving the nymph back just as he came at Kin. Kin pushed to his feet and used her attack to his advantage, moving around the nymph as he shielded his face with his arm.

He growled as he gripped Ethyrian's hand and squeezed it, crushing the male's fingers against the hilt of the blade and ripping a cry from him. The nymph lost his grip on the sword and it dropped to the ground, leaving him defenceless.

Kin raised his claws to strike.

And hesitated as several nymphs came rushing out of the woods.

If he killed their king, they would come after him and Hella. She would never be free. But if he didn't kill him…

Oberon appeared in a swirl of black mist, took one look into Kin's eyes and disappeared again.

The unseelie appeared right in front of Ethyrian and the male grunted, his mouth bursting open and blood exploding from it as his head lurched forwards, over Oberon's shoulder.

Oberon stepped back, pulling his hand free from the nymph's chest, and the male fell to his knees and then onto his side, his wide eyes staring into nothing. The unseelie looked at his bloodied arm and Kin swallowed hard as he spotted the heart the male gripped.

Oberon lifted it before him, watching it with interest as it continued to beat a few times.

When it went still, he held it out to the nymph guards and said something in the language Hella's spell couldn't translate for him.

Hella stumbled onto her feet and Kin hurried to her, gathering her into his arms.

Oberon casually discarded the heart and came to him, and Kin turned to thank him for his help and for taking the focus of the nymphs' anger off him and Hella.

He grimaced as the unseelie pressed his bloodied hand to the left side of Kin's chest.

Oberon uttered words and dipped his head as his hand dropped from Kin's chest and he stepped back.

Kin grunted as fire seared his chest and he looked down, his eyes widening as a glittering gold spark chased over his skin, searing him with a circular mark that contained what looked like a stag and a dragon, and symbols appeared around it.

"It's different to Fenix's brand," Hella murmured, still sounding a little groggy.

"You may teleport your fated one to safety now." Oberon slowly pivoted to face the guards, his crimson eyes narrowing on them.

Kin wasn't sure how to thank him. Not only for giving him a brand that meant he could teleport. Not just use portals, but apparently teleport. He also needed to thank the unseelie for taking the heat off him and Hella.

He owed Oberon a debt.

And something about the way the male looked at him as he slid his crimson eyes towards him said that he knew it and would be cashing it in sooner rather than later.

"Go," the male said. "I will ensure these nymphs do not follow you and will leave you alone from now on."

Oberon didn't need to tell Kin twice.

"Thank you." Kin scooped Hella into his arms and ran with her, placing some distance between him and the nymphs as Oberon launched his attack. When he was closer to the black towers, he stopped and looked down at Hella. "Any idea how to teleport, lass?"

"Close your eyes, click your heels and say there's no place like home three times." She was being sassy, and it was a relief to hear it, because it told him she was going to be all right.

Willing to give anything a shot, Kin gathered her against his chest.

Closed his eyes.
Knocked his heels together.
And uttered.
"There's no place like home."

CHAPTER 33

Hella grimaced as a loud bang came from upstairs, causing Annabel, the youngest witch in the trio before her, to jump.

It had been close to six weeks since Prince Oberon had gifted MacKinnon with a mark that allowed him to teleport, and her wolf was no closer to mastering the ability. Still, landing in her bedroom was better than his first teleport, which had ended with them plunging into the centre of the lake in the heart of her fae town.

"Time to wrap up." She closed the book in front of her and tucked it back into its place on the shelf behind her. "Remember I'll be gone for the rest of the week. We'll resume our lessons on Monday."

The witches lingered, murmuring things to each other, and she sighed as she turned back to face them and found them all gazing at the staircase.

Waiting for MacKinnon to appear.

It hadn't taken her long to realise that some of the young witches she liked to help were crushing on her alpha wolf.

"Shoo." She rounded the counter and waved the witches away, scowling at them as she ushered them towards the door. "He's my wolf."

"I heard that, lass." Kin's deep baritone rolled down her spine, warming her from head to toe.

Mother earth, she had missed him.

They had only been apart two days, and he had messaged her whenever he'd had the time, but she had missed him. She had even started gazing at the armchairs near the fireplace in her drawing room and picturing him there, with his legs stretched out before him. She had imagined him in her bed too, had rolled over each night only to be disappointed by the fact he wasn't there beside her.

She was done for.

She knew it.

She slowly turned to face him as the door closed behind the young witches, her heart fluttering as she caught sight of him. He smiled easily, his silver eyes bright with it and with love, and the warmth that curled through her turned into heat as she raked her gaze over him, taking in the black shirt that hugged his broad chest and huge biceps, and his onyx jeans that emphasised his powerful long legs.

Her wolf was gorgeous.

And he had been slowly working his way into every aspect of her life.

Now, she had reached the point where she couldn't imagine life without him.

Where she didn't want to be apart from him.

"Your wolf, am I?" He eased into the room, moving sensually like the predator he was, rousing the fire in her veins and making her itch to peel his clothing off him and show him that he was hers.

"Maybe." She bustled over to the counter and closed the books her students had left behind.

It still felt good to be back in her house, with her books and her work. All her precious tomes and ingredients had survived, and she'd had several customers waiting for her when she had returned, all of them eager to continue their business with her.

Kin came up behind her and braced his hands against the counter on either side of her, trapping her. "Say I'm yours, Hella."

His breath teased her nape, sending a shiver down her arms and spine, and she couldn't stop her eyes from slipping shut as she focused on him and how close he was to her, how his big body caged hers.

"Hella." His gaze shifted to her nape and she sensed the rising tension in him, saw it in the way his fingers flexed against the wooden top. He was still a moment in which her heart raced, and then he eased back and muttered, "We talked about this."

She turned in his arms when he reached for the pins holding her hair in place away from her nape, effectively stopping him. Rather than undoing her hair, he swept his fingers across her cheek, his earnest gaze holding a hint of pain that she hated.

"I'm sorry," she whispered and placed her hand over her nape. "It's so hot today and you were supposed to come later than this. I was going to change before you got here."

She reluctantly reached for the pin.

Hesitated.

Hella gazed up into his eyes, her courage failing her for what felt like the hundredth time since Kin had vowed that he would never bite her.

Never was beginning to feel like a long time.

She had enjoyed it at first. He had taken the pressure off and she had felt free to be with him, assured that he would never take things too far and try to bond with her.

But now…

Over the last two weeks, she had found herself dreaming about him claiming her and she had started wondering whether he really didn't want to do it.

And that had led to her growing convinced that he no longer wanted to be her mate.

She had started watching him more closely whenever they were together, seeking a sign that he wanted to claim her or proof that he was enjoying his freedom. He had his mate, but no bond to tie them.

Meaning he was free to come and go as he pleased.

He could leave her.

It turned out that life without MacKinnon was one she didn't want to live.

She was all in with this and it frightened her. She had never been in love like this. She had never felt so dependent upon someone else, as if they were the source of her light and life and without them she knew only darkness and emptiness.

MacKinnon's brow furrowed and his fingers paused against her cheek. "Lass? What's wrong?"

She shook her head, the same response she gave him whenever he caught her feeling down and doubting everything.

He frowned at her when she brushed his hand away from her face and walked towards the stairs, unpinning her hair at the same time to let it tumble around her shoulders. She paused at the bottom of the stairs, her hand on the newel post and her heart hurting.

"Maybe you should go without me," she whispered, hating how defeated she sounded and how her heart ached at the thought of him leaving her, even if it was only to go to a celebration at his pack's home.

And that was another thing.

He kept saying that she would meet his pack soon.

But he never took her there.

They always ended up distracted by each other and staying at her home, and then the next morning he would go back to his pack without her.

"Go without you? Nay, lass. Why would I do that?" He came up behind her and she remained facing away from him, struggling to pull herself together and vanquish the voices in her head, the ones that mocked her and made her doubt him. "Tell me what's bothering you. You used to speak your mind so freely. Now I can barely get you to say two words to me."

He reached for her and then dropped his hand to his side.

Was silent for seconds that felt like hours as they ticked past at an excruciatingly slow pace.

His voice was rough and low as he asked, "Do you no' want me anymore?"

"No! It's not—" She spun to face him and her shoulders sagged, the sudden surge of strength leaving her as her gaze collided with his and she caught the hurt in it.

She was no good at this. She had never managed to make a relationship work, and she had a sinking feeling this one—the first and only one to mean everything to her—was going to go the same way. She looked into his eyes and then clenched her fists. He was right. She used to speak her mind so freely. She never used to mince her words.

Not until he had tied her heart in knots.

She shook her head. He hadn't just tied it in knots. He had stolen it and held it in his grasp, and she was terribly afraid he meant to crush it. She was afraid he would never give her what she had come to realise she wanted from him during the last few weeks. She had witnessed Fenix with his mate, and Fenix's new friends with their mates, and a hole had grown inside her.

A hollow yearning for the one thing Kin wouldn't give her.

"Why don't you want to claim me?" The words leaked from her, trembling and sounding weak to her ears.

His demeanour changed in an instant, his frown melting away into a look that wrenched at her heart as his gaze softened. It lasted only a heartbeat before his eyes turned gold and hardened, his dark eyebrows knitting above them, and he startled her by suddenly fisting the front of his shirt.

"Dinnae want tae claim ye?" he growled and tightened his fist. "Whatever gave you that impression? Is that what this is all about?"

She backed off a step and then realised what she had done and stood her ground, tipping her chin up and squaring her shoulders, facing him in the way she should have done the moment she had discovered what she really wanted from him.

How deeply she loved him.

"You said so yourself. You said you'd never claim me," she snapped back at him.

His face darkened and he looked as if he might rage and break everything in her shop, and then he drew down a deep breath and huffed and his shoulders relaxed. "Aye, I did say that, but no' because I dinnae want to claim you. I said it because you were afraid and I needed you to know you had no reason to be fearing me."

His golden gaze softened again and his brow furrowed as he lifted his hand and brushed his fingers across her cheek, his voice going low and tender.

"Hella… I'm mad with a need to make you mine."

All her strength flooded from her and she leaned into his touch, craving more, needing the comfort of it and the reassurance that she hadn't messed everything up. Her heart warmed, beating a little steadier as his words drifted in her mind, as she gazed into his eyes and saw the truth in them. He did want her as his mate.

"Hella… lass… love…" He cast a look at his boots and then met her gaze again, adorably awkward for an alpha wolf as he stumbled and tripped on words she could see meant a lot to him. "Does this mean… Do you want… Tell me no if you want, but mean it."

"Yes," she blurted.

And felt as if a weight had been lifted from her heart.

"I thought I would never want to be someone's mate. I thought it was another way of changing me… making me different… and… it is… but not in the way I thought." She placed both hands over the one he still clutched his shirt with and held it as she looked deep into his eyes. "I know now. Being your mate wouldn't mean I was weaker or controlled by another. It wouldn't mean I would lose my independence or my standing. It would mean I'm loved by you and that I love only you, and that I wanted everyone in this world to know it. It would make me stronger… It would make *us* stronger… and it would be beautiful."

He shifted his free hand to hers and covered them, holding them to his chest. "Took you long enough to realise it."

She smiled softly. "It certainly did."

He stepped up to her, so close she could feel his heat, and she tipped her head back to keep her eyes locked with his.

"Say I'm your wolf," he husked.

"You're mine, wolf." She held back her smile when he growled at her choice of words and angled her head up, bringing her mouth closer to his as her gaze grew hooded. "Now, make me yours."

He swooped on her lips on another possessive snarl, claiming more than a kiss from her as her heart soared in response. She wrapped her arms around his neck and shivered as he banded his around her waist and lifted her by her backside, raising her up his body, and began ascending the stairs.

Hella kissed him, losing herself in each brush of their tongues and lips, anticipation building inside her as he carried her to her bedroom. When he set her down on the edge of the bed and went to cover her, she pressed her hand to his chest.

"Wait." She pushed him back and rolled from beneath him, ignoring his growl.

His gaze tracked her as she hurried to her wardrobe and opened it. She ran her fingers along the dresses, seeking one she had kept that was perfect for the occasion, and paused when she found it. She kept hold of it as she muttered the incantation and gasped as the spell completed and the long onyx gown replaced her black empire-line dress.

Another low growl pealed from Kin's lips as she turned towards him and skimmed her hands down over the metal filigree corset that cinched her waist in and pushed her breasts up.

"You kept it." He didn't look happy about it.

But she would change his mind.

"I thought I should... It's a beautiful gown after all." Hella toyed with the flowing sheer strips of material that formed the skirt, teasing Kin with glimpses of her bare thighs. "I admit I did think about getting rid of it... but then I had this idea... and I found I couldn't part with it."

"Idea?" He stared at her.

She nodded and traced one of the swirls on the corset with her fingertip. "I had a thought, you see, when I was walking down that aisle. I realised the man at the end of it wasn't the one I wanted to be standing there. He was several rows from the back and shouldn't have been there."

"I did save you... again," he muttered and then the corners of his lips curled. "You want to marry me."

She shrugged.

He growled.

"When we got home, I looked at the dress and thought... wouldn't it be a fitting final fuck you to Ethyrian if you were the one who got to wed me in this dress?" She swished side to side, tempting him. "In a shifter fashion, of course."

Kin's gaze darkened, the heat in it scalding her, and she gasped as he was suddenly before her, pulling her into his arms and kissing her. She moaned as he worked kisses along her jaw and dropped his lips to her throat, his arms steel bands around her, pinning her to his chest. He lowered his hands to her backside and groaned as he palmed it.

"You're bare," he murmured against her overheating flesh.

"And burning for you," she whispered and nipped at his earlobe. "Stop keeping me waiting."

He scooped her into his arms and carried her to the bed, set her down and twisted her away from him. He growled as he fumbled with her skirts, his actions frantic, jacking her pulse up and making her feel just as desperate as an ache bloomed inside her, a need only he could satisfy. She joined him, tearing at the strips of material, gathering and cursing them, wishing she hadn't picked this dress after all.

But glad that she had when cool air washed over her backside and Kin snarled, the possessive sound thrilling her. She gazed over her shoulder at him, on fire for him. He stoked that fire as he fisted her skirts in one hand and ran the other down the corset of her dress, and his eyes lifted to collide with hers.

"You do look beautiful in it," he murmured, his voice scraping low, relaying his desire as he raked his eyes over her again. "My mate."

He skimmed his hand around her thigh to her front as he stepped up behind her, his gaze holding hers. She shivered as he stroked between her thighs, her head growing hazy as his fingers teased her, cranking up her need until she rocked with each brush of them, aching for more. His lips captured hers and he kissed her hard as he made her hold her skirts. She twisted them in her fists, on the verge of begging him to give her what she needed.

Kin eased her legs apart and dipped his body, and she moaned as he inched into her.

She leaned forwards, eager to feel all of him, aching for more.

He gripped her hip and thrust deep, ripping a gasp from her and then another as he began moving inside her, fast and hard, pushing her to the edge in a handful of seconds. He pulled her back against him and kissed her. She cried into his mouth as he squeezed her sensitive bead and release hit her, had her trembling around his cock as he plunged into her, deeper now, riding her climax.

He groaned in time with her, his grip on her hip tightening as he leaned her away from him and took her harder. She reached behind her and grabbed his arm to steady herself as she rocked forwards with each powerful thrust, shooting through the haze of one release and barrelling towards another. He grunted and pulled his hand from beneath her skirts, lifted it and twisted her hair around it, tugging it away from her nape and bringing her back against his chest.

Her breath sawed from her, every sense she possessed heightening as his breath washed across her nape. Her nipples beaded, each plunge of his shaft feeling like heaven as she waited, as he teased her by blowing on her neck and sensitising it. It wasn't enough.

"Kin," she moaned, on the verge again, reaching for a release that felt as if it was beyond her, impossible to make happen no matter how she flexed her body and worked it against him, riding him.

"You're sure, lass? This is forever." He kissed her nape, sending sparks skittering over her skin.

"Already mine forever," she murmured. "Make me yours."

On a wicked growl, he angled his head and sank his fangs into her nape.

Hella screamed his name as fire swept through her, blazing from the point where he had bitten her and between her thighs, colliding inside her to ricochet through her and blank her mind. She drifted in the haze, lost and found at the same time as an incredible connection formed and she could feel everything he did.

All the love.

The gratitude.

The sensation of feeling honoured and humbled, and a little bit wild.

Hella put that part down to his wolf.

He released her neck and howled as he plunged deep into her and throbbed, spilling seed and triggering a third release that had her head spinning and her sagging in his arms. Mother earth. She sank against him as he wrapped his arms around her, keeping her in place on him as he continued to spill, each pulse drawing a grunt from him and a moan from her. When he bent his head and licked her neck, she shook and moaned, fire reigniting in her blood to make her wonder if him licking his marks would always have this effect on her.

Kin twisted her in his arms and flopped onto the bed with her. He tucked her to his side, his chest heaving with each hard breath, his eyes glassy as they locked on the ceiling. She smiled as she snuggled up to him, couldn't stop herself from grinning as she gazed at him and felt everything he was.

She had never felt so loved.

The look Kin gave her when he turned his head towards her said she wasn't alone.

She gripped his shoulders and hooked her leg over him, straddling his hips, and kissed him, keeping it soft and savouring it. His hands skimmed down to her backside and he groaned as he tried to deepen the kiss and she didn't let him.

She pulled back instead.

Gazed down at her wolf.

Her mate.

She stroked her fingers across the front of his throat, through the short hairs of his stubble. "So… I was thinking I should get you a collar."

He frowned at her. "Is this going to be a joke about the fact I'm a wolf and you own me?"

She shook her head, trying not to pout as he ruined it, and then sighed as she brushed her fingers across her nape and felt his mark there.

His look turned serious as his eyes shifted back to silver, and gods, she loved his eyes. No one had eyes as beautiful and striking as her mate.

"Whatever mark you want to make on me, I'll accept it, love. I want everyone to know I'm yours." He palmed her waist.

She pulled a face. "What about a magical tattoo?"

One that would say 'property of Hella' in the fae tongue sounded good, but she doubted he would go for it. He gave her a look that said he knew she was up to mischief and she decided bonds had their disadvantages too. He had felt it through their connection.

"Could get a spell for a wee set of fangs and bite me." His eyes brightened, as if he liked that idea.

The hard-on nudging her bottom said he *really* liked it.

"I think I know where I might be able to get one." She would have to pull in a few favours, but it would be worth it, and not only because her mate clearly enjoyed the thought of her biting him. She liked the thought of biting him too, and making sure the bite mark was laced with a spell that made it clear he was hers to all who looked at it. She frowned at him and stroked her palms across his chest. "Will you ever want to bite me again?"

He chuckled softly. "Lass, get those fangs and I'll no' be able to resist biting you back."

She shivered at the thought and eased down his body, pinning his erection against his stomach and rubbing it. His eyes turned molten gold and he gripped her bottom and moved her on him.

Something vibrated against her thigh and she tensed.

"Fuck," he muttered and reached for his pocket, pulling out a phone. He glared at the screen and tossed it away from him.

"Who was it?" She watched the phone bounce across the wooden floor.

"Gregor. Asking where I was with my lass."

She smiled wickedly and rocked her body against his. "I'd say we were right about here."

"Meeting my pack," he gritted and gripped her backside again, rolling his hips to meet her and not really giving her the impression that he felt an urgent need to stop and go to the party they had planned.

"Can wait." She took hold of his wrists and pulled his hands away from her bottom, leaned over him and pinned his arms above his head, bringing their faces close together. "Surely they wouldn't begrudge their alpha and his mate their honeymoon?"

"Honeymoon," he growled and then added, "*Mate*."

Her wolf liked that word. He snarled it in a possessive way that left her in no doubt she had made more than just his day, month or year by becoming his mate. She had made his life, and he had made hers too.

As much as she hated the witch, she was going to have to send Godiva a thank you note for hurling her and MacKinnon together, helping them find each other and a love that was deep and endless.

The phone vibrated again.

Hella silenced it with a spell.

She would meet his pack.

Maybe not tomorrow.

Or the next day.

But soon.

Once their honeymoon was over.

Which might be never judging by the way Kin looked at her, hunger lighting his eyes.

"I love you, mate," he husked, melting her heart.

"I love you, mate," she whispered and stroked her finger across his lower lip, tugging it down slightly to reveal his fangs. "Now show me how much."

He growled and rolled with her, seizing her mouth in a toe-curling kiss.

One she knew would last forever.

The End

ABOUT THE AUTHOR

Felicity Heaton is a New York Times and USA Today best-selling author who writes passionate paranormal romance books. In her books she creates detailed worlds, twisting plots, mind-blowing action, intense emotion and heart-stopping romances with leading men that vary from dark deadly vampires to sexy shape-shifters and wicked werewolves, to sinful angels and hot demons!

If you're a fan of paranormal romance authors Lara Adrian, J R Ward, Sherrilyn Kenyon, Kresley Cole, Gena Showalter, Larissa Ione and Christine Feehan then you will enjoy her books too.

If you love your angels a little dark and wicked, her best-selling Her Angel romance series is for you. If you like strong, powerful, and dark vampires then try the Vampires Realm romance series or any of her stand alone vampire romance books. If you're looking for vampire romances that are sinful, passionate and erotic then try her London Vampires romance series. Or if you like hot-blooded alpha heroes who will let nothing stand in the way of them claiming their destined woman then try her Eternal Mates series. It's packed with sexy heroes in a world populated by elves, vampires, fae, demons, shifters, and more. If sexy Greek gods with incredible powers battling to save our world and their home in the Underworld are more your thing, then be sure to step into the world of Guardians of Hades.

If you have enjoyed this story, please take a moment to contact the author at **author@felicityheaton.com** or to post a review of the book online

Connect with Felicity:
Website – http://www.felicityheaton.com
Blog – http://www.felicityheaton.com/blog/
Twitter – http://twitter.com/felicityheaton
Facebook – http://www.facebook.com/felicityheaton
Goodreads – http://www.goodreads.com/felicityheaton
Mailing List – http://www.felicityheaton.com/newsletter.php

FIND OUT MORE ABOUT HER BOOKS AT:
http://www.felicityheaton.com

Printed in Great Britain
by Amazon

21204721R00154